Rob R. Thompson

Ashley Bay

Fultus™ *Books*

Ashley Bay

by

Rob R. Thompson

Edited by Gail Chadwick

Cover image by Ian Jamison

ISBN 1-59682-024-1

Copyright © 2005 by Rob R. Thompson
All rights reserved.

Published by Fultus Corporation

Corporate Web Site: http://www.fultus.com
Fultus eLibrary: http://elibrary.fultus.com
Online Book Superstore: http://store.fultus.com
Writer Web Site http://writers.fultus.com/thompson/

No part of this book may be used or reproduced in any manner whatsoever without written permission except in the case of brief quotations embodied in reviews and critical articles.

The author and publisher have made every effort in the preparation of this book to ensure the accuracy of the information. However, the information contained in this book is offered without warranty, either express or implied. Neither the author nor the publisher nor any dealer or distributor will be held liable for any damages caused or alleged to be caused either directly or indirectly by this book.

Table of Contents

Chapter 1. Coming Home 7

Chapter 2. Getting Ready 55

Chapter 3. Leaving Home 91

Chapter 4. Glory Road 141

Chapter 5. Restless Moon 177

Chapter 6. These Feet 227

Chapter 7. Her Best 245

Chapter 8. First Steps 269

Though the years have gone by quickly I have always held you close through all my adventures and it's with love that I dedicate

Ashley Bay

to my sisters

Karen Dollinger

and

Beverly Crossland

Chapter 1
Coming Home

Danvers Clay was an uncle whom I had seen a time or two when I was young but who had disappeared twenty years ago in the hands of some thrice-married, two-pack-a-day barfly from up in Kittery. We never knew where he had ended up but he had left many good memories behind. My haphazard glimpse at an old photo brought back these memories and the admission that we all have our own barflies. He was Mom's brother, the youngest and kinda' screwed up but a good natured guy to those who took the time to listen. Looking around and looking back, I thought just how many years had passed since I sat here in this attic looking at these boxes set aside for days just like this one. The dust never seemed to age and the smell of old newspapers whose headlines never mattered filled the dimly lit corner of the house here on Plum Tree Cove.

I didn't know what I was looking for, just pickin' through what she had left behind. The others took their wishes a couple of days ago and as far as I could see they hadn't missed much. As I sat here on a stool way to small, I noticed the fleeting scent of jasmine in the air. It had been here for sometime far outpacing the fading headlines and dust devils. We, the children of this house had passed on our final touch and one last rose from beneath a naked elm to the silent one. The elm, a noble withered sentry of these dead for a hundred years stood guard once again as the pipes bid farewell with the drone of Amazing Grace.

A Saturday morning in a Rhode Island autumn rain and we had laid our last parent to rest. I pulled up my collar to guard lazily against the chill wind in this attic of boxed up memories. It was too warm for a sweater and there was too much of a chill in the air for extended stays without one. We, the aging silent siblings of Mary and James Swisher had nodded politely to one another and exchanged nice to meet you handshakes as the pipes played on. With the formal greetings behind us, our united tension returned us to the state of family dysfunction we had been accustomed to for so long. I had not been home in years; the town was too small and it was just too long a drive. However, I always called Mom and always remembered her on those special days but I always said, "I can't this weekend Mom but maybe next, OK." As I fumbled through the box before me, I realized that *that* weekend had finally come.

The funeral was capped off with the memories of so many years forgotten and never forgiven. The tension of family stress was over and we said our goodbyes not knowing when or *if* we'd meet again. The cars pulled out and the pink and white roses went with her as an eternal comforter. I sat in a hand me down Ford Tempo staring at a casket covered in pink and white. The mourners wished me well as they passed, the preacher nodded and it was done. I looked through the naked arboreal sentries surrounding our generations and saw the souls of those seeking forgiveness and just one last hug and knowing that many saw neither. I turned around beneath a naked elm understanding all too well that my final weekend visit was over.

The years just went too fast and I didn't know how to slow them down The future for me was uncertain and I wondered just how I would be and *why* I would be remembered at my moment. I backed up with a glimpse at a headstone one that was mossy green with age and slightly askew and I left those at rest. It had been a generation or maybe more since Dad was buried next to where Mom now rests and surprisingly the area around the graveyard had developed little. There were a couple of new homes and a stop sign that signaled modernity for this part of Warwick but not much else The selfish modern developers of this era never wanted to cross eternity; that may be their one unselfish act for I guess even the greedy fear death. I took a left down Pleasant Street and I drove past Mr. Mullins' A&P. Mr. Mullins was a good decent man a long time friend of Dad. He would always let us kids sell our junk out in front of his store so we could make it to summer camp each year. Mrs. Mullins surfaced as one of those nice little memories from those days especially when one or *all* of us kids came up short financially. As we pathetic youngsters

Ashley Bay

sat crestfallen at their storefront she always managed to find something among our trash that she just couldn't live without. It was now a mega world surrounded by video cameras and warning signs stating No Solicitation Allowed.

A couple of miles down Pleasant and with a few short turns later I pulled into the driveway on Plum Tree Cove for what I guessed would be the final time. This was my boyhood home. The driveway was never paved and the gravel still crunched as I put the Tempo into park. The sound of the crunching gravel brought back memories of bike rides, pebbles to kick, endless mud puddles and lilac bushes whose bloom was long wished for during winter nights. The sound of crunching gravel also brought back memories of Dad coming home for the final time. I stepped out of the car and crossed the road to stand opposite this home, my boyhood portal. What a journey I was about to experience; I struggled through mounting tears to look up at memories lost in the name of shame. I have wanted to take this journey for so long now and *my* time had now come. I slowly raised my eyes and looked through its front door as if it were a time machine. In a flash, I once again heard the giggles of sisters at play, sisters who were now strangers. I heard the ruffled bark of a three-legged black lab and I saw a brother heading off to war. There were countless Christmases and Easter egg hunts and centered in the midst I saw the fading face and the final tears of one lonely widow. These grounds had been hollowed by good memories and they had been desecrated by ungodly traits like greed, resentment, anger and jealousy. The doorway to regret was now open and I kicked a pebble, perhaps the same one I kicked years ago for pebbles never really go away do they.

I glanced at a plum tree a proud sole survivor of those who had given this street its name. I recalled how a chubby little boy always got caught sneaking a few of the plumper ones off the bottom branches. The young fella' thought he was *so* slick but the owner of those noble sentries, Mrs. Yowell would come out on her porch every time and chase the little boy away. She would stand there with hands on hips and with an up turned tone state, "Go on now young man I need those for *Mr.* Yowell." The young fella' was chased away for so many years until one day the little boy had grown and Mr. Yowell had been laid to rest beneath the naked elm. The young plum chaser would be nearby when a lonely widow would ask, "young man, would you like some plums?"

I stood there for several moments remembering as many of the good things as possible. I knew when we are adults we work hard to build memories we hope we never lose and when we are children we are often given memories we spend our lifetimes trying to get rid of. The battle I guess, is when all is said and done which side wins the bad or good. Looking through the oval glassed time portal I hadn't a clue to what Mom's life must have been like when she was a child nor the memories she carried as she looked upon a world she never quite fit into. Now that all is said and done is she blessed or condemned? Did she win in the end? With my hands still thrust deep, I glanced left, then right, then left again, as if I expected a car to hurl down this street town. It's not Hollywood and Vine and I sure thank the almighty for that. I thanked Him also for I knew that Mom was fine for God would never condemn the weak. I knew Mom was fine now because she had always done her best and regretted her errors so deeply that she literally hurt.

Bradford Rhode Island was a bitty town and never grew much larger than tiny. It was a wonderful town for a child to grow up in, Sawyeresk in so many ways. The main street, the busy street was called School Street for at one end stood an abandoned one room schoolhouse and at the other end stood the Presbyterian Church. Between them stood a couple of dozen homes all similar accept for structure. These homes were governed for generations by proud loving parents who wished for all their children the wonderful things in life. Their contents and residents were all similar accept for character and outcome. There was the occasional drunkard or paranoid loner and even the sporadic affair but for most part it was Hannibal Missouri. There was a field of corn a hundred yards off and the Hyde General Store near the one tiny church we all helped paint. This was Bradford as I knew it and as it will always be known.

With my hands in my pockets I walked this road again and likely for the last time also. I began a slow deliberate gate toward where,for fifty-some years the Hyde General Store had stood. I always smiled when I thought of Ms. Hyde. She never married and she died at the age of 107 in the home in which she was born. As a little boy being asked to go up to Ethyl's was tremendous treat because her one room store was the mega mart of our time. Ms. Hyde had always been old, she was old twenty years before I was born. As all could imagine she was set in her ways and would not be bothered by modern things such as television. When the neighborhood parents sent us kids to her store we would see Ms. Hyde on her screened in porch long before we came close to her yard. She would rock slowly in the hand crafted chair she kept close to the mailbox waiting on Alex *her* mailman. Whether it was the two dollars Dad had given us or just a child's anticipation we couldn't wait to get to Ethyl's. We would walk the walk of two, maybe three hundred yards for we were told not to run and the anticipation grew as we obeyed. She saw us walking and we saw her rocking. As we came close with an extra effort she would rock herself up.

Her sidewalk, which was just past the Fire Chief Gasoline pumps was a couple of stones long since overgrown. To the right of her front door stood a milk machine where a quart could be had for just 20 cents. Her door, like all others in Bradford was screened and as I recalled on this walk the screen door was the doorbell of our youth. Bang, bang-bang. Bang, bang-bang all screen doors sounded alike and I'll never forget hers. Every visitor to Ethyl's was met by her ageless white collie, Teddy and the price of admission was a scratch on the nose and a high yah', Teddy. Teddy was always especially happy to see a kid for he knew he would have rewards *far* greater than just a mere scratch on his over dented nose. The small one room store was highlighted by hardwood floors, wooden ice chests, Orange Fago, penny combs and credit for the neighbors better known as *when yah' can* lists. Ethyl's was also where we kids caught the school bus and where every Monday to start the week, Ethyl would have a bag of Bazooka Joe, Fireballs and Sugar Daddies for each of us. As we waited for the bus she would also have a brown bag lunch for those of us who didn't have one for the day. I guess she adopted us all.

When Mom and Dad sent us to shop on a *when yah' can* list, Ethyl would always have ready for us kids two butter cookies and if we ate it outside a Popsicle. The red ones were always the first to go for the older kids made sure they got there early. Outside, we have to eat this outside? Well, if *we* must *we* will. I think Ethyl had a motive or two behind asking us to go outside. To make sure we wouldn't try to sneak back inside with a dripping Popsicle, Teddy would lead us outside opening the screen door with a nose broken a time or two by each of us. He would watch us as we sat on her potato bin, he, this over fluffed timeless one was doing his job for if we kids happened to drop a piece of the Popsicle Teddy would be there to pick it up. Looking back now, Ethyl spoiled Teddy as much as she did us. As the collie's portly hulk evidenced he was always happy to see a youngster come with a *when yah' can* list.

As Boy Scouts, Ethyl's was a must stop on our way to our American History Merit Badge. We all interviewed her as the local holder of fact. It was a visit insisted upon by all our fathers but not much respected until recently when we became fathers ourselves. I began to slow my walk up the street to stand where her home still stood. Looking through all the doors my mind continued the journey to the *when yah' can* days. Though Ethyl had stopped rocking many years ago the sight of her home triggered the memories long since stored away. Her story went a little something like this.

Ethyl Hyde had been born in *this* very house on May 19, 1885 and she would be the only child of Ruth and William Hyde. As many others and I were told, Ruth was a devoted wife and cared for William until his death in 1888 at the age of forty-four. William Hyde was laid beneath the naked elm marked by a stone now mossy green from age and slightly askew. Ethyl was only three when her father died and therefore she never really knew him. What she knew was what her mother passed on to her and that's what she passed onto us. As Ethyl sat in her rocking chair passing on these stories to all of us wide eyed youths she would have on her lap a small box of artifacts from better times.

Though she never knew her dad she would always proudly reach into the box and pull out small mementos that she carried all her years. Ethyl would slowly tell her tale of Bradford and when the railroad first came and just what it was like to hear a new invention called the radio. Her voice was strong when she walked us through her life and when her journey was nearing an end she would open the box one last time for the anxious eyes of youth. Ms. Hyde would slowly reach into the box and pull a package wrapped well in ageless butcher paper and ever so delicately she would fold it back one

Ashley Bay

crinkled fold at a time. As the stories ended she gave us the explanation point, she would reach in and pull out a faded blue uniform, Union blue.

She would hold it with reverence and one could tell she had only the best of memories of a father she never knew. In a voice rough from age she would tell us, "Papa wore this uniform when he was with Mr. Grant in Virginia. He had done some fightin' at many small little towns along the way to Richmond." Ms. Hyde would pat the uniform and continue her tale. "He came home hurt before the war ended and he was never real good after that. Mama said his stomach bothered him somthin' fierce till his last day." With a smile she'd say, "They had me so I could show *you* this uniform someday young man." With those words she would then let us hold it. I've never forgotten the chills that went through me when I first touched that glorious uniform. I have never forgotten the scent of the Virginia fields that the butcher paper had long held hostage and I have never forgotten the look in her eyes as she shared her life.

As I stood just a while longer looking through the doors of youth I assumed we all still owed her money till her last day, all those unpaid *when yah' can* lists. However, I'm sure she didn't care she was a relic of what was once so good about America. Ethyl lived to be kind, *not* rich. Ethyl lived for God and not for Wal-Mart. God took her home a long time ago now but her time with a short, chubby plum chasin' young man has at times tamed his soul as he journeys to his own final corner. My hometown walk continued and I tried to rub away a chill on the back of my neck as I walked a bit further toward that corner. The homes I revisited brought back good memories all and there were no *real* regrets. The sun was still close but my soul ran one more time from house to house, from field to field and from tree to tree here in Bradford. Youthful memories of this three street town invigorated my soul and it just had to run the boyish adventures one more time.

My memory ran to Mrs.Yowell's plum trees and it ran to see the birth of Claude Sweet's brand new baby calf. My soul ran from one end of School Street and it climbed through the attic of the one room schoolhouse. My soul ran to the window outside the deathbed of Gilbert Rose to sing Silent Night one last time for our dying neighbor. Gratified, but not weary my soul returned to its owner and I washed away the chill of my childhood upon its return. There were so many wonderful memories of this little town and I didn't mind taking the occasional emotional return this road. I made my way slowly back to the car as my soul had caught up and now I waited for the memories to return to the here and now. I was no longer the chubby plum chaser; I was now a very tired man ready for rest of his own and I must say good-bye to my youth. Staring one last time at my boyhood home my memory arrived and I said good-bye to the lost little boy and to the lonely widow who never fit into the world she looked out upon.

I fumbled for the car keys and noticed that a rain had come without my knowledge and had probably been my companion for some time now. Shaking my head just a little I dried my hands as I grasped the steering wheel. I sat looking at the dashboard without as much as a blink for several moments noticing the window mist increase. I had traveled this road *so* many times over the years but had neglected it over the last decade or so, perhaps longer. I stared for several moments more at the horizon and the and of this three street town. A town that seemed so small on one hand and yet so menacing on the other would in a moment be just a highlight in my rearview mirror.

"It is finished," I said aloud. *It is finished*, the last words of Christ. These were also the words of yesterday's preacher and my words as I said good-bye to Bradford. A mile up I'd take a right on Garden Street, then a left on Spruce Road and straight to Rte. 29. I wouldn't be back and I knew in so many ways, the journey that began here ended here as well. I was caught between telling all good riddance and insisting we try just one more time to try to make it right, but we knew it would never be the same. Jealousies now usually grew from such major oversights as forgetting a $2 birthday card. I stopped crying twenty years ago over the loss of brothers and sisters and I was just too tired to give a damn anymore I adjusted my seat belt as the laughter of sisters at play faded from behind the shady pines on Plum Tree Cove.

As I fiddled for my keys some more I was reminded of how Dad did the same thing every time he got into the car. Dad was a remarkable man in his unique way. He worked hard every day of his life and never had more than a couple of dimes to rub together. I always felt that Dad had a couple of roles in life and the major one was to watch out for Mom. They met when they were young and Mom was never very strong, perhaps Dad knew that. Some would say she was even somewhat simple and seemed lost her whole life But crediting my one time faith once again I knew that God never condemned the weak. God gave Mom to Dad to take care of because God knew we kids would take care of her when Dad was called home all those years ago and that's just what happened. I looked somewhat selfish and asked special blessings for those that honored the wish.

The chill was growing as the horizon shrunk before me. I was so young when Dad died and the first preacher I ever saw was the one at his funeral. Pastor David came up to me just a bit before the service and asked if I could tell him something nice about my father. That question still haunts me, for the preacher who buried my Dad barely knew his name or much about him as a man. I think it was from that time on that I began to question Gods role in everyday life. Did God know my dad? More importantly did Dad know God? I pulled out of the driveway and left the plums and crunching gravel behind me. I soon turned and drove a short mile till I turned onto Garden Street. I had noticed during my walk and now during my drive with the drivers window down that there was a scent of a New England rain in the air. Whether it was natural or the just passing breeze there was now a growing chill in the air one that was odd for this time of year. I loved this smell though. I breathed in deeply for the scent of dead leaves, fall rain and a New England chill is one that we hold forever.

Whoosh, whoosh, whoosh the wipers were on low but made a good effort in keeping up. As I reached for the radio a nickel fell from the open ashtray, a buffalo nickel. I had forgotten about it a long time ago. It too was a story that I reca ...

"WJJL Providence 93.5 your FM friend brings you your classic gold for your drive home."

Hello darkness, my old friend,
I've come to talk with you again,
Because a vision softly creeping,
Left its seeds while I was sleeping,

Rob R. Thompson

And the vision that was planted in my brain
Still remains
Within the sound of silence...

I was caught momentarily between "The Sound of Silence" and my own darkness. *This* song and for that matter most anything by the `60s duo will unravel a lonely conscience. I turned the radio down just a bit to pursue the object of surprise, the buffalo nickel. As I put the nickel back I thought of what Simon and Garfunkel were telling me. A vision softly creeping -- what would that be like? Were my memories and are *your* memories the visions softly creeping that they spoke of? Were our dreams the creeping visions? The sounds of silence, the time honored tradition of death and the journey our souls will someday take in its pursuit. However, until silence rules our souls must complete a journey before they are at rest. The duo continued as the thunder rolled.

In restless dreams I walked alone
Narrow streets of cobblestone,
`neath the halo of a street lamp,
I turned my collar to the cold and damp
When my eyes were stabbed by the flash of a neon light
That split the night
And touched the sound of silence...

I continued inhaling the timelessness and let the song go on at an uncorrected pace. The nickel sat untouched as I looked over my shoulder and in the other direction once more as I turned onto Rte. 29. I guess I was on the journey that we must all someday take one of reflection on a life lived. Mom had taken her journey in noble fashion and Dad did so a generation or more ago. Now it was my turn so at the bequest of the duo I turned my collar to the cold and damp.

My mind was dashing here and there from this to that until it finally landed on the most recent days that Annie I had shared. I began my journey home from my boyhood home and where it would take me I did not know but it had to be taken. It's probably twenty years ago now when I, disappointed by a string of failures was blessed by Ann Marie Harrington. Annie was an amply structured auburn haired Irish girl when she walked into a room the hearts of men dead a hundred years would jump. I, being a shallow minded male quickly drew close to her. Her attention to emotional detail revealed more in me than could any stanza of Yates or Tennyson. Summer walks, picnics in the living room and an evening with Kevin Bacon and just as bad a burger rewarded weeks of fruitless pursuit of my Annie. My baby and I began our journey that night in a fall rain *just* like this one We would be joined at the hip right up till the end. She would hold my hand as she said good-bye for the final time, kissing my forehead and saying "I love you." That's why this scent of fall is so memorable for it brought back such beautiful, wonderful moments of life. There were many months behind us when one night under the full moon cover of Saco Bay our souls were united and would be so honored until the wings of heavens angels gave us our welcoming embrace. *This* road, *this* rain and *this* day is where my soul begins his journey and now leads me to you and to this night. I said to the aging face in the rearview mirror; It's a night we hope is put off as long as possible but one that draws closer with every moment of sun.

What a companion God had given this chubby young boy from Bradford. It is such a blessing for a man to have a good woman to share his life with. We primates usually realize good once it has ceased and I now saw the good. After sometime I came to understand that our union could only have been divinely blessed. For many of us men, if we look at our wives we must all be able to say what tremendous gifts God has given us. It seems like yesterday but it could have been years ago that God put Annie and I together. I learned long ago that depression and loneliness don't pay attention to the calendar so dates and times just couldn't be recalled so easily anymore. So I guess dates no longer mattered to the confused aye. I drove a few more northbound miles on Rte. 29, took the Warwick exit and in matter of minutes I pulled up to an apartment intended for a few months but a place that had now been home for many years. The place where Annie and I had started our lives.

I was tired. Sleep was well implanted and it spoke to me in a way it does till this very moment. I needed sleep but I dreaded the nocturnal curtain. The creeping visions haunted my nights and had been doing so for many, *many* nights. I pulled into our usual spot and thought of how when I was young, I had envisioned a house with a picket fence and daughters at play with an ever faithful dog. The picket fence never came, the dog was there when I was young and no daughter ever called me Daddy that I knew in this world. I had parked close enough so I could see the nondescript door on the second floor. I didn't want to walk too far -- just out, up and in. The mailbox was full of too many final notices to satisfy those who sent them so I honored none and the paper could be read later.

The apartment was like every other one for what we paid, beige carpet and popcorn ceilings and a poorly managed ceiling fan. It was cluttered with newspapers whose headlines never mattered and boxes of mementos from a handful of joy. I added some of Mom's life to it today. Tossing my keys on laundry past its prime, I flopped on a couch that Annie had bought from the thrift store just up the block. The apartment smelled bad and I was fortunate every now and then to catch a hint of jasmine making its way through the mess doing its best to cleanse from beyond an unknown portal. I laid nearly in repose and let my anxious mind find a mechanism of rest There was so much going through my mind that had to be processed and I just did not have the faculty to do it, not on this night anyway. The duo's words came back as my head sought comfort for a long road yet to come:

> Fools, said I, you do not know
> Silence like a cancer grows
> Hear my words that I might *teach* you
> Take my arms that I might *reach* you
> But my words, like silent raindrops fell
> And echoed
> In the wells of silence...

Walking alone in dreams I guess we all do that. Why cobblestone? What is the meaning of the cobblestone in their song? Brushing my head with both hands I guess I do walk alone in my dreams and I would be alone on the journey that I must take now. Was the cobblestone good or bad for a weary traveler? A ton of questions always surrounded me and were never pleased with their answers. I knew sleep was close as my mind fought the demons at the door of rest. A deep sigh, several minutes of restless legs and sleep was quickly upon me.

Ashley Bay

The last few days were hard but we, the children knew that the day we had just lamented would someday come and would also someday be behind us Mom had fought the fight and my fight was close and I had to prepare. I closed my eyes to sooth stress as much as anything but I wanted to fend off sleep for a while; it wasn't kind to me. The apartment smelled of dust, avoided wash and forgotten trash. At some point I knew I would have to get through this and move on, but when was the question yet to be answered. I shifted a worn out throw pillow and reached to turn on an alarm clock that would wake me for nothing in particular. I folded my arms underneath me and could not fend off the inevitable any longer.

In mere moments the calendar was refreshed and I found myself standing in front of my boyhood home. Noticing the scene I quickly lowered my head in shame. I felt as if I were a young man seeking a playmate and that if I looked one way or the other I would soon be at play, so I wouldn't have to go home. There were no playmates just the house and a fog covered road. The road at my feet surprised me for there was no playmate coming and I would do this on my own. In a brief second, I knew that I had to decide what was before me. Did I have the strength to discover it? Would I play or would I move on? As sudden as the lightning strikes I was frozen by the inability to decide. I had failed so often and each time it was because I decided improperly I didn't want to fail on *this* journey. If my life had taught me one thing it's that I had such a self imposed frozen factor that life was no longer fun or full of expectations. I just stood with hands at my side as the time rolled on I was frozen in time many a day.

Was it going to be fun or would I get into trouble for going further? How could I take a journey by remaining motionless? Darkness was all about me as I stood on a road once traveled by those who sought childish joy I stood silently as if in repose not wanting to look up because if I didn't look up I could never be afraid. Fear and shame were all about me, filling my mind and my mind in turn dumped all that fear and shame upon a soul once so sanctified. Sitting or standing, I did not know which and I had no landmark as to where I just was or to where I was heading. I listened for any sound that may be nearby for when it is dark we learn more from the silence around us than we do from a noisy neighbor. What will silence teach me tonight? The sounds of silence speak volumes to those who seek to be attentive and I was the best of students. The longer I stood there the greater the struggle was becoming for me to breathe. I was anxious and my palms sweaty. It was as though my nose was covered and I had to breathe through my mouth. I looked at my feet and gasped for air, struggling now to the point of choking which forced me to look up. I lifted my head in defense and *not* desire. Now that I was upright I wondered what had held me back why was I apprehensive. What would want me to stop? Was this struggle designed for me to lift my head and exit the shameful slouch? Was this a struggle between what is right and what is not? Was it shame versus trust?

The slouch of regret was behind me but my eyes were still shut. I heard what I thought was a low whisper or it could have been the sounds of an ocean hard at play with a shoreline older than God I couldn't tell for sure. There was a breeze, a scented mist from generations of fallen roses which met me as I sought to brush away that which covered my nose. My neck moved as if touched by a sneaky friend and my eyes opened like a child on Christmas morning. Before me I saw a single chair alone in a room of white. There was no dimension to the room nor was it intimidating. In many ways the chair was welcoming me from my seemingly extended journey. The chair was telling me to rest and that all was OK. I couldn't take the step that I was being asked to take. There was something holding me back a task yet to be done and I wasn't ready to rest. Why was there only one chair? Would I be alone here as well?

The ocean played harder and the shoreline fought just that much more as the water brought forth messages as yet unread by this lonely stranger Give and take, right and wrong, lost and found -- it was the sound of the ocean that was calling me with the tide coming and going. With my nose tilted to seek the sea breeze, I asked *why* I was being called. As I stared at the empty chair I thought: In the end, who wins over such questioning? Those that are right or those that are wrong? In the end who wins, the ocean or the shoreline that keeps tossing it back? In the end, who wins? The lonely or the beloved?

I turned again to the friendly touch I felt on my neck and asked: Who wins in the end? The living or the dead, the lost soul or the joyous memory? I had so many questions to ask and perhaps that's why the chair was there for me. If I waited, the answers would come *not* at my pace but when I am ready for the answer. The chair before me was in a plain room a distant resting place that came closer as my sleep drew to a close. The empty chair, peaceful now shook as if disturbed. I didn't know what to expect nor did I choose to rest. The chair was an option, I was to stay or move on the next step was mine, just mine. Why was the room quaking? Was I to enter or would it be here if I chose to return later? The quaking was steady and the sound of the ocean was replaced by the low murmuring of nearby neighbors whom I could not see. The room was quickly shrouded in a cloud like curtain by the mist and sounds of the ocean that were taking a final lap at th...

"WJJL Providence 93.5 on your FM dial. It's 5:15 a.m.and good morning with your wake up classic gold."

I was startled to say the least as I woke still breathing through my mouth. A dry mouth and a foggy mind were fed with the sounds of Neil Diamond as the list took form.

But you know I keep thinkin' about
Makin' my way back
L.A.'s fine but it ain't home
New York's home, but it ain't mine no more

Not even the chair
I am, I cried
I am, said I
And I am lost, and I can't even say why
Leavin' me lonely still...

Wow, what was that all about? I sat up as anxious about my dream as I was at meeting my forgotten brothers. I woke as if drunk from bad whisky and a worse woman. What was that dream all about, I asked again. On the side of a couch sagging with a deep indentation from many years of forgotten discipline, I rubbed my eyes. I grasped through the chills of the dream the need to avoid slamming my toes into a hand me down coffee table. The dreams had been like this many times over the years or maybe it was just a few weeks or was this one the first one altogether? Time mattered little to the lonely and I was lonely. Still, my dreams were curious and consistent every night. Since Mom's death they had been so vivid and so full of intent. Why had they begun at Mom's passing? Or was Mom's death just the bridge they needed to cross to get to me? The dreams were colorful and loud and it was as if they had dimension. If such an undefined thing as a dream can have sound mine surely did. If dreams could have depth then mine surely did as well. I walked to the bathroom and I asked the bowl the meaning of the night. Do dreams make noise? I looked in the mirror and with a spit; I asked what the shaking chair meant. I walked back in to the continuous drone of the morning golden talent and asked, If dreams have distance, then do we tire when we travel their tales?

Why would an empty room need a chair? The questions at first light were ones that could only be answered when this night brought its own rest and I with the same reservation stayed the tales course. I settled back into the dent, scratched my three day growth and turned down Neil Diamond. I looked about with my head resting on back of the couch and wanted to do so much more than allow time to eat away at me but just couldn't. With a few moments of ease I sought respite with a shower, the first in a couple of days. My mouth was dry and the shower cold so I drank the sputtering spray. As the water found its target, it seemed emboldened by the chill of the dream which still made its way up and down my spine.

A bad shave was followed by a couple of Pop Tarts and I began my day, but what would I do with it? I had, for some time now, just gone through the motions of life. I hadn't had a regular job in some time -- getting up to punch a clock in order to come home and wait to do it all over again didn't seem to make a lot of sense. The opinions of a drunken confused young man were with me again at this stage of life. I wished that I had spent more time with Annie rather then let secular pursuits cause unnecessary divisions at times. I had nothing and no one to come home to for some time, maybe a week, maybe a year, maybe longer. Recently many an employer felt that my talents were better suited to a venue other than theirs and I was happy to accommodate. This behavior was often the one I exhibited when I was young and drunk, so perhaps it *was* some time ago, time just had no meaning accept that which man gives it.

I was reaching an age where my heroes were younger than I and those who once admired me had passed beneath the naked elms of their own. What a strange sensation that is to look up to someone many years my junior. I admired those who could think, teach and preach regardless of age. I seldom paid attention to those who could sing, run and throw no matter their talent *or* their age. I was no longer sought after and seldom reached out to anymore. All the years of no had taken their share of blood and breath and I was just too exhausted to care and to scarred to risk vulnerability.

I didn't talk much anymore, either on the phone that was off the hook or nearby or buried under a stack of final notices. I did manage to write some but found myself thinking more often of what could be and all the things that never were. I went into the disgraceful example of a kitchen and made what some would call unacceptable coffee, Folgers Crystals and lukewarm tap water. The daily coffee was a crystallized blessing from Ms. Dottie McRae my downstairs little biddy of a neighbor who must have been Noah's backseat driver. Dottie didn't have any family and they must have built this apartment complex around her but she has been a good friend for several years to Annie.

I sat back down on the couch and looked about at what life had brought and what I had wrought. The once pleasant love filled quaint apartment was now one filled with entrapped pleasant memories begging to be shared. There were no longer any plaques on the wall or any photographs of wonderful days or any knickknacks that Annie had collected from our travels. I didn't have much use for television anymore either. Entertainment of a decade ago was now just decadence of various flavors. I couldn't turn on the television without being shown everything that I know at my root to be immoral. The entertainment of today was gay this and gay that or Oprah and Springer and sandal wearing, tattooed three dollar crack whores called divas. America was becoming too Springer like to enjoy what used to be entertainment. This nation's immorality had claimed the small screen, big screen and the air waves. The one solace I allowed my mind to absorb was music and a favorite one started my day:

Rob R. Thompson

I am, I said
To no one there
And no one heard at all
Not even the chair...

I loved music, for it could take a mind on whatever journey we wished for it to take. The music for me was always pertinent. The music of today is generally garbage and the older we get the more respect we have for the music of our parents so as we age we tend to revert in taste. The imagery that could come from a writer who had a message greater than his financial interests is a wonderful thing but rare nowadays. The poets of old are gone for good but scoffed at. The Hemingway's and Twains have been laughed at by the crotch grabbing, curse filled generations of today who consider classics out of touch.

We no longer read Shakespeare -- we read of Johnny and his two mommies. We no longer hear the tales of Hawthorne or Kipling -- we hear why it's OK to kill a cop or the unborn. At some point the America of our founders would hang a *going out of business* placard on the Statue of Liberty and that day is close. God where has America gone wrong? Those who need the comfort of kind words and a messenger must now look to the more corrupt side of mankind and receive just a byproduct of immorality as their comfort. I guess I had taken the finer things in life for granted though I must be honest, my definition of finer was at times up for grabs just like that of the young folks now. Perhaps, *just* perhaps the good things in life is what I must find as I continue my required trek?

The sun had been shining through a Venetian blind broken for as long as Dottie had prowled the premises. The creeping sun had elected to land on a part of the floor covered by a variety of books that once belonged to my Dad. My father's taste in books and his love of fine fiction and legitimate history are my source for that gift. I had not looked at any of those books since I sat in the attic in the house on Plum Tree Cove after his passing a generation ago. These books were, for lack of a better word "grandpa" books -- old but never aging. There were no paperbacks amongst this stack either, just well bound classics. This stack of classics held stories written at some time by those who had tremendous passion for honesty, love and their fellow man. But now they just gathered dust and the occasional kindness of the morning sun.

Dad loved a good story, I recall when I was just a little boy how he would tell stories of fact or fiction and honestly, to this day, I'm still not sure which was which. He had a tremendous sense of humor that was often forgotten because of his long days and weeks on the road. He loved to laugh and enjoyed the ever so infrequent but nonetheless pleasant things of life. I have often wondered what he would have been like if he had lived to be an old man. What would our relationship have been like if he had lived far past his ultimate fifty-six years? I wonder what he would have been like if he had had a chance to be a grandfather to his grandchildren now scattered from coast to coast.

What would he have been like if he had had the opportunity to walk the beaches of Normandy and to see the wilderness of Northern Virginia? What would he have been like if he had had the chance to see the wonders of life that he had only read about in the books now gathering dust before me? I guess Dad played his role in life and provided enough for us so we children could be where we are and in a position to take care of Mom and to walk the beaches he only read about. Wondering aloud, could we say now that Dad's wishes had been satisfied? Had he died so Mom could live? A nice thought and one that I know will be answered when he greets us all on the roads horizon.

There comes a time in all our lives when we begin to reason our being and I was now there. I had been on this particular ride for several years now and I was ready for my answer. Why was I here and why at this place and time was I doing what I was doing? What was God's plan for me? Did He have one or was I just wandering aimlessly through the congealed protoplasm called life? In attempting to answer this question many a pastor will advise the curious to just sit back and enjoy the spiritual ride while other pastors will say get in the car and drive to find what life has to offer. Still others will say that we must take the first step in order to reach our final destination. Which one is right?

God being who He is has of course given us free will, so both His and the pastoral answers are correct. We can sit back and watch or we can get out and enjoy the journey. It is *our* choice to sit in a chair in an empty room and observe or to drive and find life at every corner. The problem that I know I have faced at times is that when it comes to improving me I am lazy and will often avoid taking the first step. The more mature of us will make sure we have asked for direction before we choose a path while the young ones or those still juvenile will often set foot in a field of skunks before asking; What's that stench? Then, as we either sit and observe or sink and stink, it's often to our surprise that we receive our answers in the most unusual of ways. It will become clear to all of us that if we choose to do neither that life will indeed move on without us. We cannot just sit on the fence of life and expect to be rewarded with glory. This is a statement that should be directed at many Monday morning Christians we have in America now a days. The Christian who knows how to misquote a Bible verse or two and who will support everything ungodly is not a Christian that Christ will welcome. They are the false Christians, a Christian of convenience in other words. We need to move on from them or be at risk, yet they are often the ones we sit next to on the park bench. Perhaps the chair is meant for them, the undecided, perhaps the empty room is meant for them also.

I have watched as many a friend has died not knowing their role in life and not knowing the way of Christ. I think Dad knew his role though and I'm sure he did his best to know Christ, for that day in the attic years ago I found envelopes of tracts and scripture that he had cut out of various newspapers why did he do that if he wasn't seeking an answer. A lesser man than he would have set aside secular responsibility and moved down a path of his own choosing long ago. A lesser man would have let a widow grow old never knowing what she did wrong to be so abandoned. Dad showed us his role and I must now find mine. I had lost so much and I was afraid of drawing close to that and those who I would risk losing again. However, life is short and we eventually accept the fact that after our death there are no earthly do overs. I was so grateful that as a young man I was introduced to a peace which would serve as a seedling of faith as my gray hair grew.

I drank a bit of the tap water brewed Folgers and as if powered by an automatic pilot went about getting ready for a day without a mission in mind. Annie and I would always go for a walk this time of

Ashley Bay

morning but there are no more walks. The morning dew and the barely awake squirrels looking for their breakfast brought one of her many daily smiles as we strolled the park down the block. There was the curious fowl of dawn that followed us through that nearby park and every dog on a morning walk of their own came up to say hello. We walked as often as we could. She was always worried about those three or four pounds that I never saw but that she freaked out about. I knew she wanted me to at least make a half hearted attempt at exercising and staying in decent enough shape to at least look good for the embalmer.

Outside and down at the bottom of the stairs was Dottie's place. She was a neat little old bird who had watched out for me for some time now. Dottie sat at her window and carefully watched all who came and went from our complex mentally accepting or refuting all. She especially liked my coming home at the end of the day for I often stopped in to say hello. She would discipline me like a puppy and feed me like the birds outside her patio door. Her door was covered with a welcome sign made by a grandchild who had long since stopped paying her any mind. I knew she wasn't home because it was Monday and was Senior Day at the Chuckey's Theatre Mega-Plex, it was one of her few trips during the week and she would carry the movie with here for the week. Dottie had her week well planned around just one or two special days and Monday was one of these days. She and Annie went every now then to the classical "chick flick" at the Mega-Plex and then blame us male primates for all being "dogs." Neither was into the modern cut-and-slash, blood-and-gore so called Hollywood classics.

For Dottie it was always Bogart and for Annie any chick flick would suit her just fine as long as there was a happy ending so she would leave with a tear and a smile. I could never understand that about women. They often needed to cry to feel good leaving us male primates in the corner of the room trying to put the fire out. The walk down to the car was good enough exercise for today and it was the only exercise I had been getting for some time.

I knew Annie would be disappointed because she tried for so long to get me to lose the Hostess side effects. "Body by Hostess," she would say when I sought a new reason to sit and stare rather then walk and climb. The pattern for some time now didn't include exercise of the physical kind though I was wearing myself out emotionally. I planned as I walked what the day would be like, where I would go and what I would ignore along the same senseless route. A coffee, a *real* coffee was a requirement as was the daily copy of the Providence Times-Union a noble liberal ragamuffin. For me, a one time Christian conservative reading liberal bilge kept my blood circulating. There was a section of the paper that I enjoyed and had now read regularly for several years on the history of New England. The author was a bit of an odd duck though not surprising since he came from old time New England Yankee stock and he prided himself as being a societal observer.

J. Matthew Horton was his name and he was rather insistent that he be addressed by his full name. Old J. M. and I got to know each other over the last couple of years over our love for a good story. I submitted suggestions for stories and he in turn gave me some follow up work on others. His writing appealed to me in many ways because it was a simple style and sought to remember the days that were once so good. His writing style was one that the older among us looked forward to and the younger ignored as something that was just out of touch.

I had lived several places around the country and certainly I had traveled everywhere but for me New England was at one time America's most spiritual, God fearing region. There are others like me now who just shake our heads in disgust at how New England had become nothing but the modern Sodom and Gomorrah. From the landing of the Pilgrims to the birth of the Great Awakening New England loved and lived for God. Now, we the descendants of those founders, sit and sip our mochas seeking the love of nature and same sex unions. What have we given to America besides an up turned palm? What would God say about us now that the land that was promised to Him in Pilgrim covenant is a moral wasteland? This section of the world that the most pious settled now drips with the screams of the aborted and the blushing giggles of the newly blessed gay marriages. Massachusetts and Vermont and for that matter all of New England now live as if there is no God. The land chosen *for* God is now a Godless land pure and simple. I shook my head and at the world the Godless have wrought and pulled out onto Tennent Avenue into a world that Annie would now have to question.

Ashley Bay

    Tennent Avenue was the main route in and out of Bradford. However, if one knew the way they could skirt all this mess and avoid the modern life. The mess that I saw was the buildup of the mini-marts, video closets and gas stations. This block and the one five, ten or twenty blocks down all looked the same with nothing unique or memorable. Bradford was like any other older New England town, here forever. Everything that a person could ever want or need could be found by just heading north for a few miles. The small town feeling had been long ago replaced by the mega this and mega that and of course Wal-Mart. All were blended in with the fast food places Annie scolded me about. Where Annie and I had settled was the newer part of Bradford but if you wanted a good deal older Bradford was the best place to stop. If you wanted service and decent people, if you wanted attention and a good conversation, I would suggest driving a bit farther north on Tennent. Decency and kindness were found in older Bradford but not in this new age part of town much like society as a whole. The traffic was of consistent flow with rude out of staters and Harvard alumni. These drivers were some of the most selfish individuals that the devil could have wished for. I had spent so many years dealing with these folks that their attitude was now just an afterthought. I could barely recognize polite behavior and since political correctness prevents moral disciplining, I kept my mouth shut altogether.

    I was heading for the library that was about two miles outside of town and was built about 1900 with invested Civil War pensions. It was a nice place for any haunting rest by those of my ilk and I so haunted the upper chambers of the back room of this gothic legend. My major concern with this and many other libraries is that hardly anyone under thirty cracks the door frame of these noble sentries anymore. It was a nice place to relax amid the scent that comes from older libraries. I would sit in the upper rooms and just let the smell of the hardbound classics make its way to me without MTV interrupting. The same smell accompanied Dad's books and it was one that I wouldn't let go of. It was certainly a nice memory for those of my generation. For many of us, this is where we learned to enjoy the art of escape. This library was where I mastered the journeys that only well written fiction would take a youthful mind from the Hardy Boys to Kipling, I traveled them all. In just a few moments of nondescript travel, I parked opposite the cannon dedicated to the troops of the 4th Rhode Island and planned my route to the furthest corner of a second floor forgotten room.

I nodded to Mr. Schuster who sat out in front in the same spot that he had claimed since returning from the second of the great wars. He was a red haired silent man with a bit of limp who sat with stoic indifference to those who came bearing a friendly nod. I watched him once from my second floor loft as he just stared the seasons away and I wondered often if he was waiting for something long forgotten. The library seemed so huge when I was a young man, so gothic and almost intimidating to the point of turning this plum chaser around. As I grew, it shrunk in size but the smell of old books and the vacant looks of Mr. Schuster always stayed the same. I made my way to the day old newspaper stack and a chair in the back that overlooked the Eleazar River. This was quite the beautiful spot to sit and watch as the leaves of fall turned and the snows of December ensued. Many a deer, accustomed to man would make its way to the salt lick on the opposite bank a gift to us *and* to them from the stoic Mr. Schuster.

Sitting with an unread newspaper was how I often began my own escape into the deep recesses of mortal regrets. The aimless and daunting files of self doubt were my companions as I sat and watched a lonely fawn make its way to the banks of the Eleazar. The shuffling of the newsprint covered up the shuffling of my secular mental files. Once I had settled on Mr. Horton's tale my mind settled on just a couple of the more prominent tales of self doubt those being *God* and *self*. Did doubt in one lead to doubt in the other?

The news of the day was too real for me to use as an escape mechanism so I entrusted my regrets with the task of forming this day's escapism. If I allowed my personal loathing to form this day's tales I wouldn't have to face reality. In this day and age the papers seemed to print more stories that could be seen as entertainment than what should be seen as news, inspiration or basic respect. So skipping that wouldn't be a loss. Ignoring the usual murder or two, the political scandals and which gay celebrity married whom, I found the biweekly column of Mr. J. M. Horton. As usual the headline today stirred my fantasy instantaneously:

Forgotten Shipwrecks of Maine

Ashley Bay

The stories of the sea fascinated me as if I were a young man seeking pirate like adventures all over again. The sea gave to man at one time all he needed to sustain life and I respected those who sought to challenge it and those who found new life upon overcoming its boundaries. I knew the strength of the sea to be incredible with glorified thievery, epics of seafaring dangers and many a lost love. All of these epics were wrapped into one if you chose a life at sea. The stories of the sea could be emblematic of all our lives regardless if we saw the waters or lived without shade. One could get lost in all the stories told by old forgotten seamen now relegated to a bench in front of small town libraries coast to coast. The stories were of the clipper ships from centuries past and about the journeys of those who came seeking fame and fortune and were never heard from again. Allot like the life for the lonely regardless of their era.

The Horton headline spawned a million fables before I ever read what its author was about to say to his readers. He had a gift of empowering imagination and I was master of *that* particular task as well. A skim here and a skim there of his story was plenty for now. I would stop along the way home and get a copy for me and Dottie and I would finish a mental travail as my day came to a rest. I would be sure to finish the story before that day ended or maybe the next day but *I* would finish it. Dottie couldn't read too well anymore so I gave her snap shots of what was going on in the world about her: the news, the comics -- she was a big fan of Hagar. I would say this guy did that and the other did this and the Red Sox lost yet again. The latter made her day for despite being a New Englander she *was* a Yankee fan.

I didn't read much of the story before I shoved it back onto a musty stack but what stuck out from the story was the name Colstein Harbor. Colstein Harbor was one of those mid-Atlantic Maine villages that everyone drives through on their way to Portland. I knew this rather well for Annie and I had done our share of ignoring its existence on our way to the north coast. Annie and I had driven through there a couple of times as we headed to Augusta for a weekend drive back down the coast. Annie loved these drives, especially during the fall because of the changes of colors and the wildlife that would be everywhere she wanted to go. If one were just the slightest bit inattentive to the world around them they could easily miss Colstein Harbor. The name alone was great; it was one of those names that just sticks with you, like the name of your first grade teacher and your first dog it just never goes away. That time in life was so wonderful for us her smile could be triggered by a stupid squirrel, Charlie Brown and most often *me* - I will miss her dearly.

My time at the library was short most days but the view from this isolated perch was quite nice. With a fumble here and a fumble there of the more obnoxious headlines, I had a final look at the Eleazar and the hour had faded as quickly as the salt lick across the way. I left the sanctuary of mustiness and walked back past the gothic intimidation of the still in use card catalog and with a see yah' tomorrow nod to Mr. Schuster, I was back out on Tennent. The drive home always seemed longer then the one here. Though it was the same distance, the destination was not nearly as pleasurable. At the end of the return trip was the same old dank, neglected apartment in which I had rested for many months, maybe years or more, who knows how long.

I approached the red light at Tennent and Mathews just a few blocks from the unmentioned border that separated the old from the new section of town. As I sat at this never green long enough light, I thought how these intersections must be alike all over the country. This particular one had a donut place over there and a video place over there and some kid on the corner peddling his stuff. When I was younger, I was always in a hurry to get through these lights so I could get caught at the next one. I ask this question more and more as I have gotten older; what are the young in a hurry for? I'll never understand why the young are in such a hurry to live for age and crippled walks will be here soon enough. I wish I could grab them and say slow down, pet the puppies and talk to *your* Dotties. Slow down, my young friends and let the cherry blossoms tell you their stories. Now as timidity has seized me, the longer the light the better for me for it allowed me the time to see the world just a bit before I honked my own horn.

The donut place on the corner never changed, the videos had now become DVDs and the kid on the corner changed infrequently as well. Today it was a young girl maybe seven or eight, she had matted-hair, dirty clothes and a hand painted sign that read free puppies. The immediate need for a coffee and Boston creme far outweighed my consideration for basic driving etiquette. So as I satisfied my quest for carbohydrates, my behavior generated several undiplomatic honks by those to my rear. Well, I said to myself in a rather condescending way, my reasoning for such abrupt behavior was that Dottie would like one of those Boston cremes as well. I swung into Leonard's Donut Coral at a speed above that recommended because I was doing this *for* Dottie and not me. I was a good and decent man with only *Dottie's* needs in mind.

The manager of Leonard's was Sandi Beach a girl I had known a bit in high school but had not paid much attention to since. Sandi, as best as I could tell had been through some hard years since our school days but she had put on a brave face. Sandi had been through a series of deadbeat guys who wanted her for her connubial ability and nothing else sadly I admit I was one of those guys. It took me quite some time but I must admit, at least to myself that I fell into that deadbeat category. I had always thought of myself as a good and morally decent man looking for a similar woman to grow old with but i failed at times. Sandi was one of those girls in high school nobody paid attention to yet when a man in his later years looks back, it is them we remember with a kind smile and a wish that life for them had turned out well. I believe that when decent men mature we think of the girls we hurt, those we lied to and cheated on and we do so with tremendous regret. As the gray hairs multiply we seek to make amends to the young women we walked out on and promised to call but never did.

Sandi was in her 40s now and often looked sad and perhaps disappointed by the wakes that had come her way and at her seeming inability to fend them off. "Hi, guy," she always said with a worn out smile that seemed forced but genuine. "Sandi, how are you?" "Good," was always the reply without a hint of eye contact. She had always been kind to me from junior high through to today she never uttered a bad word toward me. "Two and two, aye?" She knew my order before I had even stepped out of the car. I nodded I hadn't even changed that in years.

Sandi busied herself behind the counter. "Sorry to hear about your mom." A pause. "*She* always treated me good."

Ugh, a pang of built up conscience and mature timidity reminded me that Mom knew Sandi's mom and had been friends with the family for decades. "Yeah, Mom was something else. She was sick near the end and maybe was ready to go. I don't think I will let those final days go anytime soon though." I thought some, "She taught us allot her last days, dignity, peace, strength she did her best to leave with us with her head held high."

I took the bag and left her a larger than average tip in hopes of making up for my lack of juvenile kindness. She smiled and bid me good day with a soft thank you. Our conversations had never amounted to much more than this kind of a shame I thought for she was at her root a good decent Christian woman. "Take care of yourself, Sandi. Maybe I'll see you tomorrow aye OK?"

Sandi tossed another smile and said, "Go and get yourself a puppy. The little one has been there all day." She pointed to the matted-hair little girl across the way.

"Don't think so. Too much trouble just taking care of myself," I said as I backed out of the double doors. Standing outside with a nod here and a nod there to fellow "carb" seekers and fumbling for some quarters, I managed two for the price of one of the Providence Times. I'll make up for it later I said with my eyes. After all, *it* was for Dottie and so it was OK. Whether it was bad driving, rude behavior or an extra copy of the newspaper, I had often legitimized my bad behavior by saying it was for the good. This behavior was unfortunately long entrenched in my nature I set the bag on the hood of a Ford Tempo that was years past its prime and made more noise than my Uncle Dave after Thanksgiving dinner. I grabbed a Boston creme and licked the chocolate hitchhikers while I aimlessly watched the world about me with an air of supremacy. I stood at the front of the car as the sunlight bounced off the rooftop. I stood there watching the traffic go by and wondering why *they*, the aimless drivers of Bradford were so arrogant. I stood with such an air of pomposity that I failed to recognize that someone was also watching me. The matted-hair little side walk vendor watched me watching her. Smacking my fingers, I thought just how much this place had sprung up and how the older generation simply stayed away from it. My head followed the cars to the left, to the right and back the other way again. The political types call it economic development but just how many Cumberland Farms and Wal-Marts does a town really need? I took the final and largest of bites and smacked my fingers without knowing that I was still being watched. At what time does the town say enough is enough and say no thank you to more video stores and discount pharmacies? When will the summer days return when we can walk home without being robbed or raped? When can we go fishing without being sued and when will the ice cream truck be met by dime waving plum chasers and not gun waving crack heads again? Everyone rushes here and rushes there and the finer, gentler side of life is passing us all by in the name of progress. Through all this mental languish I was still being watched by the vendor across the way.

The whole world has an attitude of let's hurry up and get to the next red light. All of us are in too much of a hurry to stop and smell the honeysuckle and let the jasmine touch us deep. The new approach to life is that we all have to get home and tape the shows we'll never watch. We have to be rude to the Fed-Ex guy because our overnight, cross-country delivery was an hour late. Rush here and drop off there and for many of us a blinking yellow light secretly means go faster. Whatever happened to the summertime strolls and the autumn walks with my favorite girl? What happened to our youth and to the rainbows we held in our minds because we knew the next rain storm was just around the corner? Where is the next generation of plum chasers? Where is the next generation of Yowells and Hydes? Where is the laughter of sisters at play and a nearly blind three-legged black lab? Where are the *when yah' can* lists of this generation? Where has all the kindness of man gone? To hell with them all I said smacking my fingers from atop my pious perch.

I had a wish for a few more bites of the first creme but alas it had gone to the great beyond and I knew Dottie may have to wait for another day if I went for the other. I looked sheepishly at the bag and a pang of guilt superseded my reach for the final Boston creme *but* my inner voice lost as it always did at moments like this. I don't think Dottie has seen a Boston creme yet but my intentions have always included her. As I fumbled for the last contents of Leonard's bag, I tossed a glimpse at a matted-hair young girl who insisted that her puppies were free. Why was this little snoopy girl eyeing me? I downed the second of two for Dottie didn't need the unhealthy carbo treat anyway; she had a weight problem so I was eating this for *her* benefit and not because *I* enjoyed it. Why did this little girl across the way insist at watching me with such diligence?

A strange site I thought as I glanced again at this little girl. Where were her parents? Why the puppies? Why was she looking my way? Did she expect something from me? I smacked my fingers yet again and wondered why her hair was matted and why she appeared so dirty. Why, at a busy intersection like this one, was she so close to the traffic? Wasn't anyone watching her? I grew anxious and my memory dashed back and forth to *all* the women I had known. What would this little one be like when she grew up? Was she going to be just another Sandi Beach for the world to ignore? Would she be cared for by a gentleman or battered, abused and set aside in the name of a younger, prettier model?

Maybe someone at sometime would give her just a smallest hint of God here on earth and not the minions of that which is evil. The thoughts of anger directed at the speeding, unkind, finger waving, goatee wearing wunderkinds was set aside for an open heart. The importance of the lessons taught me by Ethyl Hyde and Mrs. Yowell were never realized until moments like this when I saw a young child so emblematic of all I knew. The neighborhood preacher, Reverend Kim, would remind us all in Sunday school in the softest yet sternest of ways that God rests inside us all begging to get out. He would pass on in the most subtle of ways that we can never stand taller than when we stoop to help a child. He would share with us the view that when we act in love God comes to the world through us. The message that all the travelers in my youth taught was that at the time of our greatest apprehension we *must* show kindness to those who may just need a friend for *that* one moment. It was a tremendous message. However, I always waited for the other person to reach out first for I was just too busy. I just couldn't afford to miss the next red light so God *and* kindness would have to wait until I was ready.

I stood at the front of the Tempo and watched as cars just flew by the young girl as if she weren't there. She would lower her head and let the breeze of traffic mess up her hair just that much more. She would wrestle with the handmade free puppy sign as it blew over time after time after time to the chuckles of the elite. Appalling to even me was that some people giggled and locked their doors when they saw the little girl even look in their direction. Driver after driver just stared ahead at the horizon of unpaid bills and the rush to meet endless parental deadlines. The young girl wasn't there for many who wanted nothing more than to hurry to their next red light and not be bothered by the poorly written sign and a four foot side walk vendor.

I should have been moving on down the road myself and in fact, had my keys in hand. I had begun a slow deliberate walk to the driver's door and felt the stare of Sandi coming through the window behind me. I threw the empty bag away and tossed Sandi a smile as I again felt anxious with just a hint of confusion. Was I the only one being sent this message? Was I the only one for whom this message was *intended*? Was the message being sent as I understood it one of sharing God with this young girl? Was God speaking just to me or was I the only one listening? How many times over the years have I heard a voice just like this and said to myself maybe tomorrow instead of doing what was good and decent today. Sandi came to mind immediately, I had certainly been unkind to her many times. Thinking about some of the more glaring of offenses, I wondered who took the time to reach out to her when she was young, when her hair was matted. Was their ever a dad for Sandi, is there a dad for the little sidewalk vendor? Why would any father allow his young child, *his* daughter to stand alone on these dangerous streets? In today's world when so many men seek personal pleasure in place of committed responsibility women like Sandi are just a speed bump to the next conquest of the flesh. I looked both ways and threw half the Boston creme away so I wouldn't be accused of being wasteful.

Smacking my teeth and licking the hitchhikers off my fingers, I made my way to the sidewalk nearest my soon to be young friend. I neared the end of the entrance sign fumbling with my keys and sought something other than eye contact with the young vendor for I knew that such a look would be lethal. I watched as the traffic flung by as if seeking gold at the end of a rainbow and no one stopped even to smile her way. The people all around were dodging here and there, back and forth, all avoiding eye contact and refusing even a good day acknowledgment of their neighbors. From old trucks to new Buicks to first time, smart ass drivers all had a turn here and turn there, a quick braking and a cuss word thrust toward the car in front but not a word for the little vendor.

They were all quick and quicker and all went one way then the other. The faces of modern man ignored the simple ones who just needed a kind smile. There was beeping, honking, fumes, pollution and unkind gestures all flaring in every direction one could imagine. Despite all the action and the helter-skelter world in front of them the puppies were still free to those who would just ask, and my soon to be friend brushed her hair back one more time. I was still at the intersection when I caught her eye and she quickly slammed the return gaze to the ground as if caught doing something wrong. Now I was confused. Did she want me to cross? Did she want me to see her puppies? The mental game began as my hands fumbled the air. Should I cross or should I toss yet another till tomorrow nod her way instead? Are these puppies free or am I just fooling myself? What do I want with a dog anyhow?

The red light came and after a short lived pause and I crossed to meet the figure of a bashful young girl. At first glance, I guessed she was probably eight or maybe nine, possibly younger. She appeared dirty but could have been just a kid at play, though I noticed she made the best effort to cover the holes in her canvas shoes with pants just a bit too long Her hair was unkempt and she nervously kept it out of her eyes as she paid uneasy attention to the contents of the box. I nodded a hello her way With a hushed hello and a gaze more frequently heading to her canvas shoes than at me she sought witnesses for her noble package. I began with a businesslike good morning, "how are you?" I cleared my throat.

In a simple mumble she let me know she was "good," a low cut word that preceded the reddening of her dirty cheeks. I looked about, perhaps just as nervous as she was and I found the objects of her direct appeal. In a cardboard box well worn from serving as a carry all for some time there were three puppies, beagle pups. It surprised me that they were still there and that some finer class from up Warwick way had not claimed them. Beagles were the type of dog that nobody could ever hate; perhaps God made them just for man because of the perfect companionship that would grow from each knowing one another. Beagles *were* the Ed Norton of dogs -- annoying, not too terribly bright but loyal and friendly to a fault.

Ashley Bay

I withheld acknowledgment of the products of contention for I knew if there was eye contact with one of these pathetic examples of what used to be a proud noble beast I would be in trouble.

My young friend told me with a shy directness, "Na buddy wants dem. I foun' dem da udder day and nobody wants dem." My young friend pointed in a general way at the box of castaways.

I didn't want to look at them so I chose to look down Cooper Street to the tame intersection of Tennent and asked, "How long have you been here?"

She brushed the hair out of her eyes and said, "Came yet' day, sure hot out here and my mum got mad and told me not to stay too long."

"It's hot today too," I said avoiding the reason for our meeting huddled en masse in the box below.

"Had `tree yet'day, till got `tree today."

It seemed to me she was frustrated to the point of giving up or at least not knowing what else to do with her box of castaways. I was undergoing a moment by moment change of consciousness and felt that *this* moment was one presented to me so that I could show myself to be a kind man. This was my opportunity to suspend selfish behavior and do something nice for someone who needed a break. It was my decision to help her make *her* decision as to whether or not she should keep doing what she was doing. With a mighty gust, God gave my conscience a swift slap and the silent whisper of someone yet unknown to me gave me a shove as my compassion came forth. I shoved my hands in and out of my rather empty pockets and knew the time had come for me to look at the box below.

In a paternalistic way I said, "Hun, why don't show me what you got aye?" With a shuffle and a rumple and a ladylike curtsy, she reached for a pee-covered blanket. Beneath the cover I saw three greatly disheveled characters whose better days would be the very moment that they were claimed by people at the red lights. One was the obvious "boss," the head of the cardboard box of castaways. It was he that would dictate whose hands were allowed to touch what shipmates. The second was more passive and subservient to a nip at the ears by the first. A darker shade of each of the beagle's major color schemes were chief and yet subtle differences between the two. I knew they would be a curious friendly troublemaker for anyone so inclined to have such a pee-covered passive trouble maker wandering their suburban back lot.

The third one, still partially covered by the overused blanket was in the furthest depths of the cardboard box and seemed suspicious as to the intentions of his observer. He scooted his nose in a rather self righteous way away from any hands and toward the comfort of the corner. A glimpse out of the corner of his eye told me I best *not* mess with this one To hell with him I thought! I don't need to be treated like that by a dog covered by pee living in a box. My hell bound ego was telling me that I was being treated rudely by one of God's forgotten creatures and that I needed to ignore the needs of this one as all others had simply because *I* was being treated badly.

I fought the lethal temptation of compassion and knew intuitively that I would be in trouble if I held one; yes, holding a puppy would mean trouble. However, I took the first step and made myself willing to hear of their fate from the heart of my new matted-hair little friend.

"Where did you find them," I asked avoiding canine contact.

After a period of shuffling contemplation from the street vendor, she began, "Der mum was dead, dese were close to her and I brought dem home." She brushed the fur of the first two. "Found dem on the road home. My mum's boyfriend was goin' to bring dem to da poun' yet'day but I brought dem here instead. Dey kill puppies at da poun', don't dey?"

I scratched my three day growth and fought for a lie to answer such a troublesome question. *They kill puppies, don't they*? How was I, someone who had over the course of his life been cruelest at times to the kindest of creatures going to answer that? Rather than forcing a troubled, truthful answer I asked her to show me *who* they were. Step two of the inevitable had taken place.

With a sense of success she reached for the box. "Dis one is da one da eats eveytring." She held up the boss. He had his eyes wide open and took in all that was going on around him. He was cautious and protective and felt a duty to the others in the box for he quickly wanted an immediate return. She replaced the squirmier one and continued. "Dis one," she said pointing to the follower, "pees all da time." She patted the two on the head as if approving of their unkempt state and urinating ability. She ended her sales pitch with a half hearted point toward the last of the three "O, dis one is da shy one." My young friend seemed excited and animated for the first time in our short friendship. Like a salesclerk working for a commission she must have felt a *sale* was inevitable and she provided additional need to know information. "Dis one is da playing one and dis one is da fat one and O, dis one is small and simple like."

I did my best to avoid eye contact or get a whiff of that puppy breath that we all know too well but I was growing weak. I have found out and usually well after the fact that a conscience is a worthy foe for the guilty and habitually regretful side of man. My weakness was evident and I stammered with, "You're doing a good thing here, kiddo." A smile came from beneath the brushed back matted hair and she rolled up the sleeves of an over worn sweatshirt. Without warning and with even less of a sustainable defense, I returned to old behavior. I didn't want to commit to anything, I was afraid of *it* in some primordial way, commitment that is. I justified an early exit by looking at the car keys just removed from an empty pocket. "Kiddo, if you are here tomorrow I will stop by, let me think about it for the night." I could tell by her drooping hair that she was disappointed. There was no brushed back hair this time, just a yield to shy redness of the unwashed cheeks. My young friend neatly folded the blanket so her young acquisitions would stay warm. "I promise, tomorrow I will come by, OK."

A set of pursed lips bid me ado with, "K."

I patted her softly on the head and without losing a moment I dashed across Tennent to the lot holding my Tempo. I had to get home though there was nothing waiting for me but I just had to get home. There was so much to do in a day that held no plans and I was behind on finishing the tasks. I was in a hurry to accomplish my lethargy and set aside the time of potential charity to meet *my* needs. I had to get all the undefined done so as not to complain when the night came that all the pointlessness of the day was unfulfilled. In my mind at this point and time accomplishing nothing was the fulfillment of a day well done. I was quickly in the car and out on Tennent soon away from having to face the ghosts of those I had remembered and those I'd ignored.

The girls of years ago who were now women held a grip on my soul that no amount of sorrow could rid. To friends, family and significant others who I had made countless promises to and never honored, I now remembered more than at any time even immediately following the offense. The puppy girl brought back days of old, good and bad. There were so many in my life that needed only a friend, some truth and honesty and I couldn't furnish them with such things that would show my vulnerability. This was a mental game that I knew I would lose someday, but until that day came I would have to face the demons of my conscience. With this behavior of regretful selfishness I knew the change wouldn't come today because I was in such a hurry to get to the next red light and not take the first step. I was in such a hurry to get home, run upstairs and throw my head under whatever pillow was close and let *it* all pass. The drive down Tennent was quick, it was as if I were leaving the scene of a possible crime and I didn't want to be asked any questions by the secret bystanders. The memories of all I had harmed and told maybe tomorrow came back with a short visit to a matted-hair little sidewalk vendor. I had all my history serving as mechanisms of doubt as to my sincerity of return to her the next time. Many promises she had been told but known were kept by young or old.

I sped down Tennent to the sounds of an encroaching, supple beat of rain willed from Mom's funeral. The rain was a welcome sight for it enhanced my reasoning for having to get home for why would I want to stay out in *such* horrible weather? I passed through the contemporary part of Bradford and down over the canal I knew all too well. The chill of this late autumn had been catching up to me since the other day and now I felt the chill in my unprepared quadrants. I thought a decent rest would evict that unwelcome intruder from my seemingly perpetuating depressed condition. But how long must the rest last before I was OK? The rain beat quicker than my wipers could handle and I knew even better than twenty minutes ago that sleep would hide me from the world of God and His insistence of kindness towards all.

Ashley Bay

As usual, the drive home was longer than the one I had taken several hours before for there was nothing else to do except make plans for the same duties tomorrow. I used to be able to escape more often through the music called golden as it seeped into my tepid gray but even that was hard now. Now the music was a torrent and unacceptable to anyone who had the ability to listen. I loved the classics of my generation that the younger ones just snickered at. Music now only played memories, every song taught a lesson and brought back a neglected face. When on one of those trips, if a certain event or a certain scent came our way a memorable tune was usually behind it. The good songwriter, if fortunate to be joined by talent could tell a story and move the heart in a way that no one else seemed capable of. I sat in the car trying to remember some of my all time favorites and the reasons they were so called. There were many more than I thought and I hoped to narrow them down to perhaps the top five at some point for the sake of having something to accomplish. I'll start that list tomorrow.

The sprinkling rain seemed a torrent as I dreaded the resting place that was now just moments away. I would need to see Dottie before I went upstairs and tell her of my day and she would complain at how sad I seemed and encourage me to take a step toward moving on. I put my parking lights on just blocks from my place and with a sharp left here and a second left after that I came to the spot Annie and I had held captive for a couple of years. With my hands at 10 and 2 on the wheel I let the car run till I knew I could safely approach Dottie's place without her Boston creme Though she already knew the bag would be empty I would put on an act to mess with her a bit in order to give her something to snicker about. What story was I going to tell her on *this* day as to why my hands and her bag were empty?

I slouched in the driver's seat for a bit thinking about the mental spectrum I would record at the end of this day. How much I had done and how little I had reached out to others would be the columns in this day's journal. There were so many entries yet to be recorded -- the death of my mother, life with my Annie, the free puppies, matted-hair little lass and Dottie, Noah's maid. I was locked in place as if headed for a painful fall and I was powerless to stop the impact. I held the steering wheel tightly a sure sign of an imbedded anxiety. Dad had once told this chubby plum chaser that the best thing about a painful fall is having the opportunity to start all over again, there would be bruises but they would heal. I wish I could ask Dad now, at this stage of my life just how many times one man can start over again before he stops getting up. The question that I knew I would ask Dad someday is why start over again and again if a fall is the end result? His and *His* answer I knew, it's because we must.

I was ready to start over yet again but something was holding me back what it was time will tell I'm sure. I couldn't face the demons that countless secular disappointments always bring me and as of this day I had received my fair share of them. I had hoped that as I aged I would become braver and nobler in spirit, but I hadn't though not the fault of the spirit. I had not yet accomplished such noble bravery for I guess there were still lessons to be learned on this particular part of life's road. Plural or singular, I didn't know if there was but one lesson or thousands yet unlearned. I wondered how many lessons had to be experienced before we simply said, *Oh yeah I get it*. What I remember at such times like this is that when I was young and foolish I did young and foolish things and felt I could offer the confused mind of mine more than God could. My spirit was youthful and hard headed at *this* stage of life.

Letting 10 o'clock go I grabbed the door and soon the morning paper for Dottie. Clicking my lights it was now time to face the maid of the ages and her pesky mental floor sweeper. Dottie and I would chat and she would wag her bony finger at my ever increasing waistline and seek in her motherly way to bring me through my chapel of demons. I walked the shallow path to her door and knocked on a welcome sign made by a nephew who had long since forgotten her. My cranky friend quickly answered.

"Hi, son come on in."

Dottie always watched as I pulled in knowing that she would soon have someone to cuss at. I assumed she would be waiting on my knock, she was nagging to some but she would call it mothering to those like me. I walked through the never locked door and as always was met by the scent of freshly cut flowers regardless of the time of year. I took my customary seat adjusted the throw pillow she made years ago and readied myself for the next hour or so. Dottie usually avoided eye contact and gestured with her pudgy fingers instead.

Whether she was shy or timid I never knew but eye contact was infrequent.

"Sit down. There is coffee and some meat loaf for you to take upstairs when yah' go."

I sat down with a sigh of satisfaction and she went on and on about my behavior and how I needed to change things to live better and happier. I was so tired and sitting down in a comfortable home was a nice way to end every day, a thought was in syndication as Dottie was warming up.

Dottie, after fumbling through some bags in the kitchen waddled my way and said, "You don't eat right, never have since Annie. She would be so mad at you, yah know."

Dottie would shuffle this and that and pat the side of the chair that I was to occupy for a couple of hours. Before I could remove my initial smile upon stepping through the door, she would ask and state and declare countless things venting her loneliness at her neighbor. When Annie and I had a newlywed blowout it was here the Irish angel came to unload and it was here I came with tail dragging to make up.

I never asked nor was told much about *Mr.* Dottie I could just imagine that he must have had the patience of Job and was as silent as the evening stars.

"Here, try some of this. You'll like it, it has sugar and everything you're not supposed to have. So eat, EAT! you're all fat and bones." I just shook my head as if having a fit.

She had placed in front of me some sugar covered fancy froufrou things and I obliged her commands, feeling my fillings skyrocket as the sugar doused my raw nerves. After a handful of bites and a deposit of a pound of sugar on a rear abscess I said, "Very nice, Dottie I'll take them with me tonight." In a nervous tone that surely showed my social awkwardness I said, "Dottie, sit down, we can catch up with all *this* in a bit, OK?"

I thanked her for coffee, took a sip and looked out the corner of my eyes in suspicion of my observer and said, "I forgot the donuts today."

Dottie tossed me a she knew better smile and not another word was said about the chocolate still on the corner of my mouth.

She sat across the room on a small couch covered with handmade things from a life well lived.

"It was raining when I pulled up. Don't know what tomorrow holds though. I haven't heard the weather yet today."

She smiled and brushed off the coffee table where I had failed to use the napkin she placed there for me. In her typical manner she said, "No one knows about tomorrow my young friend. Don't let the rain get in the way of trying to figure it out though." She finished her housekeeping. "Don't let rain keep you on the couch."

I knew I had opened another door better left shut. "Yeah, I know."

Dottie was the teacher and I was her student getting disciplined for giving up on a simple assignment of not making plans for personal growth.

I ignored her subtle point and said, "Some good stories in the paper, one on shipwrecks in Maine that you might like." She fumbled to adjust the pillows behind her so she could watch the traffic out front. Dottie really did like being just a bit nosey.

"Sounds good. I'd like to read that someday, I have a bunch of stuff here to catch up on." I handed her the paper that was smeared with most of her Boston creme.

"Thanks kiddo." She stared at the floor a bit and said; "There was story I heard once as a kid, told to me by Daddy and passed on to him from some long forgotten uncle. It was only in bits and pieces and that I remember any of it is fortunate."

The quick pause in her tale was the break she needed to begin the shuffling through papers and stacks of stuff on the floor next to the couch. Our conversations were often like this some new topics, the Red Sox were sometimes sprinkled in there but most certainly those damn Democrats were a daily complaint. She would start one story, pause for a moment and finish it with the balance of one previously told though the two showed no relationship to one another.

A sip of the coffee, which I had to admit tasted so good compared to my tap water morning brew. In thanks, I asked, "Did you need anything at the store? I'm probably going out a little later." I knew she did and I knew that I wouldn't.

She still shuffled and fumbled and hesitated just a bit more before she replied in a shy voice. "Maybe a few things, if you wouldn't mind hun. I could use some help with some things."

"Sure, anytime. Is tomorrow okay? If you need it now, I can go in a few minutes." I reached for my wallet.

Our conversations were never long nor in depth nor analytical, just people talk. Our talks were small talk that ended with open ended quizzes that could be answered only with a follow up visit. I pulled out a fifty and slid it underneath her coffee cup. I tried to be slick but though Dottie was very good at avoiding eye contact except when it came to money. She was a timeless, portly soul, friendlier than anyone of my status could imagine and I was thankful she was here for me.

"You should take some time my friend and go up north to Maine the back roads and the coastal drive, yah' know, that you and Annie used to like Memories always help us with our plans."

"I was thinking about that very thing most of the last couple of days. Some time away might be good for me."

Dottie left me daily with nice pieces of wisdom and *memories help us with our plans* was one of the best something like that would never come from a Harvard type. I spent just a few moments thinking about that and how right she was and what if anything I would do about it. It was and *is* our memories that determine whether we have the strength to move ahead.

I again told her, "I was thinking about that same drive myself. Annie really did like that area up there." I paused for a second slurp. "When I saw the headline about the shipwrecks it brought back the memories of those trips we used to take. I need some work at some point, the well is drying up a little, but maybe I don't need to worry about that anymore."

Dottie, her eyes still on the stack of stuff said, "You're probably right, hun. At some time the work comes to an end."

I was telling a story of course, just trying to rationalize my way out of facing the demons that had now become obvious to my friend. If my life were left up to me I would sit and watch the days click by until the spirit called me home. I had sensed that the clock had been ticking for some time now and I was just waiting. I would sit and wonder about the existence of God until faced with my final opportunity of knowing Him or not. I guess that would be my ultimate plan getting to know Him. I would need to take a journey to find out whether or not His plan would prove to be the correct one. If I could just sit and do nothing and not be forced into thinking, what a great comfort that would be to my guilty soul but I new I couldn't do that I had to take the first step.

At times there was no more thorough relief for my depression than the tapping of the rain on the window that I stared through. The preface to the rain was a conversation like this with a friend such as Dottie. At times I would stare for hours on end having to force myself to blink because the depression was just so rooted in a spirit tired of the fight. The demons haunted me day and night but what were they and why couldn't I let them go and why wouldn't they let *me* go? I couldn't close the mental door on all the what ifs and could have beens that my secular disappointments had laid at my feet. I would listen to the mental games of *if I had only done this or what if I had only done that, my life would be better*. It is a fight that only the vile win and that the sane lament till the door of one's own satanic verses slams shut once and for all and our choice is made for us. Dottie knew the mental game and she knew I was losing the fight. She could see my eyes and read my spirit. I believed *I* was playing the game well but she could tell I was losing.

To calm the warring parties down just a bit she shuffled some home made caramel crunchy banana chews in front of me. With a pat on my head, she said with her grouchy demeanor, "Here tubby eat these." She often discredited my belt line with a smirk for she had done her share over the years to widen the very load she now poked fun at.

Whatever she cooked and put in front of me was good of course for it was mostly sugar and it would take a concerted regimen of brushing and flossing to remove those pieces that refused their final respite. I took a couple of bites and said, "I don't think I have thanked you Dottie for everything of late. You have always been very good to me," I said as my nervous voice cracked just a bit. She was a true and loyal friend.

She patted my shoulder as she took my cup for a reload of some scented vanilla crap. Though not my style or flavor the conversation made the coffee the best I had had in sometime.

"Quiet now," she demanded of her student. She put the reload in front of me and on her way back to the couch said, "You know, God puts people and places in our path to help us in our journey. I wish my friend you would remember that life is meant to be enjoyed and not endured. That, for most folks is the first thing that should be learned on our road of life but for many it's only dwelt on as the angels come." She now wagged that jagged old finger and let me know, in no uncertain terms that I had endured much of it, *my life* that is. I leaned back in her over stuffed recliner that seemed form fitted for a subject of my well earned girth. She had a quilt or a throw as she called it which had a peculiar jasmine smell that never vanished draped over the back of the chair. I was always amazed that regardless of what time of year it was that there was always the scent of flowers about her and her home. No matter how much snow or how dead the elms were, Dottie's place always smelled like fresh flowers.

A sip was followed by a second longer and more rewarding one. "I guess you're right. I wonder what people think about just moments before their death. Do they fear what's coming or are they happy or what?" I paused till I finished aloud my biggest concern. "Do you think they have regrets or are they content? Are the dead met by someone or are they all alone?" Then, I said in response to her now minutes old statement, "Sometimes enduring something is what we or *I* know best. I am comfortable in misery. I can't remember the last time I enjoyed anything Dottie, even something simple like watching the pigeons feed. It's just too hard to enjoy the simple things in life when the things we love are ripped from us day after day after day." I leaned forward a bit and set the cup down on the coffee table still without the required napkin.

"There are days Dottie when I wish the road would end and my journey would be over. I wish the road of life would come to an end and I would receive my final commandment, I'm so very tired."

Dottie adjusted her abundance and in a Yankee like manner informed me, "Don't bull shit me boy. all the Dartmouth know how language can't undo simple disappointments. When you feel bad get it out, it's like the flu. We won't get better if we want to stay sick, aye?" "When things are going bad, *really* bad." She stirred around and for once looked in my direction as I shot a stare at my muddy shoes. "We just need to pray for strength and accept the answer that God gives us and that answer *will* come, it'll be yes, no or not yet. We need to be receptive to the almighty and the lessons He wants us to learn and to Hell with our way of doing things," she concluded.

Our time together always went quickly and even though I knew I would always be cussed at I never missed a visit when one was possible. She would ramble on about how my dysfunction was leading to further dysfunction and this emotional roadblock was ruining my enjoyment of life. Her tone of voice was always without reservation and accented by a firm footing in faith.

I continued, "I don't know if I believe in God anymore Dottie. I have the same old question that the Oprahs of the world ask. Why does *He* let bad things happen?" This was a daily question. How could God let bad things happen, if He is a God of love, how can so many horrible things be going on all around me? Oprah taught us well our new shades of doubt.

With this question, Dottie would forever pickle her lips and with Irish vehemence state, "Bad things are of man *not* of God." She mumbled and continued, "The bad things we see and read about are man's creation *not* God's. God doesn't make war nor does He murder and rob. The people who usually blame God for everything are the last ones to pray and certainly the last ones ever to thank God for all the wonderful things in life. These people that blame God for the bad are the same ones that give themselves the credit when things go well. They credit themselves and blame God. How selfish is that, aye? Do you blame you or do you blame God? That is the question you start looking for answers to before it gets too late."

Dottie gave me a good question. Whom did I blame for the situations in my life; was it God or me? I knew depression was a state of mind that we can manifest to the point of being frozen in place so naturally *it* couldn't be my fault. I certainly knew too that faith left untended becomes atheistic behavior. "I question God about things but I don't believe I ever condemned or blamed Him for my mess. I don't think you're like that. You share and you have seldom given yourself credit. God and faith can relieve the pain we don't know how to handle." Dottie had a good strong voice when it came to talking about God and faith and her eyes were full of a burning spirit as she was well on her way with this tale.

"You have had a few bad years buddy just don't let them ruin eternity." With her Irish animation she continued, "The problem with many Christians now in this age of immorality is that they believe what the devil tells them and the devil's most powerful tools are depression, shame, guilt and doubt. The devil convinces us that God makes things bad and therefore gives us shame and depression. If it weren't for God we would be happy. That's the devil's weapon for modern man convincing man that God is both good and bad. The devil is subtle pork chop so pay close attention. God would never say a man is blessed then sink him into despair and shame. The devil convinces man that God is unhealthy and morals are wrong."

I shook my head in a form of passive recognition of some distant noise but not necessarily a message of any importance. "These are really very good," scooping up another caramel chew. "I'll take some upstairs when I go."

Dottie said the same thing three perhaps four times a week. When I came in with my muddy shoes and my tail dragging behind me she would do her best to fluff me up again. She was a messenger and she has often told me that the messenger is not important its the *message* that must be heard. She would clarify this often with examples such as did people follow the apostle Paul or his message? She asked me if there was anybodies message I listened to.

I had been her neighbor for so many years and I didn't even know her last name, she was always Dottie. There wasn't much in the way of signs of memories or attachment in her small apartment just her. She was friendly enough but I guess I never took the time to get to know her or anything about her life. I should take the time and do just that before it's time to move on. Dottie had lived a good long life and seemed to have little to show for it, just her messages shared with others. At one time she must have been as wide as she was tall but the years and her attention to longevity saw to a health change. Annie had told me at one time that she, Dottie, was sick and had gotten her act together, losing a lot of weight and dedicating herself to her faith. Dottie in my view was like many women; she wanted to fatten me up and then she complains about my being overweight. As one of my forgotten women had told me, a woman's job is to fatten a man up so no other women wants them.

I had tried several times to educate Annie about men, especially when we were first dating. I used to tell her, "Kiddo we males are but one DNA strand removed from swinging in the trees." I knew early on that I was going to be Annie's Ken doll though as she molded me.

When I admitted to being a simple primate Annie would always say, "Yeah I know, but you're a work in progress. What you don't want to do I'll do for you and you won't even know it."

As I had with Annie, I caught myself ignoring Dottie's comments that I didn't want to hear about *my* being to blame for my behavior so I filed her suggestions away for later use. If I admitted my role in *my* life I would see that guilt, doubt and shame were all prevalent on my emotional resume. Annie and so many others like Dottie had helped me to become a good, decent man and I would miss them so very much. Dottie was right, the power to change was inside me and not part of any government entitlement or wrapped deeply inside the blather of some self help guru on late night TV. It was my job, *my* responsibility to change and to get better and nobody else's. I had after all been given free will. God had passed on the lesson that His way was not a requirement we could ignore Him if we so desired. However, when the day does come for all of us we will be happy that we took the first step toward His way of thinking.

Dottie continued once she was convinced I was in fact ignoring her. "If I were you kiddo I would take that drive. Go up to Maine, go to where you and Annie used to go to the lighthouses along the north shore. Take the back road."

I stared with some caution at the suggestion of my observant hostess. I tossed a cock eyed smile her way from the recliner. "Yeah, that's an idea I guess. I haven't been on that road in a long time."

The brain cramps that I went home with could usually be blamed on my hostess because she did make me think. I folded up a gift and said at last, "Here's the paper but I ate your donut."

With that same cockeyed smile and just a hint of smart ass she said, "Oh, really? I would never have guessed it." A sarcastic tone in deed. With a wave of her finger she said, "Wipe your face better next time my friend."

I nodded and sat forward saying to my hostess, "I'd better go." The hour had sped by and I greatly appreciated her company. "Old woman. I've been tired a lot lately. I just can't seem to get enough sleep I just have to try it again tonight."

Dottie was still shuffling around, this time taking her task to the kitchen. She handed me a plate of meat loaf and some of the caramel crunchy chewy things. "Here take these and eat something normal for a change aye fat boy."

Her company was always good and perhaps I helped her a bit as well. She had nobody and I had been her Santa the past few years and we were a pretty good mix of forlorn complainers. Dottie, without knowing it took me back in so many ways to the memories and lessons taught to a lonely little boy from just a few miles away. The lessons of those days were kindness and patience, which, through judicious practice affixed themselves to our better nature. As determined as any ill-prepared young child may be at times to withstand moral teachings a brick or two had stuck to my foundation. Morality, regardless of our secular efforts will always win out regardless of how strong secular man fights it; right *always* wins. Our souls know what is right and what is wrong and our conscience guides them in pursuit of productive labor. That, in my opinion is why when our day comes we will all choose what is right.

I stood and laid the cup in her kitchen sink. As I turned to leave the room, Dottie placed in my hands her old family Bible. One could see that it had served a noble term of duty.

"Here, I want you to have this, I have had it here for a while and I've meant to share it with you for some time now." The cover was tattered from age as much as from use I suppose. "Annie has hers and you need yours now."

I held it as if it were an ill fitting glove not knowing which way was up. My reaction was probably the same as many others who have received such a gift, awkward gratitude. "But you ..",

She wagged her finger at me before I could finish and sputtered a profound statement my way. "My lessons are almost learned and my road has been traveled pretty well. It is my pleasure to pass the text of the journey to you." In a comfortable tone she continued, "You need it not as decoration or a trophy but as a tool for your journey."

I wanted to hand it back because I honestly didn't know what to do with it. "Can't you use this a while longer?" I asked.

In a portly gruff she said, "No tubby please keep it. My lessons are almost learned and I am close to getting them right."

This was an argument I knew I would not win and one that I would not even fight with sincere effort. A smile and a "thanks, buddy,"ended her finger wagging. I turned to grab the plate she had made for me and saw on her small table a bowl of hard candy, butterscotch and fire-balls, candy for the grandchildren who no longer came. Dottie had busied herself as I opened the door.

"I will get this money to you next time we get together kiddo."

I reached for the bowl of dusty candy and took several butter scotches. In a fond file from its mental storage I was again a young boy running to Ethyl Hyde's small country store. I held firm in my hand a list that was larger than the envelope of bills could account for. I remembered what I often heard back then and I now passed those words onto my friend. I turned to Dottie and as a generation ago said with a grateful memory, *"When yah ' can."*

Chapter 2
Getting Ready

And so it was
That I came to travel
Upon a road
That was thorned and narrow
Another place
Another *Grace*
Would save me

You are the sun
I am the moon
You are the words
I am the tune
Play me...

With crowded arms I journeyed out of Dottie's place and up two levels of stairs to my own front door remembering one of my favorite songs of all times. I had started my list. I stepped into a portal of newspapers that were days, perhaps weeks old. They were changing tint and odor via the encroaching touch of nature. Old leaves were here and everywhere and a door mat that at one time had once said welcome was now turned backward. There were cobwebs on the door frame, cobwebs of all the things I thought. Annie hated spiders and would screech the screech of the ages when one poor unsuspecting daddy longlegs would wonder through the bathroom. Hell could project no furry as the fire behind her quest to rid the world of one of these unsuspecting daddy longlegs.

I shoved open the door with my knee and dropped the gifts from below onto the table that still held a setting for two. It seemed that they had been recently used but I couldn't remember for sure. A visitor here wouldn't have to ponder too long before assuming that two, *not one* called this a home. The considerable difference in odor alone between this and Dottie's place was immediately apparent even to the most ignorant about cleanliness. The room was stagnant. There was a mix of must and dust and it was filled with everything old with an emphasis on the unwashed. I had lived in only this one room for most of my recent memory and always ended the day by saying that I would pick up the scattered piles tomorrow. I would do a wash and take out the trash *all* tomorrow, *always* tomorrow. I hadn't done much else today other than satisfying the comparative to all previous days, for today *was* the tomorrow mentioned in previous remarks. Without pause to confer with self doubt, I changed into something far more satisfactory to the qualms of my depressed state and aimed without hesitation to the ever familiar dent in the couch.

The immediate area surrounding the corner of the world that I called mine was filled with bags, trash, wrappers and unopened mail. I shoved it all aside with a forearm and flopped into my spot. *My spot*, this was never going to be taken away, this form fitted portion of a couch that had been ours for so long. Annie wanted a complete living room set that matched not the hodge-podge mix of this and that which she inherited upon our union. To anyone who has ever experienced true depression this all must seem familiar however, this was a new journey for me. A deep, daunting, haunting darkness had engulfed my spirit for some time and I was so very tired. I shifted to an accustomed spot and let my brain catch up with the demons that had been knocking at its door throughout the day. I shut my eyes, only to have them dart back and forth in search of a place to rest. A sigh deeper than all other ones forced throughout the day declared an end to this battle at least for the moment.

I was surprised at just how tired I was every day after accomplishing so very little. For me, this secular world had done little for me and I could spare little for the creator of *it*. My eyes, though shut dashed back and forth as if lost in their current state of being. My heart beat as if it were the victim of a ten-mile run. I was anxious and certainly most unkind to the pathetic example of what used to be a good and decent man. The demons of guilt, shame and doubt settled into their usual respite at the end of the couch and waited for sleep to claim me. I would fight the inevitable, which in itself was a good sign. I didn't want the demons aboard any longer and I would not allow them to join me until my resistance was at its ebb. My pastor of long ago had told me that one of the first signs of recovery is the willingness to admit defeat and I was being defeated. The possession of an inkling of strength to fight back the demons at the end of the couch was a sign that I still had some fight left.

The same pastor tried to bash into a chubby plum chaser's mind the belief that no one ever comes to God until he is willing to relinquish not only sin but also the way of looking at the life of sin. That past was something else he knew what he was talking about but my objection was that he gave little *how to* advice. Or did he? Is the unspoken *how to* the first step that a willing mind must take to turn solid hard core sin over to God? In my case what was that solid sin? Are my depression, sadness and regret the sin that God wants me to turn over to Him? One message that I saw years ago always fit times like this. "If you're up against the question of relinquishing a difficult time what would you do?" The suggestion was that I should go through the crisis, relinquish it all and God will make you fit for all that He requires of you. The point being made by that forgotten pastor was that by asking God for help we shouldn't dwell on the outcome. I wanted to fit in so I must take the journey and experience it all to be ready for what God has in store for me.

Turning toward the disconnected cable and hitting the alarm I gave in quickly to the darkness of the night. I felt sleep coming as if I were on the upward path of a roller coaster and just as quick as the coaster's descent sleep was upon me. I felt for a moment an urge to jump but quickly found myself once again in front of my boyhood home. In just a short heart beat or two I found that I was standing in a rain that fell gently at my feet. The chair in a room of white that I could clearly see before was now a fading symbol of a past rest. As I looked up and stared through the mist the vision became clearer. I didn't have to go through the front door of a childhood portal. Memories rushed at me from all sides and I was unprotected from what they wrought. In a nearby field, I saw a three-legged black lab running from place to place, looking and never catching up to his proud but neglectful owner. The lab was seeking attention and kindness for and from a lonely young man who stood quietly fighting his demons on the front porch of a pine soaked legend. The young man simply said, maybe tomorrow we will play, maybe tomorrow we will run, maybe tomorrow I will show kindness.

As I stood opposite the time portal and I heard the laughter of sisters at play, sisters who with passing years, would become strangers barely recognizable in an empty room. I saw them run and play together, separated perhaps for good *not* by the miles of life but by the progressive advances of selfishness and pride. I approached the yard covered by the hovering pines and moist from the heavy scent of lilacs that never tired the lonely heart. I stood at the foot of the stairs from which many a dream was wished and from which I bid my dad a final farewell. The scent of freshly cut grass and the sound of a frog that we could never catch always greeted the visitor. I slowly opened the door and saw before me the three-legged lab at rest. He looked up at the visitor and comforted by his appearance laid back down without seeking to question him. I stood for several silent moments in a hallway knowing that bad and good awaited a turn of a knob.

I walked through the living room door and saw a brother leaving for war. I saw a final family Christmas surrounded by now departed aunts and uncles and I saw a lonely widow looking onto a world she never quite fit into. The air was permeated with aroma of home made breads, Yankee pot roast and a vase of red roses placed below a kilted Scotsman. I didn't stay for long for there were some things I just didn't want to see again. There was pain and I let my fear hide the joys. I took a few steps through a hardwood dining room and made my way to the foot of old hand made stairs I chose not to go up for I knew what awaited me. There were rooms where sisters played and where I hid ashamed of my life and a room where my Dad took his final breath. I stared for a while at the beckoning top step but turned and left the calls behind. As quickly as I came I found myself once again at the front steps greeted by a three-legged black lab seeking a scratch on the nose fifty years past due. He had found me *he* would be my guide.

Ignoring him now as I had then, I sought the end of a sidewalk and turned left to behold a room, a room covered in white. Gasping just a bit I found it was becoming more difficult to breathe the longer I was there. I struggled successfully to brush aside the encumbrance seemingly holding my nose and I continued my journey. The room was white and as clouded as many a thought upon the day's first light. What did this scene mean and why was I witness to it now? I squinted and saw sitting in the center of the room one tiny chair, empty in anticipation, waiting for an occupant long over due. I rolled and caught myself in twilight till the sound of the ocean approached my respite. It was an ocean being tossed at a shoreline older than God and leaving behind a new message with every bite. Back and forth, hither and yon, the ocean never stops and the shore never complains and God is always a witness to the shortened shore. The question posed by many is: Are the lives of man the shoreline and the ticking years the laps of the oceans?

The sound of the ocean grew louder as if encouraging me to come just a bit closer to hear the tale it wanted to tell. Just a bit closer I did go not knowing where it was or how deep I would find it. The sound grew more distinctive as if an old radio seeking a distant A.M. station was nearing its mark. I stood with motionless hands at my side and listened to what the ocean was saying. There was growing ever more clear a voice, one that if I listened closely I would recognize. I hugged my side and was determined to listen but the echo of it trailed to my belief of what it may be. What was the voice? Was it Dad saying, " Take care of your mom." Was it Mom saying, "I did my best." Was it the lost uncles from forgotten wars telling us they would do it all over again? Was it lost loves and abused friends seeking to encourage us to be kinder and of a more gentle spirit? What was this voice and to whom did it belong?

My breathing grew labored and the blockage was more determined and not easily removed without repeated efforts. I edged a bit closer to the chair and saw before me legions of decorated angels encouraging me to *seek* for I would find and to *ask* for I would be given and to *knock* for the door would be opened. The answer was there for me if I sought it out. *I* must make the first move and *I* must take the first step on this road. The demons from my mind's closet were fighting and they fought hard because they didn't like what they were hearing. The demons that secular man has labeled shame, guilt and regret fought hard for they didn't want to *lose* their find. Their satanic intimidation grabbed my soul and I backed out of the room farther and farther from the chair. My labored breathing was accompanied for the first time in my memory by the grasp of one tiny hand. I brushed it aside now in fear. What did this hand want? Was this little hand meant for me or was it also lost? The demons of doubt and anxiety replaced the legions of decorated angels and brought instead shame and guilt in boat loads that would never find a dock and or would they ever sink. The chair was growing more distant and the voice that welcomed me now became a dot in the distance. I had not yet taken the first step.

My throat was becoming dry and water was a growing must. My feet moved as if held by the devils of the deep and all the memories of what could have been if I had been patient and learned just one last lesson now faded in twilight. My legs twitched, jerked by the demons at the end of the couch. They had assumed their traditional position in my waterlogged conscience. I tried with one last half hearted, well intentioned swipe of the ghostly grasp and was...

"Good morning, all. WJJL Providence welcomes you to this heart of gold classic from Mr. Otis Redding."

My eyes were slammed harder and I kicked with increased intensity the demons wrapped upon my limbs. I heard the tempered whistle of the forlorn crooner as I rolled still seeking the chair and the room of white. Instead I found just the docks of the bay and the morning sun mixed with the out of date banter of a morning disk jockey called golden.

The last words whispered to me before I met the dock of the bay were: *Don't let your memories kill you.* I heard with clarity the stern warning of a noble teacher. A dry mouth and several deep breaths finished the task of waking me from the last several hours of anxious rest. "Wow," I said aloud to the haunting chills from the dream still tracing my spine I batted my eyes to remove the last vestiges of sleep and with both hands rubbed my head back to front. Sitting up on the edge of the couch I repeated my morning routine. I woke to the morning sun as it peeked through the dust worn drapes. This was the most vivid of recent dreams and I had *had* my share of crusty tales of late. The music rolled on and the musings of this dated disc jockey dribbled into the recesses of my mind. Every day for some time now the dreams were becoming clearer and more vivid but their content increasingly vague. It seemed just as soon as the night began, the morning sun broke through the fog of subliminal reckoning with the heart of gold WJJL morning menace. It had been an uninterrupted rest of nearly ten hours consistent with previous nights but it seemed to last as long as the most recent of 1960s' classics.

I flicked the sleep from the corner of my eyes and scooted a bit forward to see what the skies of this day had wrought. Sun and warmth with a hint of peacefulness was going to be my lot for the day, more of the same damn thing. There were many times when I wished the rain would come so I could conjure up yet another excuse just to *be*. God was certainly doing his best in the most subtle of ways to bring a ray of sunlight back into this lost soul. I felt a bit different on this particular morning I must give Him that but why I did not know. Was there to be another message for me over this days course? Had I realized an answer from the depths of my sleep to some of my troubles? My mouth was just as dry as ever resembling the soul survivor of a whiskey and rye drunk from the night before.

My mind seemed less foggy and the imbedded inhibitions stacked layer upon layer around me seemed less foreboding as I sat watching a new neighbor take his spot at a railing outside. On the railing of the deck where Annie loved to read rested a mourning dove, whose pensive vocal allure welcomed the sun and his curious observer. I listened to my morning visitor's tempered wail and believed that this tone would be what greeted all who did as *He* had asked. Was there a tone of grace that would welcome those of us who chose God's way rather then the demon's walk? How would God show His pleasure in our choices? Would it be the tone of a small bird or the gathering of countless angelic choirs? Were they one and the same? I believed that this tone greeted all who sought an end to secular immorality and strove for faithful servitude to the God who blessed us all. The angels I assumed would sing in joy when this was learned.

"Through the travail of ages men have fought and sung for the right to be at rest with their God and with His blessings." But we must be willing to engage in that fight, for if we are passive the enemy has already won. However, I have denied myself the right that many have died for. If I have denied it to myself how can I share it with all others yet to come? I hoped to some day sit at peace with the songs of the ages as well. I was tired of the struggle with the demons and knew that *I* had a stronger ally. It has long since been *my* desires that have shaken the foundation of faith. My greed and selfishness and *my* way of thinking have kept me from opening the door to that ally. I dwelled on my role as the bird sang on and the sun glittered off his fattening breast.

My lack of faith has only compounded the selfishness of man, which in turn has shaken God from this nation. Was I to blame for my role in the building of a Godless land? I had played my secular role all too well how could I make up for it now. An old friend said these words or ones similar to me again and again when things were tough and I more impatient than perhaps than I should have been, He always said this. *Lack of faith compounds selfishness.* I recalled His words and the wail of the mourning dove as we laid our last parent to rest beneath the reach of the naked elm just days or perhaps weeks ago. The dove and the words of a long lost friend came to visit me this morning as I sat looking out onto a world I never really fit into.

There were so many reasons and *so* many endless possibilities for me to sit and do nothing except dwell on my secular failures. The trembling desires of the demons of my conscience seemed to leave me as I watched this one simple creature of God sing to me from outside the window. I guess the devil hated music of peace instead he reveled in that which the vile worshiped. Guilt, failure and doubt on this morning at least seemed to take a back seat to fresh, simple reasoning and the tepid wail from my fat feathered friend. Fresh reasoning what could that mean to someone who spent hours on end legitimizing regret? A knew way of thinking perhaps? The dryness of my mouth was gone with a patter of a smack or two of my lips. The timeless questions were mounting as I sat and listened to the tepid wail. The drone of the simpleton on the radio who called himself Golden roamed on as the dove watched his observer ready himself to get up. After one aborted try, I declared next time for sure as I leaned back for a final wisp of anxious slumber.

It seemed, though just for a moment that the viciousness of my emotional demons was tempered by the soothing comfort of my winged visitor. I rolled my head slightly askew to see the glimmer off his chest as he rose to meet another lonely soul perhaps on the floor below. I returned just for a moment to my boyhood home and the barn in which we raised our share of cranky fowl. The barn was of noble character built at a time that no one could recall. There was always a nest, perhaps two or more of mourning doves firmly ensconced in the eaves just out of reach of this troublesome, chubby plum chaser's best of youthful tosses.

I recalled just how cruel I was to God's most innocent of creatures. Cats I shot with the Daisy BB gun, the birds I chased from their homes days in construction. I especially remembered one three-legged black lab whose nose only wanted to be scratched. One's true character is never shown in better light as when it is shared with the most innocent of creatures I don't think any of us can look at a face of a kitten or a dachshund and believe that they weren't meant just for man's companionship. Do we hold the head of a dying pet or do we let them die alone in some forgotten vet's kennel? Do we knock a nest from a tree that hangs too near our Sunday wash or do we move the clothes line? Will we ask the waitress for a doggy bag for the neighbor's underfed potpourri or do we take one for the lunch of a day we have already asked off?

Do we turn our eyes from a lost and lonely stray? Do we turn our eyes from those that seek to abuse? Do we turn our eyes away from the signs that say "free puppies?" Our character is never as bold or as noble as when we seek to help those who want only to be welcomed as one of God's own. How cruel I was, what an unkind selfish young man I was. How I treated the simplest of creatures seemed to cross that secular barrier of beast and man. The cruel secular attitude landed once too often at the dinner table or in the too short and too unkind of long distance phone calls. If we consider ourselves noble for kicking a dog then slapping a loved one for petty incursions will make many of us Godlike. That is the ultimate difference in God's world and man's, man can always say he is God. I suppose that we, as we grow must recognize that we are earthly examples of good and evil entwined.

The people I hated because they interrupted what I saw as a crucial moment in my life were numerous. The women I called sluts who chose not to be with me and the family and friends I had lied to for the sake of my own selfish and greedy insecurities all were great in numbers. These harmed ones all came back to me as I watched the empty rail outside the window where Annie used to read. What lessons had I just learned from the echoes of the woeful wail of the portly winged visitor? Had he been singing to me the stanzas of amends from deserts past? This philosophical spew came from the echoing of a dove's woeful wail and the sagging remnants of a dream vague enough to confuse the apostles. The simple things I have come to see often scar the deepest and cut to the bone leaving just memories that bring tears and not anger. This was always true Danvers Clay, that skank-chasing uncle said again and again that it is the simple things that make life so much fun but it is family that makes life worth the fight. When there is no family what have we? Had I been a soldier or a traitor in this fight? Were others soldiers of their own? All of us must answer this question when we witness or are in fact ourselves laid beneath the naked elm.

Annie had tried to convince me that closing my eyes and listening to children at play always brought a smile to one's face, regardless of my effort to refute its encroach. She would thump my gut and with a smile that had more teeth than it could hold, declare that puppies and kids make life so much fun. Annie said simply watching an old couple in the park or listening to a horse in a meadow inevitably brought a smile and a wave of kind thoughts to whoever was the captive. By dwelling on things that I had no control over I made many moments of this short life unpleasant for myself and for many to whom I exhibited my pugnacious tone. Annie trained me or at least tried to and left a daily message that if we treat all in a manner that we would treat a puppy or a child a smile would always be on our face. The hurry up and get to the next red light approach to life was eventually going to make for many an anxious sleep and a lonely death If practiced with sincerity a puppy and child approach to lives problems could bring an eternal rest to commit to memory.

All this, this bulging mound of emotional clenching was due to one fuzzy breasted, over fed and out of tune mourning dove."That damn bird," I mumbled as I stood from a well forced second effort. I stood and tugged and twitched the night's sleep from various crevices and went about my first of the morning tasks. Coffee, I needed some coffee really bad even the tap water brew of norm would suffice. The rambling tone deaf occupant of the musical airwaves thrust upon my solitude and without my consent the ladies of the deep: Eleanor Rigby, Wendy and Ruby Tuesday all danced with me as I went about my undocumented morning machinations.

A shuffle and a hustle, a shower and a shave lured me back to the meat loaf and plate full of caramel crunchy chewy whatever's from my little friend on the floor below. Of course as I quickly discovered, the meat loaf would have tasted better if I had of course placed it in a better overnight location than a mere countertop and if I had taken a moment or two to brush the tools that now worked the chews. The task of the day now was to be better and happier than I was yesterday or even just an hour ago as sleep still confused me. How to be happy has always been an arduous task for me to define. Annie was my helper but she was no longer with me and I didn't know when she would be seen again. She would sooner laugh at Hagar the Horrible and the Flintstones than a multi million dollar Hollywood so called block buster. She loved life's simple things and often called Barney Rubble one of Hollywood's great under rated actors and often calling me her favorite of simple things.

She took life as seriously as the day in front of her and she would say volumes with just raised eyebrows and her puckered lips often tossed my way after a screw up was credited to my column. At such times I would think for a moment. Then, as I watched her and now as I remember her, just how all women must be like Annie. I could read countless emotions just by the way Annie folded her arms or scooted to the end of the couch at more than arm's reach. When I was with her at such times I often felt like the dog that knocked over the trash can in the kitchen. He knew he had done something wrong and he knew that despite his best efforts there was no possible way of rectifying the matter.

What a joy she was. I snickered at how she could sense that a lie was on its way days before I had even thought of telling it. She was bold and gave me plenty of preemptive warnings as to my behavior but it often didn't matter. I *was the dog* at the trash can on so many occasions. I took a couple of bites of the now more than adequately cooled meat loaf and as a few more boasts from the gas of the airwaves permeated the living room, I was ready to start my day. My mood was better today than on previous mornings that I had to admit and I sought to credit all to the ego within. As I left the apartment I brushed away the cobwebs from month's' growth and development and hours of work from their owners. Down the stairs and a couple of short quick knocks on Dottie's door brought no reply. Bingo I thought, maybe the movies or the doctor's had to be the answer to my unanswered pestering. I would see her later when she was ready.

The sun did shine bright this day and I could certainly see why the dove was so anxious to share its birth with all who would listen. A piddle here and a piddle there and I was behind the wheel of this out dated and under performing Tempo. I backed out of Annie's favorite spot and as I readied to pull out onto Tennent, I thought I saw Dottie's curtain being pulled back just a bit. She must have been lying down or whatever she does every morning rather than pay the pensive knocker any mind. I would talk to her later about the same things we reviewed just hours ago, she would need a break for a few hours. Justifying my hurried departure, I declared I would get her a Boston creme or two *she* would like that. A left on the street that bore the name of an old time preacher and I was on my way to the usual red lights and delightful cell phone wagging teenage pains.

I felt different today, rested or perhaps just more calm than during previous similar trips. There wasn't as much anxiety or negativity following me.There are some I guess that would call this relaxed state of mind contentment but I hadn't yet felt a desire to label my state of mind. Maybe a few would call it happiness or some other boorish state of peace of mind. Still others and I must say those with an Ivy League alphabet after their name would label it schizophrenia. I felt like a "D" student who with little effort, gets an "A" in his most difficult subject. For me that subject was life. This morning's drive took me through a few lights and a traffic jam at the usual road work ahead zone, a zone that demanded labor union attention year after year and was never finished. A nice way to ensure you always have a job is to never finish the task whether it was physical or emotional labor.

I neared a familiar part of the northern end of this small town familiar not only because of the age old structures but it was the location of youthful sidewalk peddlers as well. Interested only in why I was feeling good, I didn't realize until I had gone successfully through the intersection that this was the "free puppy" zone. I drove on exploring the reasoning of peace and my lack of attention to yesterday's promise. The feel good sensation immediately took a back seat to the wail of this morning's winged visitor. I had driven past the promise because I was feeling too good about my state of mind. As I remembered my rail side partner the regrets that had sifted through my mind as I sat and listened to him came back in torrents. My feel good sensation was replaced by memories of kittens I had harmed to birds I had disturbed and to that poor three-legged black lab who sought only an occasional scratch. I looked again into the rear view mirror and thought just how much a spiritual conscience was a noble foe for the selfish agenda. I began to search for a place to turn around.

My interest at this time changed from making a short library visit and sneaking the extra Boston creme to making up for damage I had caused decades ago. I drove just a bit farther seeking a place to clarify my intentions and to calm my spirit. With a look here and a glance there I found the parking lot of what I remembered used to be the Taylor Family Bakery. Now it was just another mini-jiffy-stop-n-go quick and leave place. I wanted a short few moments to clarify my intentions rather than rush to brush aside a chance at kindness. I wanted to know that I was doing the right thing.

Without using the turn signal mind you, I turned in and parked next to a van that was filled with children of various sizes, shapes, colors, and ages who all turned in unison and stared in my direction. With my hands at 10 and 2, I stared at the back of a dumpster filled with trash from this and other nearby minis. I stared, though not for long I knew what I had to do and would make quick business of it before the demons of the deep won this one too. After one of the shortest emotional free for alls I had experienced in recent memory I left this mini-whatever and with a left on Tennent I sought out my matted-hair little friend. I was anxious now to keep my word and I looked back and forth as my palms were growing sweaty. Was she going to be here today? I thought she might be gone and I again I would have failed at something good in life. I thought she might have succeeded in her task and found a home for her box characters. I was anxious for many reasons one of which was to see if her mom's boy friend had said enough is enough and treated the castaways as mere pooping inconveniences. I was anxious to know if she had found

Rob R. Thompson

homes for any of her castaways and above all I was anxious to keep my word.

I drove and drove for what I knew was well beyond the point of our previous day's meeting. I didn't see her or her sign. I knew I had blown it again and I quickly began beating myself up for not being kind to a lonely little girl and her box of neglect. I drove and drove knowing that her absence had to be a conspiracy by the cars in front of me and to the side of me. They, the drivers from all over New England were preventing me from keeping my word. Therefore, it would not be *my* fault if I failed to find my young friend it would be theirs. Light after light was going by and now were not even red they all told me to proceed or to do so with caution. Sign after sign and mini-whatever's after mini-whatever's I couldn't find her. Where was she and why wasn't she here? I went down two, three, maybe four blocks and couldn't find her. I went down side streets and up others and there was no sign of my little friend. I had promised yet another person that I would come back and failed. I promised I would return and their doubt as to my sincerity of action produced zero expectations in me and more sorrow for them.

I stopped and turned in a drive way that warned, though ever so faintly not to do so. Yeah, OK next time, *next time* I will be sure not to turn around in this guy's' driveway. My anxiety had turned now into improper behavior so I had to regroup. I posed a question that could be asked every day by anyone. Is it OK to be rude to achieve overall good? There were of course two answers to this, *yes* if I were the actor and *no* if I were the offended. I had to slow down and become reasonable in my pursuit and I would do just that at a red light longer than this one. I had not kept a promise yet again to another person, albeit a stranger. She, a little girl was lied to and she may have lost that much more trust in her fellow travelers. I was nearing the famed donut coral, brought to this community by Leonard and so well managed by Sandi the very first girl I never called back.

With my hands at 10 and 2, I was preparing to accept the guilt that was surely coming my way. I would set aside the quest of being nice to my matted-hair little side walk vendor and instead go about my daily trek. I was forced to stop at an amber cue when off to my left stood a shy little girl with matted-hair and sign saying *"free puppy."* A

Ashley Bay

smile and a peace of spirit made its way back into this Tempo and to its driver and I disciplined her ever so lightly for making me wait. I was well placed to make an instant turn into Leonard's, bumping a fellow over the hill gas burner in front of me. I had to get there in time and I was determined to keep my promise to this one and would apologize to the slightly scratched bumper later. Without tremendous delay I was out of the car and stood with increasing nervous energy as a do not walk sign commanded attention. It would not grant such permission until it was good and ready it just blinked and blinked. As I waited, it never occurred to me that so many things had worked together for me to be in this place at this time. I had to leave the house at just the right time. I had to drive at just the right pace and I had to turn around at just the right place in order to see her at *this* moment.

I wanted eye contact with my young friend. I had to let her know that I was here. Eye contact with anyone or anything meant that they had been welcomed into our world and that we respect them and their role in this God's world. I was now seeking to recognize all of them I had once ignored with this one simple gesture. I waved with keys in hand in her direction and I moved from one side to another in hopes of catching her eye as the wig-wagging sign still said no not yet. The light just would not change and seconds were minutes and a mere two minutes seemed as if an hour had ticked by. At last, rather then seeking to speed through a fading yellow light a van filled with children of all shapes, sizes, colors, and ages stopped and waved me across. I received a finger wave from the three-foot co-pilot and I looked back with a grateful heart and a high yah smile.

With a quickened pace, I sneaked up to my young friend just as she set her box near the opposite do not walk sign post.

"Hey kiddo," I barked.

In a sheepish, sleepless manner she turned herself and greeted me with a worn out smile.

"Hi," she replied.

"I told you I'd be back," I said. These simple few words released the emotions and remorse from all the years released them with wings like those of my portly morning crooner. The guilt and the shame guised as broken promises which I delivered to the doorstep of many were forgiven, at least by me and at least for now. Kindness always wins out. It just has to be put onto the field of play in this game of life. If we ignore the fruits of goodness we will forever be on the sidelines.

"I was hoping, but, yah' know...," she quipped.

"Yeah, I know," I said before she could finish.

The matted-haired side walk marketer went on with some news that I had sensed might be coming. "Yet' `day two was taken to `da pound by my mom's boyfriend. I hid `dis one in `da white barn out back."

I hadn't noticed yesterday but she seemed to have some trouble speaking. It wasn't normal kid trouble with certain words but possibly physical problems yet to be discovered or one that had been found but ignored. She was wearing what she had on yesterday and she still, with reddening cheeks, brushed her hair back out of her eyes.

With a deep breath I tossed a look into her box and saw but one remaining castaway. There was no blanket, just a small pathetic example of what used to be a once proud and noble beast. This creature had scooted nose first into a corner of the box, ignoring his observer and protecting what pride remained. Through an eye covered with gunk he cast a suspicious glare upon his spectator. Only he knew whether the look was one of warning or a call for help.

"Jut' `dis one left," she said. I don't know what to name `dis one. It pees all `da time."

In a tone reminiscent of a grouchy teacher, I stated that puppies do that. I reached in and gave him a scratch that was meant for another many generations ago and he submitted a thank you through a sand paper lick or two.

She tossed me a smile and I secretly felt she knew she had just made a sale and that everything else from this point on was verbal decoration. I had, however become my father shopping for a used car he knew nothing about. I threw my hands into my pockets and jingled change like Dad used to and I began to walk around the box giving it a full inspection. I stood just far enough back where I would not fall victim to the poetic look of the last castaway.

"Is it sick?"

"Don't know," she said."

"Where is its mother?"

"Don't know," she said.

I jingled the change and walked around to the other corner of the box still avoiding the lethal eye contact and that dreadful puppy breath smell.

"What does it eat?"

"Food," she said with a smile and in a tone reminiscent of a grouchy student. Looking over my shoulder into the traffic that was stopped at the intersection as if watching our haggling, she said, "Someone said `day would be comin' back for `dis one today." She reached into the box and picked up the object of discussion. "'Dis one's fat, hay?"

Looking into traffic as the light changed, I said, "Yeah, puppies get that way." I cast my glare at a smiling Sandi who was watching the scene from Leonard's lot. "How old is it?" I asked.

"Don't know," she said. She petted the pathetic mess and told me again that another person would be by shortly for it. She cast her eyes into traffic looking for the other customer.

The same shove that the spirit of the dove gave me this morning came back with a flush of kindness. The strength that legions of winged angels could bestow upon me would not be good enough to fend off the power of a short glimpse at the character in the face of this once proud and noble beast. I weakened and cast a glare into a box at the tail end of its duty The box had served a proud role. The lonesome soul's gut looked similar to mine at the end of an all you can eat Pop Tart buffet. The smell led me to think that he too, had questionable hygiene techniques and that his bladder was as active as its salesperson had suggested.

She held the pup as if he was but a doll. His eyes were disheveled with infection and he projected a look of hopelessness. My young matted-haired little friend projected the same appearance too. This sorrowful little one was performing this task of salesmanship for this pathetic mess, what a kind and decent little one. My young friend was reaching out in hopes of finding a friend for the castaway but *her* eyes lacked the twinkle of a hopeful future. The child twinkle that parents see, the twinkle that exudes curiosity, fun, excitement and the love for the day was missing. My young friend had no twinkle in her eyes. Instead, her eyes showed an age far greater than appropriate for someone of her meager years.

The silence lasted an eternity until the object of our negotiation delivered a bark that sounded like a one shot squeak toy. Whatever this disgraceful sound could have meant was known only to him and the one that created him. For after all, who knows what a dog means by a bark anyway? She kept her eyes pointed up at me and with a two handed demanding thrust toward me I took possession of what I knew would be a lifelong companion.

Without the expected hesitation I said, "Welcome aboard. OK honey, I suppose I'll take `dis one."

Without pause my little friend said in a proud tone, "I know."

The squirming, rather odor filled mess seemed momentarily stunned at what the world had wrought for him but with a scratch of his neck he settled down waiting for the next move.

"What should I name him do you think?"

She smiled a bit and said, "O, `dis one will be easy to name."

My new companion was squirming, grunting, farting and being a general pain shortly after my assuming clear title. In other words he was acting much like Dad's used cars. I put him, just for a moment mind you, back into the box. This action was greeted by a look of momentary despair from the little sidewalk marketer. With a finger in the air I stopped her look from progressing. "I'm taking him honey don't worry. I want to pay you a little bit for him. It's an awful nice thing you have done for him *and* for me."

She looked at me with hands on hips not knowing what to do with them. "You take care of him, OK?"

Ashley Bay

"Of course, we'll be good friends." I reached inside and retrieved what would have been money for Dottie's donuts and handed her five-dollars. Dottie wouldn't mind.

"You take `dis and get your self a little something OK?"

"'K, I'll give it to my mum." With this exchange I took a longer look at my little friend and saw the shallow hints of a past voice. There was something familiar about my little friend that touched my soul. Perhaps she just reminded me of all the friends I had lost over the years. Perhaps she reminded me of those whom I had lied to, broken promises to and just simply never encouraged. Perhaps she reminded me of the sisters who played when young and now never called. I looked at her hair, knotted and tangled a bit, shoulder length and brushed out of her eyes every now and then. A little long sleeve shirt and pants just a bit too big. I couldn't tell the color of her eyes; she seemed always to be staring at the ground or away from this nagging onlooker. What were *her* dreams like? What would life have for her? I thanked her with a wink and it was done.

Shyly but willingly taking the five-dollar bill, she asked, "You be good to him for me, OK?"

"Yeah, you bet," I said and she gave me a smile that went down to her feet. I patted her head the way a kind old pastor had patted mine a generation ago and I set about returning to the car carrying the box full of a squirming gas bag. The light had changed just as I picked up the box. The sign was waiting for me this time and would allow me to bring this character to the Tempo without delay. The light would not allow me time to change my mind, it told me to go ahead and walk.

I walked up to the car parked near the picture window of Leonard's Donut Coral and I saw Sandi staring at me and my new pooping machine. A well placed smile on her face told me she had been watching this transaction take place since the beginning. After putting the pathetic example of a real dog into the car I went inside as an unanticipated rain began. I shook the gathering drizzle from my head and asked for two and two.

"I see you made a friend," she said.

"Yeah, two friends, I think." I paused and corrected. "Two, I hope. I've been watching the little girl for a couple of days. She seems kinda' sad and lonely so I just had to stop."

I looked backed across the way and my young friend was disappearing down the opposite side. Sandi went back behind the counter and picked up the last two Boston cremes.

"She does seem sad at times," she mumbled. "I hope that she grows out of it."

Fumbling for my change and admitting my wallet was still next to the meat loaf I felt like a broke driver at a toll booth. Well, I couldn't back up so I said, "I am going to be close here" as I handed her a badly bruised dollar bill and some unused laundry money.

Through all my shuffling and mental selfishness, I had failed to notice that Sandi spoke with fond familiarity of my young friend across the way. "I don't know what I'm going to do with a dog, the apartment is small and I don't have the drive to do a midnight tinkle run every day." I stared outside to see a snoopy but jovial little lady looking in at my new passenger. Her finger tap on the window didn't stir the two pound poop producer, apparently firmly ensconced on the floor board. Sandi handed me my daily bag. "Thank you, I'll take a small black, too." Sandi had that fresh pot brewing for folks like me I guess. I was still watching the elderly finger tapper and asked Sandi a long over due question. "Can you take a couple of minutes, a break maybe?"

"I can take some time. Customers usually help themselves if they're regulars."

We took a seat at the table right in front of where I had parked and where I could keep an eye on the gathering window tappers. A puppy can calm the impatience of an angry sea and my new partner was playing his first public role awfully well. This time with Sandi had been a long time in coming, many years I guess. I avoided casual conversations with her often for selfish reasons. I hadn't taken time for her or anyone else in a long time and maybe this one act of generosity opened other doors.

We both sat and stared at the car for a few moments perhaps with some anxious discomfort but likely just searching for something to say. I punched my tongue for the right start and asked her, "How are the girls?" It was a question asked of those when I really hadn't any idea what else to say. I knew Sandi had had a couple of kids but wasn't too aware of much else. I didn't know their names or ages but she always talked of her girls.

"They're fine. Their fathers never pay them any attention though and they're at an age now where a dad would be such a joy for them. I don't think they would even recognize one another if they met on the street corner somewhere."

I took the bag she produced and offered one of the inhabitants to her. She refused with a gentle smile.

"I see one of their fathers pretty often but the other is long gone."

Still watching with tepid pride at the finger tapping old woman, I said, "I think I might go up north for a few days. I need some time away." I had ignored Sandi's tone and just begun my own as if hers didn't matter "I want to get away from all this mess." She watched me as I spoke and as I struggled for the right words seldom passing on eye contact.

"That will be good for you, I think you have been at the bottom of a heap for a long time and a journey is good for the soul." Sandi began to scold me as an old friend frustrated at another's continued misbehavior. "You've never taken care of yourself honey and allot of people care about you, yah' know. You complain sometimes but you just keep it inside until you get weird. Take your drive and let's have a nice talk when you get back aye." She threw her towel onto the nearby coffee counter not from anger but just because she could.

"I'd like that, I'm so tired I can't tell you. The days have been hard and my energy is used up, I'm so tired I just can't say."

"I know, I see it every day you come in."

Ignoring her as I have others who shared similar concerns, I smiled and threw out an impolite "yeah." A seedling of conscious rebirth can at times be a flood of other emotions once forgotten but now renewed. I had directed my kind gesture inwards at what I could do to make my life better "You're right, Sandi, thank you I feel I'm at a stage where the rewards for a life well lived are becoming scarce or worse, inconsequential."

I had lost sight of the noble vendor across the way as I became fixated on the glistening rain and the sizzle it made as car after car drove through it.

"Allot of time has gone by, Sandi, allot of things said and not said, yah' know?"

She reached for my hand but stopped just short. "For a man, at least one who has advanced beyond the knuckle dragging stage, that must be an apology, aye?"

"Knuckle dragger. Yeah, that's me, *was* me, it's awful hard for guys to grow up sometimes. We know when we do the next step is being responsible and that's scares a lot of us."

"Responsibility is hard, especially when we are not taught how."

"Well you made the best of starts this morning by stopping to talk to my girl and getting yourself a couple of new friends."

Sandi was subtle and I was still tone deaf to her hidden message.

"Can't see her anymore," I said, squinting for my young friend and coming up empty. Sandi, in a reassuring tone said she's out there somewhere I nodded an OK.

I pulled out a small piece of paper from the coupon stand behind me and gave her my phone number. It took one scribble out but I managed to remember the number that no one calls. "Here, kiddo, call me when you want OK?" I slid it her way and immediately realized that I was using the word kiddo again. That sure brought back wonderful memories of James W. Gibbons a childhood neighbor at the end of the adjoining untended field.

Mr. Gibbons was a tall drink of water of the Ethyl Hyde generation. He too was born in the house in which he would someday pass away at an age well beyond the century mark. What a man he was to emulate. He was the eldest brother of a sister born with what we call today down-syndrome. In their time it was an often a hidden condition. Mr. Gibbons received one simple task from his father on his *own* death bed and that was to provide for his sister. Mr. Gibbons would honor his father's wish and care for his sister for over eighty years. He would let the girl of his choice leave with another to sit at a quiet dinner with his sister. He would set aside big money pursuits to work the small family farm. He would set aside his love of travel to walk with his sister to Ethyl's store every afternoon. He would set aside writing memories of his own to share with a chubby plum chaser epics of character and virtue. What a good, decent, kind man he was.

Mr. Gibbons called his sister kiddo for as long as I remembered. For me the word kiddo is a term of endearment and emblematic of honor and respect. I don't believe I ever new her *real* name however for I was coached with the firmness of any grouchy teacher to call her Ms. Gibbons. Their house was at the end of our yearly trick or treat jaunt. Their farm house was built a hundred years before we were born and still stands error free. It was set just upon a small rise, visible as we neared the completion of our annual October door to door patronage. The anticipation was great as we saw their porch light come on. Our steps increased just a bit when we saw them set sugar donuts and apple cider next to their porch swing.

The stories they told us kids were glorious and brought out the wide eyed wonders of youth. Their father had fought at Gettysburg and would later lose a hand at the Battle of the Wilderness in Northern Virginia. They too, would bring memories out of a faded blue uniform for us to touch and at my age now I thank God I smelled it for that is the memory I still hold dear. That scent of the fields of Northern Virginia where my own grandfather fell is a memory burn in deed. As we children grew and as our wide eyed wonderment gave way to the selfish pursuits of girls, money and cars, the faded blue memory was stashed away. It was just a few years later when the children of Bradford were grown and the stories were considered old and boring that the apple cider was put away and the porch light was forever dimmed.

Sandi forced a smile and said, "Thanks."

A more doubtful tone I think I have yet to hear. She brushed away invisible dust from our table, said "Go take care of your puppy," and sent me on my way. She told me as she patted my shoulder that we'd get together soon. I nodded in firm agreement but some doubt.

"I'll see you in a couple of days Sandi. I want to go for a drive and will probably take the dog or something, maybe Dottie will watch him for a while."

She left me sitting at the table and informed me that she would be here when I returned. With a polite see yah' smile I left with Dottie's donuts as the rain greeted my exit from Leonard's. Of course the five minute visit had seemed much longer as I had allowed my memory to drive the conversation. I nodded to the retreating window tappers who all in various tones let me know that he, the flop eared pooper was so cute. I was back behind the wheel shaking my head dry. The rain was taking longer than I had projected and fell with committed intensity. I often wondered what I looked like as I stood or sat somewhere remembering times lost and the countless what ifs of life. Would all those friends and foe alike who watched me as I stared into my life's vault just shake and let me finish my journey unaided? Well, perhaps I owed all this work mental and otherwise of this day to the woeful demands of the morning's fine feathered friend. The day of change had begun with the choir like encouragement from a pudgy, tightly wrapped bundle of feathers.

I nodded to the finger tapping little biddy that was now on the inside looking out. I smiled as she mouthed, "He's cute."

As I sat shaking off rain and fidgeting for no reason in particular, I saw a lump of disheveled forgotten piece of ugliness on the passenger floor board looking in my direction. I looked at him and turned quickly away because I didn't have a clue as to what he needed or wanted. I was incapable of recognizing a silent call for a friend. I looked across the street in hopes that there would be a sign sent from the great beyond about how to take care of this little creature, there was none. I guess this was going to be a hit and miss experiment with this little thing. I had to take the first step.

"I spent enough on you little man so I better learn what's up aye." I placed the bag on the back seat and saw that my two pound poop producing floor board observer had lived up to his name since I last entered the vehicle. He was sitting quietly under the glove box his eyes filled with gunk and devoutly recognizing the aroma of newly arrived freshly baked Boston cremes.

Ashley Bay

I started the car and was about to back up when I looked down at my little partner and saw that he was struggling to see. His face was dirty and his eyes were covered with gunk and just plain stink of one sort or another. My spirit was touched, the spirit was Biblically pricked as I saw this small, helpless creature needing one small act of kindness. He sat there going for a ride to where he did not know trusting all around him. That trust would be me, he was for this moment placing trust in his new friend. Staring at him, I wanted him to be able to return the behavior. I wanted him to stare back at me as well. I reached down and degunked his eyes with extra napkins a gift from Leonard's. He fought for a bit but soon allowed his head to come to rest as I cleaned the mess and gave him the gift of friendship.

What a mess *it* was. I cussed him out for something that he had no control over and that cussing did its part in making me feel better. This two pound pathetic example of what used to be a proud and noble beast was in deed a mess but he needed me. With my spirit still a fire, I knew I needed him too. Pointing my finger at him I said, "Now, if we're going to get along you need to stop crappin' in my car." A lowered head was his tone. I picked him up and with an old towel made a spot for him on this gravely pre-owned bucket seat. He refused to lie down and he seemed on edge and apprehensive as to what the next step would be. What could a small thing like this little dog fear? Why was he apprehensive? A little guy like this that had come into this world unwanted and was tossed aside as others were drowned what could he possibly be afraid of? I scratched his ears and I assumed he feared being moved once again and perhaps finding no way out this time. As small as he was, he was anxious and nervous and feared being abandoned once again. So far, during his ever so young life here on this planet he had been through allot. Though he was young he showed a strong defense system. Though small, he didn't want to be shoved around. He marked his territory and declared his limits at being told what to do at least for now.

I reached behind me for a donut and found that after my carpal extraction from the bag my fingers were covered in melted chocolate. I licked the first two fingers and saw that I was under the quizzical gaze of my very short co-pilot. He had a look that said a thousand things. He wanted to know why I was doing what I was doing and why *this* human was licking his fingers? In trying to figure each other out our eyes met. We stared at one another briefly, I wondering if I should and *he* wondering if I would. His pathetic look was touching my sometimes surly soul with a master's touch and I lowered the remaining fingers to have my gift warmly welcomed by the two pound poop producer. Upon completion of his reward I withdrew my fingers and the co-pilot cuddled into the old towel. With that simple motion he gave approval to his new owner.

"A dog," I said. An out loud profession of my new responsibility. I started the car and backed up, swinging around to head left on Tennent. The rain was coming down harder and many of the drivers though still rude, insisted that I now turn my headlights on for their convenience and safety. I momentarily stared in vain at the corner where my matted-hair little rumpled friend had done her duty to find a home for this forgotten one. I guess she had gone for the day in search of some other task, good for her, for she would do well with whatever came her way. I neared completion of my turn and saw my little friend coming up the opposite way carrying a bag of chips and a single yellow rose. I waved knowing she would not see me and in my rear view mirror I saw her run across the street toward the donut shop. I saw some drivers being kinder than others as she crossed.

I felt happy. Maybe she was spending the little cash I gave her. Maybe she was feeling happy for a brief period and for the *first* time in some time. I had listened to the message and happiness was the end result of my being kind to others, not bad at all, nope not bad at all. That was a simple message from countless messengers if we are kind, kindness is often returned. The rain was growing steady and did make things a bit hard to see with or without headlights. The traffic was slowing down in both directions except for one hurry up and get to the next red light driver going the opposite direction. As it passed I did notice green plates which for all of us up this way meant Vermont.

"Figures." Vermonters are perhaps some of the rudest most arrogant people I have ever dealt with personally or professionally. The car just sped by without any concern for others just their own world was enough.

A truck that seemed in a hurry to get to the next light that would tell them to stop was not an odd scene here but in this type of weather

Ashley Bay

it was noticeable. It had to be a driver in a hurry to return the over due video and to pick up the suit they would not wear for some time. My new pal was sleeping and grunting, seemingly safe for the moment. What else is there but the moment that we are in and after all, what are *his* plans? What do puppies have to do other than sleep? What did he want to be when *he* grew up? What were his plans and goals in life? I suppose they all centered on eating and sleeping and maintaining his nick-name. The drive was a slower one not only because of the rain but the temperament of an older generation of drivers as well and I was being careful not to jar my friend. The traffic flow to my left had all but stopped. I saw in my rearview mirror some commotion highlighted by many quick brake lights. While waiting for the traffic to pick up the pace, I was able to ask myself countless questions as to the little character's future. What would I name this mess of fur and eye gunk? How do people name pets and what is the significance behind a pet's name anyway? Children are named for grandparents, old friends or perhaps an apostle or two. But how do we name a pet? I had a cat for many years that I never took the time to name. I could probably tote him around as *it* or *dog* or *you*. I guess that would be just as impolite as calling some child a matted-hair little friend.

It hadn't occurred to me that I never asked the little girl her name. Who was she and how old was she going to be? What grade was she in and what was her favorite subject? What was her favorite color, her favorite cartoon and what did she want to be when *she* grew up? This young girl who with kindness for others sought to make things better for this yet to be named castaway next to me. With my hands at 10 and 2, I shook my head in disgust at my selfish behavior on yet another day. I was rude and was too busy watching myself that I didn't see what I was doing I was attentive in only the slightest of ways. To be kind and generous it is a constant task and we must be attentive to every aspect of his behavior. If we let our guard down for even the smallest amount of time we become susceptible to the rude side of our nature. Nothing in our pursuit of goodness must get in our way.

The traffic on both sides slowed now and had nearly come to a complete stop in the opposite lane. Rather than continue a fruitless debate with my own ego I convinced myself that Dottie would be happy to watch *it* so I could take my drive. She would like the company of this furry mess and *it* would surely be stunned at this other human. The co-pilot, seemingly hearing my inner voice raised his head and agreed with what it was saying. He would approve being left alone as long as there was food and an old towel handy those were his lofty conditions.

The radio was still on low and barely recognizable as anything more than fuzz and the occasional guitar riff. The afternoon antiquated drone was no different from the slob that woke the town up every morning. The music was a little better but still repeated itself often. I turned it up a bit and caught the last few notes of a song that always brought back in droves the regrets of the past and I added one more to my list.

> Maybe I didn't treat you
> Quite as good as I could have
>
> Maybe I didn't love you
> Quite as often as I could have
> And maybe I didn't treat you
> Quiet as good as I could have
>
> If I made you feel second best
> Girl I'm sorry I was blind
> You were always on my mind
> You were always on my mind

The rain beat harder and the memory called to those the song remembered and whose tears I lamented.

> And Maybe I didn't hold you
> All those lonely, lonely nights
> And I guess I never told you
> I'm so happy that you're mine
>
> Little things I could have said and done
> I just never took the time
> You were always on my mind
> You were always on my mind

Ashley Bay

Whether it was Sandi or my Annie these lyrics brought to mind the times when I just let their hearts cry without a sign of love from me. The car windows had begun to mist and the co-pilot quickly fell back to sleep after tossing me a disgruntled glare at my ongoing rude behavior. As the rain grew steadier and the mist settled I remembered a line from an old song by a long forgotten composer. *The rain swept over the city and the thunder woke the dead.* After wiping the inside of my window I wondered if this is what was going on. There was no thunder but a chilled wind drifted deftly through the car as I sought to cover my new buddy. I brushed more unanswered memories away and believed now that Maine was the way to go. There were just far too many questions for me to answer all at once so I would put most of them on today's shelf. Some answers were given and I would work with that for now.

Yes in deed Annie loved Maine. She loved the ocean, the rural nature of the state and she told me years ago that when we retire she wanted to settle there. Of course, where I would go on this trip would be left to chance as it always was on a north bound journey up Rte.1 where one could find enough unanswered questions for the most curious of souls. I waited and admitted my soul had many unanswered questions.

As the slowing traffic delayed me I knew I would need to stop for a paper, some soda and a Butter-Finger or two. There was a mini-jiffy just up ahead so I slowed to turn into a parking lot along with others that thought of the same thing. At the crest of my turn I saw the budding appearance of blue flashing lights coming towards me and everyone else in this lot. As with most emergency scenes some drivers pulled to the side while some chatted on their cell phones or laughed as a pedestrian slipped and fell. On this day, the traffic slowed fairly well and some drivers were more polite than others. A police cruiser and an ambulance just beyond nosed their way in not too far behind me.

"The rain is getting ugly little buddy yah' know?" I directed this toward my grunting sidekick as if he would understand all I would ever say and apparently think. A quick turn and an even quicker trip inside and I had my needs plus a stick or two of jerky for *it*. I waited for the traffic flow to pick up slamming a Butter-Finger without delay. It was just a few minutes and Butter-Finger later and I was back out onto Tennent. In a mile or two I would be home to show Dottie her new friend. As soon as I could, I would leave *it* in her care and go up north leaving behind the castaway who seemed to fear just that being left behind.

The rain had stopped in the short time I 'd been inside the mini-jiffy and from just over the edge of the horizon the sun bounced off the car tops that glistened from the residue. A rainbow had made it's away across Tennent, a big thick rainbow that served as an arch for both sides. A rainbow, *so* beautiful from its origin and yet now seen as a perverse symbol of selfish sexuality. Leave it to the perverse to pervert the beautiful. From that day on Golgotha to the travels of Paul the simplicity of rainbows guided our founders. From the explorers, to that hot day in Philadelphia, to the fields of Gettysburg, rainbows have watched the blood of the patriots seep into the ground for which they died. A rainbow, if left to the imagination and to the creative moral mind will take the intellect on history's travails. It will cause us to pause and ask it where have you been and where are you going? If rainbows could speak, how would they answer these questions? The thunder came.

The ambulance and the accompanying officers had made their way well behind us all and my drive was nearing an end. As I entered the apartment complex the rain had laid a slick layer on the pavement. Just a slight skid slammed *it* abruptly into the glove box. With a thud and a well deserved grunt from the floor board we arrived home. I turned to the passenger and said, "I want you to meet a grumpy old lady, OK? She will probably insist on keeping you fat." My front seat partner seemed little interested in my intentions and sought his old towel of old as well as his previous repose. I was momentarily flustered not knowing what to grab, the donuts or the dog. I looked at both as if they were equal in value and got out leaving both behind.

A quick dodge over to Dottie's and a knock and another followed by a couple of more resulted in no one coming to be inquisitive. "Not home aye" She had been gone most of the morning. Good for her I thought, she needs to get out every now and then instead of waiting for me to come home and complain. I stood there like a reverse trick or treater; I had something to give but nobody was home to receive it.

Ashley Bay

With my hands in my pockets I fumbled at their emptiness and took a few steps forward to keep an eye on my donuts and on *it*. The rain was gone and so was the rainbow which had guided me home this day. "OK." I went back to the car and retrieved my packages, balancing my two pounds of poop producer and a Boston creme. One was being squished and the other intestinally rude. I wandered up the stairs and brushing a few more cobwebs from the door frame I introduced both donuts and dog to their new, though ever so temporary for one of them, home.

The day had gone by more quickly than I had anticipated and it was now nearing early evening. The sun had done its tour of duty and finished what the rain had begun and I was ready to call this day one that was well done. In fact, it seemed as if no time had gone by and I was still watching the morning visitor resting outside the window. The hours *had* flown by though and seemed to me to be going faster and faster as told by the number of gray hairs encircling this crown.

I couldn't believe just how fast time went as we aged. One time, when I was a boy Dad answered this timeless puzzlement with simplicity. He said that when we are young we have lived such a small portion of our lives that time goes slowly. Dad continued with as we age, we have lived a greater portion of our lives and therefore time moves faster. I went about some preemptive shuffling about and *it* sat motionlessly in virtually the same spot where I had deposited him when I first entered. He sat with sleep still in his eyes. Looking at his surroundings he must have thought that perhaps the pee soaked box on the nameless street corner would be more comfortable and certainly more aromatic. I didn't have anything to feed him and he was far too small for the jerky but now, in reflection I believe that is why Dottie sent the meat loaf home with me the previous night.

I have fed cat's hot dogs and gerbils nachos so feeding a dog meat loaf would be an OK match and *it* quickly confirmed my assumptions. I grabbed the bag from Leonard's and took my usual seat on the well body formed portion of the couch. Tossing my shoes I propped my feet on what used to be recognizable as a coffee table handed to me by a forgotten sister who had gotten it from the forgotten Uncle Danvers Clay. Still sitting in the center of the floor *it* was unsure of what to do next other than smacking his lips in appreciation of Dottie's day old meat loaf.

I smacked the chocolate off my fingers as *it* neared the edge of the coffee table. I stared forward rather than acknowledge the snoopy two pounder edging ever more near my tangled toes. With a bite or two more I finished and smacked the chocolate hitchhikers. He edged closer and with his head lowered our eyes met. I wondered if I should and he wondered if I would and of course I did. He finished and with an approving look towards his owner jumped up on the couch.

"Alright, young fella.' I can't make any promises but will do my best to be just okay." He looked back and forth at the empty bag and me as if to ask are there any more. I guess that was his answer to me if I could keep the donuts coming I would be doing OK.

I sat back and stared at the dog the meat loaf and the stack of unread mail. What a combination. I was seemingly picking up my thoughts from this morning and now wondered about fate itself. Why had the dove landed outside today? Why did I soon there after begin the thoughts that followed his appearance? Why was I insistent upon stopping and getting this little mess and why did I give a little girl just five dollars? Since I was a young man and I watched how fate comes when we least expect it, I wondered how it knew to come at all. For me I guess it came as I watched my Dad laid to rest beneath the naked elm. How things would have been different for all of us if that day hadn't happened at all at the time it did.

Leaning back and scratching *its* neck, fate once again visited me and I now sought with greater fervor a modern definition of the word. Why do things happen in the way that they do? Why do we meet the people that we do and why do we hurt the people that we do? Is all this part of one great plan to achieve an ultimate goal? If so whose goal is it that we are satisfying? These questions bounced all about me as I wondered why I now owned this two-pound stink machine. I glanced at the bag from Leonard's and thought of Sandi. Sandi was one of those women that younger guys want to spend a night or two with but once the carnal desires are satisfied they, we, *I* move on leaving behind no emotional ties. Sadly I was one of those men. I treated women as trophies and conquests as nothing more than momentary pieces of pleasure. Sandi was a girl in high school that no guy ever paid much attention to. She was plain in looks and personality and she dressed in clothes that were outdated when purchased. She was overweight, had matted-hair and bad skin. Nobody ever took her to a prom or even a Sunday show. Sandi came from up near School Street and was one of those kids picked last in gym class and made fun of on school buses. Her locker was just a couple away from mine and she always said hello and good-bye and would make small talk out of one topic or another. Sandi seldom had lunch money and instead would sit in a corner with her books pretending not to be hungry.

Boys asked her out only as a joke and girls sent her cruel notes. She studied all the time and went home to stare out onto a world she didn't know how to fit into. She often kept her tears to herself but she *always* shared her kindness. I thought for a moment, was this what my mom had gone through? Would Sandi grow to be old but sad and alone? I don't think that's what God really wants if He is the one setting the ultimate goal. I may not know about God and Christ but I do know He wants us to grow old and that He wants us to be happy and to love one another but He also wants us to accept love when it comes our way.

I guess I'm surprised I remember all this about a girl I ignored. She was nice to me and I guess we all remember kindness, usually in a retrospective way though. Our greed turns kindness into expectations and when expectations go unrealized they become anger and grudges. I expected so much more from people who were just kind to me and it was no different with Sandi. I had been away to school and had come back for the summer. I was probably twenty-three or so when Sandi and I met again after a number of years and she was working at Leonard's and I stopped by. The few short years after high school had been hard for her I guess. She would tell me she had been raped and homeless for a while and that she was treated for severe depression. As a drunken college guy home for the summer I was looking for someone like Sandi: a needy woman, a sad woman and one that could be taken advantage of, which I did.

We spent a few nights together in the Biblical sense but not days in a human sense and the summer moved on. I found other places to get my morning coffee and Sandi went to work. I got what I wanted and I left Sandi behind to her own problems. I would go to Europe and climb the Eiffel Tower; she would not. I would hike Central America and swim the Caribbean; she would not. I would go to London, Madrid and down under; she would not. I had the adventures of a careless, greedy man and Sandi looked out on a world that she did not know. How now as an older, supposedly wiser man could I ever make up for that unkindness? I had not lived the life of virtue and character shared with me by Mr. Gibbons. I had become what he was not an unkind, selfish man.

Can we ever make up for it? Can we ever reach far enough into our spirit and be sincere enough in our apologies to move on and be a better person? What is the defense mechanism that prevents us from moving on in the state of character and the nature that Christ desired and that Mr. Gibbons told of in epic form? I don't know the answer to this question nor do countless teachers, pastors and judges know. However, the discovery of the fault is often most of our life's journey and getting ready to begin the search is the *hard* part.

Fate, I looked at my little buddy and wondered if he would prefer *it*, *dog* or *hey you*. He was a sleep now and perhaps a name is not important when caught up in puppy slumber. As I rubbed his neck I recalled a small black lab pup that Santa brought one year a best friend for a five year old. He would be a friend who over the years I would grow to ignore. He would sit on the porch and often wonder when he and I would ever play again. I would come home and he would sit watch as I would soon leave not knowing that all he wanted was to be recognized. His simple request was for just a moment or two a scratch on the nose. But it was time that I could not spare. Fate! What a tool it is for those who seek a second chance in life. The black lab grew up to be alone and spent his final hours in the hands of a vet where he would die alone. I scratched my young friend's neck in memory of the one I ignored and asked again, "What's your name?"

I reflected on our first meeting and how my matted-hair little friend described her box of castaways. She struggled for words to describe this one." "Dis one eats all `da time," or " `Dis one pees all `da time," and " O,' dis one sleeps all `da time." She went on for a few moments in giving each a personality. She said, "'Dis one and `dat one and o,'dis one." She was a good little salesman, perhaps due more to her own pathetic condition than to her script or product. I'm not sure which one I ended up with, the pee'er, eater or sleeper. I rolled him over and twanged his belly and did not get so much as a rumpled grunt. Was he `dat one `dis one or o, 'dis one? Picking him up and holding him as if he were a magazine soon to be purchased, I wondered aloud, "'Dis one, `dat one, or o, 'dis one." He was the runt, the cautious observer, he was her third and final sale so he was the "O,' dis one." "O,' dis, o, 'dis, o, 'dis, O, 'dis!" I smiled and to myself muttered yeah little man. I was now the proud owner of a pathetic example of what used to be a proud and noble beast and his name was Otis.

Chapter 3
Leaving Home

    The names of all I had promised to love and care for had come back while the trembling wail of Willie Nelson faded out the back. I would concern myself with this fruitless debate of reparation later on but for now, Otis! What a great name for a dog. He wouldn't have to go through life with a fancy froufrou name. Instead, he would be the proud barer of the *manly* name Otis. I made him the same promises that I did the present from Santa nearly seventy years ago or more and as I did, I saw the wheels of life come around yet again. I found a couple of bowls one for water and the other for the remaining meat loaf. He didn't appear to be the possessor of tremendous brain power at this stage of his life so I put them in a spot where he would be sure to find them. Otis wasn't about to move from his claim on the couch unless urged by the opening of the bag from Leonard's. He was in fact so urged.

    The day was getting late and again I was weary from a trail of little activity but one that was full of a great deal of emotional work. I had overcome several things on this part of the trip and made amends for some other things. Over all, it was a job well done for the day. My brain and all its encompassing emotions had worked hard this day and as a result I was coming to appreciate the potential for emotional cleansing more than ever before. It seemed with just a seedling of effort a waterfall of emotional health is possible. But what is the effort? Would we go bowling with a brick or would we fly a kite without string? We have to identify the problem before we can recover from it as much as we find out that flying a kite is far more enjoyable when string is attached correcting a problem is easier at times when we know what that problem is. I had to take the steps to see what was causing my problems and how I could grow from their repair.

For a domestic slob such as I it's often very difficult to wash a plate or even take out the trash and for this emotional slob the task of cleansing is far more difficult. I say this of course as I look about an apartment stacked with dirty this, filthy that and whose explanation point is now a two pound poop producer named Otis. I was ready to clean house in *all* aspects of the term and I knew the surest way to let go and let God is to first say good-bye to my past. When I was a younger man I heard many times that we cannot expect things to improve if we keep up the same old behaviors. That I suppose is the best place to begin is to recognize that my behavior has caused most of my problems.

Good-byes are sometimes haunting and will for many make an indelible impression as they did for me. When I was a young boy I ran outside to see my father drive over the hill for the final time. Good-byes are usually final and if given in haste and hate are more painful then the ones given at the grave. I had to say good-bye to the old me to feel safe about my future. I recalled that as I saw my father drive over that hill that I would never speak to him again until I muttered the words well done faithful and noble servant under that naked elm. I never said good-bye to Mr. Gibbons. I never said good-bye to Ethyl Hyde or my aunts and uncles and I never said good-bye to my matted-hair little friend. I never said good-bye to Sandi, to Mr. Schuster, to my brothers and sisters or to a three-legged black lab. Am I that shallow? Am I that selfish? I guess so for my conscious has proven to be a worthy foe when it comes to pointing out my secular failures. I didn't say good-bye to so many but I will say good-bye to the behaviors that have for so long haunted me.

I suppose that our good-byes are perhaps as important as our hellos because it is that which we depart with. It concludes our time with a person at that moment in history a moment that was always meant to be. Is this why we need to treat every moment as our last? If we never say good-bye, does it mean that it, whatever *it* is, never ends? On and on went my wave of predetermined thought. I was thinking without effort of any kind. I now hoped that I could look at each moment as one that was always meant to be and not just an

Ashley Bay

accident. This quest would be one that would be handled one at a time. I went to my usual repose on the couch as Otis chased the Leonard's bag around the room with his nose. He was determined to see that the last of the chocolate was removed and he did his job well. As I lay down seeking out the cobwebbed ceiling, I realized that at times it is very difficult for me to share even eye contact with a passing stranger. Why, I asked the bag chaser in the midst of his rounds. I was ashamed or had such low self-esteem that I didn't want to recognize or be recognized. Is that why I never said good-bye, because I have never known how to say hello or to start anew? Is saying good-bye the final recognition?

I had to set all this gibberish aside and let my mind take the journey that I knew was inevitable. I will at times not hold a door for an aged widow nor will I seek to stand and give my seat to a tired woman. My memory was showing me that character and virtue are not always an enhanced trait of mine nor are the virtuous lessons of youth subject to enhancement as greed grows. I had seemingly let my selfish, introverted side always succeed over kindness and love. I had failed at the lessons Christ taught through the witness of my neighbors. A friendly greeting and a friendlier good-bye will build and hold character in place until our next visit. However, when we leave in a huff or when we avoid politeness our virtue shrinks and the hellos become downward gazes. I struggled not to sleep because I knew what was waiting for me on the barrier of night. I had opened the door on what my problems were and how they were, at one point, set aside when God gave me an open heart. How would the night look at this?

As I struggled to fight the demons of the night I came quickly to appreciate the tenacious spirit of Otis. I watched as he was determined to get the remaining bits of chocolate *just* out of the reach from a nose overly active for its size. He showed a determination in even the simplest of tasks during our as yet brief companionship. Was I that determined at even the simplest of tasks *I* faced? The answer was no, I gave up to easily at life at least until recently. I watched his efforts for a while but the weariness of my mind and the need for rest subdued me. The sun had barely set and the moon was still well beyond terrestrial reach as I pushed the coffee table farther back and laid an old shirt next to my end of the couch for my new friend. The same end of the couch called me as it had done for many nights now but there would now be a buffer. Though the hour was by some measures still young, I could not keep up its pace. I lay down as I had for sometime now, arms at my side and staring at a pockmarked ceiling. It was a ceiling that was once strewn with welcome home balloons, congratulation signs and happy birthday wishes but not anymore It was now a ceiling that saw gray stains of doubt and cobwebs of forgetfulness and it hovered over me as I welcomed the night.

I was generally content with my day's rewards one of which now sat staring at me from beneath the coffee table. I fought for a bit longer the encroaching reach of sleep because I knew what was waiting for me once I succumbed to it. Was I going to bear witness to secular lessons or the lessons that came quietly through the shades of sleep? The lessons of the day had taught me a couple of things and maybe now I was ready to hear the answer awaiting me on the other side of night. I reached for the clock and saw my new friend seek the end of the couch, obviously ignoring the old shirt. With some struggle he found the couch more to his satisfaction. I fought a bit more the tide of sleep but soon found I was standing opposite my boyhood home, my arms at my side. I kicked a pebble, possibly the same one I had kicked years ago.

As I stood in silent repose and I sought direction to the left and to the right but saw only clouds of white so the road that lay ahead must be traveled as from memory. I saw before me an oval door and heard the sounds of young sisters at play, sisters who were now strangers to this observer of family history. I heard the sound of a three-legged black lab running and looking for a playmate and seeking a hand for his under scratched nose. I knew not what direction to turn so the lab came to my side with a bark years out of tune. I stared at the oval glass and passed on to my new noble guide a scratch of his nose as the clouds of memory claimed him but I knew *we* would play again soon. I knew I had done what the spirit of any boyhood pet would want me to do so I began my journey on this cloud lit path. I turned from the door and the cloud met me like a shroud about my feet.

I saw to the right through the rising memory and at a distant pace a tall figure walking toward my boyhood home. Was it Dad returning home? Was it the lost brother? I turned back and strolled to the front of the house and looked through the door. With a bit of a squint I saw my father's face looking back on me. I bowed my head more in shame and guilt than in fear. I was filled with the shame and tears from a generations ago and they filled my face as if all were new to the senses. The fingers of God raised my chin and I saw my father speak. I could not hear his words at first because I chose again not to listen. My chin bowed again in shame. As the spirit of God raised it one more time, I saw my father speak a simple phrase but I could not hear it. His lips moved a time or two but I chose not to listen. I was embarrassed and my head dropped now in guilt and in failure. Again, with patience and tenderness, the spirit of God raised my head. I now opened my ears and heard my father speak these simple words *move on*.

The simple words of a long lost father wiped away the tears of many generations ago and many an unexpected moment. With those words I was soon opposite the home of my youth. My hands were by my side as I stood at the beginning of a road that I must now walk from memory. The tears were gone and the memories of doubt, shame and guilt remained behind a door I could no longer see. No longer was I able to see with clarity the oval glass, the tall pines out front or an apple tree that never lived up to its name. The clouds encompassed the home of youth and it was now hard to see with a final turn I said good-bye to the home that had haunted me for so long. I began walking toward the tall figure that was now at some distance and vanishing in a thick, hovering cloud bank. My chest seemed heavy as I began my journey and it was becoming more difficult to breathe as the clouds were thick and I struggled to move forward.

I felt as if someone was close and about to share a whisper so I paused to seek their words. I felt their breath and their presence was making me apprehensive and my nervousness now made it difficult to breathe. Was it a person who was to guide me or to *prevent* me from moving on? I was eager but cautious as to what was about to be said. I seemed paralyzed on this familiar road and drew back a few paces to get a better footing and prepare for my journey. I stood motionless and heard what I thought was an ocean but perhaps was just the sought after whisper. If the whisper was a message, I was avoiding it for I was afraid as to what it might be. Was it the sound of the sea hitting the shore or a gentle voice leading me? Was it the shoreline of Maine that called me or the voice of a long lost friend asking me to stay just a bit longer? The unexpected was something I could never properly prepare for I was terribly apprehensive to be a failure in carrying out the unknown. I now assumed that it was the shore of Maine that beckoned me and I sought to walk the beaches of a harbor without a name. I stood for a moment before leaving the road and waited for the traveler to come meet *me* rather my seeking the traveler. However, no one came rather I was being led; I just had to take the first step.

A twitch and a kick, a roll and a toss and I continued to gasp for air. The tension was great but the tears were gone and anticipation was the emotion I now faced. The questions were plenty and I had no reason to start asking them but I knew I should. Who was the tall figure far ahead of me now? What was that sound that tempered my uneasy spirit? There was a slight hint of moisture in the air but the road was smooth and safe to travel. My mouth was dry and my breathing labored but there was no pain. The distant voice that was coming closer came from a still unknown direction. I could feel the touch of a tiny breath or maybe it was a hand holding my shoulder. I closed my eyes to draw my other senses closer to the source in question. Who was it and what did they want? I came to see that with a small gesture and an increasingly willing spirit it was going to be a glorious journey. I stood in silent repose as the clouds clung to my feet and the nose of a noble black lab twanged my fingers. I took a step though small, it was the first of many I would take before the final wake. I took another and another and before I could take a larger, more determined one I saw off to my...

"Good morning Providence and welcome to your heart of gold station WJJL. Get up, get out and begin this day with Creedence Clearwater Revival." The riff began and my list grew.

The shrill alarm of the morning tyrant met the dawn and I sat up as if being at view. I gasped for my lost breath and felt chilled at the early morning light. The fresh morning dew made the just finished dream that much more memorable as its scent made its way through the half opened patio door. I was fearful, but now as a moment or two had passed could not understand why I was slightly set back. In a state of nausea I moved to the edge of the couch to see a confused face Otis. He placed his small head on my foot and wagged his tiny tail as if to tell me all was OK. The tightness of the chest was subdued and I sat for a moment seeking an answer as to why I felt the way I did. I struggled to know but was rewarded instead with the friendship of a two-pound poop producer with bad breath named Otis.

My heartbeat slowed to a normal rate, one that my state of being could manage. The morning musical mentor asked several questions that seemed pointless except to the sponsors. I was a runner catching his breath, I was a loner now with a friend and I was a son forgiven all rolled into one and all coming to me at once. The drone became clearer as I sought the cobwebbed ceiling and the days light attempted a slap.

> Comin' down on a sunny day?
> Yesterday, and days before,
> sun is cold and rain is hard,
> I know; been that way for all my time.
> `til forever, on it goes
> through the circle, fast and slow,
> I know; It can't stop I wonder.

Early morning sunlight came through the slightly ajar patio shade and the rays touched a piece of carpet more accustomed to dust than to sun. An autumn cold began to settle upon my shoulders as it usually did this time of year. I was almost never ill, a remarkable feat for someone who abused his body as much as I did.

I want to know, have you ever seen the rain?

I turned the radio down and answered Creedence with a yes, *I had indeed seen the rain.* Yes, it does come down whether sun or shade.

Through the rays of sun came the song of a glistening breasted mourning dove. He seemed fatter than before but just as intent on delivering his morning mail. His song this morning was more beautiful than I had heard previously and it was a welcoming beat from which my spirit could garner strength. For some time I leaned back in my seat and listened to the song of this creature that would soon leave this patio in silence. I came to appreciate the time he was spending with me; this moment was so very nice and my smile was his reward. The moment for his departure arrived before I had demanded and he left to greet another. I stood brushing my hair back a couple of times with both hands as the song subsided and the dove flew away to make another friend for the day.

Every day had begun like this for as long as I could recall. I was getting a bit weary of the early morning shakes and wished that this part of my journey would end and I knew that it soon would. Maybe it was weariness or perhaps I was becoming accustomed to it but I was ready for the morning tension to end. I took a step or two and found gushing between my toes a by product of my young friend's affection for Dottie's meat loaf. "Puppies do that." Sandi's statement was true on this morning. I looked in his direction to see him quickly close his eyes in an attempt to fake being asleep and avoid confrontation over this hygienic oversight. "OK for you little man." If a dog could throw such a thing as an I told you so look, Otis did so. I didn't mind; it was all part of a learning curve. I did what I needed to do and all was quickly healed.

I prepared a cup of tap water coffee and with a handful of forgotten Saltines I assumed my seat at a dining room table that Annie purchased a few years ago, maybe longer. We didn't have much of an opportunity to share many meals here but we always talked about the days when we would. We would talk for hours on end about the children we would have and the Easter egg hunts we would hold at a home of our own. We would describe what our children would wear on Halloween and how excited they would be as wide eyed children on Christmas morning. We would talk for hours on end about how she would buy frilly this and fancy that and how I would not allow any boy to date my daughter until well after my death. I was determined to be a protective father and to someday give away a daughter at a union blessed by God to a good and decent man. Annie always laughed at how men who were once dogs always changed when it came to their own daughters and the boys of their days.

I was going to take some time today and enjoy the scattered moments of organized thought before taking the same goal less drive. Though I thought it would be goal less I knew I would begin my trip and take the back road until I knew I could stop for a rest. The better parts of life were likely behind me but what remained should be no less enjoyable though I would have to find the joy. Memories can be a wonderful experience if allowed to be such. I guess the last days of life can be similar to the last days of school; we can still choose to learn if we wish. Graduation from both is the anticipation of what comes next. What will secular life hold for us and what will eternity hold upon one life ending and another starting?

There was a stack of unanswered mail on the table all in some form of a second, third and final notice for an unpaid or under paid bill. Dipping my Saltines I saw Dottie's Bible and wondered aloud if I should crack the timeless cover. It was an old one to be certain though I knew cracking it would mean eventually reading it so I thumbed it for now. The cover was tattered and the print faded to where only some alternating letters were recognizable. I looked at it as a cautious observer wondering if I should and its author wondering if I *ever* would. There was sticking from within its covers what appeared to be a well worn, tattered bookmark symbolizing the location of some valued piece of scripture, Isaiah 40:31.

I wasn't ready for rededication to a faith that I had strayed from for reasons of my own creation. God and I were in fact strangers because of me and my selfishness not because of His perceived cruelty. We were close at one time but as with secular brothers and sisters we now bid greetings as if strangers in an elevator. My prayers were those types of greetings; they were carbon copy forms of platitudes and condescending demands. I prayed with doubt that the demands would be answered and blessing given It wasn't until very recently I understood that to be listened to, whether by man or by God, we must at least be civil to our target audience. We seemed to let the matters that unfolded beneath naked elms dictate when we would or wouldn't talk again.When it was good-bye time we always promised we would talk again soon but the calendar clicked right on by. When it was time for a kind hello, we hardly knew one another. As I had with so many I felt that I had shamed God and rather then continuing my disrespect I abandoned the relationship altogether. It was far easier for me to be an impolite and unkind loner than a decent, kind man faithful to my God, country and family. It is easy to fail and takes the mental toughness of the generations of Moses to overcome failure and climb one more hill. How true that is for so many others I have met over the years. Perhaps I was the Pharisee who pointed out the flaws of others in the Temple while not recognizing my own spiritual state.

I took the Bible and placed it on the coffee table as a starting point for gathering my needs for my getaway. The time away could be a rebirth in a way I could begin all over again *just* one more time and *this* time I would do it right. I did have the belief that this trip may be my last opportunity to make the corrections long overdue. I was becoming more certain that my journey would take me to up near Ellsworth Maine, a tiny town which to this very day has never grown much larger than bitty. Ellsworth, like Bradford was a speed bump on the way to somewhere else and if one had the intention it could be ignored altogether. Out of all things, impatience seemed to bother me more than all other character flaws, mine or someone else's. Our impatience would cause to send by our car windows the stories of small town America. Our impatience would send by our souls the epic tales of love and glory that many had sought to instill in our young minds. This character flaw would also send by our minds the stories of those sitting alone on hidden benches. These small town speed bumps would harbor many who often, without asking, would share with anyone epic tales of character and virtue. Small towns and forgotten benches were what life should be about, I wished I had taken the time for both.

Annie loved the drive to and from Maine, why, I wasn't sure she just did. All the little nick knack stores and the small bed and breakfasts were on top of her list of all time favorite places. The drive was only a few short hours from our home here and it was for the most part along the coastline. Annie would say the sound of the sea was so beautiful, like a whisper she said. We would sit on the beach and she would close her eyes to the sound of the sea. She would breathe in deeply the smell from forgotten shores and tell me that if we listened closely we could hear the voice of the angel calling us as the sea came in. We would head east of Boston and up through Portsmouth, New Hampshire and as we crossed the bridge into Maine time stood still and as so many preachers have said, Heaven's Gate was then before us. I really didn't need a map. I had driven the circuit countless times in my head the last few months. I had heard the angels calling every time I made the trip. I needed some clothes, a few bucks and a puppy sitter and then I would be on my way. A quick visit with Dottie would solve the latter and a journey to forgotten drawers the former.

I now ignored the tap water coffee for the taste left a great deal to be desired. I made it daily more out of habit and drank only in recognition of that habit but now it was time to set aside at least that one habit. "I'll be right back," I told the grunting cautious observer and I went downstairs to ask Dottie to meet, greet and sit Otis. I was generally surprised for he didn't try to sneak out the door but chose to sit there looking at me with an I don't care what you do look. Down the stairs to her apartment, the forgotten out of date Welcome sign was now gone but the paper was out front. I knocked and after a brief wait I knocked a couple of more times but there was no answer. We had hardly ever gone more than a couple of days without seeing one another and we were now at that limit. Her days out were usually at the end of the week but perhaps the forgetful nephew stopped by. Maybe she was lying down; some of her meds always seemed to knock her out. "Crap." I slammed my hands into my pockets and was angry at my knock apparently going unanswered. I was angry because I didn't get my way and not happy for her. Before I let my selfish nature go too much further I recognized my unkindness approaching and slowed down its pace. Rather than being upset at Dottie I transformed anger into a *I hope she is having a good time mood.*

I still sought an answer at the door but set my desires aside and left her a note:

Hey kiddo, you must have found yourself a fella. Been by a couple of times, hope all is ok, got a puppy, named him Otis, crapped a couple of times already. Going to Maine so I'll see yah soon.

I stuffed it under her door far enough so she would find it if she chose not to go out for a day or two. I guess now I would have to do what I was going to do all along and that was to take the two pound poop producer with me on my trip. It would be a nice day, no rain and not much in the way of threatening skies either. A bird here and there greeted whoever would listen to their blathering and a splattering of car horns and a noiseless parking lot surrounded this small clump of Rhode Island.

I looked down and scooped Dottie's morning paper as I looked sheepishly at the door hoping not to get caught. Back up the stairs and into the door I saw Otis not far from where I left him a short time ago. He still had a look on his face that would confuse the schizophrenic. "Hey boy, let's get ready for a ride aye?" I assumed he agreed by the way his head tilted and he began to circle the floor. My youth and primate behavior taught me to pack thoroughly, sometimes without even getting off the couch. However Annie had taught some less primitive techniques and I knew I had to find what I needed from places other than a pile on the floor. I had the feeling that I wouldn't be gone too long before I found what I may be looking for; at least that's what the inner voice was saying.

I grabbed a duffel bag from a bedroom closet that I had seldom cracked. As I shuffled and fumbled for various things that I would never use I asked yet another profound question to the man in the mirror. If my inner voice could dictate actions that ran contrary to my natural inclination then what exactly was the inner voice? Is God our inner voice? Dottie had answered this many times, I guess, but it was now at this point that I recalled her prolonged explanation. She sat back one day and again without eye contact she said that the little inner voice was our guardian angel. I recalled my reaction as being one filled with pish posh and rolled eyes. Guardian angels were something that only a lonely widow created and secretly called an invisible friend. As I grayed and the years behind me mounted, perhaps, *just* perhaps Dottie had her point of view well prepared and well experienced.

I would make a choice as the days concluded as to whether or not my inner voice was the better one of my nature. The duffel bag from a musty closet still had dirty clothes from a mission trip to El Salvador that was planned a couple of years ago. The smell was a distinctive blend of mold and memories and I frankly wasn't sure which was less objectionable. I shoved a few things deep inside and found some more to pile on top of those. With little effort I was ready to make the move.

Coming back into the dining room I found a marked territory of the young co-pilot. After shaking my head, I tossed an old mold and memory coated shirt across the error in hygienic techniques. I looked at him as if I expected better and turned with a faint smile knowing that only a puppy could get a way with such freedom of urination. I washed out the duffel bag after most of the needed items were already inside and I wasn't too excited about the garments I had chosen for what I expected to be a short trip. The bag was new before I packed it originally so the only damage came from the aged clothes within its compartments and not from the week old ones I had just packed. It would be fine. Some boxers, socks, Patriots shirts and several pairs of overused and under appreciated sweat pants and I was packed. I usually forgot my toothbrush, razor and comb until I got to the car so I added them now so I wouldn't have to come back up the stairs. Annie had taught me that respect for myself would transcend the barrier to loving another and it often it started with how we took care of ourselves. She had told me as a young man that if I packed like a slob that's how I saw myself.

"No bag for you there little buddy. You'll have to get by pretty much on handouts, aye." He came to my foot and in a tone of silent reconciliation for his hygienic error rested his head on my instep. I sat down in my well formed spot and put him on the couch next to me and began flipping through Dottie's newspaper. I would read it in full at some point but for now was curious as to just how much time I could kill before heading down the road. The daily news was always the same; it didn't matter what time of year it was it was always the same. The modern news was just voyeur forms of secular entertainment and seldom news anymore. The modern day purveyors of news had decided that their social and political views mattered far more than the facts of the day. I skimmed the headlines and only saw one that gathered any interest at all:

Young Girl Killed by Hit and Run

I had a lot of things going on and didn't take much time to read trivial things like another piece about a tragedy. My brain was dotting back and forth and I was traveling three or four towns at one time so I couldn't concentrate now on what the paper had to share. I had not read much news lately and what news there was, was always bad; one could hardly tell if it was news or fiction. It seemed to be all the same and sometimes the only enjoyable part of the paper was about what wasn't real. There still was available to me the story I had left with Dottie a couple days ago about the shipwrecks of Maine but she would pack that into some distant corner of other forgotten stuff. I would bring her back some trinkets from my journey, a *this* or a *that* for her to place on some dust covered shelf and thank me often for. Annie always brought Dottie maple candy, dangerous for someone of my portly stature to leave unattended on the front seat as she napped. I thought I'd better not bring her maple candy for it may not make the trip in its original condition.

I was a guy so I knew Dottie would probably expect something like a coffee mug or a Boston Bruins hat. She would be as thrilled as if it were a box of gold from an abandoned house. As I sat leaning back I recalled the first few gifts I bought Annie. They were usually stupid in nature and intended to bring a smile and a pucker lipped laugh, which they did. When I committed myself to her I saw how her heart was so often touched by the small gestures like a single rose or a card with just the right phrase on a sad day. I played mental hockey as my house guest was becoming curious as to the eventual goal of all my moving about and I suppose curious as to his possible role in it all. The radio was still hissing away at some song that wasn't any good when it was new thirty years ago and my inner voice was now telling me that it was time to go. The songs of old which were now called hits had worn out their welcome. I unplugged the bearer of these hits feeling that it wouldn't be needed again. Maybe, *just* maybe I wouldn't need it anymore. Maybe I had heard the last of the classics and could welcome more enlightened choirs. Music for some and certainly for this aging plum chaser served as a respite for the mind. It was a mental album where the songs of our youth brought back youthful things. It is no different now as my gray hairs had multiplied and my posture had headed south. The louder I played the lost hits, the greater likelihood that my whispering guilt would not shine. But for now, I will face what my demons will bring me.

I sat on the couch and looked about wondering what I would forget because I knew it would be something but time would settle that. Looking about this musty haven I saw the phone was still off the hook and tucked away next to a chair she used to nap in. I had removed it some time ago to avoid the verbal hawkers, the collectors and their bastard children the telemarketers of one kind or another. Nothing is worse than having a one name wonder on the other end who *will not* take a go to hell for the final answer. The verbal hawkers were always Todd or Josh and never gave a last name and called time and time again meaning never to disturb.

My parents were gone, friends were few, the money grubbers were plenty and I just didn't want any of that mess. I pointed my finger at my newly acquired friend in order to tell him to stay *right* where he was and I was out the door just for a moment. Outside and down to the car I tossed my bag and saw that Dottie's apartment lights were out. I should try again but I will be gone only a few days and we will have a nice visit then when I return. I was back up the stairs and thought briefly that I saw someone else go down the other side. "A shadow or those damn birds again maybe." I was back into the home to the confused gaze of the pudgy one. "I need gas, some form of dog food, oil, paper and you probably would be happy with a week's supply from Leonard's aye." Talking to myself I looked around the apartment as if there were something missed. Was I having that gut feeling that tells us we're leaving something behind? What was my inner voice telling me that I wasn't hearing? I grabbed a couple of towels for you know who. I got a bowl for you know who as well and another bowl to match the first. I wrapped some of Dottie's meat loaf and took some chips, stale for a day or two from the week old opened bag.

"OK." Down the stairs and back up in a repeated effort I ignored the mail that had piled up on the table for when we're gone, the mail still comes doesn't it. It didn't matter if I ignore it now or later. I took the day's newspaper a Book of Common Prayer and Dottie's Bible. As I stood in the living room looking about I was a bit surprised at my last retrieval. Why had I taken these books and not one by Clancy or Grisham? Why do some people carry little pieces of scripture in their wallets and why are Bibles in hotel rooms? In a heartbeat I felt suddenly anxious for was this a message also? Fate. Why did I, without second thought, grab the books of God that I hadn't read in years? The nausea had swiftly become anxiety as I sincerely felt I was leaving behind something that I might regret As always I never seemed able to prevent regret; I just attempted to reconcile it in a half hearted head hung low effort after the victim was claimed. This regret was short lived and my defense mechanisms were strong on this day. I grabbed my wallet, some loose change for the New Hampshire tolls and some hard candy left over from the Pilgrims' first Christmas. I tossed it all into a bag whose former contents were dumped on the table to accommodate its new role.

I stood and looked about a home that was filled with guilt, shame, regret and days of loneliness. My eyes landed on Otis who scooted closer as to remind me not to forget him as I completed my packing. I was back down the stairs with the bag and another toss of a stare at Dottie's. Still nothing. I was back through the door and let the remnants of lethargy depart. "OK let's go, little guy." I picked up Otis and looked about to see what might be neglected. As I was shutting the door I stopped to put the phone back on the hook knowing that there would be no blinking light upon my return.

Down the stairs with Otis in tow, I got behind the wheel of a car that was already full of several unidentified odors likely left over from other hygienic errors. After some brief domestic corrections Otis claimed his towel from the previous day and settled in for what he anticipated would be a lengthy and curious trip. He was also passing me an appreciative look for not leaving him behind as many others had done. I sat for a bit; I had forgotten something but couldn't name it nor claim it. This sensation had been gnawing at me for some time and I suppose I would discover it when the time came. Should I wait for Dottie? Should I take one last slow walk through the apartment? I looked at her door as if she would come running out in the Bruins t-shirt I got her for Christmas, flagging me down to complain about my lifestyle. She didn't come and the sun in the rear view mirror beckoned my departure.

I sent my recollection back to the apartment and took a mental walk through rather then the physical one. My mind repeated step by

Ashley Bay

step what I had just physically accomplished. I got this, I got that, I picked that up and brought that down and I threw that away. My mind checked the sink, the stove and shut off the lights one more time. My memory had grabbed the bag and turned the radio off and the phone on. The radio was on low and the food for my pal was next to me just out of nose reach of my young co-pilot. The day was new and memories old and that was just fine for right now. I wasn't in a hurry to return to days of old it was they that wore me out. I nodded to my pal and let him know that perhaps there was nothing left behind and we were ready to go.

If I had personally accompanied my mind as it was double checking the locked door I would have heard the phone ring. If I had accompanied my mind on one last walk through the apartment rather then being in a rush, I would have heard a cracking, anxious voice: "Honey, Oh God, please be home! This is Sandi." If I had accompanied my mind to the apartment, I would have heard one more time a voice of a woman I wouldn't be there for. Once again, I would not be there when I said I would. Once again my soul knew more than my body but I listened to the flesh. I clutched the wheel at 10 and 2 and backed my way eventually out onto Tennent. Behind me, I left the sad cracking voice of a love once lost crying: "Oh God please be home!"

I would not head north today but take more of a circuitous route over to Rte. 95, taking a western trail through this half dollar state. When you go west in Rhode Island, you won't go too far before you are at risk of crossing state lines. I would come close but knew where the line ended The back roads around here were some of the ones hand made by men like my Dad who, as a proud member of the Civilian Conservation Corps, created many of our New England miles. It was an OK drive and I hadn't made it in some time. I would make my first stop at an old A&P a few miles down that was now disguised as a Mega something. One thing I found out shortly after I was old enough to drive was that distance meant nothing in New England. New Hampshire, Maine and certainly the approaching area of Rhode Island, known as the Rocky Upland had to be a nightmare to anyone who wanted an accurate map. Dad said that when these roads were made by hand there were no maps and they just kept digging and digging and digging. New England was the only place I had ever been where I could drive for one hour at sixty miles per hour and travel only forty-five miles.

When a visitor to New England gets lost amidst these miles and stops to ask directions the person they seek guidance from will inevitably give such directions using the words, "Dunkin' Donuts." Directions given to the confused driver will often sound like this: "If you need to get there, you will find the best way is to take the eventual left or right *just* past the Dunkin' Donuts and you will find your way." Well, for someone who thrived on impatience Leonard's was the only place for my Boston cremes so I never considered the latter as a reliable landmark. This would be one of those trips often taken by lost, unmotivated men and rarely by any woman we would ever know. In other words, the women we forgot would be those we remembered when left to the solace of the road. Trips like this would be not a journey as much as of revival, it would be one of farewell to the past. I would decide my destination when I got there I guess and not before. Hit and miss travel was a sign of someone who was lost and I was most certainly lost. There may in fact be a general starting point for the lost and lonely but I would let the road take me wherever it chose.

The immediate horizon would be about twenty-five New England miles away or twenty in conventional distance and measures. Situate Reservoir was the largest land locked piece of water in Rhode Island named after some well known Indian chieftain at one time. Annie and I had taken several trips here over the years and this would be my first without her. What was so nice about this area of the state was that just within a mile or two of Situate there were several cabin by the night family owned businesses. Some were old and forgotten and of course as some of the more greedy had their wishes satisfied they bought out the mom-and-pop locations. I hoped I would be able to set foot in one of these smaller less remarkable of the by the night locals.

The larger trademarked cabins were never for us nor were they the ones chosen by the locals, but they lived for the ones with the discount coupons. I remember Annie had her sight on a weekend getaway place outside a small hiccup of a town on the other side of Rte.14 called Hopkins Hollow I might stop there as well. I might visit again all the familiar places we had walked and visited over the years.

Ashley Bay

I might visit once again our old friends and places of my youth might also be possibilities. There were so many unknowns landing up here where we would often go walking, fishing and just talking about all the great adventures we would have late in life. I am going to miss her *so* much. She would, as all women do at one time or another with their significant others, come to me with a crumpled brochure and ask, "Isn't this pretty?" She would of course have the answer in mind before I offered it up so I just said, "Yup."

I would reply to such a question, as I'm sure most significant others did, through my chip covered shirt and the final seconds of some second period of a one sided game with a grunt of approval. Annie would accept this grunt as if it danced like Yates or Kipling and she would make the plans that I had so magically approved of. Annie would sit next to me with her lap full of fliers, dog eared magazines and discount motel coupons and continuously seek my grunt of approval. What a role I played and I was so proud to play such a role for her. She would as all you women do have her mind made up long before a grunt was ever sought; the grunt was a mere formality to what was the inevitable. Hopkins Hollow was one of these grunts at first and one repeated many times over the years.

I couldn't help but smile every time I thought how she would cuddle up on the couch with her stack of stuff and clip this and mark that when she knew such an activity was low on my fun list. It wasn't much fun for me. However, my joy came when I knew *she* enjoyed it so much. Her stack of stuff now rested on Uncle Danvers' night stand where she last left them still with worn out dog ears. She was and *is* my only love. Sandi may have come close early on but Annie was the one I took the walks with Annie was the one to whom I brought the rose and boxes of bad candy while Sandi watched the world go by. She was the one God put before me at a time in my life when I was preparing to move on yet again to somewhere other than where I was. She was the one who smiled first. She flirted first as I turned my head and said to my feet, "Why bother?" She was the one chosen to save my heart long before the world came into being. She was the one who softened my spirit and she helped me ready myself to walk the rest of this road that I now travel alone.

Annie asked me out first and without my realizing it, my impolite awkward grunt was an acceptance and that very first grunt was my way of letting her into my world. We courted for a while and it was nearly five months before I even tried to peck her cheek. She made me feel like I was supposed to be a gentleman and I knew after a short time that I was supposed to be nothing else *but* a gentleman. Our life together was a glorious one and it was meant to be, I guess it can only be glorious. The simple pleasures we shared with one another are now the ones that fill the back roads of this final trip. As our years together ended our memories were placed on a nearby shelf along with thoughts of our early days together. I would retrieve them often before this journey began and of late I would wander through our home touching her with kindness. As the days passed, I touched her face often and carried with me now the joy that she brought to me all these many years.

The drive so far had gone quietly and I made a quick turn into the now highly impersonal Amos Mega Market. I would go do what I had to do to make this a bit more comfortable for me and Otis and prayed that I wouldn't get behind a check writer. I didn't like this store but had no choice today; it was the only one in this direction. When we were young this was a store where many of our neighbors could find a *free puppy* of their own. The owner now was one of the new societal elites with a business degree from some school in Massachusetts. He carried himself with an air of condescension and an attitude that made casual customers feel like they owed a debt *to* him. We all know people like that I am sure and unfortunately a good deal of today's young people have that *same* attitude, the attitude that the world was finally perfected the day *they* were born.

There are I guess allot of folks like that in our society today, those who were interested in outcome and not service. Those who are not interested in anything else other than their lives and the perception of their own importance to mankind. This can be said of not only modern business but modern government as well. Where government is different than business is we can't avoid the elected. We are getting to the stage where we can no longer even get them out of office once they are in there so why bother. The odds of the modern business owner being apologetic are as great as modern day government workers saying they are wrong about a bureaucratic mistake. Some business people feel they are doing the customer a favor just by selling the same stuff as a million other retailers do. Certainly many of the politicians believe they are Christ incarnate and that we are but the temple peddlers. This Mega Market was surely of this type.

That type of behavior said allot to Annie and it says a great deal to me. Ego and selfishness have replaced compassion and kindness in much of our youth, business people and politicians. What was the turning point where we went from tales of virtue to vile tales? We have society to thank for that, for what has the modern child learned in the new type of world? What has a young person learned when fathers are no longer needed or appreciated in society? What have the children learned when marriage is now a joke and God is removed from all aspects of society? What can we expect of a child who is taught secular morality and *not* Godly truths? Annie taught me that personal style was often the result of our personal faith and that when faith is gone what style should we expect? If we had a strong dedication to God then compassion and kindness were intuitive. If our faith were weak or not important at all, then selfishness and ego would be our intuitive nature. She always said she wasn't really smart but she would say things at times that could baffle the apostles and last I knew I was no apostle.

I got what I needed and waited for some thong wearing, gum snapping, tattooed, elite wannabe to check me out and I was gone. This young *lady* and I say that with tongue in cheek made no eye contact and never said thank you. She could barely recognize the denomination I used and had trouble making the change required for the transaction. Going outside I saw a couple of younger window tappers looking at my two pound co-pilot. Otis had come to understand that being cute was an asset. In a way, he may take the same approach to life as the cashier I just left: *cute is all that matters.* In a squeaky little girl voice they beeped, "He's so cute." "Yeah he's OK, I guess. He was a stray a couple of days ago." With an attitude that was designed to show a go away sense I barked, "Bye." I opened the door tossing the bag on Otis. "Bye," the window tappers said to Otis with a finger wave as we backed our way out onto Tennent.

I was ready for Hopkins Hollow. I was ready for the valley and the lakes that could shed a degree of mental peace upon this anxious soul. I began to drive for just a short few miles to where now I knew I would head for the days that lay ahead. I suppose Otis was ready for something other than cold meat loaf too but he would have to wait to taste the pleasure of gas station bologna. I assured him saying, "Well little buddy just a few minutes and we'll stop." He tossed me a *yeah, whatever you say look* and settled into his towel without further review. If a dog could show doubt, Otis sure had in just the few hours we were partners. He was cautious but probably should be for my track record for caring for others was not great. He had been through so much in just his few weeks here on earth and wasn't sure what life would hold next for him. In his brief tenure, he had seen the death of a mother, abandonment, hunger, loneliness and he was the hidden sole survivor in a cardboard box. I petted his head and in a comforting manner tried to assure him that all would be OK on our journey. I also suggested that we both could learn something from it.

Back out onto a bit of Tennent then to 95 South for about ten miles, New England miles that is and I could take the long lost dirt road through life. We would go the back way that I hadn't traveled since I was a young man. Then it was an adventure into a tremendous growth of trees with dust and ponds bursting at the seams. If during this long confusing drive Otis piddled it was fine for the car was so far beyond anything close to a favorable odor that anything supplementary didn't matter. Annie would just shake her head at behavior like this and say a guy is always a guy. I took some beef jerky, split it up a bit for my buddy who with a nose in the air said with his eyes, I don't think so. "OK for you." He refused the spicy pepper steak but in just a short time down the road he would get some real food, which he probably sensed as he so unceremoniously hit with the grocery bag. There was no music for this part of the journey my mind was all the company I needed for the time being. There was no need to be taken on a golden journey through yesterday by a talent long overdue for retirement. I do love music so and have to thank the almighty for giving me that joy. When the talent is matched by a fan's appreciation it creates a lifelong memory.

Hopkins Hollow was a town probably before Rhode Island was a state. Many have said, at least through tradition that it was the final resting place for the lost souls of the Rocky Upland country. If someone ever got lost in this part of the state the soul would come to Hopkins Hollow to be claimed at some later date and time by loved ones. I had to find Annie or maybe she had to find me at this stage who knew or perhaps I had to let her go. I wasn't really sure what

Ashley Bay

was what but Hopkins Hollow was a place where the answer could be had and perhaps a soul lost in this world could be given direction. Maybe, *just* maybe we would meet again so we could walk hand in hand through the Rocky Upland. The trees and wandering doe would bring back our unified smile. I think she was in a better place but I had to find that place and figure out if she was going to be OK. If she was going to be OK, could I then move on?

I drove without attention to detail, beating myself up over something that I couldn't control. Why did I have to leave her? I didn't know if I was going to come closer to her in Hopkins Hollow but it seemed like that was a place to begin the search. If I could begin the search at a place where she and I had begun our lives together then maybe I could come to closure. If she wasn't there, where would she be? I would know sooner rather than later where she may be but for now I would take one step at a time. The ten miles on this southbound trek were naturally twelve and with an exit on Wakefield Road, I was on Rte. 102. I would probably plan a rest stop for both of us over near West Greenwich a few miles from the previously mentioned cabins but we'll see.

The sun had beaten the last bit of cold off the car and out of me and I was sure happy to be away from the elite wannabes. From Wakefield to 102, down a few more New England miles on an unknown road and I would come to Goyette's Country Store. Goyette's was a store that Dad and I visited many years ago and with that visit I found a life long friend. As a growing chaser, I stopped by and kept a decent relationship going with its proprietor. A stranger to this back road would be surprised when, from out of the brush Goyette's arose. However, for the experienced traveler anticipation was the sensation when it came to this particular stop. It was a nondescript store built seemingly by the leftover pieces of wood from the Mayflower. In other words it was rather old and it smelled its age. It was nondescript next to the fancy minis a few miles away with the exception of a driveway of old carriage wheels leading up to its front door. It was just a one story building that served the customer up front and served as a comfortable home out back. Goyette's was at the most twenty or so miles from our house and I came here just last Christmas and the couple before that to get some stocking stuffers for Annie's Barney Rubble stocking. I drove another couple of miles and saw the emerging unpainted frame exposed on the distant right side shoulder.

I smiled with little effort remembering the games I played with her Christmas stocking each year. Every December 25th I would hide it in a different place. The first year she was sad thinking I had forgotten but was so surprised when she found it hanging from the shower head. It was so funny seeing the childlike frustration in her face each Christmas when she went about seeking out her Christmas surprises. That prank of mine drove her nuts, one year it was hanging in the shower, the next year it was under the sink and last year it was on top of the Christmas ham in the freezer. Annie loved teddy bears and small nick-knacks and *this* and *that's* and Goyette's was the place that carried it all. I think it may have been last year but maybe more when I was here last. The time seemed to be moving on at an even quicker pace and I hoped I wouldn't lose Annie's face.

I pulled into a spot away from the door a bit to be sure to leave enough room for the next customer, which could be weeks away. I saw on the wrap around porch the same things that attracted me as a young boy. There were boxes of this and that and various old Coke machines which now served as a support mechanism for the boxes. "Are you going to be OK, do you need to do your business?" Getting just a half sleepy turn of the head I assumed the former and not the latter. I locked the doors to prevent an approach by an aggressive window tapper and left him alone for what I thought would be just a few minutes. I stood in front of the three-step approach and could smell the scents from generations ago. As I walked toward the front I was brought back to the youthful walks to Ethyl Hyde's store and half expected a worn out, nearly blind collie named Teddy to greet me There were old Coke signs hanging at a tilt to the right of a paint peeled screen door that would bang shut a couple of times upon each entry and exit. To the left were old whiskey barrels and milk churns surrounded by old boxes of car parts that Henry Ford himself had no use for. This was just the front porch, I shook my head dreading that which could possibly be waiting for the visitor out back.

Shading my eyes I peered through the screen door to see if anyone was about. "Hello, Maple, you here?" I smelled something baking or over baking as always seemed to be the case and I went inside to the sound of a screen door banging shut. The proprietor for many years now had become a long time friend. Maple Goyette, what a gal. She was as wide as she was tall. She had a hairstyle that, when it was combed came down unevenly across her shoulders. Her smile which was wide and constant revealed the need for a friendly neighborhood dentist. Maple never married and had been running this catch all store since her older brother Jeffrey was laid to rest somewhere in Vietnam. There was no answer so again I tossed in through the screen door in a timid manner, "Maple, hello." There was no answer that I could recognize just an aroma of something from the wood burning kitchen stove. A young person would have to use his or her imagination to conjure up such a store as this. However, as we age, I am sure we can all fondly remember such a vendor from the Bradfords of our own.

When you walked in to Goyette's the dim lighting always accentuated the dusty smell of items that remained unsold. There were wooden ice chests, penny candy everywhere, two-cent combs, Brasso, Sugar Pops cereal and posters of Lyndon Johnson. I shook my head every time I came in and saw some of the stuff hanging around; it was seemingly all out of date twenty years before I started first grade. There were things that just never matched their neighbors. I saw a shark's head from Key West, a collection of Rudyard Kipling's books and a beer can collection *all* on the same shelf. On the opposite wall were photographs of everything from clipper ships to her father but what was prominent was a photo of her brother Jeffrey in his Army uniform. There were photos of her mom, aunts and uncles and others of some distant forgotten family member. Old cans of this and that and a crate in a corner of every part of the room. Once found, it had to be gone through by any curious soul.

I took some candy and stood in the center of the room not sure what to do next. If she wasn't here then I would need a few things so I would toss the cash on her well worn rocking chair. A second handful of mints and I headed back outside to see a woman wide as she was tall tapping on the window seeking recognition by my still very suspicious co-pilot. My smile was back as I said, "Hey lady, I've been in side cleanin' you out." A pause as she tapped to no result. "Hi, buddy, good seein' you, hun. You got a little friend here aye?" I walked down the three steps, sliding the mints slyly into my pocket to the echo of the bang, bang-bang of the screen door. I looked through the same window at Otis as if he were a fish in a bowl.

"He seems to be a great little dog. Got him yesterday up in Bradford. Some kid was givin' him away. I had decided it was time for a long overdue drive. We're probably going up to Maine, Casco Bay somewhere up around that way anyhow."

Maple smiled and gave me a hug that was to make up for forgotten ones over recent months. "Good for you. Let's have some coffee, aye."

I nodded, hoping she would ask, for her coffee was certainly better than anything my tap water could produce. It was strong though God knows, it could melt the face of the toughest of grouches.

We were back inside to the sound of the banging screen door: bang, bang-bang, a sound that could be remembered from when Ethyl first let us into the storefront of her own. That sound was one that would bring the oldest of us back to the days of summer and our family's front porch. The neighbors all had screen doors and when the kids were called home we could hear the bang, bang-bang echo all throughout the three-street town. Maple waddled to the back and I heard her banging cups, shuffling this and that and swearing continuously in a well rehearsed way. I found a couple of chairs and moved them closer to a spot of sun that shone in from an upstairs vent and let me keep a better eye on the car.

"Why Maine?" This posed, short burst of inquisitiveness came from the side kitchen.

I fumbled for a better position and said, "Annie liked the drive and I kinda wanted to take a last trip to bring back the good memories."

Still shuffling and fumbling in the back she brought out a couple of mugs, *not cups*, but mugs a notable difference for the hearty coffee drinker. They were clipper ship mugs, she loved clipper ships. There were old photos on parts of the walls that I had overlooked before and now noticed as I sat in the sun soaked chair.

"Thanks."

Ashley Bay

I took the coffee as Maple sat down with a thud in a rocking chair that had served as a mighty helpmate for many years. She grabbed the mug and gulped in a way that some of the Hollywood elite might see as a bit unladylike, leaving a hardy slurp behind.

"There's a lot to do up that way. Daddy used to go there when we were kids," she said.

I smiled, anticipating an impending story and I wasn't disappointed. Another slurp followed by a drawn out "haghhh" and she began. She rocked slowly, giving a shove on the floor with her timeworn foot.

"Ma died when we kids were little and Daddy never made much here, just enough to always just get by," she said with a kind smile. "Dad kinda' always felt bad about bringin' Mama down this way. Life was hard here and never got better and Mama couldn't keep up." This was great for Maple always picked up right where our last conversation ended regardless of how long between visits.

Maple was silent for a bit as she gulped and smacked the blackest of coffee. "We could never keep up with the other kids never much to wear. I was always a big girl so never had many boys around." She rolled her disappointed eyes and finished with, "I didn't have to worry about the fellas *carrying* me away." With a boastful grin she said, "I like food my friend a sandwich never walks out on yah," she said with a big nearly toothless grin. "A piece of pie never cheats on yah." I nodded knowing what she meant because I was one of those men she spoke of. "We didn't have television for the longest time. Jeff joined the Army to see stuff, kinda' get away from all this and he never came home. I used to think about things yah know and Maine was one of those things. I waited for so many years for my little brother to come home but he didn't, *still* waiting I suppose."

The times I have spent with Maple over the years she always slowed her speech and choked just a bit when she thought of her brother Jeff, now dead for nearly forty-years.

"Jeff was a good brother. Daddy told him to *be* sure to come back home because he had a kid sister to take care of. He never came home, we waited and he *never* came home. Then one day the Army came with a preacher in tow and they told us he was gone. Daddy waited years and died and Jeff never came home."

Maple paused briefly but never sharing more than a brief look continued, "I'm still waiting, never went far from this place because Daddy had promised me Jeff would take care of me and I am holding *both* of them to their promise, damn 'um." She said this with a small smile that told me *she* was now taking care of her brother in many ways. She kept his memory strong for all visitors who stopped by.

The gentle smile became sarcastic when she ended with, "Hell hath no furry like a woman scorned, yah know. I'll let them both know where they stand someday."

I held the aged mug and let her know, "Yeah, I have scorned my share over the past decades, little ones, big ones, strangers and old ones. I don't know if those women ever forgave me. I asked them to but I never knew for sure."

I had a hard time figuring out just when certain women were sad or angry and Maple was one of those women.

She slowed her rock and began anew. "I was one of those girls never asked to the prom and I was never sent flowers for no specific reason other than because." Her voice never cracked and was steadfast regardless of topic. "I have sat here my whole life watching the wind claim the memories and just kinda' looking out on this big old world." With a smile less sarcastic than the previous one she said, "If I have a role to serve in this world I've never been able to find it."

I wasn't sure what to say. I never did when someone was sad or needed a hearty shoulder.

"I think it was more than just a few years ago when you and Annie were up this way that she and I had a good old talk about these things. I mentioned to her one time that I doubted God had wanted me to just sit here and watch life go by. But sit I did rocking and the years have just gone away." With a finger as big as some peoples arms she told me don't sit and rock young man.

There was a period of silence. It was awkward for me but a needed respite for Maple. Her eyes were a moist gray and she seemed to be looking for a new topic to lighten the air. In my best condescending voice, I let Maple know that her role was to make me some of the worst coffee I have ever tasted *and* that my mug was now empty. With a cake filled half grin she informed me I was a "smart ass." She sang this in a tolerable salute to my sarcasm which she and only a few others knew was my way of saying that I knew exactly what she was experiencing.

She was sad and disappointed with how life had turned out for her and said to me in a subtle way that I was given an opportunity to be kind but ignored it.

I had in front of me one of those times when I could say something supportive but said no. I was seeking a change in conversational direction so I didn't have to show my own vulnerability, and I asked, "What type of stories did your dad tell you growing up?"

Rocking back and forth in a pensive manner and maybe feeling slightly uncomfortable at sharing her personal regrets she thought for a moment.

"Hmm, Dad sure liked his stories never having much else to leave us kids he shared all these fantastic tales of woe and insight. That's a good line aye, woes and insight?"

I nodded.

"He told me tales when I was little that still have me scratching this gray head. Those are his books over there," she said pointing to the Kiplings next to the beer can collection. "Right next to my beer cans. I worked hard to collect those cans you know. I never drank a drop so the effort was even greater," she said with a shy smirk, finishing my thought for me. "He liked Kipling aye?" I asked "Yeah he thought that the freak told some good stories."

I knew as many of us New England Yankees knew, what was behind the use of the word freak.

She got up, went and grabbed one of the dusty oversized, underused books and brushed some of the dust off. She sat thumbing for a couple of minutes. "Dad loved these books, thought Kipling was a great story teller, loved his poetry too. He said he could tell more from a few lines of a hurriedly written poem than from most politicians in any speech. When I was sitting here alone one Christmas Eve and there have been *many* of those days crying of course, I found this one particular poem." Maple still fumbled and with one of many dog ears till she found the page. "It's perfect for the deadbeat guy and tells the whole story for many a lonely woman. Here, here it is. It's called "The Betrothed." Maple began to read it to me.

Open the old cigar box, get me a Cuba stout,
For things are running crossways, and Maggie and I are out.

She continued with "listen to this all you bastard men."

Maggie is pretty to look at -
Maggie's a loving lass,
But the prettiest cheeks must wrinkle,
the truest of loves must pass.

Posing in a way that would frighten the timid, she said, "When we chicks lose our luster, you men all find a different pasture to graze." She continued:

Maggie, my wife at fifty gray and dour and old - With never another Maggie to purchase for love or gold!

Maple continued with eyebrows raised and an overly soured expression aimed at only me.

And I have been a servant of
Love for barely a twelvemonth clear,
But I have been a Priest of Cabanas
a matter of seven year

A million surplus Maggie's are
Willing to bear the yoke;
And a woman is only a woman,
But a good Cigar is a Smoke...

"A man, a bastard no good worthless deadbeat man gave up a woman for a good cigar." She closed the book and rocked with aggression in the well worn chair. She looked at me as if I represented all male primates, which at *that* moment I did. "That's how shallow many men are. When looks and sex appeal go a man will look for something else." She rocked as if haunted.

She tugged a bit and affirmed that she was proud that she possessed neither luster or sex appeal. "There is no attachment of a man's heart and a woman's heart when only selfishness is involved. It is when we are frail and aged with furrows of gray when love is the strongest."

I attempted, in futility to defend us primates. Placing my finger in the air, I sought a pause in her rather vocal assessment of the male species. But alas I was reminded of my behavior and lowered that finger in recognition of her being correct.

"You're right," I said. Well, it wasn't much of a defense, I know but she was right. In a chilling desire to get out of her way just in case the copy of Kipling took flight in my direction I asked, "May I go get Otis, bring him in for a bit?"

The flush was leaving her squirrel cheeks.

"Sure, just what I need another guy running around here smelling things up," she said with a gleam. I assumed that comment was a yes and I was out and back into the bang, bang-bang of the screen door. I brought the half awake co-pilot inside to his new adventure and sat him in the middle of the room leaving him with a strained curious glare of his surroundings.

"Don't worry, he did all his business in my car."

"Serves yah right you bastard male." She was obviously still angry at the Rudyard yarn. I shook my head and was ready to listen further to her anti-male rant but it did appear as if she was finished for now. She rocked harder giving me a glare met for *all* males. Otis began his exploration of this potpourri of antiquity, beer cans and overflowing crates of various timeless things. I sat really admiring Otis in a way, for if I were seven inches high and set down in this type of place I'd start a slow pensive look about as well. I was presented with a difficult choice: should I sit here and listen to Maple promote modern feminism or daydream along with Otis? I decided, for *this* very moment anyway I would divide my time between Maple's rant and Otis' daydreams.

I began my slow come to the altar admission of male guilt to Maple. "I treated my share of women wrong that's for sure, mom, sisters, and many good friends. It is, I should say *it* was, very hard for a young man to be just friends with a woman at times. Let's look at any actress or some of lesser talent like Marilyn Monroe. Can any man be *just* friends with Marilyn Monroe? Could I look at her and say, *boy I'd sure like to play Monopoly with her*. If sex is taken out of the relationship picture what else is there?" She paused and glared. "That's what I thought for many years and I'm sure that's what the young still think."

I watched Otis as he neared completion of his rounds and Goyettes had met his approval. This Otis approach was how I thought, at least for the first few adult years of my life. I gave life the occasional sniff and moved on."I realized when it was too late of course, that if a man loves a woman, *really* loves her his goal is to make her happy to the last day." I continued my defense of the older male for some of them are defensible only when exhaustion has won. "If a man doesn't love her then there is no emotional attachment and once sex goes the relationship is over." Love her first and the rest is gravy.

Maple looked at me very doubtful of my rationality but accepted it rather then questioning it further for she was hoping to catch me in a trap Sadly, Maple admitted, "I have never been loved by a man unconditionally so I don't know."

My ego secretly knew that once again it was right. My ego justified my youthful behavior by placing blame on the other more indiscrete man of youth. I was sitting comfortably with my head laid back watching Otis and continued my pacification of Maple.

"I thought when I was young that I would marry a nice woman. We would spend sixty years together have a bunch of kids and grandchildren and die with each other as our last memory." I sipped some coffee and muttered, "Life didn't turn out that way and here I am retracing memories, looking for some things and saying good-bye to many others. I wanted to die with my Annie as my last memory. Some folks have asked whether *this* is the way it did, in fact end. I don't have an answer yet but am leaning toward the doubtful believer.

"The coffee really sucks, yah know that, of course?"

"Sure I do. You're a man and you're lucky it's even in a cup and not over your head."

I shook my head with a gruff smile adjoining it. "Yeah, I bet."

Maple picked up the tone. "Life is lonely but loneliness is optional, aye?" A bit of wisdom was dealt my way and I missed the deal of course. The words she passed out I would remember as my journey continued though. Otis by now had explored what he felt he needed to know of this place and had grown accustomed to an area of sun near my feet.

"You believe in God, Maple?"

She looked at me as if she were my near deaf aunt trying to figure out if I had actually said something. "I guess we're changing subjects aye?"

I affirmed her notion.

"I guess it depends on what your definition of God is."

"What my definition of God is?" A good question my portly buddy. I don't think I've thought about it that much. When I was young, God was taught to me in terms of a huge ominous super being who would never allow failure of any kind."

Maple had asked me a question that I wasn't sure how to answer and I fumbled for the best, yet most innocuous of answers. "Yeah, your definition." Confused a little I gave this; "I had the idea that God never allowed screw ups meant that as soon as I was old enough to know any better, I was already doomed. I messed up so often and told so many lies and hurt so many people early in life that I figured God had already erased my name."

Maple asked again, "Have you thought about what God is? It's easier to believe in something that we can at least loosely define, don't you think?"

I shrugged my shoulders avoiding the question rather than forcing an answer. "Yeah. your definition of God, dumb ass is that we can't have faith in something that we can't grasp in our mind. The opposite is true. If our definition is a negative one, then what will our impression of God be? It will be a negative or a punishing one."

There was a persistent pause and Maple said, "I guess by your pause the answer is no you have no idea of what God is do you?"

Not knowing what to say, I stammered, "Yeah I guess, well I suppose I don't ever give it much thought."

I hadn't thought about what or who God is. I just felt betrayed by something that apparently had no definition to me. Which, if I thought about it my contentious anti-God spirit made no sense. How could I be angry at something that I had never defined? This foolish anger closely resembled my fear at many of the other indefinable aspects of emotional well being. Leave it to this graphically obtuse Yankee war horse to make sense of the most complex of questions in the simplest of ways. The arguments within me began immediately and Maple watched with seeming glee as my mind opened up to the possibilities within.

How could or should something that is timeless be defined? If the timeless and limitless is defined then haven't we, in fact, given it limits? If we have given it limits it cannot be omnipotent. If I ask a neighbor to define a car, door or tree he could do that. With his definition he has limited what a tree, car or door is. With his definition he can also tell us that their respective roles are *not* interchangeable. No matter how many doorknobs or added extras they are still only what they are and nothing more. If I in the very next sentence with my neighbor, ask him to define God what is his answer? Well, many of the elitists who have sought to kill God assume that God *can* be killed and with this assumption have given God a secular definition. We know, at least we who have a seedling of faith know that *that* is not possible and this is what drives the secularists nuts for they cannot define God.

Maple watched my mental games as I admitted that faith and God cannot be defined. We have been given some good tools to understand God, but not define Him. We are expected to act in His name but not be Him. As I watched Maple watch me I knew I had drifted far into the mental abyss of thinking *and* over thinking a topic for the ages. She enjoyed the show very much.

The opposing view in my mental give and take was that God was defined for me by *this* preacher or *that* pastor or *this* neighbor or *that* event. That wasn't true. They were teaching me lessons that God would wish us to live by. I had ignored God's lessons and allowed the atheists of this world to tell me what and who God was. No wonder I was confused as to the question. Should I let someone who did not place God, faith and morality first in his or her life tell me just who God is? That seemed foolish but that is and *was* the approach to God I had taken. Is it any wonder that any definition I carried about the almighty was a negative and sometimes hostile one?

"How is God to be defined, by you I mean?"

Maple burped under her breath and reached for an itch in a most unladylike manner. With a grunt and a tug she said, "For me I had to figure out what God was supposed to do and that was a pretty easy answer. God was supposed to be good, that was the answer. God was supposed to be good. We can look around and see bad and we know right away that bad is something that God would never be part of aye. God would not be part of anything that goes against what Jesus taught us. That would be like saying God is opposing God. Why would He let horrible things happen if He is all about good?" She ended her statement with a search for a hard to find itch.

I shook my head in a yeah, I know manner, and asked; "So if we know God would not be part of anything bad we can look around and find what man has done to make His world evil? Right?"

She nodded a you betcha.

Maple continued, "We can also look at *our* behavior and figure out what is and isn't Godlike about us." She looked at me and then she reached for Otis picking him up rear end first a move that, according to his facial expressions caught him very much by surprise. She asked me, "Do you think man is evil or does God just let bad things happen?" "Hmmm, it's up to them I guess."

"Well now, that's a good question there pudgy, but if God is good, why does He let bad things happen? My nieces and friends have asked me this for years." I asked this knowing she had just presented the answer.

She was rocking at a pace that grew as she continued with her lesson to me as well as her stroking of Otis the wrong way. "Kiddo look at everything in the world: abortion, murder, tragic deaths and war. It's *all* horrible and a part of the world that is encroaching all around us. Tragedy is manifest everywhere. Why does this happen?" She was holding Otis in a way that showed he found a comfortable fold.

I was only half paying attention as I was beginning a journey that had begun a search for God as I knew Him.

"Dumb ass, God has given man free will. If man didn't have free will we would still be in the Garden of Eden. It was free will that caused man to be tossed out of paradise in the first place remember? If man didn't have free will, we would never have had the wars but free will, greed and selfishness have given us evil. God hasn't given us evil, man has. What you need to do my friend, is to figure out where you end and God begins, don't blur the two because that drives us right around the bend to the ice cream truck."

I hadn't moved my glare from the spot of sun at my feet. God is good and man is evil. If it were the other way around, there would be no God. In her abrupt anti-male approach, she made a lot of sense. There were several longer than average periods of silence and she wrestled with Otis until he became rather comfortable in a part of her abundance. Once he and she had found a level of comfort, she sat rocking with Otis as if he were a newborn which of course he was.

"Do you know what I mean?"

I shook my head a bit and told her that I believed I did. I had felt confronted with an ageless question: what and who is God?

"This to me kiddo this is the battle we see all over the world now right now, today, *this* very moment. The line between man and God has been blurred. When this happens it's harder to see what is wrong or bad or nasty and evil."

She looked at me and asked if I was still with her. "How can you be mad at God when you don't know what He is about, young man? When I was outside I saw a Bible on the front seat of your car. I know that's not yours because it's well worn," she stated with yet another smirk. She rocked and rocked some more staring the way many wouldn't like. "God is good and man is not," she reaffirmed. "That book has had some serious readers over the years, you're just the most recent carrier." She finished with, "Modern man has made God equal *to* man and therefore God no longer exists That's what's wrong with us all today pudgy. Modern man has defined God down to his level and therefore He doesn't exist anymore, man and God are equal."

"Yup, you're right it belongs to a little lady who lives downstairs from me, us, the Bible that is. I probably know you're right Maple. I really would hate to think that my problems and difficulties in life are my fault but it does appear that way." With a hellish smile I said, "I want to blame other people for all this crap."

She sat back and rocked harder as if she were a satisfied teacher. "Yup pork chop, everyone blames and no one stands up and accepts."

I was momentarily distracted by the term of endearment tossed my way in the form of a meat product but she was right.

"People don't stand up for their own lives anymore. We want more of this and more of that and we act like spoiled twelve year olds if we don't get it. The young people are all wrapped up in sex, tattoos and more sex and nothing else. The selfish young people who will someday lead this nation pursue self and reject God, country and family. They are selfish and greedy and have no appreciation for anything of traditional value. Marriage is a joke anybody can marry anything and abortion is now just a form of birth control." She scratched and concluded with, "What can the selfish possibly value?"

Maple was on a roll and I risked danger by interrupting her. She was an old time conservative woman, descended from Puritan blood and she held onto that blood gloriously. It was kinda' nice because I never knew how any man could ever spend more than twenty minutes with a woman who was a bra-burning, pro-abortion liberal.

My politics had emerged as I grew older and I settled into a position of comfortable conservatism. A conservative Christian woman at least from my experience,will tell you what is on her mind without much hesitation These women expect a man to be a man and not some effeminate type named Josh or Todd. A Christian woman will never question whether abortion is right. A Christian woman seems to know more about the world and is far less needy than a selfish, sandal wearing liberal woman. Annie was a true blue, corn fed, gun toting Christian conservative and she knew how life should be. She was raised just a few miles over the New Hampshire border and drifted down here for school *and* to find me she always confessed. She *had* to find me. I always wanted to ask the younger men I knew if they really wanted to grow old with some of the young girls they dated now-a-days. I was sure I knew the answer.

Maple was petting Otis and was doing so aggressively. She insisted with her expression that her technique of brushing his fur the wrong way was best for him. Otis, much to his credit, didn't argue and just looked at me while performing his task of keeping her busy. Though he seemed to know her action was wrong, he knew it wasn't done in anger. I also believed he knew he was doing me a favor and I would have to pay him back at some point for him shutting her up for a bit.

Maple rolled on, "What do you think your father would have said about gay marriage in Massachusetts? What about Jeff? What would war veterans say about the feminizing of American men? Did he die in Vietnam for gay marriage?" She rocked harder, holding onto Otis as if he were a half knitted quilt. "Those folks have never found God and what's bad kiddo is that they *don't* want to find Him and are making it bad for the rest of us that know Him already. The girls that kill babies and the men who marry other men want only their lifestyles and not the one taught by Jesus. "If they can't have their lifestyles, their way, they become the vilest of creatures since the medieval rat."

I shook my head and asked if she had any opinions she wanted to share with me and encouraged her to say what was on her mind. The afternoon had moved on at a fair pace. The sun's shadow had moved a foot or so across the floor but still had a distance to go before it required rest.

"The bad things kiddo, find the bad things. If you find the bad things, the good things will be easier to see. Maple grunted while shuffling in her chair."It's the bad things that are really hurting America. Daddy said that the good made this country and only the good can save it. Daddy didn't teach this fat girl much but he said we have to love God, country and family; there ain't nothin' else. If we loved just ourselves and our lives then we don't have much time for anything or anyone else, aye. If we love just ourselves and our lifestyles, than we have nothing to leave those who come after us." She reached across and handed me the character that her graphic abundance had nearly swallowed.

"I have to pee. Take this mess outside, aye."

I wasn't sure if that was an order, a request or perhaps a suggestion, but either way, with her mood I took Otis outside to the bang, bang-bang of a screen door. Otis was in a hurry to satisfy his natural needs and made quick business of it but he chose not to wander far from me, which I appreciated. He looked over his shoulder and took a step or two, then double checked to see if it was OK. He repeated this several times until he was happy just snooping a box of junk close to the porch. This old house and its proprietor had seen so much in their lifetimes and we were just one small paragraph in a lengthy chapter. I stood with my hands again fumbling in Dad like manner for the hidden quarters watching the southbound fowl traffic. The fall time in this part of the Rocky Upland was something to behold. The air, the falling leaves and the sound of southbound fowl made it a pleasure to just stand here and inhale it all. I remember so often during this time of year, Mom going on her annual pinecone trek. She would decorate all she could find so as to fulfill some special section of Christmas morn.

The pile of leaves only grew daily and shrunk even quicker as we kids would slam our bodies deep within its midst. In back of this severely unpainted, hundred plus year old home was a back yard holding most everything one could imagine encompassing most generations. Otis led me around the side of the house and with another odd look over his shoulder that said *can you believe this mess*, there was a bang, bang-bang.

A roar from the front, "I have some coffee and stuff. Let's sit out here for a while, aye."

I turned and calling the co-pilot's name for the first time I walked toward the porch. Seemingly not wanting to miss anything Otis was in tow.

"Sit," she gruffed and pointed to an old straight back kitchen chair apparently made by Lincoln himself.

"Yes ma'am, what did you make here? This is some frozen fruit that I blended with a bag of chocolate chips."

With a cautious look, I took my share while I was still brave enough to reach for the bowl.

As she was adjusting her abundance and moving the chair about she said, "The bad things, to find God kiddo you must *recognize* the bad things."

This phrase was mentioned for perhaps the fifth or sixth time and maybe I ought to listen.

"That's where we left off aye?"

Enjoying the open air freshness of the coffee I said, "Yup, this is pretty good." I attempted to reach for a bit more of her chocolate dipped fruit but the wonderment of her glare suggested I best not.

"Well there is allot of bad things I guess I," she jumped in. "The mistake I made for many years buddy, was using the word *me* and *I* when looking for bad. Using I and me meant I was looking only at what was happening *to* me. That's selfish, aye? We need to look at the bad around us and how that is making us bad." She slurped her conjured mess and said, "When we look close we see our bad adds to all the bad around us. When I say us, I mean the family, country and world, yah know. We used to be a God-fearing country but those damn Democrats did what the Romans did." She was rocking harder and the fur of the four-footed one bristled. "They slammed the spikes into Christ all over again with their love of abortion and gay marriage and seeking to end the family traditions older than Jesus himself. This part of America was founded for us Christians but man has said nope, not any more, it's time for the vile to rule. When our bad nature mixes with their bad natures our world collapses. But when our good steps forward, the vile hate us, it's good versus evil."

I sat listening to her view of history, I learned sometime ago that she was not a fan of America's political left but she used non-political examples pretty well to express her point of view.

She slowed her rock and said, "Screw politics kiddo, politicians don't recognize bad or good or right or wrong anymore, not since Ronnie anyway. I think Jesus wants us to be better people and to do that we have to see how a bad society affects us. But the politicians will never say society is bad, by gawd that could cost them a vote!" She let fly her built up throat secretions as Otis watch the flight occur."

I looked at her with some questions in tow because I wasn't to sure what she was getting at.

"Am I confusing you my friend?"

"Yup," I replied as Otis finished his snooping and assumed his rightly position at my feet. "What do you think about abortion?" A question I hadn't though much about.

"Well, I suppose it doesn't matter to me since I can't have a kid." She shook her head in condescending disgust. "You selfish man! Life doesn't know gender and the black robed bastards have said that only women know life, not men. Men ought to be just as protective of life as anyone and don't say that if you could give birth than you could have an opinion."

"If you had a closer relationship with God you would know that life is His gift and *not* a choice of a mother. What if our mothers had the right to choose and those that wanted to chose abortion? We wouldn't be having this conversation today. You wouldn't have known Annie and you wouldn't have this two-pound mess in front of us right here. If you were close to God you would be angry at abortion but the world has said that God doesn't matter and abortion shouldn't either, aye."

She rocked slowly as she stared at the treetops opposite her home. "I wish men would stand up and say abortion is wrong, I wish the young would say no to vile behavior but they won't until they experience it. I wish men would play a role in determining whether a child should be aborted, but men don't." This topic I knew was hers and she would never shut the door on it. "That's something that should be considered but not in America today. The father of the child should give permission for an abortion to be performed. The black robes and nineteen year old girls would never allow that and more and more die."

Maple was going on for some time at how little role men played in deciding whether their children should be aborted. I got the impression that Maple was saying abortion would be an asterisk in history if men stood up and said no more but free will has killed millions.

"Gay marriage is the same way. It is a vile, evil act in God's eyes and it goes against nature. But America says that it's OK and should be considered a freedom, a *right* in America. They that promote gay marriage won't believe that it's unnatural and they are the ones that are usually the tree huggers too." She slowed a little and threw another scratch my way she continued. "It goes back to those that want unnatural things must first disprove God and by doing that everything vile is legitimized. Bizarre, don't yah think? They want it all ways their way and we Christians are called bigots for even questioning them. Good-bye, America," she said as she waved to the clouds in a disgusted way.

"To hell with America. Right now we are dying and God knows it. That goes back to a question a few minutes ago pork chop is God killing America or are we?"

I looked at her and just let her go on some more before I chimed in with "I stopped for some tooth paste. Do yah have any?" I hesitated a little because I was getting her point.

"I think what you're saying is what makes me feel bad is optional for those that are good. If I looked around me and identified what made me feel bad the Godly part of me would be moved to change it."

She looked a little disheveled at my poor explanation. "Yes, honey, that's kinda' what I'm saying. What makes us feel bad is something that we naturally dislike in the first place," she continued. "If someone hates scripture why is that? If someone hates what we say about abortion or homosexuality why is that? Those that accept gay marriage and abortion are people who don't believe in the scriptures and who enjoy being evil, evil is just vile misspelled. The liberal has put self ahead of God and that's why America is dying."

I looked off at the crest of the road as if any other car might be coming here to join in on this but that wasn't the case. Scratching Otis, I heard the bang, bang-bang and Maple was back inside. For a big girl she was mobile that's for sure. Thinking about what my pudgy buddy had said, I wondered if I had been restless and depressed because something is making me feel this way, something that I wasn't willing to recognize. If I did recognize it, would I want to change it? Was I letting society and all its hellish ways determine my behavior or should my behavior affect our society? What made me walk away from friendships and rely on my untrustworthy side as an excuse for ruining relationships? Why was I driving away to find something else rather than facing the problems of every day life? What was I looking for and would I recognize it if I found it? What I came to know rather quickly was that in everything there is a message and Maple had passed many a message my way today. There is many an old teacher who taught me that and a pastor or two I could still see waving a finger my way. If it's an accident, a reward, a loss of a friend or a drive by visit with my portly friend there is a reason for everything.

I had some more of her coffee and again listened for a car that never came when I heard the bang, bang-bang.

"Here." She handed me a very dusty tube of Pepsodent toothpaste. "It's been on the counter for a while so I'll take some off."

"Mmm, thanks. I could chew this, aye?" The breeze picked up a little and the scent of cut grass and old straw made its way down this forgotten back road. "Yah know that I have been having some pretty powerful dreams for a while now. They are so vivid; they seem to be fitting one into another like pieces of a puzzle."

"Yea?"

I shook my head and said, "Yeah, it's about my boyhood home, that's what I saw most vividly anyway. In the one last night I saw my Dad. He's been dead for thirty years, maybe more."

"Ahh dreams, the nickel movies of our souls."

I smiled at that one liner. Maple said allot of little things but that one was pretty good. "The nickel movies, why's that?"

She pulled forward in her chair, scratched herself again in a unladylike manner and then she continued the metaphorical lesson.

"Dreams are always there, kinda like network TV. Can't change what'll be shown if the channel is stuck. Remember growing up the bad movies they would show on Sunday afternoons, cheap movies that we had no say over. Dreams are like that, we can't control what we're seeing each night. But even with the worst of movies dreams too have a plot. Did your dreams send you this way?"

"I don't know. They let me know that I was coming upon a long road and I had to take the journey, not much else but that."

"Look at what your dreams may be saying underneath it all is a message for you."

That was a good question. Something took me by the scruff of my neck and sent me this way and it sure wasn't the anticipation of her chatty behavior so I played along.

"Yeah, I think they did send me out here and don't ask me why they did. I just got in the car and drove."

She shook her head and a chin or two in my direction. "Dreams will tell us what's up inside us. You have a lot of things going on with you but since I first met you when you and Annie stayed out back that time I thought you had great insight into life. It makes sense that you have crazy dreams. Probably some Scotch blood in yah somewhere, you guys are supposed to be on a different mental plane than the rest of us European runaways."

"Yeah, an uncle or somebody was Scotch I'm sure. The dreams seem to be telling a story a little bit each night."

Maple stopped her rocking in an annoying way and reached for Otis but her graphic abundance prevented such a move so she readied for a second attempt. She readied and steadied herself and with another body sway forward she grabbed Otis by the rear end and laid him on her lap.

"You know, you might be living the dream, you think of that? All this could be one wild mental ride for you pudgy, you ever think of that? You're on a road looking for something, remember this road *here* and that road in your dream starts and ends somewhere."

Maple seemed to have found a new friend in Otis as well and she passed years of built up affection his way and he didn't object to it in the slightest. "We had a dog like this once, a bit bigger than this, hit by a truck a long time ago though. Daddy put him out back with a sad looking cross." She remembered her own four footed Christmas present with just as much heart.

All sarcastic opinions aside, Maple was a good, kind, decent woman and I think she only had other people's best interests in mind every time she spoke. Her opinion was brisk and sharp but had a clarity and honesty that many should emulate.

"I guess I am living my dreams, aye. What do you suppose that means?"

In her casual demeanor she enlightened me. "Dumb ass, I don't know your dream, but like what we've been talking about, there is a message behind everything. There is a *meaning* behind everything and that includes dreams. If you see your boyhood home and your Dad and you're saying hello or good-bye to that and if your Dad tells you something it's a message!" She was scratching galore now as she continued. "He wants you to do something. We spend our whole life saying good-bye, yah know." Scratching her gut and slapping it as if it was a basketball she said, "We're born to tribute and glory and then we spend our lives screwing up and saying our regrets. In other words, we're saying good-bye and I'm sorry from the day we pop out of Mama. *That's* the road that I think is in your dream pork chop, the road of regret and the road of good-byes."

I shook my head with a toned down smile. "A road of regret, wow, that's depressing isn't it?"

Maple stared out at the same road that held nothing but looming elms and pebbles kicked by the Pilgrims. "Naugh, once we say good-bye to things it's an opportunity for redemption. So, old friend in your dreams your travel could be the road of redemption."

Maple was very bright and had spent many a night reading whatever she could get her hands on. "When Jesus came, He said good-bye right from the start. He said good-bye to the old and delivered the new; you are to deliver or to look for the new if you are a Christian."

The sun had moved a bit more to the west and our conversation had waned as the sun had. The topic of discussion was paid tribute in lesser form as the day passed overhead. "So I guess all I need to do is recognize the bad things and walk the road of redemption?"

A smile showing nothing but her kindness and love for other people was the only answer I received. "Yeah, pretty much the same message that Christ began His journey with is the same one we need to follow in our lives two thousand years later, if He can why can't we."

Maple slowed her rocking and spoke once the creaking boards had stopped. "God will walk us the rest of the way. We just need to take the first step."

I looked at her or at least in her direction wanting for a positive answer to this question: "Do you think Annie will be walking the same road; I don't want to travel this if she is left behind, lost or confused somewhere. I couldn't imagine taking a journey like this if she wasn't going to meet me at its end. The life that I had lived was made worthwhile *only* after she came across my path." I wanted to know if she was going to be OK and I wanted to know that I would see her again someday. Now I was confused, was *this* but another dream.

"Yea I think so buddy, she picked you up on her journey didn't she?"

I shook my head agreeing and said, "Yeah, I don't know how she ever settled for me though. I was a Grateful Dead following booze hound with no goal and little ambition when she came my way." I passed this observation Maples way, but she didn't hear it. "Our dreams are usually a message our conscious is sending our flesh and bone our minds are controlled by our souls. The path we wish to send our souls on runs the show and the whole package works together." Maple was becoming more animated and one could tell that she was becoming weary from her teaching task.

As I sat sniffing the fields of nearby cut hay I slowed my brain to think about what she had just said our dreams are a message sent to our flesh by our conscious. Comments and suppositions like this, no matter who posed them inevitably would cause the Harvard elite to retire.

"If our souls are bad so too will be our bodies. If our souls are good, well, we have a fighting chance and we will be of a good spirit. Jesus is the tool we use to make our souls good. If we don't use Him then what *do* we use to nourish our spirit?"

That probably made the most sense of anything she had said so far. If we don't use Jesus, what do we use to feed our inner selves? Do we use sex, money, hobbies and booze or what?

"I should slow down and just pay attention, I guess aye, here." I handed her three dollars for the toothpaste and felt as though it was time that Otis and I moved on for the night. I was becoming uncomfortable with comprehension and my mind was full of what Maple had served up it had been a hearty meal for certain.

Maple sensed the impending climate change, "Where are you and this mess going to go?"

I stood up adjusting the garments that needed it. "Annie loved the coast of Maine, the lighthouses, shoreline and the sea lions being lazy. She would look at one of those big old seals and then smile as she smacked me on the gut." Maple slung back in the chair and slapping her graphic abundance with both hands, "Yeah, that was a slam harmless though, she had her claws in you from the first day young man." Maple was right about that Annie had locked onto me early and I really was powerless over it.

She stood up on the first attempt and showed a proud smile as a result of her efforts. "The drive through the Uplands is nice and if you go west on Wakefield here then take the first right past the Hobart storage you'll be on Wentworth Road. It's an old dusty thing but there is a little bed and breakfast up there an old motel more like it. Probably a good place for you and the little one. They'll take this mess for an extra five dollars a night, about four maybe five miles up that way." She gestured with her hand full of dog.

"Thanks. I'm looking for a nice quiet rest and that sounds pretty good."

"It'll be on your right sets back a bit, grayish, some dead trees out front run by an old grump widowed forty years or so, Louis Taylor."

I raised a sarcastic tone and said with condescending glee, "I guess you're sending me to somewhere nice aye?"

I stood and grabbed Otis, taking him to the front of the car. He actually seemed disappointed at losing the graphic comfort but was no longer doubtful of his observer's intentions. I put him on his front seat towel and as I shut the door I heard a bang, bang-bang. This area was actually a beautiful place to spend some time and I would be back up this way at some time in the future I thought, no red lights out this way aye. The smell brought back so many wonderful memories of when I used to walk the old railroad tracks behind the house and was nearly drowned by the flood of lilac and cherry blossoms.

The memories of youth that just the sense of smell could dredge up sometimes were so remarkable, a true gift. Whether it was the freshly cut grass, Mom's roast beef or homemade bread, each scent brought back a special moment. Maple's home and the immediate surroundings were quite antiquated in color, intentions, aspirations and companionship but a nice place to come for a visit. As I neared the time for me and Otis to share the road once again with the lost redcoats of old I noticed a light fog had begun to sneak up from behind the property. A slow moving fog was a sure sign that fall was well on its way. The warmth of the day and the chill of late afternoon caused the weather to be schizophrenic at times. I was ready and it was time to go.

I stood in a way that reminded me often of how Dad used to stand. My hands were deep into empty pockets, jingling a couple of quarters trying to make it sound like more.

Maple had made up a plate of stuff, some meat, gummy this and frosted that and she had a couple of very old cans of dog food. "Here, I put a can opener in the bag knowing you wouldn't have one aye, pay me when yah can."

"Yup, you're right, thank you, I'll bring you back something from Maine aye."

Maple had a smile of familiar doubt. "You mean you'll call sometime?"

"Yeah, tomorrow." Putting her gift on the top of the car, I told her that it was good seeing her again. I had a chance to share some kind words and I did.

"You have been a good friend for a long, long time pudgy and I'm glad I stopped by. I am sorry we, *I* didn't stop as often as I could have, Annie loved you and called you one of her best friends ever."

With a blush she returned with, "Yeah, what I wish you would do my friend is take a long look at your life and be thankful for all that you have had. Be thankful for all the opportunities you have had and all the people that God has put here for you to love and who love you. You need to let Him know that it has been a good life and not one you're sorry for."

She waddled down the three-step front porch and came over. "Just take a nice look at all your life and let the message be what it'll be and you will be thankful before you know it."

"Daddy told me that when things get real bad to just sit back and let God do the driving. He knows where He's going we sure don't." In a tone that gave little example of forethought I said, "Guess He doesn't crack up along the way much either, does He?" "Nope, smart ass, He doesn't."

She answered the question asked long ago, the question whose answer I wanted most. She patted my hand and said, "Annie will be fine, plenty of good things for her."

I nodded and told her in a familiar tone, "I was going to miss Annie so much. I can't believe that I have to go on without her." I looked sheepishly and asked again, "You think she'll be OK?"

"Of course. We women are the stable, rational ones not you *bastard* men."

I walked around to the driver's side holding her hand. I never ever knew how old Maple was or much else about her other that she was a kind decent woman who at times I didn't treat with the kindest of words. I was cruel and unkind and my thoughts were usually rude in nature but Maple was good and I knew it albeit a bit too late. Thank you God for giving me such a good friend.

"OK, young man, find the good things in life and let God do the driving. He will show you what's at the end of the road."

The sun had begun to set off to the right of her quiet little home as the settling clouds struggled from up the tree lined back lot. The birds that always greeted the sun had gone home for the day and the road was getting narrow with the encroaching darkness. I gave her a small peck on the cheek, which always made her blush.

"Thanks kiddo, I'll see you soon."

"Yeah, I know you will. You have a good trip and take care of that little piece of work you got there, aye."

"Yeah." I got into the car and was quickly at ten and two. I looked about the front seat to make sure all was in place and received a go ahead glare from my young four footed friend. I backed up looking for cars coming either way and turned to see her wave a big old *see yah soon* wave matched only by her grin. I waved and headed for my night's rest.

Chapter 4
Glory Road

Before I could manage a second look back in her direction, the road seemed to disappear with the clouds from below the hill. With a road now narrowing I searched for a tune to guide my way to where I could reach for a night's respite. I was fortunate and soon found a Gaelic blessing:

Who can say
Where the road goes
Where the day flows
-only time
And who can say
If your love grows as your heart chose
-only time
-only time...

The road was narrow to the front and dusty in the rear and I knew not what was waiting for me around the next elm looped corner, she sang on.

Who can say
If your love grows
As the heart chose
-only time
And who can say
Where the road goes
Where the day flows
-only time
-only time

A tale of choice as well for this songbird was one I needed for this short but memorable drive. I had begun on the directions that Maple had given me and was much too satisfied with her simple genius to tell her that I knew this route all too well. Wow, what a visit. Maple was one of those characters that life brings and we often pass by without even tossing a hello. She knew so much about life though many would say that life itself had passed her right by she welcomed it at every stop. How many people have there been like that in my life? How many simple geniuses have I ignored because I felt that they were only simple? Allot frankly, a good number of people I had walked by and just felt too important to even say hello to or even hold the door for. Maple was a great friend who I would see again real soon.

The road was bad, very bad even by redcoat standards. Wakefield Road is a fine example of how not to maintain progress. The same dust that choked Cornwallis now caused Otis to snort with disapproval. Otis seemed less restless now, though he was more alert and for lack of a better adjective and he seemed to have grown in the time that we spent with Maple. I felt a bit more aged myself maybe because Maple had hit so many emotional nerves and the weariness of regret was starting to catch up with me. I had been through a good emotional cleansing back there at Goyettes and would know shortly if it did any good. Otis did as he had usually done since I acquired his title after a snort or two more he nodded off to sleep. What a bum, I thought as I tossed his towel over him.

I knew this road rather well. I had traveled it many times with my older brothers and the kids in town who I thought were the best friends ever. When we could get a ride or when they were driving on their own, we came down here to drown some worms in the string of small unnamed ponds accented by abandoned shanties. It also seemed to me that everyone in Rhode Island knew Louis Taylor and every kid that ever wanted to be scared at Halloween knew of his old house a few miles ahead. Louis and his long dead wife Ruth had been in this part of the Uplands for fifty plus years and I believe that Ruth's family may have settled here long before that.

Ruth or Ms. Taylor has been lying next to Mr. Hyde beneath the naked elms for many years now. It's amazing how death does bring

Ashley Bay

the generations together; those that lived for God and country last century watched as those doing same this day became their neighbors. The development which had come to many other parts of the state had seemingly passed by this area by altogether. All that was left out this way was a forgotten shortcut to New Hampshire and the souls of Maple and the Taylor household. There were no mini-jiffies and no video depots just endless tales of virtue and character as they sought newly framed owners.

I slowed the pace a little in order to make sure that staying at the Malachi Lodge was something I really wanted to do. That was the name given to the room and board offerings of the Taylors' Malachi Lodge, what a name for a place to rest. A kid or even most adults, could imagine the hand of Satan himself resting on a sleeping shoulder when the sun set over the unnamed ponds out this way. It would be many years following that last childlike journey that I learned the meaning behind the title though. There are countless stories and even more theories as to why the small, dirty out of the way overnight lodge was called Malachi. I for one, as a kid was scared to the great beyond by walking this back road late at night to the swinging sign of the Malachi Lodge. The breeze from the scattered water would bang the sign against any tree it could find. Louis and Ruth had a son whom I had grown up with and sat next to in a couple of classes. We were both in the small Scout troop over this side of Tennent and we all would come out here and camp on the Taylors' back lot. The vision alone of those years still gave me cold chills, not for the haunting name but for the mistakes made.

A bunch of kids camping in the back lot woods on an unlit road at a property called Malachi Lodge was still memorable. I turned the radio up so I wouldn't scare Otis any further with the silent tales of confused youth. Scott McKenzie was taking us to San Francisco as I remembered their son Russell Taylor. Russell was the kid in school all us other boys would tease in the worst of ways during the week and then call him friend on the weekend when we wanted something. This is what haunted me, the cruelty of youth something passed from generation to generation. The road was straight with few turns or even much in the way of bumps or holes on this drive. My memories were causing enough of a detour for now and they provided all the bumps and shallow falls one could handle. The appearance of a shrinking road and the bouncing of the sunlight off the peeled white birch is what met me the further I drove. The reach of the old dead elm trees was so far over the road that they touched the other side such a sight made one feel as if they were entering a tunnel or a forgotten cave from childhood.

On the right side of the drive was a fence line rusted to pieces with time and impatience. My memory of youthful walks was coming back the further I drove. I squinted in hopes of improving my recollection and maybe, *just* maybe I could catch a glimpse of me. If I tried hard enough maybe I could see a lonely little guy waiting in the rain for a ride that never came. To my left off about fifty yards or so and through a buildup of dead trees and old farm equipment I could make out the tops of some old forgotten fishing shanties.

I slowed quickly to a near crawl. "Wow, I think this is it aye buddy." Otis was motionless and showed total disregard for my excitement at finding my boyhood fishing hole. *This* overgrown mess was where I learned to drown a good number of sidewalk wonders.

I knew the water had to be close but because of the overgrowth of weeds and in some cases the runaway algae seeing clearly was a task. These waters had been untouched by sun and worm so long that they had given up on life itself. If waters weren't meant to be fished or enjoyed by the drive by gawker what happens to it? When I was a boy this land seemed so huge; it was an ocean to a four-foot young man. Now, when I was taller and wider my youthful adventures seemed so small and insignificant. I knew that up a little farther there would be an old steel wheeled tractor that we would use as a landmark to find the best and least muddy trek to our boyhood oceans. Landmarks are a tool of time and I don't think we absent minded plum chasers could have learned to fish without them.

I rounded the one dogleg to the hacking of the dust gasping Otis and BAM, before me there it was my landmark of youth. It stood as a relic for decades and it served a noble sentry for the lost souls of this part of the Uplands. Still rusted and still waiting on the lost farmer that would never return, it stood as it had many years ago welcoming me to the place where memories and lessons were had. I pulled up almost right next to it and as I squinted some, it took some effort, but I was able to see the three little union soldiers, the three Green Berets, the three Stooges, The Three Musketeers and three friends for life. The three of us did everything together this was *our* spot where we could come and fish and where we would come and hate girls as a group. We could come and fish and drink our first beer and tell lies about our first girl and how much they dug us. As we played and ran and laughed and lived the adventures of growing young men we were always watched by the dumpy, near sighted kid who lived across this very road, Russell Taylor.

 The three of us played and we never invited Russell to come along on our adventures. We would have games and never ask him to join in. We would fish, hunt and drive and we would never bring Russell along. Friends were just out of reach for him. Every time the three of us came to this spot, *this* very spot we would laugh and joke and play while Russell sat and watched as fun and friends were *just* out of reach. I stared at the tractor and I dropped my hands from the ten and two and grew increasingly anxious because I knew what would be ahead when I raised my eyes. It was going to be another not so fond memory of the should've beens of life. What lay ahead were the painful memories of the harm that was passed on to the vulnerable among us. The good memories of this spot could now at this stage in life compete with the bad ones I left behind and they would lose. The car still ran with a wet gas sputter every now and then so I just turned it off and let the laughter of youth visit me. My clammy palms presented a warning though as the laughs went on by. We all know those clammy palms are overly active when we are seconds from having to face the inevitable. I looked at my palms knowing that just a stern glare from me and the clamminess would vacate the scene but it didn't. I was nervous and sad for I had left bad memories at this water's edge for someone. My youthful unkindness left a scar on Russell and many others unfortunate to be in my wake.

 A grunt and a brief look of scorn emerged from Otis as he realized the car had stopped. I looked at him as he slept and rubbed his neck as he rolled over on his back in approval. The bad memories were vivid now and I regretted my role in harming another, a feeling that I wish had prevented me from doing what I did in the first place. I looked past the noble sentry at the top of our one time fort and wondered how I could make it right now at this stage of life. Other than promising to be a better person, other than seeking forgiveness for my actions what else am I to do? The question was one of many that I had not asked for fear of being rejected and legitimizing it with the affirmation of it's much too late anyway. As I regretted all, Otis lifted his head to a sound only he could hear and I patted him to let him know that he was just schizophrenic and wasn't really hearing anything at all. He was not impressed with my canine diagnosis and sat sternly determined to let me know that something was amiss.

The night was moving on and the rambling of a now out of focus WJJL forced me to turn the radio off altogether. A cold shiver now ran up my spine followed by another short one and I felt uncomfortable, perhaps because it was so peaceful. There was a noticeable silence; birds were few and even a hard to find bullfrog was mum as the sun readied to set. Otis was doing his best to toss forward what some would call a bark but failed on first try. The scent of the dead water was picked up and delivered to the still silent Tempo and the uplifted snout of the curious sidekick.

The breeze that tripped into the back seat brought with it the smell of algae and dead trees and I turned to make sure the road was clear behind me before I continued. Otis was in obvious distress now at the tension winding its way through the car and the quicker we were on our way the better him. I had turned around to see if the same car that wasn't coming to Maple's was not behind me now. I was pleased at my all clear observation and was ready to leave when I turned to see before me a floppy hat man standing some twenty yards off. This figure was staring the years away from me and giving Otis the answer to his disturbed sleep. The look that the figure tossed our way was certainly not warm and one could imagine through the cold shiver going up his or her spine that this man was the lost farmer protecting his tractor.

He *was* the lost farmer. There were denim overalls accented by the hat, an *unbelievable* hat one that covered half the forehead and hid his timeless glare. He stood just looking at us, not moving and not seeking my intentions. I didn't know what he carried or who he was or what he wanted or if, in fact, I would run him over trying to get away. In response to my obvious high level of uncertainty Otis sat up with a startle and for the first time he sent forth what some would call a bark while others would laugh at his attempt. He followed the first

Ashley Bay

with several that were more aggressive in nature, more I think in recognition of his own voice rather than knowledge that it was doing any good to fend off any threat from the lost farmer.

The old man stared for what seemed to be eternity. There was no movement and he appeared perhaps as an apparition might. I was uncertain and acting in a defensive way. I was prepared to fight or at least say some unpleasant words to the lost farmer. The floppy hat stranger continued to stare and I was determined to teach this old man a lesson. Otis was as anxious as a growing poop producer could be and now growled rather than continue to interrupt the peace of the road with his questionable barking ability. The lost farmer swayed a bit in his aged gate but his stare was as sharp as before. In my view his look had to be similar to that given Moses when he questioned if he was the chosen one. The lost farmer gave a look that was both authoritarian and quizzical. He was curious as if he were watching three little boys at play at this old tractor eons ago. Our eyes met in a timid attempt to say, hi, may I help you? I grabbed my keys and stepped from the car and standing behind the driver's door I stood, though for a moment elevated above the stranger.

In a high pitched tone clearly stating my awkward stance I declared, "Sir, good evening, I'm just looking around at where I used to play as a kid. I'll leave shortly."

The lost farmer seemed frail and frightening; his clothes were untidy, though apparently washed. He took a small step, maybe two, likely three "Fat Maple said to expect company, you it?" He had a strong voice that triggered a distant recollection. "There's a room, extra if you'd brought a real dog, by the looks though you got a pretender there not mush else." Otis hung his head.

"Mr. Taylor?" I asked with a smile. He was a giant of a man so fierce and foreboding to us troublesome, cruel youth but he was now a frail old man wandering the same back road. He grunted a nod, "Yup boy, there's a room, yah want it?"

I shut the car door and walked to greet the poor old soul.

"Hi, Mr. Taylor. Good to see you again. Been a long time, aye."

He sauntered a bit, leaning with both hands on a handmade cane, the *same* cane he shook in my direction all those years ago. In response to silence I was thankful that he did *not* recognize me. I was one hell of a rotten kid, I was cruel to his son, his property and his life and I couldn't bear to be remembered. He extended his hand and I shook it, remembering it to be like that of Mr. Gibbons or my grandfather an old wise hand with much labor in its roots.

"Yes, sir, I'd like the room. I'll pay extra for my little friend; he's just a pup and still careless at times."

He pulled away and with the bottom of the cane, pointed my car to the driveway marked by an old milk can. "Over there, young man, park near the side of the wrap around. I'll be right there."

"I'll give yah'...," before I had offered a ride he had picked up the pace a little and headed off to meet me.

Deaf or hardheaded, it's sometimes hard to tell with some folks but it might be worth finding out. I sighed with impatience but with some relief at not be recognized. I had escaped the need for redemption by failing to be remembered. The anxiety was gone as quickly as it had come up on my first glimpse of Mr. Taylor. Though the anxious feelings were gone they were replaced with a sense of gratitude at not being recognized by the man who I had treated so badly years before. I was happy at having gotten away with bad behavior. I readied the car and knew this was not right feeling and I knew it and *it* had to be corrected. The words of Maple hit me for my sense of getting away with something is one of those bad things she told me to look for. *Look for the bad, young man especially in yourself.* Her words smacked me hard so I caught myself before I became too happy. I was glad for getting away with something and fearful of being remembered for being bad. The bad things aren't always war or death or hurricanes but most times, it's our use or non-use of the proper words. The way we leave someone can leave as painful a scar as anything else can.

I waited for the lost farmer to cross the road and get closer to the porch but he was way ahead of me. This was an opportunity to make amends and this moment was an opportunity for me to make it right whatever *it* was. I had to make this part of my life right. I recognized the bad thing which was my behavior and now I had to make amends. There may not be another chance if I didn't do it now what I had to do was prepare for this big step. I looked both ways before turning the car as if there would be another car coming and I made sure Mr. Taylor was where he wanted to be I drove slowly and let him come to a two handed rest allowing his cane to point the parking place for my car. I pulled in waving a smile in his direction as I followed the cane's direction. I backed into what was a long forgotten side yard and shut the car down for what I knew and what I hoped would be a nice visit. Mr. Taylor was standing just off to the left of the car waiting for my exit. This yard brought a flashback of memories of Halloween pranks and front yard fights. It brought back memories that showed us poking fun and teasing without mercy the forgotten Russell. We busted windows over there and we burned down a tree over there a tree whose trunk still showed evidence of the cruelty. We three brave young lads would stand cross the street and taunt and tease Louis and Ruth as they gardened and we three brave young men were merciless in our words as they went to church every Sunday dressed in what they called their Sunday best. I was the soul survivor of those three and I had to make it right; my conscience expected nothing less.

Mr. Taylor stood very business like yet in a slouched manner. He was ready for the transaction but his lean body surrendered to the slouch. I pulled on my belt and readied to leave the car when he said, "Let your friend out. He probably needs to do his deal."

"Thanks, I'm sure he does." I opened the door and a wide awake co-pilot quickly went about the task that he was destined to do, a sniff here and a sniff there and a lifted leg there.

With his cane, Mr. Taylor pointed and said, "Room's right here." He pointed to a side of the house with a small private entrance. A flower box out front held most everything except flowers.

"How much," I asked and he in turn asked in a nice way, "Can you do twenty-dollars? I'll have coffee and toast for yah' before yah go."

I was surprised at the price for I was used to a Visa and hundred dollar deposit places. "Twenty is fine." I grabbed a pathetic wad of cash and out of some guilt. "Here's thirty for me and my bud; we both thank you." I cleared my throat of built up anxiety.

Taking the money and folding it like I think all old men do he placed it as far into his pocket as possible. I leaned back on my car's hood and Mr. Taylor leaned with both hands on his handmade cane as a fresh dose of uneasy silence followed our financial dealings.

Regret and inhibitions were set aside but I *was* nervous. "Do you remember me Mr. Taylor?" I waited and waited some more as he stood and recalled all the characters that had passed his way up and down this old road. He stared with clouded gray eyes but with a fresh memory.

Our silence was broken by a stern "Yup, think I do." He eyed me up and down and his memory seemed to fill with so many highlights. Again with his cane he said, "You gotten fat, boy."

I lowered my head and stared down at Otis as he stared up. I smiled but was ashamed, not for his comments, but because he remembered me and if he remembered me he remembered the crap I caused when I was young. I welled up in memories of my youthful, harmful, cruel ways and hoped that my shameful look would be punishment enough.

"Yeah, I've been fat for a long time. It's good to see you again, Mr. Taylor."

He smiled an old man's smile and said, "Yeah," as he grunted toward the thirty-dollar room. "Room hasn't been used for a while. Need to let it air out for a bit. Maybe we can talk some."

The day was moving along but in a way I wasn't ready for it to end; my willingness to make amends showed me that a new beginning with Mr. Taylor was possible. Mr. Taylor was the place to start, I had to take the first step. My making amends to him could be the beginning of a new life for me and what so many others were waiting for. I knew I had amends to make but would it be now or later or in writing or what? I had to sort out the methods that would work best when I made my amends. I wanted it to be at *my* pace and not Mr. Taylor's and not left to the mercy of the setting sun either.

He had limped slowly to the room and opened the screen door with his cane. After a fishing expedition for the key he opened the room to the moldy air. He pushed it open and stepped back to the sounds of the bang, bang-bang from the screen door. He turned, "Let it air out a bit, hot in there, smells too. Might not bother the young one but you'd have stress. Come sit over here for a bit of shade. We'll talk some."

Old bird secretions covered chairs long overdue for a thorough cleansing. awaited us as we headed toward the chairs which sat beside the fruit cellar door.

I took the most questionable chair and for some time we sat in silence, staring at the old tractor the doorway to my youthful cruelty opposite us.

"I remember that tractor *so* well, Mr. Taylor. We used that as a landmark for getting to the ponds out back. We fished over there all summer long sometimes; all day long we would be *right* over there." The grouchy temperament that I first inferred was gone, probably never was there.

"Been meanin' to get rid of that tractor, never seemed to find the time," he said.

"It's been there along time, aye?" I asked.

A nod, "It belonged to my dad. He farmed all this up through here, at one time it was all his." He pointed with the cane up and down the road.

"I've wanted to come up this way for along time, there's a lot of memories here some bad and some pretty good. I had some fun out this way though."

I moved the chair a little to the sound of the crunching gravel. "We used to fish over there all the time," I repeated as if he hadn't heard me the first time. I was searching for time fillers even if it meant syndicating. "We would mark our path with that tractor."

The old man said, "I know, kinda' why I left it. It was kinda' nice seeing all you kids up through there, reminded me of me and my brothers. We played the same way."

My mind was now full of guilt. The man we had been so mean to years before wanted to make sure we wouldn't get lost. The man we were ugly to enjoyed seeing us at play because it brought back nice memories of his own childhood. The disrespect we showed him never interrupted his enjoyment of watching us at play.

Did our being cruel interrupt his enjoyment of memories of his better days? Was *he* cruel as a young man to some other forgotten child generations ago and we were just his paybacks? Was Mr. Taylor at an age when he could separate youthful stupidity and enjoy just participating in life's simple pleasures? The sun was at three o'clock in the afternoon sky and quickly heading to four and the thoughts trickled on.

"I remember Ms. Taylor always hanging her wash right over there on that tree" I said pointing to the front of the wrap around porch where, if a person looked closely they could still see pieces of rope around the tree branches.

He seemed to ignore my observation and segued by saying, "The sun always seemed to bounce off those old shacks over there. My daddy built them for the ice-fishermen and mom would cook for them all at the end of the day."

I watched him stare and wondered if this was what he remembered when he saw us three brave lads make our way past the noble sentry. Was he remembering the good times that he and his wife shared with all those who came here to enjoy their hospitality?

The pond's history was news to me, "Really, I didn't know that, ice fishing. I've lived here most my life and have never done that."

Continuing his story he said, "People used to come up here more during the winter than any other time. We rented these rooms just to the fishermen but the water just died one day. Someone long ago dropped some chemicals in there and the water just died. Takes something pretty bad for water to die. Died it did though."

He told the story as if he had rehearsed it many times and I felt sure that often he just sat here alone telling it to himself every night. I believed that he sat here many a similar day just wondering why the water died.

My host continued. "The water died and Ruthie went soon after, like it was connected or something."

I watched as he went on about all the life that surrounded this place at one time. There were tales of this and woes of that. His voice was strong but cracked often from lack of use. "Fishing was great for along time and for allot of years Ruthie was happy, the trees and flowers were all over her yard. If you look close, you can see some of her flowers still seeking life from the buildup of leaves and dead grass. When the water died she died in a way; she didn't plant anymore and the yard died. The yard died and she got sick. The water took the trees and the trees took the flowers and the flowers, Ruthie's fanciful flowers, when they died they took my Ruthie. That's why the tractor is still there, young man. It's *my* landmark, too."

In a polite, temperate way, I asked how long things had been like this. The old man made sounds with his body that are better left unmentioned at this point and I did what was appropriate and ignored them.

"Been close to some thirty or so years now I guess. Ruthie's been gone a long time, near that long. I have been here mostly alone for a long time. Been growin' old here, all alone for a good long time. Last visitor was Maple. She comes here every Christmas and I go there for Thanksgiving That girl can eat, don't yah know."

I smiled having just witnessed his very comment and said, "Yeah, I know I saw it firsthand most of the morning."

"Nice lady though. She talked and talked and talked, allot to say for someone who has never left the house. Maple would come and take care of the misses when she was getting' close; won't forget her for that. God has a place for her, he'll have to widen those gates but she's passing through them that I know.

"She'd come up here and preach at me like I was Satan himself camped out on this old porch. Big old Maple would stand *right* over there with hands on those hips and cuss at me like I was a stray dog. Apple in hand, I sit here and pretend to listen but my mind was right over there in those fishin' shacks. Maple is a good bird and I need to tell her that before my time runs on."

The smell of the air that had been at one time honeysuckle and freshly cut grass had turned to stagnant water and it was aging by the minute. It seemed that as the night came, the smell of what used to *be* wafted through the trees and what actually *was* landed at our feet. A light breeze banged an old chain against the guardian tractor and a bird at some distance was telling us that he had neared completion of his daily tasks.

"The breeze is nice," I remarked.

He nodded his head. "Yup, we'd sit on that old swing over there and talk about this and about that, never had much use for the television, still black and white with knobs in there." "Wow, black and white with knobs I guess it has cable too, aye?" "Cable? You have a bed and toilet and you're lucky to have a sheet that doesn't stink," he said with an old man's smile informing me of my accommodations status.

"Great, it sounds great," I said with appreciative nervousness.

Otis had found a spot of reasonable comfort under the front of the car; it was shady with lots of grass a place any pretender dog would find suitable. If one did as *I* was doing and listened to the encroaching night they could hear the distant cricket and the noble bullfrog, trying to breath *some* life back into the water but was growing weary at being the solo tenant. Mr. Taylor and his cane continued to tell the tales that once filled his now unkempt front yard. He spoke of the flowers that he would bring home every Friday to Ruth. He would speak of the nights and conversations they would share in long walks along *this* very road. Mr. Taylor complained of the weeds that never went away and he was thankful they didn't because it gave him something to do every couple of days. He too in his own way wanted to share the memories of character and virtue and with his voice one could tell he hoped someone was listening.

I was attentive to him in a fleeting way but enjoyed his Uncle Danvers like animation. He recalled how stray dogs from up Maple's way would come and help themselves to the chickens they raised. "I didn't know till Ruthie told me that they came down here to play and *not* to eat. Those dogs came and chased the chickens all day long and those dumb chickens started lookin' forward to their visits I will tell you that for sure. We had some of the skinniest chickens this part of the Uplands," he said with an old man's laugh in tow.

A breeze came across from the eaves of the shanties at the pond's edge and brought with it a potpourri of honeysuckle, algae and dead leaves and the distant sounds of young boys at play. It would be the last such breeze for the day for the bullfrog told us so. The day was still pockmarked with sun but it was clear that it was nearing an end and our conversation would soon follow. Mr. Taylor probably had been silent for a while but I didn't recognize it. I was once again on a mental journey leaving behind many a victim.

Clearing his throat with a forceful spit at the end he asked, "Where're you goin' to, you and that mess over there doin' the deal in my yard?"

"Not sure, probably Maine. My wife used to like that area up there the drive along the coast, the leaves, trees and water, yah' know. I've been thinking allot about the lighthouses up there my Annie liked them allot."

Otis finished his task and wandered with a bashful gate to the old man not sure if he was going to be welcomed or not.

"Annie would write little poems about the ocean and the lighthouses. She would sit cross-legged in the front seat as I fought traffic, rain and tolls. She would doodle and write."

The lost farmer smiled at his new two pound friend and said, "Yup, I know just what you're getting at. Women like that stuff young man all emotions and feelings don't yah know." Mr. Taylor was animated with his cane and head and was thorough in letting me know that he would never understand women either. "They seem to enjoy the simple things that life brings but they do their best to drive us nuts, don't they."

He paused for a while and stared at the pond across the way, squinting to see if those three damn little boys were still over there.

"I don't think God meant for women to be understood or they would be; they are a conundrum that the poets of the ages can't express."

In a segue that I picked up on he continued, "My daddy told us all these great haunting stories of the coast of Maine, the rocks, the lighthouses, ghost ships and forgotten seamen. He would sit right under that tree right over there," he said pointing with his cane, "he'd tell us all these great stories as this same sun was setting over the same then youthful trees seventy years ago. He and Mama built most of this house. Some was here, the back barn and back sheds over there but they built most of it."

That was news to me as well. I hadn't realized that the Taylor family had been here this long. "Really, I didn't know that. This area out here is so quiet how did they come to find this here? This must have been so beautiful before the highway and nearby smoke and the dead water and all, aye?"

"It was awful nice. My folks came from Main, a little town up there called Mast Landing just up from Yarmouth. I was maybe seven I think when we came here. Daddy wanted some farm land he was tired of struggling from season to season so he set out on his own. He knew a man who knew someone else and they let us pay this off in time, but I don't know if we ever did."

He continued in a voice growing stronger with use as the flickering porch light came on and struggled to overcome the instability that was pecking at the paint chipped surroundings. The setting sun was becoming more purplish through the elms in the yard and across the way. "Daddy was a fisherman most of his early days. My sister put together a family tree still upstairs somewhere. She asked allot of questions and sure did some snooping in her own right and found he fished off Bailey Island and all up that away to almost near Sandy Shores."

"Don't know why they wanted to move down here to Rhode Island. Mama had family in New Hampshire but this is where we ended up."

The farmer used his cane to turn Otis over and commence the sought after belly scratch. "We were young when we first came down this way; my folks met up Augusta way. I remember him telling me once that the times had gotten pretty bad so he came looking for some work down here and found this. Things seem to fall together in the strangest of ways at times. Dad came down and brought me. My sister came for a while but left when she was fifteen or so, haven't seen her in sixty years or so I bet. Family fights and stuff nasty things that are poisonous spikes. The ugliness was driven into our souls and we never took the time to remove it and heal and we missed our lives together."

"We grew up mostly here and Mama died and is buried up the road aways The war came and I went and did some fighting, joined the army met my gal Ruthie brought her here and here we made our lives."

I still watched him as he talked without so much a blink and in just a matter of a few minutes he told his tale.

"That's Malachi for yah' young man," he said finishing his talk while drawing in circles with his cane for most of the conversation.

"That's quite a story."

I had become fixated on his cane it was one circle after another the cane kept moving but Otis was pleased. It was one that I was told was passed onto him by his father. The cane had been crafted from the leftover wood from this very porch. The cane stopped only when the story was finished.

"I wondered for many, many years what happened to my sister asked my mom a couple of years before she passed and got just an embarrassed shrug of uncertainty. Never asked much about her after that. We missed our lives together because of petty family arguments. I heard through New Hampshire folks that she had gone back to Maine and settled near Wells somewhere." "Young man," he said as he hit me on the foot with his cane, "young man don't let this happen to you. Death is too late for amends, when the pastor blesses the grave there are no second chances."

"I haven't seen her in all these years and have her memory so fresh and so clear as if she was here making supper for us tonight." He moved the chair a little as if to stand or at least get ready for such a move. "I have some old newspaper clippings and old notes and stories that Dad had It's all about Maine and the folklore of the tales and people and this story and that story. I'll let you take a look before you go aye, if you want."

"That would be nice. I'd really like that I haven't read much lately." Then I asked him, hoping he would share some more of his memories, "You have any favorites, any one story or two that you've always remembered?"

He gave a tomcat smile and said, "Yeah a couple, but you'll need to find your own." The lost farmer fumbled to stand up and barked at any attempt of mine to help him. He stretched an old man's stretch and said, "The parts are cranky tonight I'm startin' to think maybe God has forgotten all about me."

The sun was about done and the porch light had been stable for several minutes now. The bullfrog had found some company and was now a member of a very vocal and experienced choir. The crickets to my rear and likely next to my room's one window were doing their best to keep up with their web footed neighbors. Mr. Taylor had risen and was staring at the driveway's gravel, gaining strength to take the necessary steps inside.

"Your room ought to be as fresh as it might get. Best get your pretender over there some food before he starts complaining openly." Mr. Taylor's direction to me was much appreciated by the one fat beagle in residence.

I stood and obeyed the order "Otis, come on boy, come on you mess let's go." He looked up assuming but not predicting that I was referring to him and he made a couple of half awake stumbling steps to await further instructions.

I went to the car and removed a bowl and a can of rather dusty Bob's Beef Dog Food, compliments of Maple. I had never heard of Bob and I didn't expect that Otis had an opinion as to Bob's welfare one way or the other. Mr. Taylor stood just to my rear and Otis showed much greater interest as I opened the can on the hood of the car. The smell of the contents may have been recognizable to some forensic specialist but not to me at this point and time. Otis wasted no time in activating his senses and knew instinctively that he and *they* were going to be pleased momentarily. The lost farmer had shifted little and seemed to be posing more for a Norman Rockwell painting than for anything else.

The breeze was awfully nice and it hit the face and neck in a way that told me I had built up a sunburn from a day of Maple and Mr. Taylor.

He leaned forward a bit and asked, "Any particular time you want to get up tomorrow boy?"

Ashley Bay

"No sir. I'm pretty tired, haven't slept real well of late so some rest might be nice."

He nodded and said he would get me up when the time seemed right. Otis was happy with the plop of a meat type substance and was letting his nose chase the bowl underneath the car. The barn to the rear of the car seemed the same as it did those many years ago still locked to keep away those who didn't belong.The woods hid the ghosts of my youth and the burned tree stumps bellowed my guilt. I was motionless until after a few more Otis slurps allowed me to pick up his bowl for future use. A few more polite stares and tidbits of this and that and Otis had finished what was set out for him to do.

"Sir, I want to thank you for the very nice conversation, I learned allot tonight. Thank you."

He tossed me a nod of gratitude. "I'll have some coffee and toast for you at whatever time you want tomorrow. I'll dig up the stories from my dad, too. I think that would be nice."

I grabbed Otis, tossing him into the room.

"Have a good night and I'll see yah in the morning." With that he waved a good night from the driveway with his ageless cane and our evening ended. I went to a room that did still bear a strange sensation of muggy stuffiness. Back to the car for the badly needed toothbrush and Pepsodent, socks and boxers. I also grabbed the day's paper and I soon joined my buddy as he watched my tasks from behind the screen door with utmost interest.

The room was still hot that's for sure but would probably be fine in an hour or two as the sun went to rest and the crickets warmed up. The decor was early `70s, from what I recall that period being anyhow. Floral this and floral that one pillow on the bed a yard sale collection of clipper ship paintings and an old Magnavox black and white with one rabbit ear "Pretty nice hey, bud?" He flipped his tale to let me know that he heard me but had not formed an opinion one way or the other as to our accommodations. As he gave me his attention, Otis had already claimed the pillow to finish the sleep that I had so rudely interrupted with his dinner. I opened the window and the breeze that had joined us outside soon came inside and refreshed the staleness. After the basic pre-bed necessities I grabbed the paper, found a new place for Otis and tried to make a real pillow with a fold here and a fold there of a pathetic example of what a pillow should be.

It was really nice to lie down; the bed was new to me. It had been the couch for so long that sleeping in a bed was a treat. The bed was new and empty. I hadn't been alone in a bed since Annie and because I was a selfish man, I hoped she wouldn't share one again. The compassionate side of me which had made a sudden and very noticeable appearance said I hope she doesn't grow old alone. The questions began with the one of should a man and a woman grow old alone? That's a tough one and one that I suppose should be answered only by the man and woman and not by a pastor or snoopy opinionated neighbor. The tension of the day was released bit by bit the more I stretched my legs. The stress began to release as I cracked my neck and popped my elbows to send it down to my legs as they kicked the stress off the end of the bed. A *pheeew* and a couple of oh mans and I picked up the day's paper, which now held news I *should* pay attention to. The news was always the same and it didn't make a lot of sense to read the tragedy of life when I wanted to move on with my own. I didn't see any need to treat this latest round of tragedy any differently. The headlines were just the ones left over from yesterday, Sox lose, unions strike and today it was the story of a young girl killed by a hit and run driver. Thanks, but no. I tossed the paper on the floor and turned toward the window to meet the breeze face to face.

My eyes shut despite my best efforts to fend off the lids' encroach and I returned to the blessings first given me on this day by a voice from the highlands.

> Who can say when the road meets
> That they might beat, in your heart
> And who can say when the day sleeps
> If the night keeps, all your heart
> Only time, only time.

My eyes fought the night a bit more as the last clefs from a secular gift bid me a good rest.

Who can say where the road goes
Where the days flow
Only time
Only time.

Otis had found a spot on the pants flopped at the end of the bed he was settled and now it was my turn. The conversations of the day were so nice, the drive was short but the journey was rewarding. I had some good memories, learned allot from the two fellow travelers and have an opportunity to practice what I was taught. I tried again and again to keep my eyes alert to whatever might come my way but it was no use.

Only time, only time

The crickets were the guests of my mind. I now welcomed the soft, soothing dedicated tone of the characters we could never find as kids. When crickets wanted to be heard they would tell us but a cricket is almost never seen. My lids were closed but my eyes darted back and forth for all they had seen today was brought back anew. Many gifts of lessons were passed on and I was thankful and looked forward to using these new lessons as I traveled. The old home of Maple's, boxes of junk and framed clipper ships that were lost to all except the artist and to us. Her books all of Kipling's, his best ones and the more unknown. The chunky and dimly lit boxes, her backyard filled with treasures and memories she didn't want to lose ever again. Her broad big smile and her soul filled with a heart as big as her appreciation for the good things in life.

The short but curious drive here to this bed, the dead pond, the forgotten tractor and the first look of one lost farmer. I have been taken on forty years worth of memories in just a few short hours. My eyes were kind and at last perhaps my mind was catching up with what I was supposed to be seeing. My eyes dotted back and forth across the front yard of Malachi's, the outstretched elms, the wrap around porch and a lonely old man wishing his Ruthie were still by his side. If I had still been attentive I would have seen Otis find one of those hard to find crickets just behind the bathroom door but secular attention was no longer of interest to me. If my eyes were still open I would have seen a raccoon make its way underneath my car and if my eyes were still open I would have read the story in the daily news.

I would have learned that a young girl was struck and killed by a car that was driving much too fast for the rainy weather. I would have learned that it had happened just before lunch time at a time when the traffic should have been slowing down. If I had taken just a few moments to read what I said was not important I would have learned much. If my eyes had been open I would have learned that the young girl was carrying a single yellow rose, a gift for her mother. If I had read the story rather than assume it was like all others, I would have learned her mother was my friend Sandi Beech. If I had paid attention to the lines written to share the story of a life lost I would have learned much. I would have learned that the little girl was my matted-hair little friend. The small one whose life had passed by in allot of ways but who took time to share so much with me was gone. The little one whose name I never asked for was dead and her last act of kindness was to share with me this two pound mess seeking a lost cricket behind the bathroom door.

The docile tone of the choir of bullfrogs was completed and as I rolled toward the wall. My eyes batted some to the beat of the frogs until I saw myself standing in front of my boyhood home. It seemed more distant now; it wasn't as clear as it had once been on my previous trips. The sidewalk was shrouded by fallen pines, the smell in the air was lilac and the sound of young sisters at play was even more distant than before. I stared for a moment at a front door accented by oval glass and with wings as a dove I was on the porch holding the knob. I struggled to get in but to no avail. I shook the knob again and again but the door wouldn't open. I was afraid and worried that I could *not* or would *not* ever get in again, I could not go home again. I must let that home go. I shook the knob and in frustration I shaded my eyes and looked through the glass. Was anyone there, would I ever be let in again? Was I forgotten about? Did my family want me anymore? I would try once again and I looked back through the glass, this time seeing before me my father's face. He was saying something. His lips moved but I couldn't hear him. His lips moved again in a simple manner but I couldn't hear him. Dad, let me in I begged. Again he looked and repeated a simple phrase. I saw his face; it was peaceful and resolute and he said again a simple phrase *move on*.

The home of youth was gone for good as my father's wish was granted. With the wings of Isaiah I was brought across this road to where I played as lad. I looked up the fog of fear sent my boyhood home to the banks of lessons learned and it was before me no more. The memories were strong and meant to be recalled but not forever dwelled upon. I was standing now facing a long road before me. I must walk it, at least for now, by myself and without a guide. I was thirsty and knew that water was close so I turned to head up this road encompassed by the scent of freshly cut grass and cherry blossoms. I knew water was close and had the sense that I would find it if I just took the first few steps. There was no sound of running water or of homebound barn swallows but I knew they were close. However, as I readied myself for the unknown my left hand felt a new arrival. It was cold upon first touch but became familiar with persistence.

I squinted a little in hopes of recognizing this very wet nose poking at my hand. A boyhood smile returned as I was reunited with my three-legged black lab coming to greet me and to receive his long overdue nose scratch. He licked my hand again and again and I scratched and scratched that anxious snout. He was so happy I was here, he ran just a bit ahead of me and sat and turned and played in a wonderful circle. He ran and ducked and the circle grew wider as he played the games that we never played when we were young. I stood silently and then took a step or two and saw he was three-legged no more. His fur was bright and new, his eyes had the love of the puppy found on Christmas morning and he ran as if he hadn't run in many years. He was before me and as dogs do tossed his head to lead the way and disappeared in his own special way, waiting for me just up ahead.

He was gone for the time being and I took a few steps on my own. To my right was a small home but it too soon vanished before I could make out any further detail and I began my walk up this narrow fog shrouded road The scent was haunting. Dampness had touched the pavement and the lawns of the neighbors had all been freshly mowed. The freshly cut grass, what a smell, we *all* remember that and for each step I took that smell was enhanced. I walked with a cautious, steady gate and with every step the fog lifted just a bit more exposing before me so much more to travel. I didn't feel lost and a childlike curiosity replaced my fear.

It was hard to tell if it was high noon or morning's dawn and I couldn't find any markers along the way to tell which it was. I stood motionless after a few steps and I looked about seeing nothing familiar, nor a daunting landmark. I saw at a short yet so far unattainable distance two figures one taller than the other. Man or woman I didn't know. I took a few more steps trying to catch up but saw they were ahead of me going in the same direction. I stopped to the sensation of stepping on something then kicking something else. Was it more pebbles or pinecones from the pines hovering as far as the eyes could see? I stopped to see what the trail had brought and before me as far as I could see were the reddest, plumpest plums a young boy would ever know. I would be thirsty no more. I reached with watching eyes for the fattest of them all. I pulled up short anticipating the glare of Ms. Yowell from her hidden porch.

I stood in the middle of this road for what I thought was hours upon hours and didn't know if I should continue or go back. I stood there sneaking one plum after another, I was an eight year old all over again and it was glorious. I had a general idea of the next few steps ahead of me but what was behind me? I wasn't sure I wanted to move on but what was behind me was done; that life has been lived. Was my father telling me this and saying that I should move on or was he telling me that he too had given up and didn't want to see me again? I walked for a distance and stopped again to ask the same question now with a twist of the head. If I went back and relived things and this time did it right all who knew me would be proud and not shamed.

Looking behind me I knew I should go back though the road behind me seemed darker and more ominous yet more familiar. A voice came to me, from where I did not know. It was gentle yet stern. "Say good-bye to the bad and look for the good, say good-bye to the past and hello to tomorrow." What to do and where to go was my quest. Man's best friend soon answered that question. My three-legged black lab had come back to me anxious and seeking to lead me on my journey. He seemed younger then I had known him to be; he was so happy and so full of joy and excitement and he was running as

Ashley Bay

never before. I turned back around and he ran ahead a few steps. He wasn't going backward but ahead on this road. I didn't move but sought his attention, "Come here boy, come here." He tossed his head and ran in the familiar circle a few more steps ahead. He repeated this exercise until he was sure I would follow him and *not* return back down that ominous road.

Follow him I would; this was a game for my boyhood friend and I *owed* him some playtime after all these years. We would make up for all the times he watched me come and go without as much as a high yah boy sent his direction. We were making up for all the games we didn't play and all the attention I chose not to give him; he wanted to play and so did I. He and I ran and we tussled over invisible ropes and he chased all the toys that he never had. He ran and stayed just ahead a number of paces so as not to lose me and I looked once again at the lifting horizon. The figures ahead were coming closer but were still to far away to be respectfully greeted. I had options now. I could go back, I could seek out the strangers or I could play with my happy friend of old.

I couldn't tell if there was an end to the road but knew I would have to take the first steps to get through a lifting fog. If I stayed here I would never know for sure what might be ahead. I took a couple of steps and sensed that water *was* coming close, a familiar sound was coming closer. I recognized the sound of a small stream where baby rainbows had been caught though with some effort and released because of their size and the heart of the youthful angler. I moved to the right side of this road and at a few paces saw a trestle marking the rainbows' home and at its crown was a bench the one I knew to be donated long ago by our neighbor Mr. Yowell. This bench was meant for those of Mr. Schuster's generation but they were all gone now. Was it now here for me?

I stood at arm's length knowing Mr. Yowell didn't want any of us kids ever to sit on his work but I was reassured so I took my seat. This was *his* bench the one he built for those who deserved a rest and not for those who had a lazy nature. However, it was empty now and waited for we had all worked so hard. I was somewhat restless but knew that a small towns, old time belief was that a restless nature was meant for the next generation as yet untested. As we age our spirit is tested and readied for the final walk as we age we become less restless. With a glare cast over my shoulder I kept my seat knowing I was no longer the untested. I arched my back to sit straight for I knew he and Dad never liked a neighborhood slouch. The bench overlooked a stream that had looked so wondrous when I was young; the rapids of youth were now just pebbles in the reality of age. I couldn't see the stream but heard it trickle, trickle, trickle. The rainbows were there as well and *their* parents were there all seeking greater waters which they would find as they too followed the rainbows Through the settled fog and a home in the distance I heard the quiet call of, "time to come home, it's suppertime!" My sister was calling me home, I could hear in the distance the school bus coming and honking for all those who were late. I felt a cold chill from an unknown guest but it was just a cold shiver ending at my shoes. The cold shiver could be interpreted a million ways and I had not yet settled on my favorite definition of the pimply intruder.

I sat for awhile and was getting tired but I soon recalled the old train that ran behind our home, I could hear it coming. The slow chug-chug-chug of the coal burner. There was a rush coming from down the unknown road it just had to be that train. It seemed it was getting colder and the fog was growing thicker but I strained to hear that the train. The train was something that all we kids looked forward to watching for the conductor always waved. We would run as fast as we could to see it chug on by. It could be heard from miles away as the old coal burner approached all the town's freshly washed white sheets. The whistle would blow and the chugging could be heard as it came near us from around the bend. Chug-chug-chug and the whistle would blow and all the small town dogs would send back howls of their own. The train came and I knew if my sister tried to call her voice drowned out by the smoke belching monster.

The road was damp and my feet were chilled. The stream sent its trickle, trickle across the rapids of my youth. I was getting colder and felt I should go on but in which direction? This was a nice rest but it was time to go. Where had my childhood friend gone? I pulled my collar up near me as I stood. The scent of mounting generations came across the fields of hay. The fog surrounded my feet and drifted up till it was about my waist. I wasn't sure why all this fog was here and what it meant. Is the fog emblematic of being lost? I again felt the call home from my sister, *it's time to come home* was her cry. I couldn't find

Ashley Bay

the direction in which to start, I was confused and had trouble seeing. there was no sign and no signal to follow just the belching encroachment of the LA&L. I was confused but not frightened. On one hand I had a voice calling me home and on the other hand I had an old friend showing me a different way. I was sure I would be safe either way.

Would I stay and wait for the train would I go home to my sister or would I seek the goal of my boyhood friend? I looked behind me and saw the bench was gone and all I had was the sound of water. Where was it going? Where was it coming from? It's when it stands still that it seems to die and the frogs sing no more. The water has to move to live for what happens when water just stands still? I backed up because I couldn't step forward and risk a fall all too familiar. As I stepped backward, I heard the crack of a whip or maybe it was a car door instead. The sound was strong and direct; maybe it was a tree branch breaking as it reached a bit farther. I took another step backward my foot feeling first for a safe landing A toe touch here and another one there and I eased back into a comfortable position. Another crack of a whip greeted me or maybe it was a distant door slammed shut by an angry sister. She would call me no more for she had tried once too often. Crack, crack, crack went the unseen whip.

I was ashamed knowing for if I would go home I no longer knew the way. I was ashamed because I again was afraid of taking a chance and doing what had to be done. But I couldn't I was told to *move on* and that I wasn't welcome there any longer. The inhibitions came back and I wondered why my parents no longer wanted me there. My feet shook as I stood uncertain near this small stream. The sound of the water told me I was close so I had better not step any closer. I felt the rush of a wind across my face and I reached down and felt the nose of my boyhood friend, he had found me. I didn't need to look for him and I didn't need to go back. I scratched his nose and patted his head. My friend knew my fears and came to comfort me and he had always been a noble friend I just never saw it. I heard the whine of a lonely friend and stooped to find him. My feet shook and I heard a distant bang, bang-bang. I was startled, for this sound was new. I turned around and heard a voice but it was unclear. The voice came again and again it was in the distance. Was it the figures on the crest or was it my sister or was it Dad telling me come home? Who was it that wanted me to answer? I stood silently and let my head drop to my chest and listened as the voice grew healthy and my friend of youth went away.

The secret voice became louder as the road vanished from beneath me.. "Young man, young man wake up your coffee's ready."

A rolled grunt and a bang, bang-bang and again "Young man, it'll get cold!" He tapped on the window frame with what could only have been his cane. I woke like Dracula sitting straight up and meeting Otis at the foot of the bed with *that* look on his face. He looked as troubled as ever, though beagles seldom look anything else but. His sorrowful look could mean only one thing and as I gained my wits I soon noticed his morning surprise waiting for me near the television. I wasn't troubled and accepted his silent apology as an error that he would soon learn to correct. I was thirsty the dream had sapped my energy and the now fleeting memories of the dream just blurred its intentions.

I had fallen asleep fully dressed and slept most of the night nearly in the same position I dropped off in. Otis made it clear that he regretted his hygienic error from the previous night by tossing several woeful looks my way hoping I would forgive him. I did as he wished.

"Ok little buddy; I forgive you but not next time aye." He was pleased and said so with a couple of good morning thumps of the ever fattening tail. I swung my feet to the side of the bed and stepped on the paper, which kept from me the loss of my matted-hair little friend and I stood to begin my morning routine. The dream had ended to the rude awakening attempts by Mr. Taylor. It was rude *only* to those who slept through it and not to those that woke when he called them to his front porch for the coffee and toast he offered.

My routine ending, I saw my pitiful little friend in need of a hurried visit to the front yard. Letting him out I watched as he made quick business of what must have been a centurion buildup. Otis was as quick at his morning routine as I was and was quickly off to whatever growing dogs do after taking care of their morning duties. I threw a bit of water on my face and thought a shower would be appropriate but convinced myself that when this day's road ended I would accommodate my built up bodily porous secretions at a motel named for an even number.

Ashley Bay

Mr. Taylor was pleasurable at first light. But, as with most of us as the day wears on shadows bring from us the unpleasantness that comes from being weary. He was dressed the same as he had been yesterday and from what I recall, the same as he had been the last time I saw him when we ignored his only son some forty or more years ago. I stood near the doorway; it seemed that most men, after a certain age, all dress alike, admiring our own adornment I tugged what needed to be tugged. Making my way through the wake of another bang, bang-bang, Mr. Taylor was already sitting and listening like a hawk for his prey.

He said, "Here young man, found these upstairs." He waited for me to come up from behind and he continued, "Thought you might like to take them with you. These go back many years to my own father."

The lost farmer handed me a stack of old newspaper clippings, yellow and ripped at their edges from years of being ignored.

"Hey, this is nice, thank you. Is this about what we talked about last night?"

He nodded in a manner that I took to convey a yes.

The morning chill was comforting this time of year, for it brought the scent of honeysuckle, which was probably my favorite of all earthly scents. It wasn't too over powering yet one could tell that something good was in the air. The chill brought the sounds of the hardy survivors looking to extend their lives in the fading pond across the way. The chill brought pulled up collars, piles of fallen leaves that were never in the same spot and the wheezing of southbound fowl. The old man poured the coffee and I was sure thankful it was as thick as his New England heritage. Good, hot, jet black coffee on a fall morning so nice it was.

"Thank you sir. I've been looking forward to this."

I watched Otis out of the corner of my eye just to make sure he stayed out of trouble, though he was nothing but a door stop in training. I had yet to decide if I would move on in a bit or ask for another night. To be sure, I was tired enough just to sleep for a while; the weariness from all the months and years was mounting. With a hearty gulping slurp I said, "I slept pretty well last night Mr. Taylor."

He shook his head and said, "A lot of folks do just that out this way Not much noise other then the curious critter or two." The coffee was strong. It had been made for decades by the hands of a widower not used to taking care of himself since the days of Bastogne.

"Not many visitors, aye?"

"Nope. Maple every now and then. Hard to feed that girl though; sparks fly when *she's* at the table." He scratched his head and said, "But not a better soul in these parts than that one." Mr. Taylor seemed so much less ominous than when I first saw him yesterday facing me and the vocal Otis. He was frail but friendly to the core. As I sat and listened to his stories, I thought just how nice it would be to stay for a few days right here in this chair. How nice it would be just to sit and watch the compounded silence of the days that used to be. If I stayed I could go between here and Maple's, my mornings there and evenings here, that would be a nice break. She would complain about bastard men and *he* would defend our species. It was relaxing just sitting here and listening to the sounds of the memories brought back by looking at the pond across the way and the tales of one lost farmer.

The days had grown in number since I was one of three chasing ghosts across the way. I knew too, that the numbers of days behind me far outnumbered those that now lie ahead and I would someday be the Mr. Taylor of my generation. Would anyone come visit me? Would I have a Maple to complain about? Would I someday be host to a younger man seeking to make amends of his own?

Otis had found his morning assignment some poor bull frog seeking any place of respite that didn't resemble the beagles wet nose. Otis would also be the one on this particular day in charge of sniffing the backside of an old milk can. Once he found that to his interest he'd soon moved elsewhere. He would make sure to record for posterity *his* can though so all others would know that Otis had been here. As the day's curiosity wore on he would find the shady underbelly of the car out front and wait for his next task.

Mr. Taylor slapped a big old gob of apple butter on some wheat toast as dark as the pond across the way. I smiled for this I remembered so well. Mom showed me that apple butter is good for everything a cure all even for the most depressed mind. "Apple

Ashley Bay

butter! Wow, I haven't had this is so long, thanks." Otis became curious as to the newly arrived aroma.

"You know who makes this don't yah," he said with a kind gesture toward Maple's opulence. "Where you headed to from here, young man?"

"Real good this is real good. I think Maine, maybe Casco Harbor haven't made up my mind yet. Kinda' letting the road decide for me. I have some good memories of Maine and I wanted to go back there. I remember that I first went up that way when I was a little guy. We spent the summer along the Casco shore."

"Yup, the road is a good choice, a good teacher too," he said. "The road never leads us wrong and it always takes us somewhere."

He slid the chair forward a bit slurping his coffee so as not to miss a drop. "The road might take us but it's up to us to decide what turn to take when we start our journey though. Lots of options. My daddy took a few side roads and that's what built this house that gave you such a good night's rest last night. If he hadn't made a choice you would never have had that tractor to guide you three."

I was sharing the apple butter hitchhikers with a pitiful excuse for a dog and thought just how he was saying in his own way was just what Dottie and Maple had shared not long ago.

"Don't be too cautious in life, young man. Take the first step when one needs to be taken, don't just let things pass you by."

I sipped some more coffee enjoying the finest brewed in along time and chimed in. "There is some things I have to do before I get to Maine. I don't know how important they are but they should get done."

"Annie liked Maine. She loved the lighthouses and the shorelines the rocks and the sounds of the ocean late at night. The times we went there she seemed to return to the childhood of her own. She would dance in the sand and find the biggest of shells to share with me. She loved it so much, I just want to see that one last time." I sat back in a cool breeze and the scent of jasmine reached me again from an undisclosed starting point. There were freshly cut flowers sending me a greeting from somewhere but I couldn't find it and assumed that it was the nearby untended field. A deeper breath and a deeper one still were met by the kind smile of Mr. Taylor. He knew the all about the familiar floral visitors and the cold chill which had made its way to my neck. It seemed that he knew what I was experiencing and he was happy that I was taking part.

"Yeah, take your girl for another walk up there boy." Mr. Taylor shook his head. I agreed "Yup, I know there are some great stories up that way." In a follow up he let me know that there were some good ones in the stack he gave me and encouraged me to take a look when I could. He handed me another portfolio of clippings that he had taken some effort to gather for me the night before.

"Thank you. I'd like to take a look if I could."

The sun had begun to shine just a bit through the jagged elms across the way and a single bird could be seen in flight making its way through the rays of morning light. I thought, how strange to see just *one* bird; all should go through life with a friend. He probably had a task to perform as well and was just late in getting started. The feathered guest may have been looking for a friend that was also gone for good. I didn't want to leave this place of rest right yet but seemed I was called by a curiosity at what the end of the road held for me. Mr. Taylor and Maple had told me that there are always rewards at the end of the road *if* of course, we take the right route.

"It's been a nice visit, Mr. Taylor. I relaxed a lot and the rest was great."

He nodded and asked if my buddy had found the accommodations to his satisfaction. Otis, now well under the Tempo accepted some bread tossed his way covered with a big old slab of apple butter. The growing canine seemed to know when he was the topic of discussion and made his way to my side, tail going in steadfast delight once the gift found a spot of rest.

"Yeah, I think he likes it out here."

The morning conversation dotted back and forth with politeness and small talk about the trees and loves we both have lost. The road was winding and full of dust and entanglements but it wasn't too far to where I wanted to stop next. It was an hour's drive in New England time to Baker's Brook a small pond where Dad used to take us as kids to break in our brand new Zebcos. The morning was midway and I felt a pang of guilt at having to make the most difficult choice of the day so far.

"I think we'd best move on, Mr. Taylor." I leaned forward in the chair and flapped Otis' ears. I stood and tugged at various parts to make sure they were ready for the continued journey and found that they were. I had one last thing I needed to do.

Mr. Taylor didn't stand and pointed to the pond across the way. "A lot of memories over there for all of us."

I knew now that he had indeed remembered me and what *used* to be me. He remembered the daggers I used to toss at his boy and the unkind words that we all showed him and his family all those years ago. He leaned a bit forward in the chair and pointing with the cane he said again, "A lot of memories in those waters. You boys played so hard at times, me and Ruthie used to laugh at all the times *you* fell trying to jump that ditch."

"Yes sir, there are memories," I agreed.

"Some good and some bad; the bad *are* forgotten and the good remembered," he said. A smile, though faint, came across his nearly toothless face.

"A lot of years have gone by Mr. Taylor," I dribbled back with hands thrust in my pockets and a posture that showed apprehension. I cleared my throat as my eyes welled.

He nodded and said, "Only one type of water is worth remembering and that's the water that cleanses us. It's never too late my son." He stood up as quickly as his old bones allowed. "The water that cleanses is the type that never dies, it cleanses us and helps us start each day like it was a new life."

I was feeling a dig at my heart that I knew came only with emotional growth and a spirit begging to get out. I looked at the old tractor and back at the forgotten farmer. I held my eyes tightly on his dipping chin and placed my hand on his shoulder. "Mr. Taylor, sometimes I wasn't real nice as a kid. I wasn't always kind to you and your family. For all the hurt feelings, for all the pain I caused you, I am deeply sorry."

He stood, this time unaided and placed his healing hand upon my shoulder as well. He seemed stronger and more attentive. "Son, don't take regret with you on this journey. Just take with you the knowledge that all is forgiven and no matter how hard it is, just look for the best in everyone." He nodded without passing on any other words of forgiveness; his nod said it all.

Reminiscent of a younger man, he took my elbow and walked me to the car at stronger gate and on our arrival he handed me his cane. "I want you to take this with you I won't need it any longer." I shook my head with a I can't tak... before I could deny his gift he shushed my concerns with his words, "I won't need it any longer."

I wasn't sure what he meant by his words but I accepted his gift as a tool to use on my walk. It was crafted with character and virtue both which would come in handy for my trip. I nodded a thank you.

"Otis, come on we got to go." Otis came running the best a fattening beagle can and with a shove of my shoe he hopped into the front seat. I took the cane with some hesitation obviously but it was a gift offered by an older man who had just forgiven my youthful cruelty.

"Yah might want to drive a little slower than you had thought. The road can show you things that you would have otherwise missed. Too many people now-a-days just drive without looking."

I smiled because I knew just what he meant, "OK ,I'll go slow and check things out along the way." I had retrieved all I had set inside the tiny room and put the paper on the floorboard in back.

I got in behind the wheel and Otis, his paws on my knee wanted to say his thank yous as well.

"A nice little friend yah got there. He'll be with you a long time."

"Yes sir, I know. I have that feeling, too." Some more kind words a final handshake and I wished him well. He wished me the same.

I drove out slowly and recognized for the first time that leaning on the other side of the wrap around porch was the old sign for the Malachi Lodge. What a great name for a place of learning I would find out later through this old King James Version that Malachi was called the Socrates of all the prophets. Malachi said to his students that we can all learn from how we talk and how we reason our status of life. Malachi's prophecy of old is a testimony to God's grace. Now I know why this little home, marked with love and respect was named Malachi. A last look in Mr. Taylor's direction and a quick wave. He nodded and Otis and I were on our way to see what the road might hold for us.

As we had spoke over coffee the years seemed to catch up in gentleness rather than the mounting piles of regret that I had lived with for many years. I had soothed the impolite nature of the rest that I often wrestled with and the morning brought amends and forgiveness. How nice those two work together: amends and forgiveness. I may be able to do this one person at a time, but can others serve me with the same graciousness? Did it matter what others did or did it matter what I did? I knew the answer to that and saw no reason to wrestle with it further. The willingness to make amends, I guess will calm our greed and make a person more willing to see his or her own errors that need correcting and not so much others' faults. Mr. Taylor had said let God work on others as He has on you; don't rush Him.

In between our sips of very strong Quaker ground coffee, which he had received from a recent visit by Maple, I had packed up what little stuff I had and moved the newspaper to the front seat. I was almost ready to toss the paper but once again saw the front page headline. I would read it at our next stop or maybe tomorrow, when I get around to it. I would take the time to learn about the tragedy of another. The rest at Malachi was nice and the day was either well underway or on the other side of midway I couldn't tell. I drove slowly toward the next stop, feeling rested but acknowledging the encroachment of age. I looked next to me and saw that Otis was making himself ready for continuing the journey and I felt a need to take one last look about at the adventures of youth.

I let my mind wander to the forthcoming generosity of whispering lilacs and gave my final stare at the dying pond and forts of old. The bullfrog and his colleagues had returned for the day and they were bidding me farewell also. I squinted some and saw three young men no longer boys walking away from the water. They waved good-bye with a smile to Louis and his bride Ruth. The good-bye I suppose was to say thank you for all the fun times, as the young men would return no more to the forts of old. I watched as one would die before his time and I watched as one would go and never be seen again. The figures vanished and left just one remaining who stopped, took his hands out of his pockets, turned and with a smile and waved good-bye to his boyhood.

I also said my farewells to the pleasures created by the youthful mind and knew there were still some miles to travel. In our adult years we often regret youthful joys, spending countless hours trying to overcome them. Some of us may take them to the sheltered eaves of squeaking rocking chairs while others never loose the ties. I watched as the last remaining pirate of old encountered on his walk from the water the lost soul of Russell Taylor as the whooperwill cried on.

Chapter 5
Restless Moon

I left Mr. Taylor's with a genuine smile and felt the day was going to be a good one, one of the best in some time. Making amends for the wrongs of old loosened my spirit and encouraged me to look for the good that might be there. I could literally smell the anticipation in the air for what the day might hold. Joyful anticipation was something that I believed only kids experienced while waiting for Christmas but it's there, always there for everyone. I felt good and secure in the choices I had made on this day and felt that I would be more aware of what would come next, at least as far as opportunities for kindness. That was something many of us overlooked on our way to enhancing opportunities for selfishness, at least I always did till now.

The opportunities for good often fall victim to human greed and I sure had to be careful of that. As I drove past the side of the Taylor household that I seldom saw as a young man, I thought that there were other things I could have said to Mr. Taylor. There was something else I could have done to show my sorrow for being rude and crude. I could have asked if there was work that needed to be done around the house and I could certainly have asked about his son Russell. The far side of the Taylor property was often the subject of the ghost stories of older siblings. Brothers, cousins and such told us of those stories of the ghosts of the lost redcoats and the devils that greeted everyone who dared approach the Taylor household. That's why many of us knew that deep down inside our youthful imagination, Mr. Taylor was either a redcoat or the devil. Being young and dumb we hated both and showed our hate in actions and speech but it was losing our selfishness that we were afraid of for if we had taken the time Mr. Taylor would have seen to that.

Those amazing stories of youth. Which ones are real and which ones are passed on for the sake of entertaining the young? Are they harmless in the end? Were Santa Clause and the Easter Bunny entertainment or folklore or are they real? We have to make this distinction not only from society but in our minds as well. Are the devil and God folklore as well and passed on for the weak minded only? What's good and what's bad? The job for us as we leave these back roads is to separate fact from fiction. What is the depth of the fine line that rests between folklore and faith? My mind was all over the place however but I was learning how to calm it down as I grew. I was slow and deliberate when I slammed on my mental brakes to make sure I didn't collide with any other emotions along the way. I didn't want to drift too far from how I left Mr. Taylor; I knew I would be tempted but I would win.

The road heading west from Mr. Taylor was one on which I drove slowly to be sure. It was new in so many ways and offered endless opportunities for an imagination of any age. I did want to enjoy this drive and hoped there would be no more red lights. My patience was back and I didn't want it threatened right now. I would look carefully and enjoy the ride to see what may be to the side of the road as Mr. Taylor had suggested. I wanted to let my eyes see what might be there and not what actually was there In order for memory to work we must have faith in the past so for faith could work in the here and now. I must take time to define God in order to grow and experience His love. That's what I felt Mr. Taylor's message was to me: slow down and let God come on in.

The radio was off and Otis was sitting contently staring at the dashboard as if there were hidden treasures calling for his determined sniff. The mind is a dangerous tool for the weak and I was walking dangerous ground when left alone to my own will. Whether it was I or Otis contributing to the atmosphere I felt my trembling spirit falling victim to the growing attitude of doubt. Why wait for God? I had questions of why didn't I know then what I am seeking now? Why was I rude so often to so many people over stupid things? Did I show Annie the love that she so deserved? Was I being punished for my past transgressions or trained and prepared for the future?

The most recent question I posed came back as quickly as I had tossed it out. I ignored it but it was persistent and ran about my soul like a newborn pup. I wondered if God were real, for if He was would I have instinctively acted in a more loving manner? If God is real, then the devil or evil must also be real. If good and evil were real which one did I most often seek in my life? Well the answer to that was clear. Though I hadn't always been good my inner voice knew when I had acted in a way that was something other than kind. My inner voice would tell me you should have done better, you could have acted more kindly and you should have been more patient. Though I listened often to the *negative* inner voice, I ignored all too often the *positive* inner voice but I began to learn to change that.

These questions were bouncing back and forth and the content feelings of just moments ago as I departed Mr. Taylor's were being beaten back by doubt and self-flagellation. I tried to shake the pesky doubt out of the way but with little success my peace of mind was run over by runaway doubt. I had been rooted in spiritual doubt for so long that I had little resistance to direct combat with the enemy of the deep. The question that now sat behind me in this trembling Tempo was if God is real why had I ignored Him? We all we ignore God for one reason or another and these reasons all seem so well thought out when we publicly issue them. I drove on now a handful of miles from the trusted prophet and now wished I had stayed with him just a while longer.

This underlying question as to whether God is real was answered by my hollow soul and by that shameful inner voice. My inner voice at times was the demon from the deep and this time it answered the question with, Hell, No! Of course God isn't real. Just look at your life. Look at who you are. God is for the weak minded *not* for you. So my inner voice of doubt had told me God cannot be real and as far as I know the only thing that would ever say God is dead is that which opposes His teachings. My inner voice had fallen victim to the devil himself. Only the devil could convince man that God is dead. Only the devil could take root in society and convince its members that things such as the most vile are OK because God is dead.

I guess that's maybe what Maple and for that matter what Dottie had told me. Look for the good *and* the bad things in life. If you find the good then you know God is there and the same is true of the bad where bad exists it's likely evil has been rooted somewhere in the neighborhood. The friends I have set aside so many times tried to tell me in their way that all good things in life are of God and all bad things are of the devil. Maple, in all her abundance told me that things the good book called vile such as the killing of the unborn could never be of God. Therefore they can only be of the devil. As I drove I wondered is free will the devil dancing is way through our lives?

OK, I had found out that my inner voice if left to its own growth would become hell bound quickly if not properly trained. The road that I was now on was as straight as I could see but a choice would soon come. There wasn't much in the way of a horizon or clue to what may lie ahead and the landmarks were indistinguishable if present at all. The road was much like my soul for right now I was uncertain as to what direction I would go I would have to venture a little further but not much to know. I knew if I concentrated on the road I wouldn't have to fight the mental battle. If my soul just stayed undecided I would experience neither glory nor hell. Right? In other words if I ignored the demons it meant that they weren't there and if I ignored God He wasn't there either. But I had learned enough now to know that *that* wasn't true I would know that God would do His best to teach the neutral and the devil his best to steal the spirit.

The elms crisscrossed this part of an under used and often forgotten Rhode Island back road and they swallowed me the further I drove. I was hoping that the radio would shake out the troublesome question of God but I was out of reach of anything other than tormented static. Back to the subject at hand, I had an uncle, not the skirt-chasing, beer drinking Danvers Clay, but Paul Richard. He could answer questions like this with ease but he had a difficult time counting to ten. I wondered how he might answer this question and how he would fend off the demons. The clumsy minded usually have such insight into the profound that it *is* sometimes spooky, Uncle Paul was such a man.

I thought for awhile and believed if Uncle Paul were asked this question he would stretch back in his chair, tug his sweater and say, "Well, if you ask someone the same question at twenty-one and again at seventy-one, you'll get much different answers."

Ashley Bay

I drove deeper into the tree hollowed back road and wondered if Uncle Paul would be correct with his answer. Did my feelings about right and wrong change as I got older? Did my belief in God change because of my age and experience? There was no horizon ahead and no turns either, just a road growing more ominous the further I drove. Uncle Paul was a far better philosophical actor than practitioner but he would have been right about this. When I was young, I had the air of elitism about me like many New England twenty year olds do at *this* time and any other time for that matter. I knew that the best day the world had ever known was the day that I was born. I acted as if I knew it all and those who got in my way were inconveniences and a hindrance to my aura. When I was young, I was rude to all who got in my way and ignored the simple teachings of Christ and His minions because it was my life and *not* His.

I didn't have time or patience for family or friends or for a friendly, nearly blind, lame three-legged black lab. The road was narrow and I suppose so was I. I rolled down the window down a bit so both Otis and I could get some fresh air from the usual and growing unusual car smells. The latter we both must have our columns debited for. My side kick approved and slid near the window a nose rather small but ready to sniff whatever might come his way and he did so in between gusts of road dust. The road held no turns and the sides held no water. It was just a flat, dusty back road *so* without distraction, my mind posed questions to its owner. I answered the first part knowing that all young who think they know, ultimately find out they don't. That is why Mr. Taylor told me to watch for what's on the side of the road; there is something there even if we can't see it.

The road was so dusty. The more I looked about I sensed that we may never have come down this way when we were young after all, but who knows. The road went on and I asked. If I was debating God, then should I ask if the devil is real? My mental ghosts were dancing from topic to topic looking for a bridge and an answer. Maybe we can look at those times in our youth to answer that one. As I aged and my life experiences taught me that there was so much more to this world than *my* opinion, some cruelty left the scene. As I grew and chose the good things, the devil began to leave as well but the fight was tough. This question had made me think back to not only my younger years but to just a few hours ago as well. Did I let the devil go far enough away from me so as not to be a *total* victim to him? Whom had I been rude to and was I now a man who believed more in good than in evil? Yes, I was. I don't think I was that selfish; after all I really did have a good, caring heart I just had a hard time showing it every now and then. Recognizing the four footed, floppy eared beneficiary of such a change in my behavior.

It made me think back to when I was taught by well meaning people that if I screwed up or if I was mean to that lonely three-legged black lab then I would go straight to hell. Did they really mean that or was it just a lesson? It was a lesson I know that now and I am forever seeking a lonely lab. All those teachers just wanted me to know that being compassionate is what life is about and that being unkind and disrespectful is not for *this* life. My parent's just wanted me to grow into a good and decent man and pass that nature onto my own family when one came. If I was taught that I was hell bound would I try to disprove it? Well, not when I was young but as I grew my actions would disprove that belief for me. As we grow and mature and see life I had a sense that kindness is intuitive Well based on these perceived teachings I assumed I was doomed right from the ripe old of age of eight or so. If I believed from such a young age that I was evil and that heaven was and would always be out of reach, then a relationship with God was not necessary. That was only the case during those early years and I now thanked God every day that I was no longer of that age of confusion. The road went on.

With this sense of always being wrong and unkind I was never shown that redemption was possible and I never sought another way of life. However as I grew older I also grew spiritually because the seed of faith was planted all those years ago. I did fall from the goal of the New Testament, that yeah we screw up but Jesus came so that we may have life again. The older I became I saw many around me fall further from me, not because of anything else other than my actions and lifestyle. They grew and became for the most part children of good and I still had the demons of doubt firmly locked into my mental files. It wasn't until Annie had dug me out of the emotional trash of life that I began to *see* life and all its wonders and those wonders weren't *my* doings but His. The road widened as I traveled further from Mr. Taylor's place and the more my mind grew in peace the ominous horizon shrunk. I guess I just had to be opened minded and when I am I become less selfish and less selfish means I show Gods love.

With my hands at ten and two and the road still without a clear direction, I thought that was one hell of a load for a young person to carry, one screw up and your doomed approach to life. How can *any* young person carry with them through life the sense of eternal damnation? When a young person embarks on life's road feeling that regardless of whatever happened, he or she was hell bound from the very start how could they ever recover from that? If a young child has a spiritual relationship removed and never receives an opportunity for redemption then that child will live a long, painful life. I had lived this painful life for many, many years and then the life became an angry one with my anger directed at everyone in my path. I was so angry at life but not for too long, I had been shown love and kindness and I changed. I drove with clenched hands and a mind lecturing its owner as to all the lost years. As we know when a childhood is full of pain it is transmitted into adulthood and that's what I'm now living. Were my childhood pain *my* fault then or was my life my fault now? Well, I guess I would find the answer to that at some point but the underlying question now at this stage was what *had* I lived for? If I died what awaited me at the end? The mind went on and on and on.

Many years ago a friend said to me that if we don't live for God then what are *we* living for? If we go through life just concerned with our own selfish interests what happens when we die and that pursuit ends? If we live just for ourselves then what do we leave behind when we die? Old Terry Sullivan, he had lived for a while across from Annie and me and he was another bright, kind person who had a beautiful family life. In one of our Sunday pre-game conversations, he asked me if we don't believe in God, then we can't believe in the second "o" in His name good. Dottie, Maple and now Mr. Taylor all followed up on that question from years ago Did I believe in good? Terry always had a smile when he informed me that good was just an extension of God. If I were to take what Terry, Dottie and Maple had said to me then I might in fact be developing an understanding of His world. Good is a simple extension of God, pure and simple. If we show kindness then we can't prevent the spirit of God growing inside of us it's natural. If I find good I have found God and therefore the opposite must be true. If I find God I have found goodness. Pretty basic but all I have to do now is to define what is good. The road went on and on and on.

The drive continued and it had now been about a half hour or so since my morning departure. My mental journey had been through all that it had in a short time. I had defined God in a mere half hour. I thought about all the selfish greedy people out there and how so many of them had screwed me over the years. Those bastards! My eyes were all over the windshield and I slowed the car. It just goes to show how quickly we can destroy all our progress but letting the devil in. I was determined not to lose any more ground though. I saw Otis was asleep again and my mind was battling the devil or its weaker side for a definition of goodness. I would win.

I reached over and scratched Otis behind the neck. "Buddy, what does good mean to you?" Otis showed little desire in answering the question posed him and left it to me to discover for myself the question of the apostles. The road was starting to narrow some again and there were still no identifiable landmarks but there was an arch that seemed to point to an impending right turn.

I would come back to this looming topic before too much longer I was sure but I felt the demons were on their last lap with me so I wanted to bid them good ridden. They had fought a good fight but they were losing. I glanced at the road now ahead of me and from deep inside the memory bank came a hint that perhaps my brother and I had taken this drive once some thirty years ago perhaps longer, or was it less? We had maybe come in from the opposite side or had come out here when he first learned to drive but it looked familiar. Regardless of how, when and why, this looked familiar. I guess I would know for sure once the drive was complete and then everything once seen is in fact familiar. If my memory was accurate then there would be up on a hill to the right an old barn and a pasture where my brother had taken a summer job caring for the animals.

I took the curve that came upon me faster than expected and I was disappointed to find no barn no horses and not even the smallest hint that any such things ever existed. I was heading north now and within a few miles of southern Massachusetts. People who had even the slightest amount of Puritan blood always clenched their teeth when they neared that state. I was headed on a western loop well outside of the Boston area, purposely avoiding the mess the liberals have created. That city and that state would be a test for this conservative that's for sure. If I had not chosen a Christian path, I would be fine but I did choose Christ and I do know better. However as history would some day reveal this state had done as much to kill God than anything else since ancient Rome. Rhode Island was great; it was so small and country like and quickly behind me. However, I knew that most of the next few hours would be spent going through one of the most anti-Christian portions of America. The traffic would be offensive and so would the people behind the wheels, cash registers and toll booths. There would be no Maples or Mr. Taylor's anywhere in the Massachusetts I knew. The demons would be willing to come back if I failed this test on his turf.

The sky was brighter and the sun was to my rear so it gave the appearance that it was already late afternoon. I could see at a distance of maybe a mile or more a slow rising hill that I would be forced to navigate. This too brought back memories of when I would go fishing and I'd walk everywhere; there was *always* a distant hill to mount. The road then as now was always dusty, even during the heaviest of rains it was dusty. The sight of a hill would flood the imagination of all the buried treasures I would find on the other side of the hill. It never failed that when I was outside on foot that the rain came at such a pace that Noah himself would delay his departure for higher ground. I smiled because I remembered that when I was a boy I always looked forward to what might be on the other side of any hill regardless of rain.

As I drove exiting the mental anguish of just moments ago I was full of expectation again as to what I might find on the other side of the upcoming mound of mud. Just for a moment, it was as if I were a boy again for I didn't know what was on the other side of the little hill now in front of me. It was like the day before Christmas, it was like waiting for the tooth fairy and it was like catching that first fish with Dad. Anticipation was something else; it was marvelous and always sought after and it became a greater commodity with age. The little hill seemed never to gain on me so I thought a bit more. Anticipation was a wonderful emotion for a new couple and for a new father and for grandparents waiting for that Sunday visit. This dirt road and this one small hill out in the middle of nowhere was *my* anticipation brought back to life. This was just a small out of the way portion of this back road in a forgotten piece of Rhode Island but I was anxious to see it none the less.

    I slowed down a bit because I wanted the sensation of anticipation to last a bit longer. It was like the buzz from a couple of beers that I spent a generation trying to recapture. Though I hadn't had the former for decades I always remembered it that buzz. The sensation was great and getting better all the time the closer the hill came. What was going to be on the other side? It's not as if there was anything behind me so I could take my time, the hill was now about three-quarters of a mile away. I was driving slowly enough now that Otis was disturbed by the sound of the crunching gravel beneath the wheels. The pudgy co-pilot sat up and wondered what the problem was that was causing such a diminished speed. The hill was a half a mile away and the trees shrunk behind it. What would be on the other side now that the trees were gone? Was there gold, was there a forgotten fishing hole or would the lost redcoats still be seeking forgiveness? Would my sister be there calling me home for dinner? Would my childhood friends be there on their way to the lost farmer's pond? Would my Dad be waiting for me in his old beat up station wagon? I began to climb the hill more slowly than I thought was possible and keep the car moving forward. Otis was now rather curious as to my intentions and showed me with his questioning tilted head.

    I slowed to a near crawl and Otis was more than curious as to my intentions. He was fidgety and thought that perhaps he would be left beside the road for some other stranger to abuse and neglect. I slowed more and neared the side of the road facing the last of the rusted out, under appreciated barbed wire majesty. Before I knew it, I was on top of the small hill and to my surprise there was just emptiness on both sides of the road There was no sister, no father and there were no friends just the emptiness that had been there a generation ago. The outstretched arms of the Upland elms were now gone altogether and before me was the blighted forgotten country side of Western Massachusetts. There were no horses, no water and no lost farmer seeking a friendly neighbor named Maple. I was sad, I *really* was as I quickly met the other side of the hill and saw before me a rusted old neglected sign welcoming me to Massachusetts. "Crap" a truer sentiment was seldom expressed when one familiar with New England read such a sign. My anticipation that had been built up by a wish for something nice was quickly thrown to the ground by imminent reality.

Almost as if he too knew our new position, Otis passed on a discontented grunt circled three times and went back to his previous repose. We went down the hill at a speed a little greater but due more in part to gravity than to sincerity and desire. I looked solemnly as I passed the welcome to sign and was genuinely surprised that there was no fee for admission. Everywhere else in this state of a once noble and historic breed took whatever it could from *anyone* it could. This state had taxes for everything else so I was flabbergasted that Massachusetts didn't have an entrance fee for all those crossing the border. *This* state, founded by those seeking a new land for Christ had done everything they could to take from man and from God.

My life experience reminded me that it was about another three or four miles before the small town of Webster would come across my way. Webster was another small New England town that had been accented with modern wannabees. This little town had been forgotten by tradition as the modern day conveniences replaced kind neighbors and elite vendors. Webster had all the discount stores that seemed to mark progress and that closed the doors on more polite service and free smiles. Webster would be a nice place though to stop and let Otis perform his duties for a few moments. The day's drive would go north from there on Rte. 495 and I would probably grab a night's rest at an even numbered motel somewhere up by Framingham. Framingham would be about as close to Boston as I would care to get. In short order, I needed to make the plans for a stop just before 495 for both my young friend and I would need to explore the great outdoors and do so quickly. Webster was my first choice but I would play it by ear and by smell.

A night's rest would be a great time to answer the question that I had posed to myself not long ago: *is* God real? I insisted on using the real time definition and not the past tense, this was noticeable progress. It didn't matter if God was real at the time of Washington or Constantine but it mattered if God was real right now here in the tailing off Rocky Uplands. Is the same God that Washington prayed to in the woods of Valley Forge joining me on this journey? Is the same God that met Paul on that road or spoke to Lincoln traveling with me and my floppy eared co-pilot? The time spent outside under the patient sky tonight would allow me time to settle the request from Maple as well. "Look for the good and look for the bad in life," the words of wisdom from my portly friend. These questions had to be answered first and at that point when I had found a decent solution I would know whether God is real. One thing that I always recognized about my behavior is that I was one to analyze everything thoroughly. If I could review the things in my life that were good I could see how my behavior towards others may have been anything but. I would analyze all but me.

The grass was getting greener and more artificial looking and the gray orbital sky far to my right showed me Boston was well in the midst of another day of tax therapy. Otis was no longer curious as to what was on the other side of the hill and neither was I. He was safe in the knowledge that he wouldn't be tossed to the side of the road so he could finish his fifth nap of the day. We both knew or at least I sensed that what awaited us now was the real world. I had been on a fantasy ride for so long and had been pampered by good friends but I was now on my own. How I handled this would be a determining factor to many other things. The impolite drivers, the murderers, the rapists, gay marriage, runaway abortions and governments telling us useful idiots that all was OK. This was and *is* what society shows us *is* the real world. Perhaps the question that should be asked is: *is* God real in America? I would see the answer to this come first.

I slowed and took what was the first paved road since taking the dusty back side exit to Maple's yesterday morning. Pavement and asphalt are the signs of modern well intentioned man, the same modern man that showed us signs for strip clubs, discounted tires and Jesus saves *all* within arm's length of one another. A stop sign was just ahead and a road sign telling me where to go to get where I needed to be all with arrows showing me this way and that way. There were so many options and none were pleasing. "Ahh, modern man my little friend." There are signs that tell us how to get where we're going and then charging us to get there but nothing to tell us about our journey. Modern man will charge us for everything we do but will never appreciate our visit; selfishness at its finest is modern man and modern man is the poster child for anti-God behavior.

I drove and drove dreading the gray cloud of modernism off to my left however, *it* was growing larger with each tire rotation. I remembered what Dottie had once said in her mumbling Irish style that life is like a pile of road signs. There is a beginning and an end and unless we follow a specific set of directions there is nothing that guides us on our journey. Perhaps that's why so many people like me have gotten lost on our way. Perhaps that's why Dottie gave me *her* road map in a King James cover? I always wondered what it might have been that guided the explorers before there were maps, compasses or road signs declaring to all that this is a toll road. How did man get anywhere before he had to pay for the privilege of traveling this modern world? In the same vain I wondered what man did before there were any religions, *not* God but religion. Where did man go for direction in life before there were religions? Has God existed long before religions ever came into being? Were religions the roads signs of man's spiritual world? More questions for a melted gray matter already out of business as Boston loomed before me.

Well, I couldn't answer those questions, at least right now and I knew no matter how much I sought guidance from the growing grunting mess next to me he wouldn't be able to shed any light on the issue either. It was also my experience that there was only a small group of people who believed they could answer such timeless Godly questions and they taught up the road in Boston. I said this with a smile of course for those up in Boston only felt like *they* knew the truth about God. The atheists and agnostics were always the first to share their well thought out ideas of God and salvation. In others words the skeptics would always open their mouths first when it came to faith. I could speculate like everyone else who sit in the pews and lecture rooms as to the answer of God. I would only be confused though by those standing up in front of their students and their congregates. The finished products that come out of college classrooms and out of many services each Sunday seem more lost than ever. If they are lost and have the sense that it is the Church that sent them a drift then why *would* they return to the fold?

As I drove more and more into this bastion of modernism I came to see that man actually *confused* man more about God than God confused man about God. This journey, this drive through some of the most pleasant and now some of the ugliest parts of New England would enlighten me. It would help teach me the good and the things that God might consider not so good. It was as I had always sensed up to man to decide what is and isn't good and it is how he is taught that will help us see. If man is taught that immorality defined by God is moral in man's eyes *then* God doesn't matter anymore. If man is shown that cruelty defined by God is protected by man's law *then* God doesn't matter. In other words God shows us what is good and right in this world and man shows us what is bad and evil. I drove on through the light seeing both and leaning toward one.

I have believed that man has always relied on his own free will or opinion and his own intuitive guiding spirit for direction in life. Where has that gotten him though? Where has my free will taken me? How successful has man been in using his own free will? How successful has he been in building a world of peace and love based on his own opinions and world views? I just had to look at the day's headlines to see the answer to these questions. The theory that had been gaining a foot hold in Christian America was that secular man had killed God all over again and this was becoming clearer the older I got. When I was young I had no reason to believe in God or His morals because *I* knew everything so whatever God needed to know about the world He just had to ask me. Youthful, untested ego, God faced no greater test than that especially in *this* modern world, ego was God's primary seed of opposition in modern America. I wouldn't be sorry to see it go that's for sure. The drive became less pleasant as I neared the Webster turn off but I was nearing an understanding that man's free will is the test of what is and isn't evil in this world. I had to learn to see my free will and God's will.

The road was becoming more adorned with signs for everything, the elms were replaced by two for one discount coupons and all you can eat buffets. With hands at ten and two the mental debate had begun as I looked for what Mr. Taylor had suggested. He wanted me to keep my eyes on the side of the road for what may lead me to my next mission. The side of the road had taught me something this morning, it taught me that when the grace and beauty of God is left behind the subtle ugliness of man takes over. The elm trees were replaced by the flash of neon lights of selfish man. If this theory were actually the way it is and has *always* been, then we can say that man has always been at his root an atheist. If man has always had in his nature selfish free will, then it was now clear that man has always been at his root atheistic. If man has always been at his root ungodly, then man has always been at his core evil in nature.

"OK little guy, I guess I have just solved the mystery of the universe, aye." Otis wasn't impressed.

These were largely the political and social views that I had carried for many years and ones that at times made Annie shake her head. She shook her head, not in disagreement but in frustration; how could I believe such things yet give myself little credit for moral strength? I was my biggest enemy, not anyone else. This part of the journey had opened my eyes to the question I had asked for along time. Man was the one who gave the world evil things and it was man who had the opportunity to accept or refute God and morality. Had I accepted or refuted God, was the new question I had to find an answer on this trip, there would be no other time. I guess I turned my back on God when things were bad and credited myself when things were good. When man turned from the world there was only one way to go. When man turned to the world there *too* was only one way to go.

I shook my head knowing that I had just feed the mighty beast named doubt a big heap of Bob's Beef but it was badly needed. I had refuted God and His ways so I could live a life that by all means was an immoral one for many years. Would God forgive me when my day came to leave *this* life? Would He welcome me back into the fold or would He point the other direction? Was he watching me the whole time as I screwed up one part of life after another just waiting for me to come back around? I guess I knew the answers because the day for my calling was coming closer and we all knew it. That day *was* coming closer but I drove closer to the doom that awaited Otis and me and asked aloud, "are all men atheists?" I knew the answer to that as well. If they refuted God and His teachings what else could they be but atheists? With all that we now see in magazines and TV is America now atheist?

Perhaps I was getting too analytical as Dottie had said was a trait of mine and this trait was too unhealthy for me, I thought too much she said. I was too restless. I should just let things be and let people be who they are and I shouldn't define everything. Dottie had reminded me that when we are the most confused it's because we have spent years analyzing the simple things to a point where there is no longer any definition at all. Like marriage and like life society has analyzed both to the point where neither has much meaning anymore. Like God and *like* evil, man has analyzed both to where they are equal in meaning.

I voided Webster from my mental map and took the first on ramp leading east on 495. This may bring me closer to the Boston area but it was a quicker route to southern Maine. I would give up momentary ugliness to reach the prize at the end. I had thought enough for the morning and though it was fruitful I needed a rest for a short time. I knew there would be a rest stop some six or seven miles just ahead and Otis and I would disembark there for a bit. The traffic was as busy as I had thought but less than I had wished for. I needed to see other people so more cars the better If one looked closely they could see a honk there and belching hippy wannabees there and bouncing hip hop everywhere. I continued my analyzing of the question for the ages but was happy with my answer and left it at that for a while. God *was* real and had always been with man but man has not always been with Him, simple.

I heard Maple's voice screeching from the back seat and she was saying, "God and the devil have always been here because there has always been good and bad; it is *man*'s choice what side he wants to join." She would do as she did often and conclude her statement with her favorite term of endearment for me, *dumb ass.*

"OK, Maple I got it. Good job."

The green and white signs told us the rest stop was about two miles ahead and I was sure ready to use the tax payer paid facility for some stretch time. This road was never new, for its always paved over and becomes just covered up faithfulness; paved roads never yield memories as good as the dusty ones do. Modernism has taken away the dust too I suppose.

"God and the devil have always been here, aye little man?"

The words of Maple and those of an old time preacher came to me every now and then. Pastor Kim once said the closer we get to God the more vulnerable we are to the voices of the deep. If the preacher was correct is the opposite of this true as well? If we are close to evil does that mean we are more vulnerable to the voice of God? That's a tough one even Maple couldn't answer, for all we have to do is look at our neighbors. Let's look at the vile acts all around us; can we say they are *close* to God when they seek what they do? Well, little buddy I guess it does come down to believing in good and evil. If we don't believe in good, then evil doesn't exist, aye; both are the same. I was directing my lecture series at Otis who seemed rather dismayed at my endless blather but tolerated the ride none the less. The rest stop was just up a head and I concluded this portion of the debate with, in a society like ours now it's apparent many feel that both God and the devil do not exist. With this supposition morals are lost.

I was about a mile away from the rest stop named for an officer killed in the line of duty just last year a young officer who I hoped knew the difference between good and bad. I was sure he found out first hand what God and the devil were all about that day he was called. The road ahead was highlighted by the dark looming gloom of the Boston skyline and I was a little less apprehensive at having to skirt it. I took the inside lane and saw just up ahead a lone figure walking toward the rest stop's entrance. He was walking slowly with head held low and a back pack with just one strap attached. There was, for a brief moment a question running through my head at just how long this young man may have been on his trek but I didn't suppose it was any of my business. *Look to the side of the road*, the words of Mr. Taylor returned as I passed the young man by.

His solemn desolate figure reminded me of *me* many, many years ago when an aging, chubby plum chaser had succumbed to homelessness and was hitching the back roads of southern Georgia. What a time that was for the lonely and how great the desire to die was. Though he looked like me in many ways, he was nothing like me in so many more. He had just started his journey and I felt mine was nearing an end. When I was his age my choices were few and the faces who called me friend were fewer. As I sped by him his gate was not disturbed by yet another hurried east bound driver. Looking back to those days of mine, I must have been twenty-two or maybe twenty-three and I was a rabid drunk when I had given up on my life. What was *this* young man's story? I had said good-bye to the balance of my years and just walked out and hit the road, I had give up. The mental illness was so great that being a loner was a far greater pleasure than being a member of this world who had only laughter for me.

At that time in my life when I was a wandering soul, it didn't seem like there was much use in keeping my education going strong. I had failed at everything and had no plans to continue the same old struggles. I had been a failure in every aspect of life: money, family, love and God. I saw nothing but continued disappointment ahead of me so I gave up. I was just a young man, troubled beyond one's comprehension and I was seeking a way out. I hit the road and said good-bye to what I had known. I hopped on I-10 and left Florida behind me and I had not thought much about that time since. I long wanted to file it away with a lot of other trash. I would walk and hitchhike most of the way from north Florida through the better part of those Southern states.

What a nasty taste for life I had and I really wanted to seek a slow painful way out of what had been a miserable first few years. My illness compounded my ego and vice versa and both then were beyond retrieval. Severe depression that is not addressed may lead a person to sit and stare out that window not knowing how to fit in. Those years, now far in the past still left a horrible taste and were something I seldom thought of privately for I just shook my head when I did regretful that they had existed at all.

In an attempt to shove those years aside once again, I said to my pudgy co-pilot, "The rest stop is just up there a bit and yah' can go then." Otis sensed he was an excuse and thumped his tail anyway. The road narrowed quickly and with little reflex I pulled up into the rest stop and parked far enough away from any other car so Otis could do his business without the rolling eyes of curious old ladies. He would have to be quick about it for I too, needed to par take of the public accommodations. I opened the door and with little prodding he was about his business with little care for the rolling eyes from Vermont. He did his best to sniff, think and sniff and think for a while as if he was searching for just the best of all places for leaving a deposit for future use.

He found the best place and was true to his promise and made quick work about it and with a prideful look he came back to me. I

Ashley Bay

locked him back into the car when he was ready and I was onto my task. The rest stop was nearly vacant so I felt assured of his safety but I was in and out in relative short order just to be sure. In going back to the car I noticed the soulless hitchhiker coming up the ramp. I took a spot on the hood of the car which provided a nice perch for looking down onto Rte. 495 from this large grassy knoll. I was on my perch overlooking all that went before me and this too reminded me of one former drifter and how he used to sit under the bridges of the South and yell and shake a fist full of vulgarities at all who passed by. I shook my head again in shame. What a time that was how this plum chaser ever survived was not my doing but God's. Having lived through that there is no one that can ever tell me that God does anything by random, He had a purpose for me then though I drifted from it. What a time that was and it lasted so long and how many times had that plum chaser died inside until he rose from the ashes like the Phoenix can't be numbered. The times that I took a steak knife to a wrist only to be so drunk that I cut the steering wheel of the car I called home instead. I *was* the Phoenix. God had saved me but had my life been worth saving? What did he save me for?

The plum chaser of old had wound his way from the shelters of Jacksonville to the fields of Waycross, Georgia. He had slept in rooms of two hundred to three hundred of the most drunk, lice infested, screaming, tremor filled human specimens one could imagine. The plum chaser of old had dipped the well too often and there would be no further help from those who wished him well. When his last eight dollars were used the bus driver said no more this is where you are on your own and he set about the open skies. The plum chaser of old walked and walked till his feet bled from open blisters and his rotten socks had infected the wounds. He slept in abandoned gas stations and in open fields under any restless moon that would have him. The days were long, filled with the laughing unkindness of passing teenagers. The nights were even longer, filled with the screams of all the dying dreams of his youth. But it was there where he slept in a field filled with the creatures of the night that he wondered what had gone wrong. Why was this young man in this condition and where were those that had expressed love for him? Why had affection overlooked him? That thought still banged around as I sat on the hood of this car; why had love never come my way in those early days? I looked over my shoulder and saw the lone figure from the highway approaching the rest room doors. Was he thinking the same things? Was he the plum chaser of *this* day and age?

I brushed aside the much crumpled sad excuse for a mustache and brought Otis out to spend some time on the grass in front of the car. I resumed my reflection once Otis was content with his opportunity for additional sniffing and an opportunity for new friends. I watched him seek higher ground as I returned to the Southern fields. The plum chaser had walked many a dozen in terms of miles and had only the clothes he wished to leave Florida with. He was dirty and filled with lice and his wounds were hidden as well as visible and they were deep widening emotional scars. He had as his possessions a comb and a photo from his childhood that now lies with his mother beneath the naked elm the one that always made her laugh. He also carried a nickel, a Buffalo nickel that once belonged to his father the last earthly tie he had to him. These possessions were his world and all that would be found if *he* were to be found. He slept the sleep only the insane lamented and walked the back roads of small towns so the dead would not be disturbed. The mental games were making him even more depressed and the depression led him down that afore mentioned lamented path to *his* final stone. These bad memories are not healthy for someone wishing satisfaction but they heal those who wish to be healed. I so wished.

Otis was happy and his tail sure showed it as a young child from a nearby car wanted to make a new friend. Otis, doing his duty agreed with the strongest of approvals. Otis was happy for the moment and so was I for I was cleansing myself of the bad that had to go before there was room for the good to grow. I was letting go of the plum chaser once and for all, maybe one of the hardest things I've ever had to do but I was getting close to doing just that. I had done a lot in life but there were so many scars that surfaced at times when I was the most vulnerable. I watched the scene before me unfold. The little girl giggled as Otis said hello the way growing puppies do and her parents a stand offish couple from Vermont asked their young child not to get dirty as she played in the grass with a puppy.

The laughter brought Georgia back to the hood of the car. The homeless plum chaser sought out food and water during the day from

Ashley Bay

those who would seek to pass onto him simple words of kindness and a moment or two that affirmed his importance in God's eyes. He was often left alone on the side of the road waiting for that one sign that good existed and evil did not rule his world. The plum chaser was sure that evil existed for it had tailed him for most of his life and the final, ultimate choice could be one that only evil would supply and *that* choice now awaited him. He just had to take that first step. These roads I traveled now reminded me so much of the tales of the lonely plum chaser seeking a kind heart from among the unknown ghosts of southern Georgia. I recalled now just how lucky he was, lucky *he* found one such voice.

The puppy wandered, the child giggled and the ghosts haunted me a bit more. The story goes on that one of the days as he was nearing the end of the fight for life he was sitting alongside a road without shelter from the torrents of rain. He sat now with nothing but the clothes on his back, the Buffalo nickel and a piece of glass from his last beer. There would be no steering wheel this time to stop the mission he meant to accomplish. He sat and wondered about what life hath wrought and about the dreams that were born in that small town that still nestled beneath the pines. He wondered what his last thoughts would be. What, after all are the last, the *very last* thoughts of those who are about to cross the final bridge? Are those thoughts ones of regret or love or sadness and shame? For him it would be obvious what those thoughts would be, they would be ones of regret. It was obvious he had failed in life and now he must do it a favor and leave the regrets behind. His mind worked without hesitation as he wondered what became of his sisters. What had become of his brothers and his mom who was now but a lonely widow? He sat and asked anyone who chose to listen, why had he not met the woman who would be his till the last day?

My thoughts were shelved momentarily as the character without form came and sat at the picnic table a few paces to my right. The Vermont couple feeling even more troubled viewed the traveler and without hesitation asked that the young girl leave Otis behind and come to the car. I knew what that meant and I knew how *that* felt. The stranger shouldn't be seen or approached, that's what those words meant. The child should be shielded from the likes of the man without form who was just a bit too close for their comfort. I watched as the young elite couple scurried to be on their way. As they packed up and backed out in one steady flow, Otis received a good-bye finger wave from his new friend.

As I watched Otis watch the car, I nodded in the strangers direction He out of uncertainty avoided the eye contact sent forward for the sake of recognition. My thoughts returned to the lonely plum chaser on the Georgia back roads as he prepared for a last task. The questions continued as to why and how come the plum chaser had ended up where he was. All the tears and questions that couldn't be vanquished were left unanswered as he prepared to bid this world a final good-bye. He couldn't do it anymore, fifty miles from anywhere and hundreds more from somewhere else and he wondered if his body would be found and if it were, would they know who he was? Had he mattered? What did those who wished him well call him now?

The plum chaser wanted to know if he should die in a place where he would be found so those that had expressed love would know the results once and for all. Should he die in a place where he would not be found until the creatures of the night had claimed enough of his carcass to make remembering a coin toss? The choice was a life changing one to be sure and one that would be made in a simple stroke. The plum chaser decided that he would cross the road and seek the restroom of a gas station some distance a head whose closeness was marked by a nearby road side sign. The dirty restroom would be the place and only those who sought similar ends used it. The story was told that he went down the banks of this under appreciated state road and crossed the way as the evening rain began to subside. The road sizzled to the sound of the drying rain and the laughs of the passersby.

The young man knew that death was close and that he would soon be wherever the lost souls of man went to be claimed, whether it was Georgia or the Uplands of Rhode Island. The rain was more persistent than the forecast had indicated and the drizzle made a steady gate impossible at times but he took those steps. The young man up to the end wanted to show all those who watched from afar that he had a man like walk and took the steps proudly. The plum chaser walked proudly as he was shown the way by the demons of

Ashley Bay

the deep to his ultimate final resting place. He believed that the rain was a way of washing the dirt from his face so he turned it skyward and he saw the ever so slight emerging moon. He walked and walked some more until the station was just ahead a few hundred yards to his right. He didn't want to be seen by those who thought they ruled his rest so he was to encircle his final home from behind. He began to cross the field that would take him behind the building that he had marked as his final resting place. It possessed no glorious architecture or gothic theme and there would be no choir bestowing a garden of roses when the job was done.

The rain had begun to turn the banks of the ditch muddy so climbing them in a state of ill health was difficult but he persisted. The plum chaser tried once and fell back to the laughs of the passing geniuses. He then tried once again but slipped into a gathering pool of water and was covered with filth that the devil had no need for. He stood and exited the ditch and would approach those who ruled his rest from a forthright position and ask for a key so he could cleanse his flesh. The plum chaser exited the filth of old and staggered into a road no longer full of the laughing ones. He stood at the edge of fleeting reality and was met by a small white car that had nearly clipped him before his self-designated time.

He showed a spirit of severe disrespect for the driver of the most intrusive of careless vehicles. "How dare they?" he asked . The car continued for just a few feet ahead and quickly slammed on the brakes. The lost soul knew there would be a confrontation and he was ready for it. The plum chaser was angry because he had been so rudely interrupted by another car that showed disrespect. The anger was great and the disappointment was even greater for the plum chaser had failed at even this final task, that of ending his life. How could anyone be so rude and keep the lonely from seeking peace? He would show his anger and hope that he could soon be about his goal.

The rain was all but over and the summer heat had turned the moisture of the road into a cloud like curtain. The summer moon still peeked through the mist as if it were watching me it seemed to have a glare that no man could ever dim. The arrogant plum chaser approached the car from the passenger side hoping there would be a snub nose that ended his fight for all the dreams that were never met. He approached with his head aimed at his feet so he could not anticipate what might be awaiting him. As he saw the passenger window come down, he looked in with the cruelest of looks He reached deep down inside for what he knew would be words that would embarrass the saints.

He bent to look inside at the driver who so rudely and without consideration prohibited his glass gashed wrist from bleeding all over the rest room of The Outbound Gas Station. With a nervous attempt to brush the mud and weeks of dust and shame from his shirt he looked in and with a gruff "hey" saw the face of a woman nearly seventy years old. His confusion was obvious for he had prepared to fight the most aggressive of Southern tattooed red necks but instead looked into the face of a bespectacled blue haired grandma. The plum chaser didn't know what to say or where the conversation might go if he said anything at all. Enduring the palpable tension, he saw this woman's purse sitting close to the window where even the clumsiest and most out of shape criminals could make a clean get away.

The arthritic driver said with an aunt like smile, "You look lonely young man. Would you like a ride somewhere?"

The plum chaser was left momentarily silent by such a bizarre request from a complete stranger who had no idea what type of person he had become and who she asked to help.

The plum chasers ghost gave me a break and allowed a return to reality. As I sat on this abused and misused Tempo but my thoughts of the plum chaser were set aside so I could move to a nearby picnic table with Otis in tow. He was enjoying the assignment of sniff and pee on a knoll that we knew we would not see again. Though he was a bit confused as to the sudden departure of his new found four year old friend, he was ready to make another friend. The homeless stranger who had joined us noble ones upon this grassy knoll was a table away smoking a butt that he had found in the grass beneath his table. His age was probably not much older than twenty-five but he could have been a allot younger for street life has a unique way of aging us before our time. He wore a dark t-shirt that had seen far better day's years ago with a logo that had lost its luster. His pants weren't of concern, for at least he had some after all I had seen many a person who claimed the title homeless who was without the proper south of the border attire.

Ashley Bay

His face was unshaven of late but it appeared that some effort had been made to acquire the occasional trim and bird bath wash. Dirt was ingrained and the exhaust from the passing drivers accented the sweat and grease from weeks of thoroughly unwashed skin. He had a look of near defeat and definite weariness but there was a trace of resoluteness, which for all of us is the seed of hope. I saw sitting not far from myself the plum chaser of old. I cast the same look upon him that was cast upon me more than a generation ago or longer. The look had ingredients of pity, peace and ugliness and the first thought that came to my mind was that he should get his act together. Those were the same words often tossed my way well meaning or not. The kinder side of my soul would win this argument for I soon returned to the plum chaser of a generation or more ago.

Otis had found a place of comfort underneath the table and was lying at my feet apparently not in any hurry to resume the front seat towel. I peaked down and was happy to see that his growth was now well underway. He would be healthy and he would be a fine friend for as long as we were allowed each other's company. A quick glance at our neighbor and I was brought back to the tale of the lonely plum chaser on Georgia's back roads.

He had been offered a ride by a little old lady when he was far from nowhere on a lonely last journey. The problem as he saw it was what did *she* want from him? There has to be a catch to this old hags kindness. Why would someone, a complete stranger at that and an old crank bitch of a woman as well, why would she want to help him? She *must* want something. His mental state had been tortured for so long by the demons of the deep that he was mad when someone didn't help and bitter when they did. I recalled that the fear of people was tremendous; I just didn't want to be hurt, I didn't want their sorrowful looks and complaints. The pain was great and I was taken back to the voice of the one who called himself a golden memory as my list was almost done.

    For I've been lonely
    In need of someone
    As though I'd done
    Someone wrong somewhere
    I don't know where

Come lately...

As quickly as dreams end I was back to the picnic table and thought just how many times I had behaved like this young man in front of me. I was so bitter at every aspect of life I demanded and refuted all at the same time. I had believed that people could be and would be nice to me *only* because they had selfish motives and because I assumed their intentions were selfish I formed a negative opinion well ahead of time. I could ask myself the same question: did *I* help people because I wanted to or because I had other reasons in mind? Was I like the little old lady of the plum chaser era or was I like a spoiled little child who would clean his room not because he wanted to but because he would get a reward when he did. The story of the lonely plum chaser continued when he said *yes* thank you he would like a ride. Now as my gray grew would I offer one to this soul?

He got into the front seat at the driver's insistence and not the back which he suspected would be the place of least danger for the driver. This was a kind move because she showed no disgust at his appearance or smell and both were highly objectionable. The car was air conditioned and clean, pleasing to the senses of the plum chaser.

She pulled out onto a road that bore no other encroaching laughers and said, "You looked very lonely I thought you could use a ride somewhere I'm only going up about ten miles but I will take you that far."

He was confused for now the immediate desire to end it all in an out dated and under cleaned bathroom had succumbed to thanking the air conditioner.

He said with a breath catching gasp, "That would be nice. It's been a hard few days."

The smell of cleanliness was such a joy. When one sleeps in the fields with the creatures of the night and when one bathes in rest rooms outdated before Sherman's Southern march, cleanliness is a joy. The car smelled of flowers, jasmine or roses it surely didn't matter it was sanctity enough. There was no sign of the source but it sure was nice. The artificially grateful plum chaser looked anxiously about to see what he could escape with that may have some value. The kindness shown him was fighting with the evil that he still bore witness to.

He wanted to distract the driver so he spoke. "I think I am going to Atlanta, not sure yet, maybe even farther north," he said while looking at the ashtray change in hopes of not causing suspicion.

She seemed to sense his restlessness yet her smile was resolute. "Atlanta is a long ways. What will you do there?"

The plum chaser stopped his roving eyes and sat as if he had been asked to split the atom.

"Do?" "I have no idea. I hadn't thought that far ahead. I just have to get away from where I am," he said with a bit of a nervous laugh. The chaser's goal was not to have to answer such questions but since she so rudely interrupted his gashing he had to think about those questions now as if they were all new. The rain had ceased to be a concern and off to the left we could see the purple and pink that welcomed night and said to the day, *well done noble servant, well done*. The moon still shown lightly through the setting pink and the gray sky was soon to envelope us and all who followed this pair up this once lonely road.

I stumble bummed through a series of gasps over her question and just simply said, "I don't know. I have no idea what I'm going to do." "I used to have some goals but had no luck at getting anything done and family seemed to turn their backs long ago. I didn't seem to live up to *their* expectations."

She drove without much of an expression other than the transfixed smile on the road and an occasional finger of explanation at the setting pink. She let me know in a gentle way that I would never get anything done if I didn't set out to do something. She continued to show examples of how some of the greatest of any profession had far more failures than success's. I just happened to gather all my failures at once.

"I wasn't much good at anything and wasn't shown much in the way of encouragement so here I am." With a graying stare I passed these final thoughts on for this section of road.

The washed up morning hack called golden came back to me and continued with the timeless line of another who was lost.

> And so it was
> That I came to travel
> Upon the road
> That was thorned and narrow
> Another place
> Another grace
> Would save me...

She went on about the shortcomings of Lincoln, Washington, and even the apostle Paul. Her review of historical figures had little to do with my current state of affairs but I believed that she must be at her root correct about her view. I thought to myself how true it is that failures are easy and will never be hard to find and therefore, failures are easily accomplished and require little effort. The difficult road is the road to success and it's not easily walked; it's often thorned and very narrow for the song says so.

She concluded her little talk with, "It's much like belief in Christ. Believing in bad is easy but following and living a life of goodness is the hard thing." She rocked and thumped the steering wheel, being a follower of good is hard job.

The chaser kept his glare steadfast on the passing leftover crops as she went on about the easiness of failure. The driver went on about how tough it is to be good but it is the most rewarding part of life and the reward is, after all, what's worth living for. She went on and on about the points that needed to be clarified between failure and success and good and evil.

I had wanted to end my life. I had wanted to end the pain that life's failures had brought me. I had *had* enough of loneliness and shame but she came along when she did.

> Another place
> Another *grace*
> Would save me...

Ashley Bay

Grace saved me that day. The long hand of God reached into the mind of one of the most wretched of souls and pulled out a heart that was forever changed for the better. God touched the spirit of one who had called the demons of shame and guilt master and God had won. Death was my goal but she had to come by when she had and life was her gift. I had set out to do something that was the greatest of all sins and was stopped from completion by His grace. I had failed at failure but had begun my first steps toward succeeding in life.

"Things have been hard lately and don't know much about starting again. Too many hard times to think about and I'm really so very tired."

His eyes had stopped dashing from side to side looking for things of value and now gazed out the window at the passing the fields of wheat that seemed to line all of southern Georgia. He was shy and didn't want to reveal too many feelings to a stranger, for she too might think him weak. The drive was short but the offer of kindness would be something he would take with him through *his* final journey. He sensed that the ride would soon be ending but she kept driving and kept the pleasant, albeit one sided conversation going.

She kept the traffic at bay and told me, "I'll take you up to a truck stop about ten miles ahead. Maybe you can catch a ride there to Atlanta."

A second kind gesture from this little old stranger whom I knew I'd never see again. She was driving like little old ladies drive and she said in nearly a whisper, "You got to give life a chance, young man. You're too young to give up on God's gift now."

His eyes did not leave the passing wheat as he thought about the meaning of the phrase God's gift.

"I have spent so many years watching the young ones around me give up before their journey even starts. It hurts us old ones, to see young folks waste away."

There was no smile and there was no recognition from him as to her comments for they were just words and they didn't apply to *him*. I just couldn't see myself competing in this world anymore. I was impatient for perfection so I gave up altogether when it didn't happen over night. As he sat in her car, looking out onto a world that I never quite fit into he had no reason to care for God's gift. He was willing to say no thank you, you can take this thing called life back. There wasn't even a thank you for her kindness; there was just bitterness toward the subject of her comments. He didn't want to hear about God moving on or giving love and goodness one more chance. I just didn't want to hear it! I was captive in her car so I was going to hear her words whether I wanted to or not.

This Yankee plum chaser was getting angry at her and at all those who dared preach God to him. This egotistical plum chaser was convinced that only the self righteous dared preach God. I believed that only those who believed they were heaven bound could have the gall to preach Godly ways I was angry at all who laid Gospel at my feet for if they knew who I was they wouldn't bother. The more she went on the angrier he became and the angrier she perceived him to be the further she drove and the more she talked.

Upon the road
That was thorned and narrow
Another place
Another *grace*
Would save me

She was going on and on about the words that had been passed on to her from generations of pastors and lessons learned. She was playing her role and was delivering that message first delivered in Judea, *to* him a wretch on this thorned and narrow road of southern Georgia.

You are the words
I am the tune
Play me...

The little lady and the words of Christ were played so well together that I couldn't help but listen. How dare she tell me about God? What right does she have? Doesn't she know who I am? Doesn't this lady know that I'm not for God and He isn't for me? As our time together passed I think she knew exactly who I was and *what* I was and that's why she was sharing those words of time. What strange and unkind human fool would take time to tell a filthy stranger that

God has a gift for him? These and many others were the thoughts running at jaguar pace through his mind as she began to slow to the hints of road side signs. This kind, elderly woman would drive him nearly twenty miles to the West Folkston Truck Stop, well out of her way and she didn't seem to mind much. This kind, blue haired woman from a time and place of eons past showed more spirit than anything a soul a third her age could ever muster. The plum chaser condemned her for all she offered and resented that *he* had been her good deed for the day. The confused and lost young man vented some more but the broken glass would be picked up no more as the ride came to an end.

To those who lived in Folkston proper, West Folkston was trailer trash central. These small back water Southern hiccups of a town were scattered ankle deep from Alabama to where I would soon rest. This particular little town was a place where red neck wannabees would go to seek their training and grow old as friends with those they once lamented. The little cross road was a location where trucks from north and south would continue east and west so *I* did have a better than average chance at a ride to anywhere but where I was. The three or four red light societal backwash was where the odds were pretty good that the plum chaser could lie himself into a ride farther north and I think she knew that too.

My vehicular host saw the end was close and began to slow her pace of scriptural teachings. The traffic was a little tougher now and she pulled into a spot close to the restaurant that is the central point for truck stops like this one all across the nation.

Without losing her smile she said, "Here you go young man this is the best that I can do for today."

I was double checking the travel worthiness of my brown bag when she reached over the visor and handed me ten dollars. With a voice that echoed from generations ago she said, "Take care of yourself you'll be needed someday."

I had not held a ten dollar bill in so long and especially one that was a gift that I looked at it as if it were alien.

"Thank you. It's nice of you. I will try to get better; it's so hard though."

With that he, *I* exited her car with a sense of incredible guilt and shame mixed with what I now recognize was expectation of me from a stranger. I thought she expected me to live on and that through her God expected nothing less as well. I nodded and mumbled what I thought would be interpreted as a final thank you and took a few steps toward the front double glass doors. I stopped and turned for a wave but found her car was gone as quickly as it had come upon me. I had never asked her name nor did I know where she was from nor did I ask to return the money someday. How rude I was to the woman who had just saved my life.

The plum chaser was left standing in the parking lot of this truck stop a first hand witness to goodness. That memory has never left him, it has never left *me*, what a blessing that woman was. If it weren't for her at that time and at that place in my life all that has come forth from a different man would never have been. Fate. Her time with me was short but it forever changed who I became. The time and patience of a stranger, an unlikely stranger at that, was so important that it can't be expressed in mere secular words. My thank you to her, whoever she was has been expressed in the things that I can no take pride in but which I now do in *His* name.

As I looked at the 495 traffic I had to admit that I believed that those times that I considered good and rewarding were few but they were glorious none the less. I looked at Otis, the victim of my recent change of heart who just gave me a look that showed unconditional appreciation and expectation. A second thought came my way: maybe things aren't that bad after all. I had been through allot in life but I persevered. I failed at many things still but learned to appreciate the small things that life gave me. Otis was growing but still seemed bothered by the comings and goings of the big trucks and the growing amount of noise throughout the rest stop. A scratch behind his neck and I informed him, "Probably time to go, little man."

I stood and picked him up and went back to the nearby Tempo. I plopped him into the front seat where he would have a sense of certainty. The words of all my guests from previous hours came back to me, look for the good and look for the opportunity to be the good that others are looking for. The goodness that others are looking for is the grace God bestows on us, at least according to Maple and I bore witness to that many years ago on a rainy summer's day in Georgia. If one is not good he must then in fact, be seeking selfish or un-Godlike things and therefore be emblematic of evil. The line between the two was now clearly drawn by my own experiences. The useful, though confusing statements from my guests had to be put to use at some time and *now* was one of those times. I walked over to the wandering soul who sat a picnic table or two away from us and asked if he needed a ride somewhere. He tossed me the same look the plum chaser tossed that little old lady a generation or more ago. The look on his face was one of frustration and how dare you interrupt what my ultimate plans are.

The wandering soul took a final few puffs on a butt that had none left in the first place he tossed it some distance and kept an eye toward 495. I knew that stare, I knew what he was thinking and it was now my turn to share a ride. He was more jovial than the plum chaser ever was when they walked the same forgotten back roads. He had glasses that had been taped far too many times to count and his face hid what the chaser knew was a deep dark depression.

His eyes still had some luster but the cloud of doubt was circling quickly and it wouldn't be too long for him either.

"I am going up toward Framingham. Can take you up that way?"

He sat finishing a second butt that could barely hold a light and had yet to meet my stare with one of his own. This one he had found with others he placed in an overused baggy tucked in a simple brown bag at his feet. I was happy to have a chance to try the role that God seemed to hold open for me with the words of a stranger. *I* was now needed.

"Framingham, yeah that's OK, not too far from where I'm going."

He stood as if leaving a successful job interview and with a respectful effort brushed the fragments of month long residue build up from his pants. I guess God needed me for this task at least.

The day was moving along nicely and I did need to pick up the pace a bit to stay on schedule and reach the shore just past Wells in a day's light. My passenger rolled up the much crumpled bag and made his way to the passenger door of the under appreciated white Ford Tempo. He waited for me to enter first and then he got into the front seat. Recognizing a new guest Otis was soon at the rider's feet. The look that he had after the first few moments showed the same satisfaction with the air conditioning that I had those many years ago. He breathed in deeply the air that he thought of as fresh as we backed out and made our way back down onto 495. The overwhelming exhaustion that follows those on the streets is so great that total sleep and near collapse comes when the slightest comfort is found. I could sleep the sleep of the ages when I was given just a few hours of uninterrupted and safe rest. My passenger must have felt the same way.

The young man closed his eyes and laid his head back on the rest as we exited the rest stop. "I'm sure tired," rumbled on out of him.

With an easy traffic merge, I found a desire to begin a conversation begun a generation ago in rural Georgia; it was now my turn to continue it. I had become the unknown little old lady and the new guest was my test subject. I must recognize him as an important part of this world and that he *too* had a role to fill.

"Where you coming from?"

The question went unanswered till he simply muttered, "Down South."

I wanted to identify with him in some way so I replied, "I spent a lot of time down that way in my younger days, most of my college was in Tennessee."

No answer, just a nod and a lost stare out the window as he watched the fields of western Massachusetts go by.

"Where are you heading, anywhere in particular?"

No answer came from the passenger. Otis was watching both of us not sure if he was going to get an answer either so he turned his head back towards me waiting for the next move. I let the traffic dictate if there was going to be any conversation between us but discovered it would be Otis who would get the ball rolling. The growing furry mess knew how to get the needed attention and with a bowed, droopy face he went to work.

The young man reached down and with a scratch behind the abundant folds of ears he said, "Beagle, aye?"

Ashley Bay

"Yeah, his name is Otis."

A smile came across his face. "Otis is a great name for a dog, like the Andy Griffith Otis."

"Yeah, this one drinks toilet water though."

The conversation was awkward and directionless but the silent pane between us was cracked by the poop producer. The rain that had been promised by the last several golden jockeys was now hit and miss and probably a complete miss altogether. As we started to drive farther east toward Boston and the coast the sun shown through a rear window and the gray mist from man's modern liberalism was now before us in the Boston sky. I had to admit that at times the breeze was always nice as the fall season came and summer, especially near the ocean, was never that bad either. The torturous threat of Massachusetts rudeness could be set aside by a few moments with the breezes of fall and drives like this.

"What's waiting for you up north, anything good?"

My young passenger just shrugged and said, "Some family up New Hampshire way but don't know where though. We haven't talked in a long time. They gave up on me long before I ever did."

He continued his scratch of those big ears. "My family was never that close, seemed to grow apart when we grew up, grew up and grew apart." He looked back at the mess on the floor and segued; "He's cute, do you know how old he is?"

"No, not really. He's been with me for a while. I never had a birthday party for him."

As I let the road dictate the mood my young passenger had taken up the conversational duties. Talking had never been a strong suit of mine and I knew I would soon run out of words if I was left a solo act. I never could find enough to say to an automated teller so I was happy he started the ball rolling.

His statement that his family grew apart was certainly one that I could agree with it was sad but it was so true. My brothers, sisters and I have had plenty of silent years. Though, as we age and as the years behind us have begun to out number those before us we have grown closer. At times when we gather we sit and dwell on all the bad days behind us but add more to the stack as we say farewell. Whether it's ego or unrealistic expectations of each other, we have let the years go by and we are now just nice to meet yah' strangers.

The guest had searched the ashtray for a smoke and then asked more directly. I said I didn't imbibe but I would be happy to get him a pack or two at the next exit. Whether it was a good gesture, I don't know but it was received as a kind one from my passenger and he said so. The next exit was whatever one I chose and I now battled the thoughts that encircled my guest. Should I ask him why he is alone on this part of the highway? Should I get too intrusive in his life so he would get as angry with me as the plum chaser had with the kind elderly women in southern Georgia? Should I just shut up and take him where he wanted to go and leave him to the whims of others?

I was attentive to the road but tried to be a pleasant host as well. I think Otis was doing his best too though he wasn't sure what his role was for this part of trip, he faked it pretty well.

"I am heading up to Maine for a day or two. Otis has never been there so thought he'd like a trip to the ocean side."

Another nod and a hushed, "Maine's nice," as he reached to scratch the young one, himself a four footed, floppy eared hitchhiker named Otis.

The traffic was growing somewhat frantic as we neared the area of the state when the lunch time Boston inbound was becoming a greater pain. I usually kept conversation to a minimum when dealing with such delightful highway partners as inbound Boston traffic but remained attentive. My passenger was awfully quiet as had been the plum chaser many years ago and I did wonder what the little old lady would have said back then if she were here now. Should I ask or shouldn't I? Was he going to respond respectfully or shun the words of kindness as I had?

Would he get ugly if I asked questions that may be over the line? Acting on a hunch I asked, "Are you feeling OK, you're lookin' a bit gray. It's easy to get sick when you're out here for a while."

He went back to watching the fields as they flew by. "I'm OK, just real tired yah' know?"

Ashley Bay

I nodded in agreement while switching lanes for the next available exit. I knew the answer OK was an answer that was given when the real answer was too long to describe.

"Yup, I know, I surely do."

We had gone perhaps fifteen miles or so from the rest stop when I took an exit to a mini-jiffy named for a Tiger or at least at one time it was. We pulled in to a row of several cars from several states all filled with dogs and kids.

"Come on, let's get you some smokes, aye?"

A smile was his thank you.

"Get what ever you want to eat or drink too."

As we exited I noticed that we were parked next to a car load from Vermont all shapes, sizes and screech levels and whose nose was already thrust high.

"Thanks," he said and made a picked up pace grasp for the double glass door. Otis watched with anticipation as we got out of the car for he knew as I did that he would be the beneficiary of the chocolate hitchhikers from a day old Boston creme.

My new friend asked how many and I said three of this and a couple of that and told him to be sure to grab some water. There was a mind burning memory of going days or even weeks without water when I was on the streets. I had gone so long without water that when a glass finally came I needed to ask for help in holding the glass. He nodded a thank you that was mixed with a hint of embarrassment for needing help with the basics of life. The visit was short and as we rejoined Otis to the watchful gaze of the Vermont squealers he grabbed the book bag that he had been carrying and put all but a pack of smokes deep inside. I broke a Boston creme a bit and gave Otis what he expected. I looked his way and the other and made sure all were ready and we were back out onto 495 in a short burst.

I again asked what he had already answered once. "Any family around that you might want to call?"

"Nope, none close anyway. Some up north but not worth seeing, that's what they tell me anyway."

I shook my head knowing exactly what he meant. "Life goes by quick and it's always good to try to make things right because someday we all wake up dead. Then what do we say?"

"I don't think many would notice if I lived or died right now. Can't turn to many more for help. All I get is snap out of it or grow up or a man has to be a man." The passenger popped the smokes and talked to the window.

I could never understand how families just simply say no and move on as if they were all that mattered. He lit up one of his discount smokes.

"Depression, I guess is something I was told I needed to snap out of," he said.

He rolled down the window and asked if he could smoke after he had already lit the first of the pack. I agreed, not for my pleasure's sake but for *his* comfort level. If smoking would help him open the door to what might be inside then maybe, *just* maybe he would give himself a second or perhaps third chance. I didn't expect to be a miracle worker but somebody would be for him why not me. Just as the old woman did for me years ago I wanted to help open the door for him.

However for him as with me he had to take the first step, *he* had to want to recover. The Framingham exit was said to be eight miles up and a motel named for an even number was just another five miles past that.

I paid closer attention to the empty road ahead of me and I shared my story just a bit. "I was in a similar state a good number of years ago and was ready to die. I had given up on life and all the things that were possible for someone my age. All the dreams I had dreamt when I was a little boy never came true and all the cars and women and all the money just never happened like they did in my dreams. I was the poster child for depression and bad luck and my family had said more than once *to hell with him*." I wanted him to know that I had, in some form seen a similar fate early on. There was a silence lasting for me a few passed cars and for him a few long drags on the first of the pack. "The only way I could have ever moved on was saying goodbye to everything and everyone. I did that and sucked it up, it was one of the hardest things. Even after a period of years approaching my family was still difficult because I knew they'd never believe it."

He smoked as if he were starving for what the Camel had to offer for long drags were all he had. I continued my sermon as he puffed away and as Otis sneezed in disagreement with the new odor.

"The problem was that I had not separated reality from my dream world and I had wanted my dreams to come true because I didn't have to work for them; *they* were just there, *they* came without my asking. Dreams were always easier than reality because they could change every night so my ambitions could change every night."

As I took the time to switch lanes, I noticed a small smile appear as my guest looked out at the last of the passing Massachusetts wheat fields. The smile stayed till he noticed that it was now less than five miles to the Framingham exit. I continued to confuse the obvious to some yet complicated for him.

"We don't get disappointed by our dreams. They don't cheat us or lie to us and they can take us places that our own lives often can't."

A slight pause as a driver up a head couldn't decide which lane could slow the rest of us down the most and decided that he best pull over to think about it.

"I had to move on into reality and for the lost ones, like I was that sometimes is very hard."

With a squinted look, one could see deep into the horizon and see the smog and yuck coming from the bastion of abortion and gay marriage, Boston. The frequent traveler who possessed a conservative nature knew that just off to its left was the bastion's devilish offspring Cambridge and both were too close for my liking so I gripped 10 and 2 tighter.

He had finished most of the smoke and tossed it out the window. Otis had long since finished his chocolate delight and was anticipating my next move. There is nothing as nice as the look on the face of pets, confused *yet* excited as to what they may see next. Otis could pass onto me the looks that expressed a thousand emotions but none of them greed or hate. He wondered if I would and I wondered if I should and at the next stop of course, I did as another Boston creme failed to make the journey safely for any amount of time.

I had discovered long ago that Otis was a true fan of anything that had even the remotest chance of being sweet.

My canine confession was broken by the words, "Dreams are cool though," the long awaited reply from my passenger and his tone was an educated one. "Dreams are seldom edited and I'm seldom disappointed unless they're interrupted."

I had a smile that seemed as if I was born with it and couldn't remove it with the best of efforts. I think he understood what I was saying. Once he understood, I think *I* at last understood the words of all my friends, look for good and share it and the love of Christ will have been spread. The day was now approaching the post noon hours and the gap to Framingham had narrowed. I asked where he thought he might like to get out and he said anywhere up ahead would be fine.

I had hidden from him a motive for this particular exit. I had seen for many miles now the large roadside billboards for Framingham's First Baptist Church. Annie and I had attended services there a couple of times and I grabbed the exit for the church would be within view of our separation. True to form, I saw at a distance of a few hundred yards the steeple of one of the finest churches in the area. First Baptist was one of those churches that had a nice broadcast every Sunday which Annie and I listened to when we were on the road to elsewhere sometimes.

Close to the church, in sight anyway, was a mini-jiffy so I pulled in there and said to my guest, "I guess this is it, aye?"

"Yeah, this is fine."

As quickly as it had started the ride was over and I believed I had made a positive impact in this young person's life. He gave a quick look about and seemed pleased for his setting was shaded with a couple of picnic tables across the road from the church.

The tables were important to me for I had placed them there years ago for the weary traveler such as my guest. He was busy making sure his bags could make another round of gravel crunching and I

Ashley Bay

reached above the visor. I grabbed what cash had been stashed there and gave it with pleasure to my young friend.

"Here, you'll want to take this. You'll need it before all is said and done. I'm talking to you like someone else did many years ago to me. Go take a seat over there at those tables and just think about things for a while. There is no hurry to be wrong and just remember you'll be needed some day."

He thanked me and exited heading to the double doors of yet another nameless mini-jiffy. The time together with a young forgotten stranger was a good one, at least for me for perhaps I had made amends and passed on good will all at the same time.

As he was nearing the doors, I asked. "What's your name?"

With a head hung rather low he said, "Paul" he said.

"Paul," I said with a widening smile not in fond remembrance of an uncle but rather of an apostle who became such a voice for Christ only after being on the road for many, many days. In a final utterance to the empty front seat, "A great name, that's a name of a man that God changed for the best of *all* man kind, so take care of yourself." He nodded and disappeared.

I was back out onto the main way when aloud I recalled. "Take pride in your name, you'll be needed." I watched as he made his way inside the mini-jiffy and if I would have stayed just a bit longer I would have seen him turn around to see an empty parking lot. The words of Maple came back like a board to the head: look for the chance to do well and to be the good others are looking for. What a few moments that God had given me this day and I knew I had done my best to do what He wanted done.

This was one of those opportunities I long remembered as being a turning point in my life. I helped someone just because I believed it was the right thing to do and I wanted nothing in return. It was in between so many other chances forgotten but *this* one stayed well entrenched till the last day. I saw, at last that good and bad did exist and both were at our finger tips any time we wished to activate them. The bad and good that impacts other people are also at our disposal; that's just how much we can impact our fellow travelers. I swung around in the church parking lot and saw there was a back entrance to 495, which I took rather than be conventional. I was but a few miles from the motel with an even number and I was ready to lie down for awhile. The day may have just started for many others but mine had moved so fast and was at its end. There had been so much recollection and feigning that my mind and spirit were now very tired. I was feeling tired and looked I thought far older than when I had begun my journey.

The days too were moving by at a pace that I couldn't keep track of. I was older in so many ways now not just in looks. My bones had become frail, my hair more gray and my vision questionable for night time use. Otis too looked older certainly fatter than when our journey had begun. He was likely to soon sit on his stomach and not the part of his body that God had intended for such purposes. The traffic was getting heavier and the smog from the distant Boston skyline was growing in its threat so a quick nocturnal landing was required. A decent meal and a good night's rest would do wonders for me especially if it was anything like Mr. Taylor's Malachi Lodge. There was a chance to drive some distance past our chosen respite but not today. There would be a chance for further thought but not right now either. I just wanted to lie down for awhile and reflect on all that had been accomplished.

Otis had reclaimed his rightful place in the car and made a half hearted search for his towel a search that he soon threw aside in exchange for rest. As I neared our stop I wondered what the young man would do. Was there anyone looking for him? Was *he* looking for anyone? Were there brothers and sisters who were now strangers and no longer heroes? Where would he go and what would he become? Those were the same words asked in silence buy the little old lady many years ago on the back roads of Georgia. That choice I guess was not mine to make, it was his. He too had free will and he could always say no to what is put in front of him just like I had. I had said no to choice and opportunity for many years myself but I hoped that his fall from grace would not last nearly as long as mine had. A question I had always wanted to ask Dottie frequently was: is man's selfish free will man's way of saying no to God's wishes? I said no to God and that's why I could not recognize Him at times. The barrier was now though crossed and I sought Him more.

Ashley Bay

The free will debate had been part of my inner recesses for a long time and now it came for a visit one more time. If man didn't have free will what would we be like? Would society be what it is today if free will were just a fantasy? Is free will God's way of separating the wheat from the chaff, the good from the evil and the righteous from the selfish? I kept my hands at ten and two and explored my new understanding of free will just a bit longer as the gloom cleared. This had to be the answer I looked for all these years, for if man had no free will then we all would be evil or righteous. Man has the choice to be just as good and just as evil as he wishes, it is *our* choice, only ours. It's also our choice how to respond to those traits as well. We can choose to live to the best of our ability the life that Christ teaches us or we can live a life of immoral behavior and ask forgiveness seconds before the dirt's shoveled on our face. What life path is more sincere? Will God notice? We can also choose to live a life that is opposite of the one Christ wishes for us that too is also our choice. We can have at the center of this life sexuality, immorality, selfishness and an attitude of elitism in all that we do.

I drove and drove further still pondering the questions that theologians for centuries have asked and in so doing missed the exit for the even numbered motel. I was not stressed or full of anxiety at my oversight for my spirit was becoming calm. I knew it was calm because I had listened and helped someone in His name. I felt good for helping a lost soul at this point in his confused search. I was patting myself on the back and I didn't want to do that too much for I could overdose on that as well. The road was crowded and filled with anxiety from any number of states but I flowed with the wind and not the traffic. The traffic and Boston skyline heightened what anxiety I did have and so I chose the next immediate exit rather than let the pot boil out of control. I prevailed as I went a few miles more and took exit 16B marking the best possible directions to Jack n' Jill's Motel and Restaurant. A place like that I thought didn't sound like they would object to a fat beagle named Otis spending the night.

The motel was but a mile or two at the most off 495 in a nice shady part of what may have been at one time a well traveled service road. A couple of cars out front and the old neon sign without the flickering O that called visitors like Otis and me for their thirty-nine dollar special. The restaurant may have been pleasant at one time but it looked now as if that time was a generation ago. I parked off to the right of the main door so if Otis was prohibited, he would be snuck in later unbeknownst to the proprietor. I went inside and the cling-cling-cling of the little bell above the door that brought a delayed "be right up" from the back.

I leaned on a counter that had the usual items such as a map that highlighted all the tourist traps in Massachusetts and a little rack of fliers as well as a stack of tracts from Framingham's First Baptist Church. I studied the olive drab curtains, the carpet that matched and furniture that was as old as the little lady that who made her way up from the cavernous back side of the motel.

"Hi, I need a room for one person for one night."

"You talk too fast, young man. Slow down and one more time for me aye I'm an old woman and don't care about anything too much."

I stared and smiled and used a bit more of a deliberate tone during the second round of my nocturnal request. She shuffled for a registration slip and gave me a pen from a can marked Bob's Dog Food and I heard a couple of snippy ankle biter barks from in back. "OK son that's forty-four altogether and I won't charge you for your dog. He must be small." If he poops, you clean it. The room will air out." She mumbled some words that Webster couldn't make out and continued with "People make more of a mess and stink than do most animals, yah' know."

I was making out the little slip and she looked over her specks and smiled and with a Cheshire cat grin said, "Everyone who wants to hide a pet parks right where you did. I learned that long ago."

I nodded and smiled, "OK you're right. He's Otis a beagle. Don't know how old now. If he poops, I'll clean it. He's pretty good though."

She took the cash and hunted for the change. "Beagles `day ain't real dogs, kinda' pretenders is all."

As she shuffled for a couple of dollars I nodded and knew I had heard comments like that somewhere before but couldn't put together the when and where.

"Yeah, he's a wannabee for sure."

Ashley Bay

I handed her the registration, sliding it her way as she handed over the key to room 2. I thanked her; she returned a polite nod and wished us a good night's sleep.

"No rush to get out tomorrow, out young man, take your time."

There were no window tappers at the car and Otis was sincerely happy to see me upon my return for he too was anxious as to whether or not this room had Nick-at-Nite. The room was nearby so with a turn and jiggle we were quickly inside. I was happy that the air conditioning was on and Otis was happy to begin a new round of sniff this and sniff that. The room was scented with Lysol and it was musty but it did have more than just the one flip flop over used pillow on the bed; it *had* two. Otis sat just inside the door and watched me as in one swoop I grabbed my bag his food and Dottie's newspaper. I walked back inside and with a wig wag of his tail I closed the door for the night.

I prepared a bowl for my young friend and after a long, long shower I began to study the face of the man in the mirror. I hadn't taken the time to analyze the face that looked back upon me in many years. I hadn't shaved in awhile and the face that was beneath the built up whiskers had aged significantly since I last looked at. The lines under my eyes were deep and dark and the gray was growing by the day from temple to temple. I wanted to wash the wrinkles away but saw that there were only deeper, darker, older ones beneath them. My eyes were weaker than I had understood them to be and they had less shine than that of a younger man. I looked with some disappointment at the man in the mirror and asked what had become of his youth. I had drunk and fought and lied my way through so many of the years and when I was near the end God gave me Annie. I had wasted so much and now that my years were closing, the years that were left to enjoy and share life were few in number.

I knew when I was a little boy that the mirror is a time portal for all the souls who had at one time or another stared at the silent observer and wondered the same as I had. When I was a boy I looked into the same portal of *that* generation and I dreamed of what I would someday be. I looked at the young pudgy face of a little boy who had dreamed of being a cowboy and wondered if he would ever ride the Great Plains. He wanted to ride the range and save the settlers from the Indians who only sought their end and quash a life of peace. The little boy wondered as he stared into the mirror just what *this* cowboy would accomplish. The drama and the adventures were all about the young man as he escaped the sadness of his day by taking the simple journey by the hanging time portal.

The graying man of *this* day looked deeper into his frame and looked for the dreams of the far away plum chaser. The little boy had wanted so badly to live the adventures of the cowboy and now as an old man, I looked back upon that dream. When I was young I wanted to be a cowboy but as I grew dreams of adventures were replaced by fear, loneliness and regret. Now as an old man and the regret filled years were more or less behind me I reviewed the dusty trail. As an aging man I can say I have climbed the Eiffel Tower, the Statue of Liberty and the volcanoes of Central America. I have sat alone at a homeless man's funeral, I've held a dying baby and I've saved a runaway. I have shaken the hand of Ted Williams, the *same* hand that shook the hand of Babe Ruth. I have walked the beaches of Normandy and the peach orchards of Gettysburg. As a man I have met five presidents, head butted Eric Clapton and *I've* kissed Cher. I have ridden a camel and an elephant and I've delivered a litter or two. I have slept in a Governor's mansion, in the finest Paris hotels and in the open fields of Georgia. The trail was now narrowed and the Great Plains were in fact behind me. A gentle breeze touched me as I smiled back into the mirror at the graying old man for I realized that it's a cowboy I've always been.

I drew back from the man in the mirror and was pleased that after all is said and done I had achieved a boyhood dream; I had lived as a cowboy after all. Why had the years gone by so fast and why had I been so wrong about so much were the next questions. Could I make up for it before my time ran out? Did it matter if life went by quicker than we wished or should our death be what we should worry about? I rested my hands on the sink and took a closer look at the face again that would never be all that his youth had dreamed of. Would I be a dad? The answer was *yes*, history would show me I would call a little one daughter and four I would call son. I shook my head in a combination of disappointment and distress at the unraveling of time. I stood back and looked deeper into the mirror and this time I saw my father, brothers and uncles and wondered how many times had they stared and wondered the same things. Had I done well? Would I be missed? The shaking head of distress became once again that of doubt and shame and I turned quickly from the face in the mirror as if offended. I didn't want to face those fears anymore; there were better ones in me and I was just beginning to find them.

I went to the bed and was met by the curiosity of Otis as he sat waiting for his towel to be tossed in a place he could claim for the night. The hours had ticked by at such a pace that morning and night seemed to have blurred and the blur helped me ease the tension between the two. The recollection of the day was not on the morning with Mr. Taylor nor with the young stranger. It was with who I had become the boy in the mirror from so many years ago was the seeds for a good and decent man. The lessons that I had learned through all the trial and errors of my journey had in the end paid off. The young man who had shared the most recent of trips with me was the beneficiary of the seeds of good implanted in my spirit. I settled atop the covers and satisfied the silent wish of Otis and the appreciation of good was quickly sifted through.

The mind of mine which had been through *so* much, had once again replaced the good with the remnants of doubt and shame. They are mighty foes for the weak but I knew that they would be overcome more easily each time. I also knew that I might have to face these foes just a while longer but not to long. The mind of madness that I had so long considered traditional, lamented everything good and positive that could happen to me. The mind played this game the same way when it came to goodness lamenting the bad things that our conscience insisted on. In other words our good nature will with the prick of the spirit question our goals when we go astray. Astray no more, I grabbed the paper that was now two or three days old which I had pilfered from Dottie's stoop. Lying back I fluffed for comfort the pillows as Otis jumped seeking his spot near my feet.

The sun was going down as best it could and what was left of it was making its way through the sliver of curtain. Maybe it was a street light or moon or some form of other light. I laid the paper across my chest and made an effort to read the box scores now a couple of days old. Baseball was once a great game but it had become the poster child of greed and selfishness and those who played often saw the fans as a mere inconveniences. When I was young, a player was with one team their whole career now a player is up for bid and loyalty was is just the almighty dollar. Where are the Brooks Robinsons and Duke Sniders of this day and age? I wasn't a baseball fan but was always amused at how Dad always followed the Sox and how year after year he always said, "Next year *is* the year." That year did come for some but for others it was just too late. Baseball is emblematic of the nature of America at its root; it was still good but on the surface greed and selfishness had become the dress code.

I was disgusted anew for the news was all the same this for sale, that person arrested and Hagar the Horrible never winning a fight. Flipping and folding the paper so I could better read the front page I again laid it across my chest. My eye sight was growing questionable without the benefit of a strong Edison and well groomed bespectacled adornment. Otis was content and I was getting there but the demons of the deep kept the pinpricks of my mind alive and well. Had I done enough for the young man? Did I provide enough support so he could pick up his own mantle? Were my words the right ones? This was the new game but it ended quickly because I had made the effort to be kind and show goodness. I wanted the debate to be on not what I had done wrong but on what I had done well and so the clouds lifted.

The room was one that didn't include a remote control for obvious reasons and the television could only be turned on and over by the old fashioned way. I guess the room would remain silent, for the ambition to get up was gone and I didn't want to bother Otis so I would leave the TV off for *his* benefit. I needed my glasses which were firmly ensconced in a place somewhere in the Tempo so visual comfort could wait as well. My eyes had been getting bad for awhile and my youthful pride hammered away at the common sense that insisted on wearing them. What I did read as I picked up the paper was the scriptural thought for the day:

"Don't go into battle without the breastplate of righteousness."

That was a head scratcher, the breastplate of righteousness. What a great vague thought for the confused to contemplate. What could that possibly mean? I stopped my eternal sarcasm for I knew the answer. Pastor Kim from a million sermons ago drilled that into us pack of impatient eight year olds. Righteousness is the underlying message that comes from all the teachings within the words of Christ. He expects us to face our demons of the deep with the breastplate of righteousness in other words face our demons with the truth of Christ. The truth of Christ was *and* will always be rooted in love and mercy. The pastor had tried to teach us plum chasers that we would be tested by the demons of man but the love of Jesus would win in the end. The pastor had tried to teach us that the demons will fight and they will win many battles until we get tired of them It is when we get tired that we reach out to the one who can defend us and that is Jesus Christ, the breastplate.

Jesus was our defender when it came to the demons. He knew man was at his basic nature is too weak to fight the evil that man himself can muster up. I was giving a "figures" head's wag to the scriptural quote because I had carried this paper with me for a couple of days now maybe more and when I was ready to read it this was the first thing I read.

I didn't want to pay a great deal of attention to thinking about this quote so I asked, "Maybe I should turn on the tube aye boy?"

The breastplate, what an antiquated tool good for many a Roman but what about all who face the modern battles? The paper credited no pastor or scriptural text but it did seem to me that it had to be somewhere between Genesis and Revelation. What is a breastplate for and why was it used? The Romans used them and so too the American Indian. They were used to protect individuals from incoming arrows and other attacks from their enemies. The demons of the deep can thrust many an arrow such as shame, guilt, doubt and regret so the *breastplate* was as pertinent today as a millennium ago.

The breastplate protected the soldier from the enemies of their era so how did it apply to us today? I grabbed a pillow and rolled it up to better prop my head. From what did we need protection from at this time and in history that our military couldn't handle? It didn't make much sense for me at this time of day as my demons were winning the fight and I was defenseless against that at least for now. I shoved the paper to the other side of the bed and it landed front page up as I fell victim to the nocturnal call. The enemy I faced was far different from the spears of the Trojans thrust in the direction of the encroaching legions. They had breastplates that would fend off the weapons of their days and I guess God was in His way giving us weapons for our days. My mind was growing weak and susceptible to what might be nearby and what was nearby was a story days old and on the front page of the paper.

My eyes dodged back and forth over all that I had experienced this day and all other of recent memories and they landed on a far off shore. The shore was one that had played many a joyous role in my life and one I had wanted to see again before it was too late. I stood there anxious to know if my boyhood home was at all close to where I now stood. It wasn't the home of my youth was gone for good. I was no longer disappointed and took upon my shoulders the joys from youthful expectation as to what the road ahead may now hold for me. Sleep called me and I wanted another night's rest to ease the stress of all the harm I had done to myself. God called me years ago to share His message, He had been waiting and I had now answered His call.

Chapter 6
These Feet

    As with us all we seem to be the most vulnerable to the soul's voices the very moment before sleep takes us away for the day. Did being this vulnerable mean that we listen to *their* voices and later adhere to *their* messages? We yawn and our eyes are watery as sleep comes but the fight lingers, the nose itches and the body makes noises better left unmade. We kick our legs to get the last couple of end of the day stretches out of us. We yawn and yawn some more and the highlights of the day have as much value as the day's undone to-do lists. I rolled to stare momentarily at the shadows dancing back and forth across the dimly lit ceiling; my breastplate was gone and the demons of the night rolled on in.

    In what seemed to be mere seconds I was standing in repose to the sounds of a trickling brook. It was a brook whose locale could have been an arm's length or a day away. The sound of the water never increased in volume; it was constant and of low flow. As I stood on this road, there was a distant sound that grew stronger as I raised my head from a shameful slouch to one of an attentive intention. I was determined to find out just what this sound was and where it was coming from. What the sound was could only be surmised through the use of a more attentive ear and a couple of curious steps. As I stood a bit more restless than I was before, I guessed the sound to be coming from an owl; it was an owl making his call. Why an owl? What a blessing this creature is for a silent night. They're one whose face is almost never seen and whose home was never knocked from the perch by a plum chaser with a persistent aim.

    I stood restlessly not knowing the direction of the brook or the song of the owl who had been calling many home on this same road for as long as this water ran on. The road was draped with a moist cloud like curtain and it reached out to all who chose to travel its course. The voices of covenants thousands of years old seemed to echo through the song of the owl and land at a point not too distant from me. I turned to make my way to wherever the road might lead me and away from my boyhood home. *It* had been set aside with the wish of a loving father and the greeting of one happy three-legged black lab.

As I began my walk, I saw at some distance before me two figures one taller than the other. Near to them were two more followed by two more still all walking hand in hand at a pace that marked no rush and no hurry and no knowledge as to where they were going. The road was smooth and my walk was not at my pace but guided by the song of the owl, the trickling of the brook and those far ahead. At what seemed to be a pause, I was met by my noble three-legged black lab that sought and was given a well deserved scratch on his well healed nose. I could breathe deeply and as far as the lungs allowed as there was the scent of freshly cut grass and honeysuckle from a thousand mountains. I squinted just a bit and the figures before me were coming closer but were still at *some* distance. I began to see more figures than I could count; they were two by two by two and yet by two again. The walk was less arduous than when it had first begun some time ago and my companion a noble lab was attentive to the duties that lie ahead for him and me.

Our journey was one seemingly destined from the beginning of time but not promised until I had taken the first step. If I had not been willing to be curious I would still be staring at a past wishing it never had been. I was learning that I must first let go of the past in order to accept the future. I didn't want to stop now there was so much more to learn. I wanted to go faster than the road would allow me and faster than the black lab permitted. Both the road and man's best friend were allowing me only so much at a time. There was no sun and no shade to speak of and the ground seemed well traveled and forever healed. There were no rough spots or pot holes that I could see and the dew seemed honey sweet. The road was fresh to the touch and the song of the owl was as clear as he had been at *his* first song. I took a few more steps on this road and then a few more before I sought permission from the feathered guide.

Ashley Bay

The road had gone from one that was made modern by the world of man to a land that was highlighted by tall grasses and rolling hills. I halted in my gate and with some notice I found that the trickling water had stopped. I was concerned, for perhaps I had gone too far. My friend had moved on in a flash and I was full of anxiety and doubt as to my doing the right thing. Had I gone too far or not far enough? I froze in my steps and the fear that was gone now came back in fingers that wrapped around my neck. I backed up a couple of steps and listened more closely but still there was no water and the owl had ceased in his task as well.

Frozen, yes I was I said to the visitor who I knew had to be close. The chill ran up my spine and through my hair. What did they want and should I go? Leave me now, I have to go I told the fingers. I must go now I said to that which was now upon my shoulders. I beckoned with little effort for the creature to let go of my neck but it did not; it seemed to steady me and I knew that it was not a creature but a guiding hand. Was it the hand of an old friend or was it a stranger showing compassion and just wishing to calm me down. I backed up a few steps further and still I heard no water; there was no owl or the honeysuckle of the ages. My fear had overcome the joy they brought me. The grasp was loosening some as I backed farther from the crest of the cloud's hem and stood as they once again shrouded my journey. My fear had over taken my faith in the road before me and I was back to where I knew I must once again make a choice. I was lost all over again and my expectations were replaced by anxiety and fear of the unknown and my secular concerns had won out over the eternal journey of faith. My feet jerked to shake the weight of retreat from them. They jerked again and the grip was gone from about my throat but I was as lost as ever as I stood frozen in time. I was paralyzed and the only thing prohibiting my growth was my own fear. The vision was fading from me and a new one was coming as my eyes grasped for a narrow view of the room about me. As my eyes struggled with a wink and blink I awoke in a room full of dark.

It wasn't a dream this time or what was it? I was full of confusion for was I awake or still dreaming? Had the road I just been witness to disappeared and was I now in an alternative place? Was the room dark and was it light outside or was it day time and dark inside? The next time I rolled over would I do so to the flickering light of a morning sun or to the curious shapeless figures before me? I was too busy trying to figure out if I was asleep or awake when I felt a furry lump next to me. Otis was awake and I was here he seemed to quiver as much as I fought the shakes myself. Why was he afraid at what *I* had dreamt? I knew now that I was awake and I rolled into a human like form and struggled to find the switch for a fifty watt light. It came on and Otis was seemingly fearful at having been left alone or so he thought for such a long period of time. The dog, man's protector and best friend was actually afraid of the dark. In this night's dream I had returned to a boyhood question: where does the body go when the mind leaves on such a journey? Does the mind live forever or does it leave when the body does? Is the mind the soul and separate altogether from this earthly form? Had my furry friend realized that I was soon leaving him? Did he fear that he would end life much as he had begun it alone and seeking companionship? Why was he afraid and why was I accepting the message the night had given me?

I sat with my hands a quiver seeking to brush my thinning hair forward. The light was on but there was such a chill coming in from all about me that I sought a worn out cover. It was going to be a short respite from the fellow travelers for the journey must continue. The nausea was back but I laid my head down again to where I had awoken and was comforted by Otis and his dog like demeanor. He had now become far more than a two-pound poop producer looking for a home. He had become a noble care taker and companion for whatever our journey may be. He didn't want to be left alone nor did I and I pulled the covers closer to my graying crown.

I lay staring at a ceiling that had not seen a good dusting in years but whose color was neutral enough to soothe even the most helter skelter of minds. I thought I should try to finish my sleep for I knew it would be a long angry day if I remained awake now for the balance of this yet undetermined calendar element. The rest didn't wait and was quick in coming and days, weeks, perhaps months of tension filled anxiety was laid to rest. I returned to a long unpaved road which now met the tamed unconscious. The sight was new and the clouds were gone.

I found myself standing at the crest of this hilly road looking down at a farm land centuries old and a land pot marked by modern ranch style dwellings. It looked familiar in *so* many ways to me and all others who had studied from this same hilly crest. Should I walk or should I wait? I didn't know what to do for this was new to me gradually the fear was gone but the scene was still new. I had learned the lesson of not fearing the unknown so I chose to walk on. As I strode my first few steps I repeated the most supportive phrase for the discouraged, *walk on*. Where was my boyhood home? I would see it no more and that question would no longer be asked. Walk on, I did so just a few steps at a time but I did so now with some strength. I did so with my head held high and a smile seeking a recipient. Those words brought back a hint of a familiar tune sung by my father throughout the house on any Sunday visit as he struggled to make one more day without pain. Walk on I did with a glory filled spirit and a heart filled with loving memory for all that life had brought me so I walked on. The sounds of trickling water and the fog that covered surroundings of a once known and proudly traveled childhood trail were gone. As I stood I saw fields of honeysuckle, they were so beautiful and were as far as the eyes could see. The hill before me rolled more and more but this traveler would tire *no* more, I walked on. The naked elms could be seen but were at a great distance. It all looked familiar in a way for it was all brought from the deep recesses of a well rested mind.

I looked at the horizon and saw rolling hills all about me there were fields of uncut hay and apple trees as far as one could wish to see. I could see at best just to the bottom of the first hill and no farther though. The horizon was cloud covered and ominous, if one chose to use that word but I didn't for the future was no longer fearful. I looked and squinted in various directions and saw at many, many yards the end of this dark and dusty road. At *that* end one could make out the figure of a person walking at a deliberate pace towards me. Who was it? Will it be a stranger? Should I leave? Am in some kind of trouble that only running away could settle? The tempered wail of a lone owl once again greeted me, serving now I thought as a landmark rather than background noise for the inattentive. He was behind me calling from an unseen perch.

I looked with some anxiety at where this owl was declaring his song but saw no perch that would allow such a harmonizing decree. Was I hearing things or was I being directed to turn around and see what maybe behind me? What would I do if the stranger before me arrived before I could move away? What would I say if I met this stranger? Would they ask why I was standing alone on this road? To be safe and *not* be thrust into a confrontation with the figure coming towards me I better turn around and see what was on the other side of this dark and dusty back road.

I turned slowly about and I looked at my feet. They were covered with ages of dust from the grounds traveled for seventy-nine years. *These feet*, there were so many roads they have traveled and so many tales that they could tell. I stared as if they could tell a thousand and one stories and I smiled because I knew they could. *These feet* they have walked the beaches of Normandy and the peach orchards of Gettysburg. *These feet* they have climbed the Eiffel Tower, the volcanoes of Central America and the pyramids of Mexico. They have walked the grounds of the White House and they have rested alone at a homeless man's funeral *these feet*.

These feet. I looked with fondness as some of the dust cover had begun to lift from the soles. I looked as some of weariness left as well and the bruises were healed. *These feet* which have stepped ashore at the Atlantic, Pacific and Caribbean they have walked many a mile and skied when they were very old. They have danced with my Annie, with my forgotten daughter and they have walked behind casket after casket after casket. The have knelt at alters throughout the world and they have lacked cover when the demons of the deep claimed them as their own. *These feet*, what a glorious source of remembrance we have been blessed with. They have climbed endless hills and walked countless roads to reach for dreams that were just out of sight and discovered ones never wished for. *These feet* though tired and weary, battered and bruised they never gave up *These feet* have walked with my bride on one special day after another from coast to coast and just around the back yard. The have bounced babies of all ages and they have cradled the heads of many a dying pet, *these feet*. They have walked the white crosses of Arlington and they have danced the Tennessee waltz with a colicky child. Where would they take me now, *these feet*?

I had turned to see the other side of the hill and could see nothing but the fog from previous days. There were no trees, no clouds, no fields of wheat nor the woeful wail of a mourning dove. There was nothing more behind me; all now was laid before me. I took a step, small at first followed by several more and my feet had stopped once again. The sense of night or day was no more but I felt the lick of my hand by a familiar soul. I couldn't find him nor feel the nose seeking an overdue scratch from the neglectful plum chaser but I knew he was there. My hand sought the friendly companion but couldn't find him; the clouds all about me hid his whereabouts but his wet nose was persistent. A lick here a sniff there and another lick, lick, lick and finally a short to the point yipe brought me out of the sleep induced dream to the much demanded attention of a two-pound poop producer named Otis. I lay there prone with my head over hanging the side of the bed and leaving me face to face with Otis who apparently was in great need of urinary relief.

The day was at more than mid-morning when I was stirred, at least according to my judgment cast through the greenish curtains. A good sleep had come at last and I did feel that the anxiety and depression rooted in lack of rest would be gone for this day's journey. I had gotten through the stages I needed to and I could move on now in peace. As a preemptive strike, I had asked the owner of this delightful hideaway if I might be an hour late checking out and she had told me all would be fine. Still fully dressed I rolled to let Otis meet is urgent need and was back inside as soon has he acknowledged completion. Otis was grown now and seemed a shade of what he had been at the start of this journey. He was certainly fatter and now if upon a closer examination he had acquired many canine gray streaks of his own.

I was amazed at how time moves quicker than our secular abilities can mange. My life had gone so fast and I had come to the realization in just the nick of time that it does go by quick. Life had seen so much from the days as a boy wandering the woods of hidden Bradford to walking with my Annie along the beaches of Maine. I was seeking those walks yet again and I would have them but they wouldn't be in Maine. The days had moved so quickly that my memory watched now as a mere attendee at a holiday parade. The trek was new but it seemed to have lasted a life time. Otis was just a pup one day lost at the corner of a busy intersection and before I knew it his gray beard was in place. The fragile cautious observer who fought my attention that first day could not manage a day without it now. After our brief stay outdoors I sat in a chair facing a wall mounted mirror just above eye level. I sat as many do or at least I assumed they do wondering about the outcome of our rests. I was wondering not necessarily about the next few hours but the past several thousand. The dream, which I had had for many nights now were coming together in one general overall message. I felt confident that it would be repeated and clarified each and *every* night until it was understood completely the question was how much longer would it last.

The dream had garnered at first some fear and anxiety but now at this stage I showed not even curiosity but just acceptance. I was learning something and all that I had to was sit back and enjoy the ride for the dream would end soon and I could move on. I began to question my drive: should I go or should I stay here and rest for a few days and then go back and to the snoopy Dottie? Has my dream been telling me to move forward or to stay where I was? Can I go forward with a clear mind and an ambition that is not relegated to the backseat of a depressed state of affairs? I hope so. I was ready for the emotional turmoil to end that's for sure. Otis, with a swish of his widening appendage saw my indecisiveness and let me know that he would be there under the chair if I needed to talk. A smile for him showed my appreciation and he went about his task of being idle.

I scooted down in the chair a bit and looked for a remote that I knew was nowhere to be had and even if there was one, the TV was an antiquated turn the knob model. The mental game started again: was TV fact or fiction? Even the nightly news is hard to figure out. Are they telling us the news or what they want us to take from the news? Back and forth with one mental game after another I sat forward shaking my head clear and thought a walk would be a good idea. If news is fiction then can life itself be labeled fact or fiction? Do we do and act the way we are meant to act or how we wish *others* to perceive us? Fact or fiction, I must admit it's hard to figure out at times but I didn't want to wait till the end to find out that life is real. The same is true of faith. Are God and religion the same? Are they real or fiction? Is God what the pastors tell us He is or what the lawyers say He isn't? The dreams that we all have, the dreams that I have been having are they fact or fiction? Is the story being sent to us through our dreams something real or is it something meant to make us feel a certain way? If the latter is true, then who is manipulating the dreams? Is it my subconscious or is it in fact, God?

Can my memory bank of neglect and regret be producing the nocturnal broadcast that I experience each night? In other words are my guilt and shame driving my dreams? Is it a large file of horrible behavior that is replaying each night as I wander the edge of life? If this was the case then my dreams are making suggestions as to how I should act and what the next steps should be for me. I was learning that I don't need to hold onto the past because it can be such a boggle to enjoying the here and now. Letting go is tough when pain and shame are seemingly what the first half of my life was about. However, by *not* letting go those negative emotions will follow me through the second half.

The dreams were telling me this now as I was nearing the last days of my life the days ahead were fewer and I wish I had learned some of these lessons years ago. Is the road in the dreams emblematic of my life lived, mistakes made and of the good that lies ahead if my behavior is corrected? I had no idea what the answer to any of this might be but believed God must be providing these questions knowing that my nature was a curious one and that I would seek to find. "Seek to find," an out loud question was acknowledged by a thump of a fat tail from beneath the chair.

There were so many questions that had come my way and some had begun to be answered. However, there were still some signs left to find. Now that I had begun to settle on what my next move would be I could settle in and seek a few more answers before the inevitable. I thought I would go for some distance on 495 and let the road decide if I should continue north or turn around and go back home again. The important question had been answered though, would I be of a state so I could take the first step? The burning desire that was with me when I began the journey had been tempered as I recalled the visits with fine friends and as I learned the lessons from my dreams. I leaned forward and thought I might read the paper that I had dragged with me for some time now; this might clear the balance of cobwebs. I fumbled and shuffled and was finding what I wanted to read, such as the horrible news of the Sox latest curse and how Hagar just couldn't get it right. I wanted to read just enough to say that I had but needed to read what was still hidden on the opposite page which I ignored.

I shook my head at how poor my vision had become as I had aged. When I was younger I could spot a faded dime from fifty yards and now it's hard to see one without numerous aids. It has become so hard to make out the small print designated for the real news and so hard to avoid the king sized font dedicated to the latest gay marriage honeymoon spectacular. In other words, society has become one dedicated to sensationalism and not morality, what was real and honest was given font size 4. It has become one dedicated to the trivial and not to growth and good deeds. Dad would be so disgusted at what the world called news these days for he was one who respected those who truthfully informed and not those who selfishly bemoaned for their own agenda.

The newspapers and writers of old were proud to be Godly *and* American and wrote stories that spoke boldly of the faithful American family but now it was just pure dribble. I remember fondly when we could say God in public and how we could say Christmas was a Christian celebration and not just a generic holiday. Yet with this new age dribble modernism has defined God as something that is offensive and should not be used in public for it may offend the immoral. Was part of my life lived as if there were no God because of what I had seen, read and been taught? Maybe, if that was the case then what can we say as to the underlying religious intentions of those institutions? Their goal may be the removal of God and faith from America so the immoral can thrive and I was caught right in the middle of their game. Did immoral America want my soul condemned for the sake of their own selfishness? How can people be satisfied with someone wanting to inform them of the daily dribble that emanates from the streets of modern America? I just shook my head when I thought of how the news makes its way to us poor, average, everyday non-elitist types. Are we even aware of what the real news is anymore or do we just accept the fact that taxes are good, abortion is OK and a man can marry a man? Man was no longer moral nor apparently did he even care. I guess for some of us morality will matter only the very second after our death.

Ashley Bay

The newspaper was showing the wear from being packed and carried about for a few days so I best make this the last attempt to see what was new. A fold here and another crease there and I felt an urge to begin where most things do at the beginning. Gazing the headlines I skimmed over old weather forecasts that were wrong as usual, the news that was important not so long ago and the comics. The news of the day of this paper and likely today's and next week's would be the same. It would highlight the complaint filed by a civil rights group because of the Book of Romans and bits and pieces as to why *this* would be the Red Sox year. The paper would say that modern hip-hop is the best ever and that another church has closed because of abuse. The news would take the reader on a journey from newly opened strip clubs to what priest likes little boys. If there are those around who would doubt this view all you have to do is watch and read. With another thump of a fat beagle's tail, I declared, "Jesus, it's time for you to come back my friend it's been long enough."

I couldn't find the story on the Shipwreck of Maine which I had dog eared for just such a moment and that moment was gone and so was the paper I looked, skimmed, and repeated the behavior and found myself transfixed to another headline much smaller than all others of course. The headline couldn't compete with the projected importance of all others already discussed. The real news is like this story it's overshadowed by the sensationalism of who cares news. Despite the efforts of the professionals in question I was drawn to the headline that I had avoided. Set amongst all the trash was the story of a little girl and I wondered if I should take the time to read this. Should I read this story because it was *just* a story or because it didn't seem of importance and was likely placed in the paper as column filler? Should I read this story because it may be about something real and not about sex, drugs and the damn Democrats promoting their ilk?

I set aside the comics and the same old junk and turned to the story of the little girl for it may be a story of meaning. If this was the nature of the story then I was confident that not many people would read it for many sought vile news and not heartfelt stories. With all the growth that I had recently experienced why did I want to feel bad by subjecting myself to the forgotten sadness of life? Why did I want to read dribble and feel bad? My life had been so hard at times and now as my journey continued I just didn't want to be hurt anymore. My life was hard and I just couldn't bear the news of any more tragedy. However, as I edged to the napping stage I was shoved by my conscience to break the first paragraph of the story. I stared at words that would, at some point, whether today or next week form a message that would make some sense.

The eyes weren't what they used to be and the glasses I refused admitting the need for were still in the glove box used only when I came home. Vanity "ugh" for a portly, beyond the prime primate is a foolish thing but it still wiggled through the cerebral cortex. The unfortunate headlines came to rest upon my chest as I sat briefly seeking the attention of a grunting, tale thumping mess. The story that I thought would be one of hope and happiness for folks like me was all but that.

The story told all who could take a few minutes from their ever so busy, get to the next red light lifestyle that a little girl had been killed by such a driver. The driver had done his or her business and sped from the scene fast for they just couldn't let the everyday people get in their way. The story went on to say that on that day the road was slick due to the rain that had come through Bradford a day or two or perhaps longer ago. I chose only to read the first few lines of this story for I wasn't ready for the end result, the opening was bad enough. The story wasn't going to end well so if I put the paper away and ignored the sadness then it never existed at all. Ignoring it meant that it never happened so I didn't have to respond. Put it away I did, at least for now. However, if I had taken the time to read the short story I would have learned so much more. I would have learned that the little girl had been running across the road to see her mom who worked at Leonard's Donuts. If I would had taken the time to finish the few small paragraphs dedicated to tragedy, I would have learned that day ended the life of this little girl. If I had taken just a few more moments, I would have learned that her mom was Sandi, my friend Sandi had lost her little one, the shy artist from years gone by.

I shifted my girth to a more comfortable dent and if I had taken some time to read these forgotten words I would have learned so much more. The story shared with all those who spent a couple of minutes between the animal rights debate and the new property tax

Ashley Bay

bill was the life of Ashley. I settled back in the chair to let my mind and soul take me back to the day years ago when I learned the truth about Ashley Bay. The day could have been yesterday or years ago but it was *so* real that the time and place didn't matter. I was coming through Bradford late one summer day when I stopped into Leonard's, knowing that my friend Sandi was there. I was far younger than I am now and it was long before Annie ever came along to calm this wandering primate. Sandi was always faithful to our friendship and seeing her would be a nice thing to do.

I was coming through town on my way to some place far from anywhere responsible and ignoring the calls from my mom for a visit. I was young and I knew my mom would always be there so I just told her I would stop by soon, words that she took comfort in but ones she knew were artificial. There had been nearly three years in between visits with Sandi after our one summer together where I got what I wanted and left her to be and I moved on to my adventures. I stopped by to say hello and try to excuse my behavior in the best of possible ways without seeking a commitment. I couldn't recall what I was driving or where I was going but I was drawn to her on this *one* particular day. I went in and was received not by a cold hearted bastard stare but a delightful heart filled smile and, "Oh my God! Kiddo so good to see you, dumb ass." I was set back a bit because I wasn't expecting anything other than the cold hearted bastard smile *but* dumb ass was OK.

I had a string of small talk ready for her and readied my excuses as she gave me a nice cup of coffee and a couple of Boston cremes. That's *the* day the habit began. Sandi and I began our small talk in between her wrestling with real customers and her own awkward feelings. She told me that she had been at Leonard's for several years now and of course I knew that. I stood forlorn in the lobby watching her as she busied herself by keeping the customers satisfied. I felt like a lost pup in an overused cardboard box wanting someone to pat me on the head. I wasn't sure what to do and was throwing my looks about the lobby when I saw at a table near the far window a small framed little girl three, maybe four years old at the most.

She was sitting with dangling feet fully absorbed in her coloring book the first of an afternoon full. I watched without obvious rudeness as she used one color after another, deliberately using one color till it was needed no more. She would neatly line up the used ones because they had been faithful to her task. Her tongue stuck out just a bit as she delivered to the paper each color in a delicate masterful fashion. Purple was frequently used and she moved back and forth between red and yellow till at last she noticed a curious observer looking much like a lost pup.

I was awkward to say the least and tried hard not to get in the way of Sandi and her work, I wanted to talk to her some so I picked a table that was opposite the young foot-dangling artist. I scooted the chair out, then in and sat there with my coffee and bag of hitchhikers. I had settled in for what I hoped would be a nice visit and began to open the bag for the first of two. The bag crinkled like a chip bag in a movie theatre and loudly enough to get a couple of raised eyes from the little foot-dangling artist. She gave me, typical of her, a puckered lipped look to the noise coming her way. I reached in and pulled from the bottom a fresh chocolate drenched Boston creme. As I shoved a better part of the specialty into my oral crevice, the three year old's raised eyes met mine. She giggled in a very lady like fashion as I left most of the chocolate all about my sad excuse of a mustache and most of the creme on my blue t-shirt.

I tried to act casual, pretending all that she had just been witnessed to was, in fact the way that everyone eats Boston creme's. The young artist was not convinced and showed such a look of doubt with the raised eyebrows. As I sought the napkins, Sandi had noticed the error in donut technique and had placed a stack of napkins before me.

"I think you're entertaining Ashley," she said.

"Ashley?"

"Yeah. Ashley, this is a good friend of mine. Dumb ass this my daughter Ashley."

A smile dodged across my face and I said, "Daughter aye, how cool, Ashley nice to meet you young lady."

Ashley nodded in a leg dangling blushing manner. "Hi."

"I didn't know you had a child Sandi, so nice." "What are you coloring over there little buddy?"

Ashley Bay

The young artist just shrugged her shoulders and added a bit more red to her hidden work. When her work had reached the point of satisfaction where she could hold it proudly for public view she showed me it was a small farm.

Young Ashley had held before me a picture of a long road with a small barn in the foreground.

"That's so nice Ashley, awfully nice for sure."

Her smile was still blushed but full of pride now as well as she satisfied her pudgy donut eating neighbor. I packed up my girth and moved to a chair on the other side and much closer to the young artist. She seemed happy and was expecting such a move all along.

"Would you like a milk and donut maybe there kiddo?" I knew the answer before asking for the answer is the same for any child and for that matter most adults. She cast a look at her mom and so did I. "What yah say Ma?" I asked trapping her and leaving her with just one possible escape route.

With just a short pause and a puckered look from Sandi, chocolate milk and a fat jelly donut found its way to my new friend. Ashley lined her crayons up so they wouldn't interfere with her new task and so they were also close at hand for any color emergencies. She nodded a thank you and I nodded you're welcome and our friendship began. Whatever small talk that we adults pass on to young children is usually the most enjoyable because it brings us back to our own youth. We talked and laughed at stupid things and she let me color with my tongue hanging and using her suggested color schemes I too produced a nice farm scene.

When my young friend had an error with her milk, Sandi said, "Ashley Bay, you know what to do."

She nodded and quickly cleaned up the spill and grabbed a second cup. I later learned that her middle name was Barbara and that her mom just called her Bay for short. Ashley later whispered to me with rolling eyes that she liked Bay better then she did Barbara. I learned that she had been here hanging out with her mom for a while everyday and that she liked animals and taking walks along the long road that was near her home.

"I'm impressed. You have some *fine* qualities young lady. You make your mom proud *I* know."

"I know too," she said wiping remnants of strawberry jelly from her face with one of many, *many* napkins laid before us both.

I also learned that she was waiting for her mom's boyfriend to come get her so they could go home and this made her seemingly very nervous. I also learned under her breath that she didn't care much for her mom's boyfriend. "He yells allot."

"He drinks beer and shouts allot, I don't like that," she revealed.

I was about to reassure her that all would be OK when Sandi told her to get her things ready for her ride had just pulled up. This made Ashley very nervous. She dropped her crayons and book and had difficulty opening her Winnie the Pooh book bag. The ride for my young friend didn't come in but instead stayed out side and beeped the car horn several times in what could only be described as an impolite fashion. This guy didn't want to be bothered by coming in and saying hi to Sandi or getting the child, beeping was his statement, beeping was his demand.

Ashley Bay began to pack up her small book bag far more jittery than sitting here talking to this relative stranger. A longer beeping car horn that came from the boyfriend increased Ashley's anxiety. She was packing her crayons and her books and told me I could keep her picture of the small farm scene.

"A nice gift, buddy thank you. I'll see yah' again. OK be good, aye?"

Another multiple beep came from the guy outside and I cast what could only be interpreted as a go to hell look out the window at him. Ashley was growing nervous and spilled her unfinished milk and was embarrassed now.

"Don't worry buddy I'll take care of it for you."

"`Tank you, `don't want to get him mad, `daint good to do `dat."

She hugged her mom and smiled at me as she went to sit next to an impatient driver. Her speech was worsened by the nervousness from having to go with someone she didn't like. I watched out the

Ashley Bay

window as she climbed into the passenger side and as they backed out all I could see was the top of her head. It would be the last I would see of her for many years until that day on the corner with her box of castaways.

My primary concern was why Sandi was with such an apparent idiot but that was something I could blame myself for. I sat back down after wiping up my new friend's milk and folding neatly the gift she had given me. Sandi had been finished with her customers for some time and had just been interested in watching me with her daughter.

"What a nice little girl you have Sandi."

"Thanks, she is awful special, kind, nice and healthy, everything a mom could want yah' know?"

Sandi and I spent the next couple of hours talking about our school years about our parents and about where life has now taken us. I wanted to ask her about Ashley's father but it seemed inappropriate, probably not something she wanted to talk about anyway.

"I'm looking forward to being a father someday. I have to grow up first; a wife can't raise a husband *and* a child at the same time."

"That's true, I always thought you would make a great father, you're kind, decent and reasonably healthy, everything a woman would want, sort of."

I nodded in agreement especially at the *sort of*.

"We never have had much of a chance to talk about things. You left me kinda' high and dry."

"I know, I know." I couldn't disagree with anything that she would say over the course of the next few minutes so I just listened.

Sandi went on to say that she had always cared for me but I never showed her any attention except when it came to three summers ago. She said that I was the most selfish she had ever known me to be but had never held that against me because she knew the truth. I left her back then and she had no way of reaching me to tell me what was going on I just disappeared and went on with my own dreams. I climbed my mountains and I never knew what became of her. Sandi told me that she felt I didn't care if she was OK or if her feelings were hurt or how her life was progressing. Sandi went on and on and was thorough in letting me know I was cold and unkind in all ways possible that summer some three years ago. Sandi never let on in a direct way but allowed me to eventually discover the truth when I was ready. Sandi, many years ago now, told me that she just didn't think I was ready and she didn't want to lose me as a friend. The time would come when I would find out what she had held back from me all those years.

Though it would be after the fact, she would with ever so subtle of signs teach me what I needed to know. Sandi never held a grudge and with a heart full of love and kindness always shared a piece of her life with me. Though it was far after the fact and I never knew until the gray had been overcome by glory I had shared a piece of my life with her as well. Sandi always held good memories of our time together and told me once in a small hand written letter that she had always loved me and wished me nothing but the best in all that I did.

That day many years ago was my first meeting with the life I had shared with Sandi. That day many years ago in a crowded corner of Leonard's Donut Coral was my first meeting with my daughter Ashley Bay.

Chapter 7

Her Best

As I sat ready for another night's rest in this small yet overstuffed yard sale special and again remembered all the times I had forgotten to remember. Ashley was my daughter whom I would never know and it now came flooding back that perhaps I had shared some times with her over the years and I hadn't known it. That is a question that only the end of this journey of mine could some day answer for either I would be shunned or we would travel the road together. Either Ashley would forgive me or I would not be known to her. I shuffled the paper to the side of the bed where any possessions of mine could be gathered if they needed to be. The sun was halfway and it didn't matter much if it was half up or half down. The paper was still only half read though and I was curious about many things that still went mostly ignored by my ego and by my underlying fear of the unknown. Those too could wait as I was coming close to completing my list of lessons learned.

Why hadn't I spent more time with my matted hair little friend? Was I doing my best to just be friendly and do what I felt would *not* be seen as cold hearted? Was the matted hair little side walk vendor the Ashley with whom I had shared those moments many years ago? Was the little girl who had given me such a fine two-pound friend *my* daughter? Was the little girl who now lays dead my daughter whom I had ignored in life? Would I ever have a chance to make amends for not being her Dad? Why hadn't I offered her a ride home when I could tell the rain was about to start that day? If I hadn't given her the money perhaps she wouldn't have worried about buying something. Perhaps if I had just driven by and not bothered she would be alive today. Was her death *my* fault in some way? Did my kindness kill her?

The other side of my doubt took its turn; maybe it wasn't the same girl, maybe just maybe it was someone else. Little kids that age kinda' all look alike and maybe it wasn't the same girl after all. Was I still in a dream state and all this bad news was just part of some other plan to make me be a decent father? I was just projecting allot into this and for no reason what-so-ever other than not wanting to face an all new round of regret and shame. Perhaps, *just* perhaps there were other matted hair little girls named Ashley wandering the streets of Bradford. Did it matter in the long run if it was my fault or not? The little girl is dead and maybe she was in a far better place than the lone corner in a bad part of town. This feeling certainly bothered for why did I think death was better. Should I be the judge of that?

Did it matter if it was *my* matted hair little side walk vendor who died? If she did die why was I concerned for she had played such a small, insignificant role in my life and I in hers. The mental games went back and forth over the very real tragedy that took place with someone who was alive just moments before I had a donut. I looked over at Otis her gift to me he had seemingly grown so much during our time together and she had saved him. If it had not been for that young girl, he too would have fallen victim to the sorry bastard who now accompanied Sandi. The same bastard who had beeped his horn so rudely that day waiting for a little girl and her crayons was the only daddy Ashley ever knew.

Otis was not the last pleasure that brought a smile to her face the last smile likely came when she purchased a tiny yellow rose for her mother. I didn't want to think about this for it couldn't be true for I had sought to do well and her death was a result, *that* God would not allow to happen. Why would God ask me to seek to do good only to have misery be the end result? I grabbed the paper and went to the bed seeking another day of what I hoped would be a quiet rest. There would be no knock at the door or an impatient motel manager as she said all would be fine. I knew I would take the second day and seek the long awaited rest and escape the result of my good intentions. The day was at halfway at least that's my claim and I wanted to walk the road of youth in hopes of an answer to this latest of problems. The day was young still but I was so much older now and was tired and curious as to what the road of my dreams held for me. I didn't want to sleep because that would throw the whole schedule off so I stood and wandered the yard sale special.

I went to the mirror over the top of an outdated and over stained, never moved oak wannabee dresser. I saw before me a man of tremendous sorrow. His eyes had been cloudy for so long and now his hair had achieved the gray fullness that had trickled aboard during this journey. His face aged at a pace that seemed at one time never to come and now seemed never to stop. I leaned over the dresser top and looked closer at my observer and at what life he had wrought. The years seemed to come and go like the swish of a butterfly's wings and I just couldn't slow it down any longer I was defenseless. The breeze of life was flowing by and I now just waited for it to bring me along. The gray was here to stay and the wrinkles and lines of sorrow and regret were well formed as I backed away to seek the door that led me from this time to another.

The feet failed to work as well as they had in days past and I would need at some point the help of Mr. Taylor's cane but not yet I said with defiance. Otis was nowhere to be seen and perhaps he had just claimed a more comfortable spot in some hidden place of *this* hidden place that I had not yet found. I stepped outside and saw to the end of this row of rooms a fenced in road that edged the banks of a now small stream. This story of this once noble waterway was told to me some days ago by the woman who had the job of cleaning the residue of folks like me. As I stood here, I could hear the trickle, trickle, trickle of the once proud spring taking the rainbows to where they call home. I was sick to my stomach and knew that the smell of anything but enclosure would do me well and I went about improving my health. I began a slow walk down the row of forgotten rooms to the fenced in weed engulfed road and the banks of fallen leaves.

Locking the door to the best of my ability I lifted my collar to offset this fall time New England mid-day chill. A walk would do me good and it would bring back a few more final thoughts and wishes. I walked past a number of rooms which had an occupant or two but for the most part had been left unvisited often. The leaves were falling about me as the wind that came from the north did its best to rid the sad examples of noble sentries of their colors. I walked with increased stress on my stature to the gate that marked this once traveled road and was greeted with a well rusted Do Not Enter.

Odd to say, for how could something seek company if it insisted that all stay away. The sign reminded me of the world in which I had lived for so many years I sought attention and visitors but shut everyone out. I would be the one who sat alone at parties and would be a part of the fun things of life only vicariously and then criticize those who laughed legitimately. The road that was long out of the business of welcoming travelers was at times like many of us who choose not to answer the door. The road looked tired and it had done its duty well it just needed rest and to be left alone for awhile. The empty cart path was like those of us who refused to visit a sick friend; it just didn't want to be bothered until it were ready. As I neared the gate, I thought the empty path is very much like those of us who refuse to stop and help a stranger along their way; we just didn't want to get involved. We have all our own Do Not Enter signs expressed with hung shoulders or turned away gazes.

I leaned on this metal warning sign and entered as it said at my own risk a road that one could see headed off to a dog leg left about a hundred or so yards ahead. The grass was knee high in some places and if I looked with some attention I could imagine that I was not the first to make such a walk. I felt like I had an expression of confusion as I took a few steps toward the inevitable dog leg but it was just weariness. I could make out tire trails long out of use but I could tell they were still there. The expression I held was one of why is this area unkempt and why had so many at one time traveled this way. What was at the end of this road that attracted them? The old leaves crunched underneath my girth and they were plenty and so was I so the crunching was easy. The leaves had built up over the years and I could smell the scent of days of the built up forgetfulness. We can imagine that smell if we take just a moment: old leaves and peeling bark, a chill in the air, ageless uncut grass and trickling nearby streams. There was an occasional bird and perhaps a bark but all that seemed at a distance that I chose not to find. The sight and sounds were remarkable and ones that brought me back to walks I had made like this one all the years before. The walks that I had taken when I was young and the days I would sit out behind my boyhood home

Ashley Bay

watching the trickling streams to the scent of new born cherry blossoms.

I recalled as I walked more slowly than previous years how as a young man I made similar treks in fields back home. I would be the loner seeking a message to life's puzzles with my mind's endless journeys taking me from one grand adventure to another. The years had passed by me by the dozens but the puzzles were still the same and I knew that the journey at some point would be coming to an end and I must find the last piece. I walked a bit further and without knowing it had accomplished the dog leg without fear of the unknown. This was at one time I'm sure a very nice little meadow area and I could see dogs at play with their attentive owners. I could imagine families long ago enjoy Sunday afternoon's *right* along these very banks and the rainbows hidden by the flowing waters saving them for the downstream freshman angler.

The grass was still higher than many a farmer would have appreciated and I could both see *and* smell the coming water. The trickling of the water, heading somewhere and coming from the unknown.Water was such a rest to the anxious mind that could be why it's such a life source. I walked a few more steps much slower now and with the aid of some nearby rails I remembered how I as a boy used to just sit and watch the water. When I was young, I would sit and day dream as I watched the streams go by wondering what it had seen and just how long it had been traveling. The walk was a nice one now and I saw scattered about the encroaching banks the buttercups of youth, *not* mine but theirs. The ones we used to hold beneath our chins and if we saw yellow we would be loved by the one we were with, Annie always saw the yellow Sandi did not. A smile came to me from generations ago. How nice the memories were that the mere sight of these tiny weeds brought back to me the joys of life. I had been so troubled for many years but now as I age I had learned to set aside the bad memories for these simple pleasures of life.

I stood silent for a moment and in the distance I heard a bark, knowing it wasn't Otis for he could barely put the energy behind a mild grunt much less a canine tone of this pitch. There was no direction in which to seek the friend of man and his tone soon vanished at the end of the road I walked another few yards and saw the topic of my trip and the place where I might sit and cleanse my spirit some more. It was perhaps at one time a nice little piece of water that enjoyed its share of picnics and youthful avengers but now, as with us all, its agile days were behind it. No longer did the stream easily make its way over rocks and limbs and no longer did it move gracefully move from one bank to the next. The water now was older and struggled in its journey but still showed a glow of magnificence that only the blessed could imagine. I stood above it looking at what used to be a proud example of flowing truth and I could look down both sides to where I would not go and to where I had come from.

To the end of the path that I would not journey there was the sun a plenty and where I thought the dog might be sending a greeting from. I looked at the stream below and saw the increase in size due to the rain from previous days and I followed the cascading branches of a limb that came from an upstream tree. I watched the stream carry the hapless limb down past to where I had just entered. As I watched the limb go on to meet others on their way there through the gate I saw a small figure slowly making their way past the Do Not Enter sign. The figure was faint and was sure slow in their walk but all I knew was that I wanted to be left alone. I didn't want any company on this part of the trip. I had talked to so many and now just wanted some privacy to finish the thoughts that never seemed to end.

There was no need to know if I would have company or not I didn't know if this person was just going to walk by or return from where he or she came. I knew that this person would inevitably make their way to me and insist on being chatty I had that knack. He or she would ask countless questions as to what, where and how come. I would be polite and move on with the tension that had sent me this way but I would show only polite attentiveness to this forthcoming stranger. I turned my attention back to the hapless limb trying to make its way past a convoluted abyss. The hapless limb escaped its trap and floated to a point where I lost sight of it and I began looking up stream to find another doing the same. As I looked for another hapless one I felt a cold chill sent by the slow gate of a nearby visitor.

I had no need to wait on the slow moving figure because I didn't want to talk to anyone and it was only being kind to avoid being rude. I had had my fill of nosey, snoopy people and I was done with them for now. What bothered me most was this person's walk it was *so* slow, *so* very slow. Wasn't there somewhere this person had to be in a hurry? Why so slow, so deliberately slow a walk? I was so uneasy at their pace for if the person was coming I wish he or she would hurry up and do so and just get it over with. I wanted to be alone and didn't want the unpleasant rude company of a stranger to break the ugliness that my mind was walking me through. My experience showed me that strangers could be a pain to the selfish mind and today *I* wanted to be selfish. I stepped back out onto this forgotten path and headed to where I thought I wouldn't have to face the stranger a place that was out of the way. I acted like a little boy not wanting to get caught so I hid from the forth coming guest. I picked up my pace a little and moved a few more yards through uncut weeds to out guess the intruder as to my location. I picked up my pace even more so as to out walk the figure and was around the back side of a small grove of trees out of sight to all except the tones of the distant bark.

The grove by some definition was a couple of dead scrub oaks but for this aging wonder seeking boyhood forts it was a forest. If I sat here and held my head quietly at an angle, I would not be seen, all could pass me by. There was one amongst this forest that was far greater than all others I hadn't seen in many years one like this. This beast had out lived many of my ancestors and many of its own and had been laid to rest at the time that this water had begun to die. I went to its aid and sat upon its broad trunk resting my arms upon the throne made by two of its appendages and held my head to the sound of the trickling rainbows.

I knew from where I had hidden, with my feet toward the unknown and my back to the stranger that I couldn't be seen and therefore not bothered. The whisper of more south bound fowl grew as I looked skyward for their tune and as I lowered my gaze I saw the frail smile of an elderly woman She was soft a foot and traveled quicker then I had thought and was upon me before I knew it. She was slightly slouched from age and breathless from the walk but her kindness was meant for all who wanted it. She wasn't evil or vile as I had let my mind project and was dressed in typical mother like clothes, covered by a hand made white sweater. She smiled a smile that was so familiar among all those who I had wished good-bye generations ago. It was a smile of and for a friend and one without the need to be ugly and unkind. I smiled slightly and asked if she would join me on this roomy throne of old. Her head was ensconced in gray as though she had always been this way and she was small of frame and her face seemed pale to all who saw it. She said with a low soft voice that she had been walking for some time and was a bit tired and appreciated the rest.

I scooted over some to make a little room and *I* was now more nosey than caring when I asked, "Out for a walk, are you? Why are you out this way? Not much out here."

She didn't hesitate long when she let me know that she had seen me come out of the room and thought I looked lonely. "I thought you might want a little company. Was I right?"

A question like that is one that the lonely never really know how to answer. Did I want company? I nodded so she couldn't see it. It was a polite smile but my inner voice was wishing she would go away. I was lonely and perhaps my aggravated mind was due to *being* alone more than anything else. A mind game like this is a hard one to win, I was lonely but solitude was all I had wished for. I hated isolation; however I had hurt so many people I couldn't face hurting any more so I sought solitude. Being alone was the best for everyone so I replied, "Yeah, a little lonely I guess."

I ignored her at first like she was just an inconvenience, she was probably just a nosey little crank. Instead, I just began our time together with an observation."This was probably a nice part of the world before secular neglect took over."

"Secular neglect. You mean the world, right?" She gave her head a small nod of confirmation so I did see it. She had taken a seat on the edge of the noble trunk; it was more of a lean than a seat. She was too dignified to jump upon the fallen tree. My guest looked down at the fallen bayberries at her feet and said the next round of many words. "Yeah, at one time it was *very* pretty out here. When I was a little girl I used to come out here and collect pine cones and acorns for Christmas. I used to walk right up this way." She continued, looking sometimes longingly at the end of the road which still needed traveling. "We never had much money so I would decorate them and give them as paper weights and little nick-knacks for my sisters."

With her eyes still on the end of the road she added, "I miss my sisters an awful lot some days."

I knew what she meant for so many of the hometown generation of mine had done the same thing when they were young. Because money and opportunity were so scarce they would turn toward the heart rather than the wallet for memories. The children of her generation grew up knowing that it was what came from the heart and not the shopping cart that created the deathbed memories. That generation of my guest knew where kindness came from so much better than any of us now a days could imagine.

My companion left the yet to be traveled horizon and returned to the fallen bayberries. "I miss them allot sometimes." Her head was low when she asked, "Do you think they're OK?" I watched her and seeking an answer to her question I said, "I'm sure they're fine."

The goal of the heart is not always the case much anymore. Today's affection is often attached to the dollar sign. The children of this nation will in many cases attach being loved to what their parents can buy for them and not what grandma can make for them. The treasures at the feet of my guest generation were often the most valuable because a gift made by hand showed the greatest of love and personal care. The aunts who brought the homemade gifts to us were some of the ones first neglected but the ones now remembered and usually still sitting proudly on a shelf somewhere These little mementos will tell us far more about love than what could be spent on some toy from some mega-a-world. These discounted plastic gobs of junk would never mean as much as the personal gift made with diligent time and attention from a loving aunt, grandmother or mother.

I followed up with, "Christmas, I know mine as a kid was pretty cool It was probably my favorite time of year; yours must have been something awful special too." I looked at the gate at the far end of this path and said, "I came out here to just see what was here I guess I just needed a nice walk. I'm up there with a room for the day and a dog of some sorts."

She nodded again. "Yeah, I saw the cutie last night. We had allot of animals growing up and my kids always brought the strays' home. We always had them around the house."

The wind was more chilled than when I first began my walk but the scent of wild flowers was new to the throne of old. The scent was beautiful and flowed evenly from one end of the throne of old to the other. There wasn't a sign as to where the scent came from but I was glad it was here. My companion kept her eyes fixed on the road yet to be seen as if she were looking for something *or* someone.

"You headed up north, aren't you." she affirmed.

"Yeah, maybe. I was headed that way but I'm not sure where I may end up. I've been gone either just a day or a year but I've learned so much. The time reminiscing with old friends has been good."

The setting that we both now enjoyed flooded me with files from the past. The good times of childhood came and over took the bad ones that I liked to dwell on. The memories of childhood games, toys and vacations overtook my pettiness and negative feelings. The true affection that I have for brothers and sisters now took a back seat to petty infractions of years ago.

I wanted to tell all those I knew to just sit back and see what I now saw. Sit back, those of you of a certain age and think back to where you may have been raised and to those who did their best for you. Sit back now as your hair is also grayed and remember with fondness the honeysuckle of youth. If you're like me and was fortunate and grew up in a rural part of America anywhere from coast to coast take a journey to back to that time. Take a trip back to your youth, you gray bearded one, to the pets, to the flowers and freshly cut grass and to the always full plum trees across the road.

Can you remember the smell in the air that walked with you as you made your way from house to house during your Halloween jaunt? Can you recall the days when you would be walking the fields behind your homes and you were met by the smell of a roast beef dinner? Can you recall the scent of the grass as it was cut just after a summer rain? The smells of youth never leave us; they stay until we are ready to move on ourselves. The scents of youth are the photo albums that never get lost in a move. I have become so impressed at our nature and just how our minds respond to decade old aromas. We respond to those smells fifty years old with clear dexterity but we may have trouble remembering where we left the car keys.

It's just amazing just how the mind responds to scents and I ask you to take yours on such a journey. I recall the perfume that Annie wore when we first met and the smell of a football game in late October. I sat here with my elderly guest and for a short time, my memory took me on an all new journey through the finer things of my youth. She reminded me in her stillness that those years weren't as bad as I made them out to be after all. I was regressing to the finer moments of my younger years and not regretting the ugly ones. My guest smiled at me with graying eyes seemingly knowing without asking what I was experiencing. This is what this little spot along the banks of a forgotten stream did for me it brought a close to the years of regret and replaced them with peace. The gentler memories of youth are what had come to me as a silent gift from my guest she brought them as a gift knowingly or not. My new friend was quiet; she sat looking at her fingers every so often wondering if she needed a trim before she moved on.

Catching my eye she said, "Maybe later."

She looked with a growing glee down the road yet to be traveled and told me, "I raised my kids in an area allot like this with allot of trees and small streams. They all love animals now and could never have enough pets around the house back then." She had a blank stare and her eyes seemed sad. "They seemed to like it allot. I hoped they did anyway." Her gaze was still fixed on the end of the road and she asked an unforgettable question, "I wonder if they'll miss me when I'm gone?"

I was silent and looked at her with a heart that I had not known before and sensed there was allot of pain deep inside her. Why was she out this way, apart from her family and friends? Why was she so sad and why did she think that there was no love from her children? I sought to comfort her but had no clue on how to do that or if I should do anything.

I looked at her head held low and said, "I'm sure they will, I *know* they will. My mom passed some time ago and I miss her dearly, I can tell you that for sure." I hoped that the words of a motherless son would comfort her as she began to weep for her own children's affection as if a stranger.

I looked down towards the growing grass and breathed deeply as flowing jasmine met my words. "All kids, unless they are dead of heart, always miss their mom no matter the problems they may have had."

She looked at her nails again and passed on a small smile. "Not yet, soon though, soon I will have to go."

I wasn't sure what she meant by that repeated phrase but it had come again. She still seemed sad as she went on with her story of doubt despite what I thought were comforting words.

"There are times when I never felt that my kids loved me. It seemed I was a bother to them and their lives and that I was always in the way. I felt the snickers and under the breath laughs at times but I never let on. I was too shy and maybe I deserved it anyway. I knew they didn't want to come over at times and I knew I was invited at times just for courtesy" She stared again at the road yet to be traveled. "Not yet, soon though I must go."

I began just to watch her actions and listen to her words rather than to seek out answers I hoped would help. "I hope they'll miss me. I sure miss them, I know that for sure. It's been so hard to let them go I can see them all around the table playing that silly game."

I knew how she felt for I had seen how Maple was treated and I sensed as I grew up just how bad at times I had treated my own mom. I was the one who snickered at her frailty and I put off visits because of times I felt she would be difficult, I knew just what my guest was saying.

I stared now at the feet that had walked so many journeys and I took another look at the relationship with my own mom. I was for the most part a cold hearted young man who was cruel and often merciless toward her when my days were young. I laughed at her weaknesses and while I ignored my own. I was disappointed at her abilities to learn and I approved of my constant failures. I was rebellious and hell prone in all that I did and I spoke and turned to her only when I was in trouble. Yet, despite my words, my actions and deeds she always said she loved me. With all my unkindness and all the years I never called, she always remembered me with a kind card and the words I love you. I wondered if all young people are like this, I wonder if my brothers and sisters feel the way I do? Were the children of my new found friend like me and did my mom leave this world with the same questions my guest had? *I wonder if they'll miss me when I'm gone?*

To break the unease I asked, "The flowers smell so good don't they?"

She nodded and said, "My late husband planted all kinds around the yard. Tulips were always near the barn we had out back and every now and then a few roses would come around." She looked again at the end of the road and asked once again, "I wonder if they will miss me when I am gone?" Her eyes seemed sad and lonely and they brought back memories of a lonely widow who sat and stared out upon a world she never quite fit into. She continued, "My kids grew up so fast I didn't have time to tell them how sorry I was for the pain I caused them. They grew apart and I never had a chance to say how sorry I was for all the mistakes I made. I wish I had told them just *one* last time just how much I loved them and how proud I was of them. I wish I had *had* just a little more time."

I watched her without an exchange of words as one small tear was followed by several more and I thought how regret is often carried to grave no matter what our age. I thought as she dabbed the tears just how the one thing about us humans that never ages *is* our tears. The ones we first shed when the doctor brings us in and the ones we shed as the preacher blesses our souls are about the same. They are always fresh and never show signs of weakness. My guest seemed to be a woman who had fought the good fight and still wondered if it was enough to leave this world and all she blessed it with *with* a feeling of peace. She seemed afraid to leave behind all those who perhaps needed just one last hug.

She continued, "My kids grew up so fast. Before I knew it, I was old and walking this road looking for away to say I'm sorry for my mistakes" Looking at her fingers, she asked again, "I wonder if they'll miss me when I'm gone?" Her voice was no longer weary, "My kids grew up and grew apart; they seem so very far apart I think I did this to them." My guest looked both ways of this now frequently traveled path and I think she thought she should go back *rather* than go forward. Perhaps my friend felt that if she could return she could make things right this time.

I had this same thought most of my days: should I go forward or go backwards? This thought even made its way to my dreams. I believed that going back was easy, for it kept us from having to decide or *not* decide what to do with life. I was surprised that regardless of age and condition, tears flowed just as easily as ever and choices were often just as difficult. For me it seemed that regret and shame and perhaps even guilt rode with us to the day we take our last walks. I have wondered for so many years just why at the time when we kneel at the grave of a parent we are blessed one more time with the tears of our own shame, guilt and regret. Blessings these tears are for they teach us just how much deep down inside past the corridors of ego we loved and respected and will forever miss those who bore us.

As we kneel at their graves we thank them with the tears that fall next to the naked elms for all that they did for us. We thank them with a final kiss for all the lessons learned and all the small moments of kindness now remembered. We ask forgiveness as the pastor blesses their grave for all our unkind words and for all the under the breath snickers and for all the forgotten special days. We pray to God as we know Him and to the fallen one in hopes that we are forgiven and that they *both* welcome us into His kingdom. We ask in prayer that as we age we may come to understand that they *will* meet us at the end of our own journey someday and that all *was* forgiven.

She had not moved since taking her seat on the timeless wooden throne her eyes were all that moved. "I loved my children so much and wanted to do so much for them but I failed all the time." She looked right at me and with hazel eyes filled with tears she asked, "Is this why they snickered, because I failed them, because I didn't do good at times?"

I didn't know how to answer other than to follow the inner voice. "Kids don't hate their parents they love them but it's never shown until the very end sometimes. When a parent is at rest surrounded by her kids and reaches for the angels the earthly transgressions are forgiven."

Ashley Bay

She looked above the tree line and watched as a flock of south bound geese make their way over us. A smile momentarily replaced the years of tears that had been meant just for *this* conversation. "I love animals," she said in a girl like manner. "They never criticize us."

I tried to calm her with words I had wanted to pass onto another at one time but this was the time. "I know now as an older and a supposedly wiser man that my parents were often right in what they said and did. I don't know what life was like for my mom when she was young; she never said much about it and she did seem very sad at times. We kids, my brothers and sisters, did grow up and did grow apart but that is because of our own egos and nothing our parents did. I think that's the same for *you* as well. Kids become adults and they just grow apart and the relationships of siblings change for the better or they don't it's not *your* fault."

I looked now at my fingers as she kept her eyes on the path yet to be traveled. "I guess when I'm a parent I will wonder what I could have done differently and I will wonder if they too, will miss me when I am gone."

The scent of jasmine was again at my chest and a breeze that bore a double rainbow in anticipation marked the trail that my guest still needed to travel. The morning had become early afternoon and I knew that I had been locked out of the room and Otis was being held hostage until a day's rent was paid. The sun was more than half way and she looked up again at what would be another flock of south bound feathered friends.

She stepped off the wooden throne and in a refreshed voice. "Your mother loves you and is *so* proud of you young man. You have done so much. The years have gone fast for all of us my sisters are gone now and their husbands are now with mine. The homes we made for my children have been sold and sold again and the pets are gone now too."

I watched without a word as she took a couple of small steps towards the path. I stood and followed to see if she needed help in some way. My guest seemed to be regressing and I worried about whether she was going to be OK or not as she went about her journey.

I asked, "Can I help you with something? Do you need to go somewhere?"

"No, I'm OK now," she said as she took my hand.

We walked a few steps to the path that was more visible one way than it was the other. She held my hand tighter and walked a few steps she was warm to the touch but told me she was fine.

"I'll be OK now, I just needed to rest and needed to talk a little bit." She was slouched when we first met but now stood tall in knee high grass.

"Can I give you a ride somewhere?"

My question was answered by a kind soft smile. "No *my* boy I'll be fine now, I'll walk this path just a bit farther and I'll be home soon."

I nodded and said, "Alright, you take care of yourself. It was so good talking to you, you helped me in allot of ways today."

She again smiled softly and said. "All we moms do that." She left me with a few of words. "You take care of yourself too and make things right with your God. We'll meet again someday sooner than later." I thanked her for the nice talk and still holding my hand she looked at me with a warm timeless smile rather than tears of moments ago and said, "I can't believe how much fun it's been."

She headed down her part of the path and I looked skyward at one last southbound friend. Her pace was a little quicker than before and her posture was now proud and strong.

We bid farewell and I watched as she began her journey through the part of the path that was full of cherry blossoms and honeysuckle. I walked a few steps back to where I needed to go at least for now, through some of the most unkempt and overgrown grass I had seen in some time. As I walked but a few yards I saw yet another south bound flock of fuzzy fowl and turned to show her. It had been just a moment or two but she was now gone and all I saw before me was the double rainbow at the end of the path. The clouds were growing darker on my end and the skies were opening up towards where my friend must have been headed. I began to head down my part of the trail back to the room and likely a very anxious portly beagle. I walked a few paces and turned around to see if she had rounded the

Ashley Bay

corner or perhaps was sitting down again. I didn't see her. I stopped and edged my eyes a little farther to see if perhaps she had fallen but she was not to be seen.

I hadn't great concern for she seemed strong of character and would probably be fine but I was curious. I walked a few steps closer to the little stream and still saw no friend. The scent of honeysuckle was strong and so beautiful I didn't want to leave. The scent wafted through every pore that sought comfort and I didn't fight the intrusion. I hadn't noticed in my initial walk but Cherry Trees and the whiteness of their blossoms edged the entire bank of the stream just past the throne of old. I walked a few more steps and still saw no friend looking at both sides of the stream and the rainbow that had crossed the water at some distance began to fade just a little.

I walked a few more yards to the wooden throne we had just vacated but she wasn't there. With a little patience I saw nestled where she had sat one tiny pink rose. An oddity to be sure, it must have fallen or been left there by some other earlier traveler I couldn't be sure. She may have dropped it as she continued her search for those elusive pinecones. I picked it up and was growing more concerned as to my guest and her welfare she was so sad and seemed so disappointed. Would she be OK? Had she been hurt and I just couldn't see her? For many years, especially my younger ones I had ignored similar silent cries for affirmation from my own mom but I hoped I had helped my *new* friend today as she sought answers. To the sound of the fading feathered fowl and the growing glow of the transient rainbow I turned to head for completion of my own journey.

I had a peace of mind because I hadn't found her injured so felt assured she traveled on and was welcomed to wherever she was headed by those who loved her. I walked at a much slower gate myself back toward the starting point of this most recent of points. I felt older each and every day now and knew that the cane so joyfully passed onto me by Mr. Taylor would be handy as I continued my trip. I too, was now more slouched than at any point but continued my walk. I felt satisfied with my actions of this one very special moment in my life, I had handled it well, I had made *my* amends. I had shown kindness and gentleness to one of the weaker of God's children and I believed He would approve. I felt that I had assured my guest that all would be well with her children and that they would miss her very much when she was gone.

My path back to Otis and the day ahead was nearing conclusion when I felt a gust of wind from behind that shared with me the scent of past generations. From faded roses to tulips and the oft-loved winter time roast beef dinners. The smell of homemade breads and lilacs outside the kitchen windows, apple blossoms, freshly cut grass and a just decorated Christmas tree. The breeze wrapped its way around my soul and the memories of the finer things of my youth were forever imbedded as the pain of those days was gone once and for all. In my time with the unknown guest I had set aside all the disappointments from those childhood days and remembered the fun they brought. In my time with the unknown guest, I forgave the transgressions I felt my parents had passed onto me and I in turn asked for their forgiveness for mine. In my time with the unknown guest, I asked my mom for forgiveness for all my faults and for being a disappointment to her. As my path narrowed and one southbound fowl followed the sun I was forgiven.

The scent of life generations old brought back the finer things and my willingness to seek forgiveness for my role in life brought closure too much of my pain. My path to the poop producer was less overgrown now and behind me the rainbow smiled as never before. There is not and will never be any memory that does more to bring back times of long ago like the scents from our youth. As I stepped through the Do Not Enter gate the rainbow left and the last two feathered fowl said so long to their new found friend. I lifted the pink rose and was reminded of the tears that had fallen at what I knew were recent grave side farewells. I knew too that I would see many more of these simple gifts from the creator before the journey of my own came to and end.

The time with an unknown guest was one that I felt had to be taken with someone but she was the one whom God had sent me. My walk now was of a certainly more labored pace than when my travel had started long ago. Aches and pains were in places that I had not remembered from years passed and my vision slowed as I had seen what was before me. I shared my slow gate with curious birds and a cautious squirrel or two and then I was back to the room where rest awaited. There were no notes of "Pay up or I'll keep the dog" on the room's door an act of kindness from the folks up front. I struggled with a motion that showed the fumbling for my keys was successful and I unlocked the door to the greetings of a canine's anxious bladder. I shared with Otis the opportunity that he had longed for and God only knows for how long. He was across the lot next to a forgotten trash pick up before the keys were even back in my pocket. He was grateful.

The mission before me now as I saw it was whether I should stay here or make my way farther north. I was still tired in so many ways and rest would be nice but I was ready to move on. Otis, who was certainly far older than I remembered him being would appreciate a rest or at least a clue as to where we may be heading. He and I wanted less travel now and more direction in life as the sun set on these learned days. The old dog waddled more than he sprang and slept at intervals only man could dream of. The bed looked so good to this aged, portly preponderance a generation or two removed from his finer times and I soon called it mine. There would be no knock on today's door for the rent would be collected when it was and no sooner. The bed looked so good that I had to lie down and let the trek of my life catch up to all the unanswered questions that I still had but were fewer in number. The paper that still had to be read and the clothes that seemed so out of date could all wait for their time. I needed rest and rest is what came. I sat on the edge of the bed and thought how Otis had been a friend for so long. I had tried to make up for the cruelty to another by giving him a good and decent life. I stared out the door and in his mounting years Otis looked my way and with a throw of his head chose to follow the path of the unknown guest and for now I would be seen no more.

Otis, when he chose to return would find his way with tremendous effort to the end of the bed and for safety's sake, I let the attached lamp glow through the night. I kicked loose the sand and regret from this journey for the final time and was now making plans to finish this trip as my need for rest came to a close. I stretched, rolled and folded a time or two the excuse of a pillow and quickly faded off to the great folds of sleep. The fading glimmer of the attached light bounced through the files of the encroaching message, a message that would within a short time become clear as to its meaning. The night was young or the day was old; when one is tired it is hard to tell if one is beginning or the other is ending and I was there. The chimes were tickled as the tiny pink rose lay on the forgotten dresser and I went to sleep assured by my guest that my mother had done her best.

The night became indistinguishable as I found myself on the crest of a long dirt road. The trees on both sides of this well traveled path were well groomed and the flowers showed their talent to all who would travel their way. I stood with my hands at my sides and there was no longer the mist that had once surrounded these feet I could see clearly. The sky was clear and so too was the horizon in all directions. The sun shone with the beams of glory from every angle that I and all who would follow this road could see. Beams of glory are by some measure songs from the angels and by others still it's called God's grace. Regardless of which one, we seek to call ours a beautiful highlight that is left to help mark our way. For those of us who have traveled the road of youth and now look for a new way, God's grace is what has led us to this point. At *this* age on *this* road I now sought God's grace.

I stood at the base of what had seemed as an insurmountable hill when I saw a figure coming from a distance at a steady pace. I looked to my right and thought I saw coming through all around the budding blossoms many a traveler, I was not alone any longer. People were coming from all over and as far as I could see, I couldn't make them out but was not anxious. The sun had never set on my journey and the wishes of years ago were put aside in favor of the needs of others such as love and mercy; *they* had won in the end. There was no hesitation in the questions I posed to whoever listened and I had waited for their answer. An equal number on my left side matched the figures coming from my right at a distance of some unknown measure. They were coming from so far away. What were they looking for? Where were they going? Dottie, Maple and all the others were right; *good* wins in the end we just have to find it. Is good what all these others are also looking for? The good things in life are the most addictive for the pure of heart and the bad things most addictive to the selfish mind. This journey has showed me on which side I stood. When one without selfish demands seeks to show love and mercy for his or her fellow man, the way Christ has shown us, good wins and we have all been blessed When Christ wins, man wins and when man wins the world loses and man has overcome the world. As I stood on this road I asked; Had I overcome the world?

I and those to the left and right all walked to the bottom of a shallow rising hill and over us all was scattered the chords of heaven's music No longer were the clouds hovering but angelic choirs showered us all. I stood again with my hands at my side watching those from all sides coming at a steady pace to where I now waited. The sound of the owl had faded from my time and a new sound came from all around me and the fellow travelers. The wail of regret had gone and the troubled sorrow that came from such a tone was gone as well. I stood motionless with my head looking upon these well traveled feet. They were so close now, *so* close. I heard a light hum and stood as silently as mortal man could trying to hear what had always been said since my journey began. The hum that had been with man from Isaiah onward was now mine to bear witness to. It belonged to all those on my right and left for they have all made journeys of their own and had their souls cleansed as well.

To my right there were thousands by thousands by thousands more and the same to my left and as far as my eyes could see. Coming from all corners of the field of honeysuckle was a tone that led many up this last hill The field that I had once knew as barbed and scattered with dead water was now *so* beautiful. The range I had walked all along was a beautiful song filled valley. The music was nearly harmonic and none of the choir was out of tune. I shed the cold chills and was guided by growing translucent warmth of my fellow travelers. Through it all I listened and I heard:

"For the sake of the sorrowful passion have mercy on us and on the whole world"

"For the sake of the sorrowful passion have mercy on us and on the whole world"

The numbers to the right and left grew and grew. Now many more thousands had been added and the song increased in its pitch.

"Eternal Father, I offer you the Body and the Blood"

The fellow travelers were coming closer and from behind me as well, I slowed and they began to pass. All had arms outstretched being welcomed on top of the hill and they encouraged me to join them in song and I did.

"Holy God, Holy mighty one, Holy Immortal one, have mercy on us and on the whole world"

The tone was clear both near and far and to my left and right I saw thousands by thousands by thousands more. I was not encouraged to come with them but I knew I could not go back, they were waiting on me to decide. The crest ahead was mine and the first step must be mine as well. A favorite song of youth came back as I was waiting for my soul to catch up to this mortal refuse. I set aside the ageless choir for one last secular tune and the one that would say it's OK for me to move on I added to the list.

"Step into my heart
Leave your cares behind
Welcome to My world
Built with you in Mind"

The Lord my God had seen *me*, for all time, as part of His Glory and His creation He would never leave me. He so loved us that He had built upon that shinning hill a glory that we could all experience and achieve it was there for all of us to see. I now saw. The lessons taught by the preachers from centuries ago could be seen in the faces of those to my right and to my left. The lessons shared with those who sought knowledge could be seen in their walks as well as heard in their song. We had all learned because we had an open mind and we all taught because we all had a willing heart. We had done our best. I was still nervous and I knew I had one last final decision to make but I was close. My list grew by one more.

"Knock and the door shall be opened
Seek and you will find
Ask and you'll be given
The key to the heart of mine"

Ashley Bay

The choir was small at first and its location was uncertain but I felt surrounded by the glory it gave to those who listened. I had that choice to make now but was still so uncertain for would I be alone once I reached the top of the hill? What and who would be there if I went ahead? The choir was so beautiful that it was hard to resist but I held strong as I looked again at my feet as if to ask them to please, *please* take just a few more steps. I just stood there as the choir grew and surrounded me at the end of this long road and the sang:

"Holy God, Holy Father, Holy Immortal one, have mercy on us and on the whole world"

"Have mercy on us and on the whole world"

I was guided by the voice of the angels. I asked a simple question in hope for just one answer; would they be there? Would they *all* be there or would I be alone? Would I have to wait? Would they miss me when I was gone? So many had started to pass me by that I had to ask. Would I be left here on this last road all by myself? As more and more began to pass me and before I could take a step backwards to change my mind a hand took mine. I couldn't see them for the choir was still so large but they seem to step aside and let my guide come through. She came under my arm with a smile as wide as the heavens she was so beautiful. Her cheeks were rosy and her hair was full of Baby's Breath. I knew now upon seeing her face I would not return, for my Ashley would show me the way. Ashley held my hand and walked me to a point where she was to leave me ever so briefly one final time. It was just a few steps forward to encourage me to take the last few steps with a willing heart.

The memories that had never been allowed were presented to me as our hands slipped each other's grasp. Ashley held my hand until she slid away silently and to where I must climb this small crest with those who came from all sides. The song was so beautiful; the scent of honeysuckle, jasmine and cherry blossoms was all about me and the sky was *so* blue hand painted by the creator. The clouds had lifted long ago and before me I saw as far as the eyes could see the hand holding spectacle of all those who had followed me and whom I had followed. They traveled in pairs and by hundreds and by thousands and thousands more, we were all heading to the same crest and we were all seeking what was on the other side.

I stood a final time with my hands at my side looking again at these well traveled feet on their final trek. The voices of the forgotten ones were now remembered as the woeful wail of the owl was replaced by the angelic choir of the heavens. It was then that I knew my journey had come to an end. It was then that I knew.

Chapter 8
First Steps

I had died on a Tuesday with my Annie by my side and she had held my hand giving it up *only* to the angels so they could take me home. She held it as she had done when God joined us together many years ago. The angels had called me home this day but God had blessed me with one last walk through life and all the lessons learned. I had been blessed with one last look at the errors made and the love I had shared. I had been given one last special opportunity to visit old homes, old friends and old dreams. With the love that has been learned and shared, I knew Annie would be just fine. She patted my hand and kissed my forehead farewell as I joined at last the choir of the ages.

"For the sake of His sorrowful passion, have mercy on us and on the whole world."

"For the sake of His sorrowful passion, have mercy on us and on the whole world."

The morning dew on this day was light and the dove flew one final time to the rail outside to where we would sit and read. I had been blessed with the memories of fine friends and the times they shared with us. They were all gone now waiting for me at the end of this final journey just at the top of this last little hill.

The memories were glorious ones. I had lived a wonderful, beautiful life and I was so thankful. I left behind *no* regrets and I left behind ones who could share a smile and a laugh when they thought of me. Though my chair would now be empty, my love and my spirit would be with them until the rainbows met us all. The sorrow would last for a time that could never be measured and on this day I was proud the pews were full with those who had long been friends and allies and those who had made amends. Annie sat proudly with our children and our grandchildren were as far as the eyes could see. Sandi sat alone near the rays of morning sun remembering a fine and loyal friend. There were some tears but mostly smiles and hugs in remembrance of someone many called a good and decent husband and father. The son of the pastor who had married us some fifty years ago stood over my humble remains and let me know that I had, in deed done well as a true and noble servant of Christ. I had done well.

The regrets and doubts which traveled the road with me *all* these years left as a feathered witness to the goodness of the ages. Shame and doubt flew to meet the rising desert sun and would return no more. *Good and decent servant of Christ* the timeless words for all mankind and I had sought to hear those words my whole life. Now as my spirit nudged the neck of my Annie and as she smiled to the chilling touch, I heard these words at last and heard them when they meant the most. The shroud of death was shed as my tears for all my wrongs were forever wiped away by the Son of sons. I watched as friends and family remembered the good times shared and all said they knew we would meet again, really soon. I had done my best to help set aside the shame and guilt that secular lives often bring and I was reassured at *this* moment that I had done so.

The songs played and the tears were mixed with smiles as photos brought back memories of the life we had shared together and of the walks we had taken. These memories told so well our story as my list neared completion.

"of holding hands and red bouquets and twilight trimmed and purple haze and laughing eyes and

simple ways and quiet nights and gentle days with you."

I had been blessed with so many to love and share the glory of life and the grace of Christ with, what a glorious beautiful life this has been! I had been *so* blessed and now my journey was over, the road was traveled, bumpy at times for sure but wonderful to the end and now I must go home. The angels sang and the rays of sun lit the valley as my sons bore me with pride and respect and their heads were set high as they set the bronze casket down for the final time. The pastor, with some kind words blessed my grave and with a final kiss from my Annie she tossed a tiny pink rose to rest for eternity upon my chest. The sun was near its mid-day peak and I was laid to rest on a fall time morning beneath the naked elm next to a stone mossy green from age and slightly askew. My family, now several generations deep stood holding hands as a lone piper bid farewell with the timeless wail of Amazing Grace and my list was thus complete. The mocking shrills of the demons named doubt and regret were gone for good at the hands of most eloquent of verses.

> 'Twas *grace* that taught my heart to fear
> And *grace* my fears relieved
> How precious did that *grace* appear
> The hour I first believed

Some tears were shed, yes of course at this our final dance but the pipes played on.

> Through many dangers, toils and snares,
> I've already come;
> 'Tis *grace* hath brought me safe thus far,
> And *grace* will lead me home.

I turned to finish my journey and was met by Ashley who reached for me on this final walk, with a chill to some I returned to give a final kiss to my Annie and as she tucked her neck the kilted one bid farewell to her beloved one.

> When we've been there ten-thousand years
> Bright shinning as the sun
> We've no less days to say God's praise
> Then when we'd first begun

I was saved and just had to be reminded of that as my final hours were ticking. I had to be assured during my final dream that I had done what was asked and had lived the best I could as He had wished. The rainbow that had greeted Him that day on Golgotha now greeted me and many more on this beautiful day on our road to glory.

The rainbow lit the journey and the corners of these elms as I was guided to the crest of the last dirt road by my Ashley Bay the daughter I never knew. She stood with a smile for the ages and she reached for my hand again, she was *so* pretty. Her hair was brushed back and full of flowers and she was wearing a dress all of white. She took my hand and began to show me the way. There was no studder and no stammer now and I wasn't scared nor was I sad. As we began our walk slowly toward the crest many whom I had known along the way soon met us. Ethyl Hyde smiled as she stood with her father and the supplier of endless plums Ms Yowell met us on the road as well. There were aunts and uncles and Mr. and Mrs. Gibbons. She was healthy and whole now and laughed the laughs she never could. There were friends long forgotten and family never known and we walked together towards the horizon that was there long before man *ever* dreamed.

We saw to one side of our path thousands by thousands and to the other side of our walk thousands by thousands still as far as the eyes would see. We were one, we were a family and the songs of the owls became the lost angelic choir that now guided us and we all sang:

"Hallelujah, hallelujah, hallelujah."

Those to the right and to the left, those dressed in union blue and rebel gray walked and asked blessings upon the world. Those children who were never allowed to be and those who came home before their time were joined with the saints of the ages. Those who had died so others could be free were joined by those who had been freed. The lonely and the lost had become the loved and saved and all sang as one:

"Hallelujah, hallelujah, hallelujah."

Those who had walked this life alone and those who sat at windows hoping for a visit that never came joined us as we walked on. There were those who had been the victim of life and many an unkind word. There were the Russell Taylor's and the Maple Goyette's, her brother Jeff and Dottie Noah's maid. There were those who had been the victim of the worst natures of mankind and they too sang. To our right were fields of white and to the left it was the same. No more pain, no more lame or blinded walks. Those who could not see *now* saw and those who knew a rose only but its touch breathed deeply the glorious scent and those that knew an owl only by its song sang with us all:

"Hallelujah, hallelujah, hallelujah."

The dying who did so with no tears shed for them and the sick who had no visitors were joined by their fellow man. There were the aged, the young and all in between as we came from horizon to horizon through fields filled with the green newly made and never to fade we walked on. We came from all sides of the crest and only a mind true to faith could imagine its beauty. We stood near the rise and I lowered my head for what I knew would be the final time. Ashley took hold and held my hand for the few final few steps to the right and to the left all joined hands and the angelic choir began anew.

"For the sake of the sorrowful passion, have mercy on us and on the whole world."

"For the sake of the sorrowful passion, have mercy on us and on the whole world."

The tears I shed now were not ones of pain, regret or shame but tears of love and peace. I stood motionless as the words shook the chills from me and I felt a gentle hand on my right shoulder. Before me I saw just a few more steps that needed to be walked, I was close now but there was still just one question. I took one step with head still lowered at these refreshed well traveled feet. I felt a second smaller but no less loving hand on my left shoulder. My parents had welcomed me home. I looked up and saw a proud father, his limp was gone, and he was holding the hand of his wife no longer cancer bound. They were just a few paces ahead and waited for me to make my heart willing and take the last of the needed steps into glory. I *was* willing and I was tired no more. I had left behind me on this *road* of life all the hardships exchanged for lessons learned and love shared. I had made the trip and had been told all along that I had done well and that I was a true and faithful servant but I didn't believe it till this very moment. The question was answered.

With a hush Mom and Dad walked hand in hand to the crest and turned to wait. They were joined by thousands times thousands times thousands again and the angelic choir grew in size and in timbre. They waited for us all, we were the children who never grew and the sick who never ran the course. We were the lonely, the broken hearted and those who sat staring out onto a world they never quite fit into. We were those who did our best and tried to show love in all that we did. We were those who were shunned and ignored by all but *one* and we were those who sought peace and freedom for our fellow man.

I lifted my head to see standing behind me all who waited their turn and there were rainbows, doves and a light welcoming all. A smile made its way to me from my loved ones just up ahead and to all others from theirs as we began our last few steps. I took my last step and *then* my first step. Many asked was it their time, should they go? Those that were ready went and I was one, I was so ready. As I took my first willing step I was met again by a small hand taking mine. Ashley was walking with me over the crest of our last hill and as her tiny voice was added to all the others she tugged at my fingers wanting to stop. She looked briefly at me and with eyes as blue as the sea she turned to look over her shoulder. With a clear voice she gave the valley a final call, "Otis, Otis! Come on boy we're going home."

Printed in the United States
29430LVS00002B/45